*Muttering softly, his eyes blazing with fury,
he started toward Mrs. Lewis, and began killing her.*

Alex remained still in the corner of the kitchen, his eyes glued to the scene that was being played out a few feet away.

He could feel the pain in Mrs. Lewis's neck as the dark-skinned boy's fingers tightened around it.

And he could feel the terror in her soul as she began to realize that she was going to die.

But he could do nothing except stand where he was, helplessly watching, for as he endured the pain Mrs. Lewis was feeling, he was also enduring the pain of the thought that kept repeating itself in his brain.

It's me. The boy who is killing her is me. . . .

BRAINCHILD
An excursion into absolute terror
by the bestselling master of fear
John Saul

BY JOHN SAUL

BRAINCHILD

John Saul

BANTAM BOOKS
TORONTO • NEW YORK • LONDON • SYDNEY • AUCKLAND

BRAINCHILD

A Bantam Book / August 1985

ISBN 0-553-24975-4

Published simultaneously in the United States and Canada

Bantam Books are published by Bantam Books, Inc. Its trademark,
consisting of the words "Bantam Books" and the portrayal of a
rooster, is Registered in U.S. Patent and Trademark Office and in
other countries. Marca Registrada. Bantam Books, Inc., 666 Fifth
Avenue, New York, New York 10103.

PRINTED IN THE UNITED STATES OF AMERICA

H   0 9 8 7 6 5 4 3 2 1

To Shirley Osborn, with love, affection and appreciation

PROLOGUE

The late-August sun blazed down on the parched hills with an intensity that was usually felt only much farther south, and south, the sixteen-year-old boy thought as he moved stealthily through the scrub-oak underbrush of his father's vast *rancho*, was where he and his family should have gone long before now.

But his father had insisted on staying.

All year, since the Treaty of Guadalupe Hidalgo had been signed, his parents had been quietly arguing about what to do.

"They will drive us away," his mother had said over and over. She had said it again only this morning, her tall figure held firmly erect as she sat on a ladderback chair in the shade of the eastern wall of the hacienda, dressed, as always, in black, despite the heat of the morning. Her hands, their long slender fingers betraying nothing of what she might be feeling, worked steadily at the needlepoint with which she occupied herself during the few moments of each day that the pressures of the

1

hacienda allowed her. But his father, as he had every other day, only shook his head.

"In Los Angeles they are honoring the Spanish grants. They will honor them here, too."

Doña María's eyes had flashed with impatience, and her mouth had tightened, though when she spoke it was with the respect she always paid her husband, and had taught her daughters to pay to both their father and their brother. "They have not found gold in Los Angeles. There, the land is worthless. Why not honor the grants? But here, even if there is no gold, they will take the land. In San Francisco the ships arrive every day, and the city is full. Where will they go?"

"To the goldfields," Don Roberto de Meléndez y Ruiz had insisted, but Doña María had only shaken her head.

"Most of them will go to the goldfields. But not all of them, Roberto. Some will see into the future, and want the land. And those men will come here. Who will defend us?"

"The presidio at Monterey—"

"The presidio is theirs now. The war is over, and we have lost. Our troops have gone back to Mexico, and we should follow them."

"No!" Don Roberto had replied. "We are not Mexicans. We are Californios, and this is our home. We built this hacienda, and we have a right to stay here! And stay here we shall!"

"Then we shall stay," Doña María had said, her voice suddenly placid. "But the hacienda will not be ours. The *rancho* will be taken from us. New people are coming, Roberto, and there is nothing we can do."

And now, this afternoon, they had come.

From a hilltop two hundred yards away, the boy saw a squadron of United States cavalry appear in the distance, making its leisurely way up the trail toward the whitewashed walls of the hacienda. Nothing in their manner indicated a threat, and yet the boy could feel danger. But instead of mounting his horse and riding home, he tied the animal to a tree beyond the crest of the hill, then crouched down into the brush.

He saw his father waiting at the open gates, and could almost hear him offering the men the hospitality of his home. But the riders did not go inside. The squadron waited while one of the stable boys brought his father's horse. Don Roberto mounted, and the squadron, with his father in its midst, started back down the trail toward the mission village a mile away.

The boy moved as swiftly as he could, but it was slow going. There was only the one trail, and all his instincts told him to stay off it, so he made his way through the tangle of dry brush, hiding himself as best he could in the clumps of oak.

He watched as the squad drew close to the mission, and for a moment his fear eased. Perhaps they were only taking his father to a meeting with the American commandant.

No.

The squadron passed the mission, and continued another hundred yards down the trail to the enormous oak tree around which the village had originally been built. Under its mighty branches, Indians had camped for untold centuries before even the Franciscan *padres* had arrived.

Suddenly the boy knew what the squadron was going to do, and knew there was nothing he could do to prevent it.

Nor could he leave. He had to stay, to watch.

As his father sat straight in the saddle, one of the men threw a rope over the lowest branch of the tree, while another tied Don Roberto's hands behind his back. Then they led the black stallion under the tree and tied the free end of the rope around Don Roberto's neck.

From his hiding place in the brush, the boy tried to see his father's face, but he was too far away, and the shade of the oak was impenetrable.

Then one of the cavalrymen lashed the black stallion's flanks with a riding crop; the horse reared, snorting, and came stamping back to earth. A second later it was over.

The black horse was galloping up the trail toward the hacienda, and Don Roberto de Meléndez y Ruiz's body was swinging under the embracing branches of the oak tree.

The cavalry squadron turned and at the same leisurely pace started back up the trail toward the hacienda.

The boy waited until the soldiers were out of sight before he picked his way the last fifty yards to the floor of the valley. He stared up into his father's face for a long time, trying to read in the eyes of the corpse what might now be expected of him. But there was nothing in the twisted grimace of pain, or the bulging, empty eyes. It was as if, even as he died, Don Roberto still hadn't understood what was happening to him.

But the boy understood.

He turned, and faded away back into the brush.

It was late in the afternoon, and as the sun dropped toward the western horizon, long shadows began their march across the hilltops. Far away, the boy could see the beginnings of a fogbank forming over the ocean.

Below him, the last of his family's servants were drifting out of the open gates of the hacienda, their meager belongings tied up in worn *serapes*, their eyes fixed on the brown earth, as if they, too, might be in danger if they so much as glanced up at the guards who flanked the courtyard gates.

Against the inside of the western wall, still protecting herself from the fading heat, his mother sat calmly on her chair, her daughters flanking her, her fingers still occupied with her needlework. Every now and then, he could see her lips move as she offered words of farewell to the departing *peones*, but none of them replied; only one or two even had the courage to nod toward her.

Finally the last of the servants was gone, and at a signal from their leader, the guards slowly swung the heavy gates closed. The officer turned to face Doña María. His words carried clearly up the hillside.

"Where is your son?"

"Gone," his mother replied. "We sent him away last week."

"Do not lie, Doña María. He was seen yesterday."

His mother's voice rose then, and the boy knew her words were for him, as well as for the man she faced. "He is not here, señor. He is gone to Sonora, where he will be safe with our people."

"We'll find him, Doña María."

"No. You will never find him. But he will find you. We are not afraid to die. But you will not gain by killing us. We will not leave our land, señor. My husband said we will stay, and so we shall. And you will kill us. But it will do you no good. My son will come back, and he will find you."

"Will he?" the squadron leader asked. "Get up, Doña María."

As the boy watched from the hillside, his mother rose to her feet. Drawing their courage from their mother, his sisters, too, rose.

"My son will find you," he heard his mother say. "My son will find you, and he will kill you."

The squadron leader jerked his thumb toward the south wall. "Over there." He stepped forward, the bayonet fixed to the barrel of his rifle jabbing menacingly at Doña María and her daughters.

Doña María stood firm. "We are not afraid to die, but we will not be prodded like cattle." She turned and carefully set her needlework on the chair, then took her daughters' hands in her own. She started across the courtyard, her step firm, her back as rigidly erect as ever.

She reached the south wall, still bathed in the afternoon sunlight, then turned and began to pray. As her lips began to move, the boy on the hillside closed his eyes and silently mouthed the words he knew his mother was speaking.

The first shot jerked his eyes open, and he blinked twice before he could focus on the scene in the courtyard.

His mother still stood, her head up and her eyes open, but her right hand was clutching at her breast. A moment later, blood began to seep from between her fingers, and a crimson stain spread across the bosom of her dress.

Then the quiet of the afternoon was shattered as his sisters' terrified screams mixed with the angry rattle of gunfire, and a cacophony of sound echoed off the hacienda walls to roll over the countryside beyond.

His younger sister was the first to fall. Her knees buckled beneath her, and the motion itself seemed to concentrate the gunfire on her. Her body twitched violently for a moment as the bullets slammed home, then she lay still in the dust.

His older sister screamed and her arms reached out as if to help the fallen child, but she only pitched forward, falling facedown into the dirt as the rifles spoke again.

Doña María stood against the wall alone now. She faced the squadron with open eyes, gazing down the barrels of their rifles with a calm serenity. "It will do you no good," she said again. "My son will find you, and he will kill you. We will never leave our land." Then she, too, sank slowly to the ground. A few seconds later the squad emptied its rifles into her lifeless body.

It was past midnight when the boy crept down from the hillside and slipped through the gates of the hacienda. A strange silence hung over the buildings; the night creatures themselves seemed to honor the dead. No guards patrolled the grounds, nor had anyone covered the corpses. The squadron had left long ago, searching out the families of the overseers to deal with them as they had dealt with the family of Don Roberto.

The moon hung low in the night sky, its silvery light casting strange shadows across the courtyard. The crimson stains of his family's blood were faded by the half-light to nothing more than grayish smears on the whitewashed walls. The pallor of death on his mother and sisters seemed only to be the peace of sleep. For a long time the boy stood silently praying for the souls of his parents and his sisters. And then, with his last prayer, he put his grief aside.

He was changed now, and there was much to be done.

He picked up his mother first, and carried her body out of the courtyard, then up to the top of the hill, where he buried it deep within a tangle of brush.

Beside his mother, he buried his sisters, and then sat through the rest of the night, his mind numb as he relived the horrors of the day that had just passed.

As the first light of dawn began to bleach the darkness of the long night away, he rose to his feet and looked down once more on the hacienda that had been his home.

His memories, and his mother's words, were etched on his soul, as the blood of his family and the marks of the bullets that had killed them were etched on the walls of the hacienda.

Nothing would ever erase the images in his mind, or soften the hatred in his heart.

Nor would he ever leave the village that had been his home.

And forever after, night after endless night, he would awake from the dream, shivering.

Always it was the same. Always he was in the hills above the hacienda, watching the slaughter of his family; always he heard the words of his mother clearly, and understood what it was that he was to do.

Was it real? Had it all happened exactly as he saw it in the dream? The shots. The screams. Crimson stains on whitewashed walls.

Always the dream returned. And he knew what he must do. . . .

PART ONE

PART ONE

CHAPTER ONE

La Paloma was the kind of town that absorbed change slowly. Tucked up in the hills above Palo Alto, it had grown slowly for more than a hundred years, yet its focus remained as it had always been, the tiny plaza of the old Spanish mission. Unlike most of the California missions, Mission La Paloma had never been converted to a museum or a historical monument, becoming, instead, the village hall, with its adjoining school now serving as a library.

Behind the mission there was a tiny cemetery, and beyond the cemetery was a collection of small run-down houses where the descendants of La Paloma's Californio founders lived, still speaking Spanish among themselves, and eking out meager livings by serving the *gringos* who had taken over the lands of the old hacienda generations ago.

Two blocks from the plaza a smallish, roughly triangular piece of land dominated by an immense oak tree lay at the confluence of the main road through La

11

Paloma and the side roads that wandered through the ravines into which the village had spread over the years. The patch of land had existed undisturbed because the original settlers, starting with the mission priests, had elected to leave the massive oak in place and route the roads away from it. And so it had remained. There were no sidewalks or curbings along La Paloma's haphazardly meandering streets, and though the village that had grown up around the mission had eventually spilled over into this unnamed, unpopulated area, the plaza had remained the center of town.

Now the area surrounding the oak was known as the Square. And the huge oak under which generations of La Paloma children had grown up, had climbed on, hung swings from, carved their initials into, and generally abused beyond all reasonable horticultural endurance, was neatly fenced off, surrounded by a well-manicured lawn crisscrossed by concrete walks carefully planned to appear random. Discreet signs advised people to stay off the lawns, refrain from picnicking, deposit litter in cans prettily painted in adobe brown to conform to La Paloma's Spanish heritage, and the tree itself had an ominous chain surrounding it, and a sign of its own, proclaiming it the largest and oldest oak in California, and forbidding it to be touched in any manner at all by anyone except an authorized representative of the La Paloma Parks Department. The fact that the Parks Department consisted only of two part-time gardeners was nowhere mentioned.

For now the computer people had finally discovered La Paloma.

At first, the thousands who had flocked to the area known as Silicon Valley had clustered on the flats around Palo Alto and Sunnyvale. But tiny, sleepy La Paloma, hidden away up in the hills, spreading out from the oak into the ravines, a beautiful retreat from the California sun, shaded by towering eucalyptus trees, and lush with undergrowth except up toward the tops of the hills where the pasturelands still remained, was too tempting to ignore for long.

The first to move to La Paloma were the upper echelons of the computer people. Determined to use their new wealth to preserve the town's simple beauty, preserve it they had, spending large sums of their high-tech money to keep La Paloma a rustic retreat from the outside world.

Whether that preservation was a blessing or not depended on whom you talked to.

For the last remnants of the Californios, the influx of newcomers meant more jobs. For the merchants of the village, it meant more money. Both these groups suddenly found themselves earning a decent income rather than struggling for survival.

But for others, the preservation of La Paloma meant a radical change in their entire life-style. Ellen Lonsdale was one of these.

Ellen had grown up in La Paloma, and when she had married, she had convinced her husband that La Paloma was the perfect place in which to settle: a small, quiet town where Marsh could set up his medical practice, and they could raise their family in the ideal environment that Ellen herself had been raised in. And Marsh, after spending many college vacations in La Paloma, had agreed.

During the first ten years after Ellen brought Marsh to La Paloma, her life had been ideal. And then the computer people began coming, and the village began to change. The changes were subtle at first; Ellen had barely noticed them until it was too late.

Now, as she steered her Volvo station wagon through the village traffic on a May afternoon, Ellen found herself reflecting on the fact that the Square and its tree seemed to symbolize all the changes both she and the town had gone through. If the truth were known, she thought, La Paloma would not seem as attractive as it looked.

There were, for example, the old houses—the large,

rambling mansions built by the Californio overseers in
the style of the once-grand hacienda up in the hills.
These were finally being restored to their original splendor. But no one ever talked about the fact that often the
splendor of the houses failed to alleviate the unhappi-
ness within, and that, as often as not, the homes were
sold almost as soon as the restorations were complete,
because the families they housed were breaking up,
victims of high-tech, high-tension lives.

And now, Ellen was afraid, the same thing might be
about to happen to her and her family.

She passed the Square, drove up La Paloma Drive
two blocks, and pulled into the parking lot of the Medical Center.

The Medical Center, like the fence around the Square
and the chain around the tree, was something Ellen
had never expected to see in La Paloma.

She had been wrong.

As La Paloma grew, so had Marsh's practice, and his
tiny office had finally become the La Paloma Medical
Center, a small but completely equipped hospital. Ellen had long since stopped counting how many people
were on staff, as she had also long since given up trying
to keep books for Marsh as she had when they'd first
married. Marsh, as well as being its director, owned
fifty percent of its stock. The Lonsdales, like the village, had prospered. In two more weeks they would be
moving out of their cottage on Santa Clara Avenue and
into the big old house halfway up Hacienda Drive whose
previous owners had filed for a divorce before even beginning the restorations they had planned.

Ellen half-suspected that one of the reasons she had
wanted the house—and she had to admit she'd wanted
it far more than Marsh or their son, Alex—was to give
her something to do to keep her mind off the fact that
her own marriage seemed to be failing, as so many in
La Paloma seemed to be, not only among the newcomers but those of her childhood friends as well, unions
that had started out with such high expectations, had

seemed to flourish for a while, and now were ending for reasons that most of them didn't really understand.

Valerie Benson, who had simply thrown her husband out one day, and announced to her friends that she no longer had the energy to put up with George's bad habits, though she'd never really told anyone what those bad habits had been. Now she lived alone in the house George had helped her restore.

Martha Lewis, who still lived with her husband, even though the marriage seemed to have ended years ago. Marty's husband, who had flown high with the computer people for a while as a sales manager, had finally descended into alcoholism. For Marty, life had become a struggle to make the monthly payments on the house she could no longer really afford.

Cynthia Evans, who, like Marty, still lived with her husband, but had long ago lost him to the eighteen-hours-a-day, seven-days-a-week schedule the Silicon Valley people thrived on, and got rich on. Cynthia had finally decided that if she couldn't spend time with her husband, she could at least enjoy spending his money, and had convinced him to buy the old ruin at the top of Hacienda Drive and give her free rein to restore it as she saw fit.

And now, the Lonsdales too were involving themselves in one of the old houses. In the next two weeks, Ellen had to see to it that the floors were refinished, the replumbing and rewiring completed, and the interior of the house painted, activity that she hoped would take her mind off the fact that Marsh seemed to be working longer hours than ever before, and that, more and more, the two of them seemed to be disagreeing on practically everything. But maybe, just maybe, the new house would capture his interest, and they would be able to repair the marriage that, like so many others, had been damaged by the demands of too much to do in too little time.

As she slid the Volvo wagon in between a Mercedes and a BMW, and walked into the receiving room, she put a bright smile on her face and steeled herself to avoid a quarrel.

There had been too many recently, over too many things, and they had to stop. They were hurting her, they were hurting Marsh, and they were hurting Alex, who, at sixteen, was far more sensitive to his parents' moods than Ellen would have thought possible. If she and Marsh quarreled now, Alex would sense it as soon as he came home that afternoon.

Barbara Fannon, who had started with Marsh as his nurse when he'd opened his practice almost twenty years ago, smiled at her. "He just finished a staff meeting and went to his office. Shall I tell him you're here?"

Ellen shook her head. "I'll surprise him. It'll be good for him."

Barbara frowned. "He doesn't like surprises . . ."

"That's why it'll be good for him," Ellen retorted with a forced wink, wishing she didn't sometimes feel that Barbara knew Marsh better than she did herself. "Mustn't let Doctor start feeling too important, must we?" she asked as she started toward her husband's office.

He was at his desk, and when he glanced up, Ellen thought she saw a flash of annoyance in his eyes, but if it was there, he quickly banished it.

"Hi! What drags you down here? I thought you'd be up at the new place driving everyone crazy and spending the last of our money." Though he was smiling broadly, Ellen felt the sting of criticism, then told herself she was imagining it.

"I'm meeting Cynthia Evans," she replied, and immediately regretted her words. To Marsh, Cynthia and Bill Evans represented all the changes that had taken place in La Paloma. Of the fortunes that were being made, Bill's was one of the largest. "Don't worry," she added. "I'm not buying, just looking." She offered Marsh a kiss, and when it was not returned, went to perch uneasily on the sofa that sat against one wall. "Although we *are* going to have to do something about the tile in the patio," she added. "Most of it's broken, and it's impossible to match what isn't."

Marsh shook his head. "Later," he pronounced. "We agreed that for now, we'd only do what we have to to make the place livable."

"I know," Ellen sighed. "But every time Cynthia tells me what she's doing with the hacienda, I get absolutely green with envy."

Marsh set his pen down on the desk and faced her. "Then maybe you should have married a programming genius, not a country doctor," he suggested in a tone Ellen couldn't read.

While she tried to decide how to respond, her eyes surveyed the office. Despite Marsh's objections, she'd insisted on decorating it with rosewood furniture. "This isn't exactly what I'd call shabby," she finally ventured, and was relieved to see Marsh's smile return.

"No, it isn't," he agreed. "And even I have to admit that I kind of like it, even though I flinch every time I think of what it cost. Anyway, is that why you came down here? Just to terrify me with the idea of your shopping with Cynthia Evans?"

Ellen shook her head and tried to match his bantering tone. "Worse. I didn't even come down to see you. I came down to pick up the corsage for Alex." Marsh looked blank. "The prom," she reminded him. "Our son? Sixteen years old? Junior prom? Remember?"

Marsh groaned. "I'm sorry. It's just that there's so damned much to keep track of around here."

"Marsh," Ellen began, "I just wish . . . Oh, never mind."

"You wish I'd spend less time here and more at home," Marsh finished. "I will," he added. "Anyway, I'll try."

Their eyes met, and the office seemed suddenly to fill with the words that both of them had spoken so often they knew them by heart. The argument was old, and there was, both of them knew, no resolution for it. Besides, Marsh wasn't that different from most of the

husbands and fathers of La Paloma. They all worked too
many hours a day, and all of them were more interested
in their careers than in their families.

"I know you'll try," she said. Then she went on, her
voice rueful in spite of her intentions. "And I know
you'll fail, and I keep telling myself that it doesn't really
matter and that everything will be all right." Once
again Ellen regretted her words, but this time, instead
of looking irritated, Marsh got up and came to her,
pulling her to her feet.

"It will be all right," he told her. "We're just caught
up in a life we never expected, with more money than
we ever thought we'd have, and more demands on my
time than we ever planned for. But we love each other,
and whatever happens, we'll deal with it." He kissed
her. "Okay?"

Ellen nodded, as relief flowed through her. Over the
last years, and particularly the last months, there had
been so few moments like this, when she knew that she
and Marsh did, despite the problems, still belong together. She returned his kiss, then drew away, smiling.
"And now I'm going to get Alex his flowers."

Marsh's expression, soft a moment before, hardened
slightly. "Alex can't get them himself?"

"Times have changed," Ellen replied, ignoring the
look on her husband's face and trying to keep her voice
light. "And I don't have time to listen to you recite the
litany of the good old days. Let's face it—when you
were Alex's age, you didn't have nearly as much to do
after school as he does, and since I was going to be in
the village anyway, I might as well pick up the flowers."

Marsh's eyes narrowed, and the last trace of his smile
disappeared. "And when I was a kid, my school wasn't
as good as his is, and there was no accelerated education program for me like there is for Alex. Except he's
probably not going to get into it."

"Oh, God," Ellen said, as the last of their moment of
peace evaporated. Did he really have to convert something as simple as picking up a corsage into another

lecture on his perception of Alex as an underachiever? Which, of course, he wasn't, no matter what Marsh thought. And then, just as she was about to defend Alex, she checked herself, and forced a smile. "Let's not start that, Marsh. Not right now. Please?"

Marsh hesitated, then returned her smile, though it was as forced as her own. Still, he kissed her good-bye, and when she left his office, she hoped perhaps they might have had their last argument of the day. But when she was gone, instead of going back to the work that was stacked up on his desk, Marsh sat for a few minutes, letting his mind drift.

He, too, was aware of the strains that were threatening to pull his marriage apart, but he had no idea of what to do about them. The problems just seemed to pile up. As far as he could see, the only solution was to leave La Paloma, though he and Ellen had agreed a year ago that leaving was no solution at all. Leaving was not solving problems, it was only running away from them.

Nor was Alex's performance in school the real problem, though Marsh was convinced that if Alex only applied himself, he could easily be a straight-A student.

The problem, Marsh thought, was that he was beginning to wonder if his wife, like so many other people in La Paloma, had come to think that money would solve everything.

Then he relented. What was going wrong wasn't Ellen's fault. In fact, it was no one's fault. It was just that the world was changing, and both of them had to work harder to adjust to those changes before their marriage was torn apart.

He made up his mind to get home early that evening and see to it that nothing spoiled his wife's pleasure in their son's first prom.

Alex Lonsdale leaned forward across the bathroom sink and peered closely at the blemish on his right cheek, then decided that it wasn't a pimple at all—

merely a slight redness from the pressure he'd put on his father's electric razor while he'd shaved. He ran the razor over his face one last time, then opened it to clean it out the way his father had shown him. Not that there was much to clean—Alex's beard, a month after his sixteenth birthday, was still more a matter of optimism than reality. Still, when he tapped the shaver head against the sink, a few specks appeared, and they were the black of his own hair rather than the sandy brown of his father's. Grinning with satisfaction, he put the razor back together, left the bathroom, and hurried down the hall to his room, doing his best to ignore the sound of his parents' argument as their raised voices drifted in from the kitchen.

The argument had been going on for an hour now, ever since he'd left the dinner table to begin getting ready for the prom. It was a familiar argument, and as Alex began wrestling with the studs of his rented dress shirt, he wondered how far it would go.

He hated it when his parents started arguing, hated the fact that as hard as he tried not to listen, he could hear every word. That, at least, would be something he wouldn't have to worry about when they moved into the new house. Its walls were thick, and from his room on the second floor he wouldn't be able to hear anything that was going on in the rest of the house. So when the shouting matches began, he could just go to his room and shut it all out. Every angry word they spoke hurt him. All he could do was try not to hear.

He finished mounting the studs, shrugged into the shirt, then began working on the cufflinks, finally taking the shirt off again, folding the cuffs, maneuvering the links halfway through, then putting the shirt on once more. The left link was easy, but the right one gave him more trouble. At last it popped through the buttonholes, and he snapped it into position.

He glanced at the clock on his desk. He still had five minutes before he had to leave if he wasn't going to be late. He pulled on his pants, hooked up the suspend-ers, then eyed the cummerbund that lay on the bed. Which way was it supposed to go? Pleats up, or pleats down? He couldn't remember. He picked up his hairbrush and ran it through the thick shock of hair that always seemed to fall across his forehead, then grabbed the offending maroon cummerbund and matching dinner jacket. As he'd hoped they would, his parents fell silent as he appeared in the kitchen.

"I can't remember which way it goes," he said, holding up the garment.

"Pleats down," Ellen Lonsdale replied. "Otherwise it'll wind up full of crumbs. Turn around." Taking the cummerbund from Alex's hands, she fastened it neatly around his waist, then held his coat while he slid his arms into its sleeves. When he turned to face her once more, she reached up to put her arms around his neck and give him a hug. "You look terrific," she said. She squeezed him once more, then stepped back. "Now, you have a wonderful time, and drive carefully." She shot a warning look toward Marsh, then relaxed as she saw that he was apparently as willing as she to drop their argument.

"Gotta go," Alex was saying. "If I'm late, Lisa will kill me."

"If you're late, you'll kill yourself," Ellen observed, her smile returning. "But don't rush off and forget these." She opened the refrigerator and took out Lisa's corsage, along with the white carnation for Alex's lapel.

"You should've gotten red," Alex groused as he let his mother pin the flower onto his dinner jacket.

"If you wanted a red carnation, you should have gotten a white jacket," Ellen retorted. She stepped back and gazed proudly at Alex. Somehow, he had managed to inherit both their looks, and the combination was startling. His dark eyes and black wavy hair were hers; his fair complexion and even features, his father's. The combination lent his face a sensitive handsomeness that had earned him admiring remarks since he was a baby, and, in the last few months, an unending string of phone calls from girls who hoped he might be tiring of Lisa Cochran. "Don't be surprised if you and Lisa don't wind up the king and queen of the prom," she added, stretching upward to kiss him.

"Aw, Mom—"

"They still have the king and queen of the prom, don't they?" Ellen asked.

Blushing, Alex nodded his head, checked his pockets for his keys and wallet, and started for the door.

"And remember," Ellen called after him. "Don't stay out past one, and don't get into any trouble."

"You mean, don't drink," Alex corrected her. "I won't. I promise. Okay?"

"Okay," Marsh Lonsdale replied. He handed Alex a twenty-dollar bill. "Take some of the kids out and buy them a Coke after the dance."

"Thanks, Dad." Alex disappeared out the back door. A moment later Ellen and Marsh heard his car start. Marsh arched his brows. "I don't believe he's actually going to drive all the way next door," he said, unable to suppress a smile, despite the fact that it was Alex's car that he and Ellen had been arguing about all evening.

"Well, of course he is," Ellen replied. "Do you really think he's going to pick up Lisa, then walk her down our driveway? Not our Alex."

"He could have walked her all the way to the prom," Marsh suggested.

"No, he couldn't," Ellen said, her voice suddenly tired. "He needs a car, Marsh. After we move, I just can't spend all my time ferrying him up and down the ravine. And besides, he's a responsible boy—"

"I'm not saying he isn't," Marsh agreed. "All I'm saying is that I think he should have earned the car. And I'm not saying he should have earned the money, either. But couldn't we have used the car as an incentive for him to pick up his grades?"

Ellen shrugged, and began clearing the dinner dishes off the table. "He's doing just fine."

"He's not doing as well as he could be, and you know it as well as I do."

"I know," Ellen sighed. "But I just think it's two separate issues, that's all." Suddenly she smiled. "I'll tell you what. Why don't we compromise? Let's wait until his grades come out, and see what happens. If they get worse, I'll agree that getting him the car was a mistake, and you can take it away from him. I'll cope with the transportation problem some way. If they stay the same, or improve, he keeps the car. But either way, we stop fighting about it, all right?"

Marsh hesitated only a second, then grinned. "Deal," he said. "Now, what say I help you with the dishes, and we try to put together something with the Cochrans?" He offered his wife a mischievous wink. "I'll even drive over next door and pick them up."

The last of the tension that had been vibrating between them all afternoon suddenly dissipated, and together Ellen and Marsh began clearing away the dinner dishes.

Alex carefully backed his shiny red Mustang down the driveway, then parked it by the curb in front of the Cochran's house next door. He picked up Lisa's corsage, crossed the lawn, and walked into the house without knocking. "Anybody here?" he called. Lisa's six-year-old sister, Kim, hurtled down the stairs and threw herself onto Alex.

"Is that for me?" she demanded, grabbing for the corsage box.

"If Lisa isn't ready, maybe I'll take you to the dance," Alex replied, peeling Kim loose as her father's bulky frame appeared from the living room. "Hi, Mr. Cochran."

Jim Cochran raised one eyebrow and surveyed Alex. "Ah, Prince Charming descends from the castle on the mountain to take Cinderella to the ball."

Alex tried to cover his feelings of embarrassment with a grin. "Aw, come on. We're not moving for two more weeks. And it's not a castle anyway."

"True, true," Cochran agreed. "On the other hand, I haven't noticed you asking if you can rent Kim's room. We'll happily throw her out."

"You will not," Kim yelled, aiming a punch at her father's belly.

"Will too," her father told her. "Want a Coke, Alex? Lisa's still upstairs trying to make herself look human." He dropped his booming voice only slightly, still leaving it loud enough to fill the house. "Actually, she's been ready for an hour, but she doesn't want you to think she's too eager."

"That's a big lie!" Lisa said from the top of the stairs. "He always lies, Alex. Don't believe a word he says." Lisa, unlike Alex, had inherited all her looks from her mother. She was small, with short blond hair swept back from her face so that her green eyes became her dominant feature. And, being not only Lisa, but her father's daughter as well, she had chosen a dress in brilliant emerald rather than the more subdued pastels the other girls would be wearing. Alex's grin widened as she came down the stairs. "Hey, you look gorgeous."

Lisa smiled appreciatively and gave him a mock-seductive wink. "You don't look so bad yourself." She stood waiting for a moment; then: "Aren't you going to pin the corsage on?" Alex stared at the box in his hands, his face reddening as he handed it to Carol Cochran, who had appeared from the direction of the kitchen.

"M-maybe you'd better do it, Mrs. Cochran. I . . . I might slip or something."

"You won't slip, Alex," Lisa told him. "Now, come on. Just pin it on, and let's go. Otherwise we'll be here all night while Mom takes pictures."

Alex fumbled clumsily with the corsage for a moment, but finally succeeded in getting it fastened to Lisa's dress. Then, true to Lisa's words, Carol Cochran began herding them into the living room, camera in hand.

"Mom, we don't have time—" Lisa pleaded, but Carol was adamant.

"You only go to your first prom once, and you only wear your first formal once. And I'm going to have pictures of it. Besides, you both look so—"

"Oh, God, Alex," Lisa moaned. "She's going to say it. Cover your ears."

"Well, I don't care," Carol laughed as Alex and Lisa clapped their hands over their ears. "You *do* look cute!"

Twenty-four pictures later, Alex and Lisa were on their way to the prom.

"I don't see why we have to stand in the receiving line," Alex complained as he carefully slid the Mustang into a space between an Alfa Romeo and a Porsche. Before Lisa could answer, he was out of the car and opening the passenger door for her.

From a few yards away, a voice came out of the dusk. "Scratch that paint, and your ass is grass, Lonsdale."

Alex grinned and waved to Bob Carey, who was holding hands with Kate Lewis, but paying more attention to his Porsche than his girlfriend. "You tore the side off it last month!" Alex taunted him.

"And my dad nearly tore the side off me," Bob replied. "From now on, I have to pay for all the repairs myself." He waited until Lisa was out of the car and Alex had closed the door, then relaxed. "See you inside." He and Kate turned and started toward the gym, where the dance was being held.

"We have to stand in line because you're going to be student-body president next year," Lisa told Alex. "If you didn't want to do that kind of thing, you shouldn't have run."

"No one told me I had to. I thought all I had to do was have my picture taken for the annual."

"Come on, it won't be that bad. You know everybody in school already. All you have to do is say hello to them."

"And introduce them to you, which is stupid, because you know them all just as well as I do."

Lisa giggled. "It's all supposed to improve our social graces. Don't you want your graces improved?"

"What if I forget someone's name? I'll die."

"Stop worrying. You'll be fine. And we're late, so hurry up."

They hurried up the steps into the foyer of the gym and took their places in the receiving line. The first couple to approach them were Bob Carey and Kate Lewis, and Alex was pleased to see that Bob seemed as nervous about moving down the line as Alex was about standing in it. The two of them stood for a moment, wondering what to say to each other. Finally it was Kate who spoke.

"Isn't this wonderful?" she asked. "All year I've been looking forward to tonight, and I'm never going to forget a minute of it."

"None of us will," Lisa assured her.

And none of them ever did. For none of their lives was ever quite the same again.

CHAPTER TWO

The last thundering rock chord was abruptly cut off, and Alex, gasping, glanced around the gym in search of Lisa. The last time he'd seen her—at least fifteen minutes ago—she'd been dancing with Bob Carey, and he'd been dancing with Kate Lewis. Since then, he'd danced with three other girls, and now Bob was standing near the wall shouting in Jennifer Lang's ear. He started outside, certain that he'd find Lisa out on the lawn catching her breath. As he reached the door, a hand closed on his arm. He turned to see Carolyn Evans smiling at him.

"Hey," Carolyn said, "if you're looking for Lisa, she's in the rest room with Kate and Jenny."

"Then I guess I'll have a glass of punch, if there's any left."

"There's loads left," Carolyn told him in the slightly mocking voice Alex knew she always used when she was trying to seem more sophisticated than the rest of the kids. "Hardly anybody's drinking it except you and Lisa. Come on out to my car—I've got some beer."

Alex shook his head.

"Oh, come on," Carolyn urged. "What's one beer gonna do to you? I've had four, and I'm not drunk."

"I'm driving. If I'm driving, I don't drink."

Carolyn's head tipped back, and a throaty laugh that Alex was sure she practiced for hours emerged from her glistening lips. "You're just too good to be true, aren't you? Not even one little tiny beer? Come on, Alex—get human."

"It's not that," Alex replied, forcing a grin. "It's just that my dad'll take my car away from me if I come home with beer on my breath."

"Too bad for you," Carolyn purred. "Then I guess you can't come to my party." When she saw a slight flicker of interest in Alex's eyes, she decided to press her advantage. "Everybody's going to be there—sort of a housewarming."

Alex stared at Carolyn in disbelief. Was she really talking about the hacienda? But his mother told him the Evanses weren't letting anyone see it for another month, until it was completely refurbished.

And everyone in La Paloma, no matter what he thought of the Evanses, wanted to see what Cynthia Evans had done with Bill Evans's money.

At first, when the rumors began circulating that the Evanses had bought the enormous old mansion on top of Hacienda Drive, the assumption had been that they would tear it down. It had stood vacant for too many years, was far too big for a family to keep up without servants, and was far too decayed for anyone to seriously consider restoring it.

But then the project had begun.

First to be repaired was the outer wall. Much of it had long since collapsed; only a few yards of its southern expanse were still standing. But it had been rebuilt, its old wooden gates replaced by new ones whose designs had been copied from faded sketches of the hacienda as it had looked a hundred and fifty years earlier. Except that the new gates were wired with alarms and swung smoothly open on electrically controlled rollers. And then, after the wall was complete, Cynthia had begun the restoration of the mansion and the outbuildings.

Almost everybody in La Paloma had gone up to the top of Hacienda Drive once or twice, but the gates were always closed, and no one had succeeded in getting inside the walls. Alex, along with some of his friends, had climbed the hills a few times to peer down into the courtyard, but all they'd been able to see was the exterior work—the new plaster and the whitewashing, and the replacement of the red tiles on the roof.

What everyone was truly waiting for was a glimpse of the interior, and now Carolyn was saying her friends could see it that very night.

Alex eyed her skeptically. "I thought your mother wasn't letting anyone in until next month."

"Mom and Dad are in San Francisco for the weekend," Carolyn said.

"I don't know—" Alex began, remembering his promise not to go to any parties after the dance.

"Don't know about what?" Lisa asked, slipping her arm through his.

"He doesn't want to come to my party," Carolyn replied before Alex could say anything.

Lisa's eyes widened. "There's a party? At the hacienda?"

Carolyn nodded with elaborate casualness. "Bob and Kate are coming, and Jenny Lang, and everybody."

Lisa turned to Alex. "Well, let's go!" Alex flushed and looked uncomfortable, but said nothing. The band struck up the last dance and Lisa led Alex onto the floor. "What's wrong?" she asked a moment later. "Why can't we go to Carolyn's party?"

" 'Cause I don't want to."

"You just don't like Carolyn," Lisa argued. "But you won't even have to talk to her. Everybody else will be there too."

"It isn't that."

"Then what is it?"

"I promised my folks we wouldn't go to any parties. Dad gave me some money to take some of the kids out for a hamburger, and I promised we'd come home right after that."

Lisa fell silent for a few seconds; then: "We don't have to tell them where we were."

"They'd find out."

"But don't you even want to see the place?"

"Sure, but—"

"Then let's go. Besides, it's not where we go that your mom and dad are worried about—they're afraid you'll drink. So we'll go to the party, but we won't even have a beer. And we won't stay very long."

"Come on, Lisa. I promised them I wouldn't—"

But Lisa suddenly broke away from him and started pulling him off the dance floor. "Let's find Kate and Bob. Maybe we can convince them to go up to Carolyn's with us for just a few minutes, then the four of us can go out for hamburgers. That way we can see the place, and you won't have to lie to your folks."

As Lisa led him out of the gym, Alex knew he'd give in, even though he shouldn't. With Lisa, it was hard not to give in—she always managed to make everything sound perfectly logical, even when Alex was sure it wasn't.

The headlights of Alex's Mustang picked up the open gates of the hacienda, and he braked the car to a stop. "Are we supposed to park out here, or go inside?"

Lisa shrugged. "Search me. Carolyn didn't say." Suddenly a horn sounded, and Bob Carey's Porsche pulled up beside them, its window rolled down.

"Over there," Bob called. He was pointing off to the left, where a small group of cars already stood parked in the shadow of the wall. Following Bob, Alex maneuvered the Mustang into a spot next to a Camaro, shut off the engine, then turned to Lisa.

"Maybe we oughta just go on home," he suggested, but Lisa grinned and shook her head.

"I want to see it. Come on—just for a little while." She got out of the car, and after a second's hesitation, Alex joined her. A moment later Kate and Bob appeared out of the darkness, and the four of them started toward the lights flooding from the gateway.

"I don't believe this," Kate said a moment later. They were standing just inside the gate, trying to absorb the transformation that had come over what had been, only a year earlier, a crumbling ruin.

To the left, the old stables had been rebuilt into garages, and in the bright whiteness of the floodlights, the new plaster was indistinguishable from the old. The only change was that the stable roofs, originally thatched, were now of the same red tile as the house and the servants' quarters.

"It's weird," Alex said. "It looks like it's a couple of hundred years old."

"Except for that," Lisa breathed. "Have you ever seen anything like it?"

Dominating the courtyard, which until recently had been nothing more than an overgrown weed patch, was a glistening swimming pool fed by a cascade of tumbling water that made its way down five intricately tiled tiers before finally splashing into the immense oval of the pool.

Bob Carey whistled softly. "How big do you s'pose it is?"

"Big enough," Alex replied. Then his eyes wandered to what had once been the servants' quarters. "Wanta bet that's a pool house now?"

Before anyone could venture an answer, Carolyn Evans's voice rang out over the rock music that was throbbing from the huge main house. "Hey! Come on in!"

Glancing at each other uneasily, the four of them slowly crossed the courtyard, then stepped up onto the broad loggia that ran the entire length of the house. Carolyn, grinning happily, waited for them at the elaborately carved oaken front door. "Isn't it neat? Come on in—everybody's already here."

They went through the front door into a massive tile floored entry hall that was dominated by a staircase curving up to the second floor. To the right there was a large dining room, and beyond it they could see through another room into the kitchen. "That's a butler's pantry between the dining room and kitchen," Carolyn explained, then raised her voice as someone turned up the volume on the stereo. "Mom wasn't really sure it was supposed to be there, but she put it in anyway."

"You going to have a butler?" Kate Lewis asked.

Carolyn shrugged with elaborate unconcern. "I don't know. I guess so. Mom says the house is too big for María to take care of by herself."

"María *Torres*?" Bob Carey groaned. "That old witch can't even take care of her own house. My mom fired her after the first day!"

"She's okay—" Alex began, but was immediately drowned out by the others' laughter. Even Lisa joined in.

"Come on, Alex, she's a loony-bin case. Everybody knows that." Then she glanced guiltily toward Carolyn. "She isn't here, is she?"

Carolyn giggled maliciously. "If she is, she just got an earful."

At the top of the stairs, María Torres faded back into the darkness of the second-floor hallway, her black dress making her nearly invisible.

She had been sitting quietly in the large bedroom at the end of the corridor—the bedroom that, by rights, should have been hers—when the first of the cars had arrived.

No one, she knew, should have come back to the hacienda for hours, and she should have had the house to herself and her ghosts from the past. But now her reverie was shattered, and the pounding din of the *gringo* music, and the children of the *gringos* she had spent her life hating, filled the ancient rooms.

She had been in the house since seven o'clock, having let herself in with her own key as soon as Carolyn had left. She had spent the last four hours drifting through the house, imagining that it was hers, that she was not the cleaning woman—no more than a *peón*— but the mistress of the hacienda: Doña María Ruiz de Torres. And one day it would happen; one day, sometime in the vague future, it would happen. The *gringos* would be driven away, and finally the hacienda would be hers.

But for now she could only pretend, and be careful. The *gringos* were strict and never wanted her to be alone in their homes. She must leave the hacienda without being seen, and make her way back down the canyon to her little house behind the mission, and when she came back tomorrow, she must give no hint that she had been here at all tonight.

She glanced once more around the gloom of the bedroom that should have been hers, then slipped away, down the back stairs, the stairs that her ancestors never would have used, and out into the night. Then, as the *gringo* revelry went on—a desecration!—she kept watch, her ancient anger burning inside her. . . .

"Jeez," Bob whispered. "Last time I saw this, it looked like the place had burned. Now look at it."

The living room, across the entry hall from the dining room, was sixty feet long, and was dominated by an immense fireplace on the far wall.

The oak floor gleamed a polished brown that was nearly black, but the white walls picked up the light from sconces that had been wired into them at regular intervals to fill the room with an even brightness that made it seem even larger than it was. Twenty feet above, huge peeled logs supported a cathedral ceiling.

"This is incredible," Lisa breathed.

"This is just the beginning," Carolyn replied. "Just

wander around anywhere, and make sure you don't miss the basement. That's Daddy's part of the house, and Mom just hates it." Then she was gone, disappearing into the mass of teenagers who were dancing to the rhythms of a reggae album.

It took them nearly an hour to go through the house, and even then they weren't sure they'd seen it all. Upstairs there was a maze of rooms, and they'd counted seven bedrooms, each with its own bathroom, in addition to a library and a couple of small sitting rooms. All of it looked as if it had been built and furnished nearly two hundred years ago, then somehow frozen in time.

"Can you imagine living here?" Lisa asked as they finally started down toward the basement.

"It's not like a house at all," Alex replied. "It feels more like a museum. Hey," he added, suddenly stopping halfway down the stairs. "I don't remember this place ever having a basement."

"It didn't," Kate told him. "Carolyn says her dad wanted his own space, but her mom wouldn't let him have any of the old rooms. So he dug out a basement. Do you believe it?"

"Holy shit," Bob Carey muttered. "Didn't he think the house was big enough already?"

At the bottom of the stairs they found a laundry room to the left, and beyond that a big empty space that looked as though it was intended for storage.

Under the living room, occupying nearly the same amount of space as the room above, they found Mr. Evans's private space. For a long time they stared at it in silence.

"Well, I think it's tacky," Lisa said when she'd taken it all in.

Bob Carey shrugged. "And I think you're just jealous. I bet you wouldn't think it was tacky if it was your house."

Kate Lewis raked Bob with what she hoped was a scathing glare. "My mother always says the Evanses have more money than taste, and she's right. I mean, just look at it, Bob. It's gross!"

It was a media room. The far wall was nearly covered by an immense screen, which could be used either for movies or projection television. Along one wall was a complex of electronic components that none of them could completely identify. They were, however, apparently the source of the rock music, and they could barely hear Carolyn demanding that it be turned down for fear the neighbors would call the police. Nobody, however, was paying any attention to her, and much of the party seemed to have gravitated downstairs.

What had elicited Lisa Cochran's criticism, though, was not the electronics, but the bar opposite them. Not a typical home bar, with three stools and a rack for glasses, the Evanses' bar ran the entire length of the wall. Behind the counter itself, the wall was covered with shelves of liquor and glasses, and each shelf was edged with a neon tube, which provided a rainbow effect that was reflected throughout the room by the mirrors that covered the wall behind the shelves and the bar itself. The bar, by now, was covered with bottles, and several of the kids were happily filling glasses with various kinds of liquor.

"Want something?" Bob asked, eyeing the array.

Kate hesitated, then shrugged. "Why not? Is there any gin?"

Bob poured them each a tumbler, added a little ginger ale, and handed one of the glasses to Kate, then turned to ask Alex and Lisa what they wanted. But while he'd been mixing the drinks, Alex and Lisa had disappeared. "Hey—where'd they go?"

Kate shrugged. "I don't know. Come on, let's dance." She finished her drink and pulled Bob out onto the floor, but when the record ended, both she and Bob scanned the crowd, looking for Alex and Lisa.

"You think they got mad 'cause we had a drink?" Kate finally asked.

"Who cares? It's not as if we need a ride home or anything. Forget about them."

"No! Come on."

They found Alex and Lisa in the courtyard, staring up at the stars. "Hey," Bob yelled, holding up his glass, "aren't you two gonna join the party?"

"We weren't going to drink, remember?" Alex asked, staring at the glass. "We were going out for hamburgers."

"Who wants hamburgers when you can drink?" Bob replied. He reached down and pulled a bottle of beer out of a tub of ice and thrust it into Alex's hands. Alex looked at it for a moment, then glanced at Lisa, who frowned and shook her head. Alex hesitated, then defiantly twisted the cap loose and took a swig.

Lisa glared accusingly at him. "Alex!"

"I didn't even want to come to this party," Alex told her, his voice taking on a defensive edge. "But since we're here, we might as well enjoy it."

"But we said—"

"I know what we said. And I said I wasn't going to any parties, either. But I'm here. Why shouldn't I do what everybody else is doing?" Deliberately he tipped the beer bottle up and chugalugged it, then reached for another. Lisa's eyes narrowed angrily, but before she could say anything else, Carolyn Evans's voice suddenly rose over the din of the party as she came out of the front door with her arms full of towels.

"Who wants to go in the pool?"

There was a momentary silence, then someone replied that no one had suits. "Who needs suits?" Carolyn squealed. "Let's go skinny-dipping!" Suddenly she reached behind her, pulled down the zipper of her dress, and let it drop to the patio. Stripping off her panties and strapless bra, she dived into the pool, swam underwater for a few strokes, then broke the surface. "Come on," she yelled. "It's great!"

There was a moment of hesitation, then two more kids stripped and plunged into the water. Three more followed, and suddenly the patio was filling up with discarded clothes and the pool with naked teenagers. Once more, Alex glanced at Lisa.

"No!" she said, reading his eyes. "We were only coming for a few minutes, and we weren't going to drink. And we're certainly not going into the pool."

"Chicken," Alex teased, shrugging out of his dinner jacket. Then he drained the second beer, put the bottle down, and began untying his shoelaces.

"Alex, don't," Lisa begged. "Please?"

"Aw, come on. What's the big deal? Haven't you ever skinny-dipped before?"

"It's not a big deal," Lisa argued. "I just don't think we ought to do it. I think we ought to go home."

"Well, I think we ought to go swimming," Alex crowed. He stripped off his pants and shirt. "I didn't think we ought to come here, but I came, didn't I? Well, now I think we ought to go skinny-dipping, and I think you ought to go along with it." Peeling off his Jockey shorts, he plunged into the water. A moment later he came to the surface and turned around to grin at Lisa.

She was gone.

The effects of the two fast beers suddenly neutralized by the cold water, Alex scanned the crowd, sure that Lisa must be among the kids still on the pool deck. Then he was equally sure she was not. If she'd made up her mind not to come into the pool, she wouldn't change it.

And Alex suddenly felt like a fool.

He hadn't wanted to come to the party, he hadn't really wanted the two beers he'd drunk, and he certainly didn't want Lisa mad at him. He scrambled out of the water, grabbed a towel, then dried himself off and dressed as fast as he could. As he started into the house, he asked Bob Carey if he'd seen Lisa anywhere. Bob hadn't.

Nor had anyone else.

Ten minutes later, Alex left the house, praying that his car wasn't blocked in.

*   *   *

A quarter of a mile down Hacienda Drive, Lisa Cochran's quick pace slowed, and she wondered if maybe she shouldn't turn around and go back to the party. What, after all, was so horrible about skinny-dipping? And who was she to be so prissy about it? In a way, Alex was right—it *had* been her idea that they go to the party. He'd even argued with her, but she'd insisted. Still, he *had* drunk a couple of beers, and by now he might be working on a third. And if he was, she certainly didn't want to drive home with him.

She stopped walking entirely, and wondered what to do. Perhaps she should walk all the way into the village and wait for Alex at home.

Except that her parents would be up and would want to know what had happened.

Maybe the best thing to do was go back to the party, find Alex, and convince him that it was time for them to go home. She would do the driving.

But that would be giving in, and she wouldn't give in. She had been right, and Alex had been wrong, and it served him right that she'd walked out on him.

She made up her mind, and continued down the road.

Alex jockeyed the Mustang around Bob Carey's Porsche, then put it in drive and gunned the engine. The rear wheels spun on the loose gravel for a moment, then caught, and the car shot forward, down the Evanses' driveway and into Hacienda Drive.

Alex wasn't sure how long Lisa had been walking—it seemed as though it had taken him forever to get dressed and search the house. She could be almost home by now.

He pressed the accelerator, and the car picked up speed. He hugged the wall of the ravine on the first curve, but the car fishtailed slightly, and he had to steer into the skid to regain control. Then he hit a straight stretch and pushed his speed up to seventy. Coming up fast was an S curve that was posted at thirty

miles an hour, but he knew they always left a big
margin for safety. He slowed to sixty as he started into
the first turn.

And then he saw her.

She was standing on the side of the road, her green
dress glowing brightly in his headlights, staring at him
with terrified eyes.

Or did he just imagine that? Was he already that
close to her?

Time suddenly slowed down, and he slammed his
foot on the brake.

Too late. He was going to hit her.

It would have been all right if she'd been on the
inside of the curve. He'd have swept around her, and
she'd have been safe. But now he was skidding right
toward her . . .

Turn into it. He had to turn into it!

Taking his foot off the brake, he steered to the right,
and suddenly felt the tires grab the pavement.

Lisa was only a few yards away.

And beyond Lisa, almost lost in the darkness, something else.

A face, old and wrinkled, framed with white hair.
And the eyes in the face were glaring at him with an
intensity he could almost feel.

It was the face that finally made him lose all control
of the car.

An ancient, weathered face, a face filled with an
unspeakable loathing, looming in the darkness.

At the last possible moment, he wrenched the wheel
to the left, and the Mustang responded, slewing around
Lisa, charging across the pavement, heading for the
ditch and the wall of the ravine beyond.

Straighten it out!

He spun the wheel the other way.

Too far.

The car burst through the guardrail and hurtled over
the edge of the ravine.

"Lisaaaa . . ."

CHAPTER THREE

It was nearly two A.M. when Ellen Lonsdale heard the first faint wailing of a siren. She hadn't been asleep—indeed she'd been sitting in the living room ever since the Cochrans had left an hour earlier, growing increasingly restless as the minutes ticked by. It wasn't like Alex to be late, and for the last half-hour she'd been fighting a growing feeling that something had happened to him. The siren grew louder. A few seconds later it was joined by another, then a third. As she listened, the mournful wailings grew into shrill screams that tore the last vestiges of calmness from her mind.

It was Alex. Deep in her soul, she knew that the sirens were for her son.

Then, inside the house, the phone began to ring.

That's it, she thought. They're calling to tell me he's dead. Her feet leaden, she forced herself to go to the phone, hesitated a moment, then picked it up.

"H-hello?"

"Ellen?"

"Yes."

"This is Barbara, at the Center?"

The hesitancy in Barbara Fannon's voice told Ellen that something had gone wrong. "What is it? What's happened?"

Barbara's voice remained professionally neutral. "May I speak to Dr. Lonsdale please?"

"What's happened?" Ellen demanded again. Then, hearing the note of hysteria in her voice, she took a deep breath and reminded herself that Marsh was on call that night. "I'm sorry," she said. "Just a moment, Barbara."

Her hand shaking in spite of herself, she laid the receiver on the table next to the phone and turned toward the hall. Marsh, his eyes still bleary with sleep, stood in the doorway. "What's happening? Something woke me up."

"Sirens," Ellen breathed. "Something's happened, and the hospital wants to talk to you."

His eyes immediately clearing, Marsh strode into the room and picked up the phone. "This is Dr. Lonsdale."

"Marsh? It's Barbara. I'm in the emergency room. I hate to call you in this late, but there's been some kind of an accident, and we don't know how bad it is yet. Since you're on call . . ." Her voice trailed off uncertainly.

"You did right. I'll be right there. Does anybody have any details at all?"

"Not really. Apparently at least one car went off the road, and we don't know how many people were in it—"

"Maybe I'd better go up there."

There was a hesitation; then: "The EMT's are with the ambulance, Doctor. . . ."

Now it was Marsh who hesitated, then grimaced slightly. Even after five years, he found it hard to accept that the emergency medical technicians were, indeed, better trained to handle such situations than he himself was. "I get the picture, Barb. Say no more. See you in a few minutes." He hung up the phone, then turned to Ellen, who stood behind a chair, both hands gripping its back.

"It's Alex, isn't it?" she breathed.

"Alex?" Marsh repeated. What could have put that idea into Ellen's head? "Why on earth should it have anything to do with Alex?"

Ellen did her best to steady herself. "I just have a feeling, that's all. I've had it for about half an hour. It *is* Alex, isn't it?"

"No one knows who it is yet," Marsh replied. "It's an automobile accident, but that doesn't mean it's Alex." His words, though, did nothing to dissipate the fear in her eyes, and despite the tension that still hung between them, he took her in his arms. "Honey, don't do this to yourself." When Ellen made no reply, he reluctantly released her and started toward their bedroom, but Ellen held onto his arm, and when she spoke, her eyes, as well as her words, were pleading.

"If it isn't Alex, why did they call you? There's an intern on duty, isn't there?"

Marsh nodded. "But they don't know how many people might have been hurt. They might need me, and I *am* on call." He gently disengaged her hand, but Ellen followed him into the bedroom.

"I want to go with you," she said while he began dressing.

Marsh shook his head. "Ellen, there's no reason—"

"There *is* a reason," Ellen protested, struggling to keep her voice level, but not succeeding. "I have a feeling, and—"

"And it's only a feeling," Marsh insisted, and Ellen flinched at the dismissive tone of his words. He relented, and once more put his arms around his wife. "Honey, please. Think about it. Automobile accidents happen all the time. The odds of this one involving Alex are next to nothing. And I can't deal with whatever's happening if I have to take care of you too."

His words hurt her, but Ellen knew he was right. Deliberately she made herself stop shaking and stepped away from him. "I'm sorry," she said. "It's just that . . . Oh, never mind. Go."

Marsh offered her a smile. "Now, that's my girl."

Though her husband's smile did nothing to alleviate her pain, Ellen picked up his wallet and keys from the dresser and handed them to him. "Marsh?" she asked, then waited until he met her eyes before going on. "As soon as you know what's happened, have someone call me. I don't need details—I just need to know it's not Alex."

"By the time I know what's happened, Alex will probably be home," Marsh replied. Then he relented. "But I'll have someone call. With any luck, I'll be back in an hour myself."

Then he was gone, and Ellen sank slowly onto the sofa to wait.

"Jesus Christ," Sergeant Roscoe Finnerty whispered as the spotlight on his patrol car illuminated the wreckage at the bottom of the ravine. "Why the fuck didn't it burn?" Grabbing his flashlight, he got out of the car and started clambering down the slope, with his partner, Thomas Jefferson Jackson, right behind him. A few yards away, Finnerty saw a shape move, and trained his light on the frightened face of a teenage boy.

"Far enough, son," Finnerty said quietly. "Whatever's happened, we'll take care of it."

"But—" the boy began.

"You heard him," Jackson broke in. "Get back up on the road, and stay out of the way." He flashed his light on the knot of teenagers who were clustered together. Most of them had wet hair, and their clothes were in disarray. "Those your friends?"

The boy nodded.

"Musta been some party. Now, get up there with them, and we'll talk to you later."

Silently the boy turned and started back up the hill, and Jackson followed Finnerty down toward the wreckage. Behind him, he heard car doors slamming, and the

sound of voices issuing orders. Vaguely he became aware
of other people beginning to move down the slope of
the ravine.

The car lay on its side, so battered its make was no
longer recognizable. It appeared to have turned end for
end at least twice, then rolled until it came to rest
against a large boulder.

"The driver's still in it," Jackson heard Finnerty say,
and his stomach lurched the way it always did when he
had to deal with the victims of automobile accidents.
Stoically he moved forward.

"Still alive?"

"Dunno," Finnerty grunted. "Don't hardly see how
he can be, though." He paused then, well aware of his
partner's weak stomach. "You okay?"

"I'll throw up later," Jackson muttered. "Anybody
else in the car?"

"Nope. But if someone wasn't wearing a seat belt,
they'd have gone out on the first flip." He shone his
light briefly on Jackson's sweating face. "You wanna
help out here, or look around for another victim?"

"I'll help. 'Least till the medics get here." He approached the car and stared in at the body that was
pitched forward against the steering wheel. The head
was covered with blood, and it looked to Jackson as if
Finnerty was right—if the smashup itself hadn't killed
the driver, he must have bled to death by now. Still,
he had his job to do, and clenching his teeth, Jackson
began helping his partner cut through the seat belt that
held the inert body into what was left of the car.

"Don't move him," one of the emergency technicians
warned a moment later. He and his partner began
unfolding a stretcher as the two cops finished cutting
away the seat belt.

"You think we haven't done this before?" Finnerty
rasped. "Anyway, I don't think it'll make much difference
with this one."

"We'll decide that," the EMT replied, moving forward and edging Jackson aside. "Anybody know who he is?"

"Not yet," Jackson told him. "We'll run a make on the plate as soon as we get him up to the road."

The two EMT's slowly and carefully began working Alex's body out of the wreckage, and, what seemed to Jackson to be an eternity later, eased him onto the stretcher.

"He's not dead yet," one of the EMT's muttered. "But he will be if we don't get him out of here fast. Come on."

With a man at each corner of the stretcher, the two EMT's and the two cops began making their way up the hill.

The crowd of teenagers on the road stood silently watching as the stretcher was borne upward. In the midst of them, Lisa Cochran leaned heavily on Kate Lewis, who did her best to keep Lisa from looking at the bloodied shape of Alex Lonsdale.

"He must still be alive," Bob Carey whispered. "They've got something wrapped around his head, but his face isn't covered."

Then the medics were on the road, sliding the stretcher into the ambulance. A second later, its lights flashing and its siren screaming, it roared off into the night.

In the emergency room of the Medical Center, a bell shattered the tense silence, and a scratchy voice emanated from a speaker on the wall.

"This is Unit One. We've got a white male, teenage, with multiple lacerations of the face, a broken arm, damage to the rib cage, and head injuries. Also extensive bleeding."

Marshall Lonsdale reached across the desk and pressed the transmission key himself. "Any identification yet?"

"Negative. We're too busy keeping him alive to check his I.D."

"Will he make it?"

There was a slight hesitation; then: "We'll know in two minutes. We're at the bottom of Hacienda, turning into La Paloma Drive."

Thomas Jefferson Jackson sat in the passenger seat of the patrol car, waiting for the identification of the car that lay at the bottom of the ravine. He glanced out the window and saw Roscoe Finnerty talking to the group of kids whose party had just ended in tragedy. He was glad he didn't have to talk to them—he doubted whether he would have been able to control the rage that seethed in him. Why couldn't they have just had a dance and let it go at that? Why did they have to get drunk and start wrecking cars? He wasn't sure he'd ever understand what motivated them. All he'd do was go on getting sick when they piled themselves up.

"It was Alex Lonsdale," Bob Carey said, unable to meet Sergeant Finnerty's eyes.

"Dr. Lonsdale's kid?"

"Yes."

"You sure he was driving it?"

"Lisa Cochran saw it happen."

"Who's she?"

"Alex's girlfriend. She's over there."

Finnerty followed Bob's eyes and saw a pretty blond in a dirt-smeared green formal sobbing in the arms of another girl. He knew he should go over and talk to her, but decided it could wait—from what he could see, she didn't look too coherent.

"You know where she lives?" he asked Bob Carey. Numbly Bob recited Lisa's address, which Finnerty wrote in his notebook. "Wait here a minute." He strode to the car just as Jackson was opening the door.

"Got a make on the car," Jackson said. "Belongs to Alexander Lonsdale. That's Dr. Lonsdale's son, isn't it?"

Finnerty nodded grimly. "That's what the kids say, too, and apparently the boy was driving it. We got a witness, but I haven't talked to her yet." He tore the sheet with Lisa's address on it out of his notebook and handed it to Jackson. "Here's her name and address. Get hold of her parents and tell them we'll take the girl down to the Center. We'll meet them there."

Jackson looked at his partner uncertainly. "Shouldn't we take her to the station and get a statement?"

"This is La Paloma, Tom, not San Francisco. The kid in the car was her boyfriend, and she's pretty broken up. We're not gonna make things worse by dragging her into the station. Now, get hold of the Center and tell them who's coming in, then get hold of these Cochran people. Okay?"

Jackson nodded and got back in the car.

Lisa sat on the ground, trying to accept what had happened. It all had a dreamlike quality to it, and there seemed to be only bits and pieces left in her memory.

Standing in the road, trying to make up her mind whether or not to go back to the party and find Alex.

And then the sound of a car.

Instinctively, she'd known whose car it was, and her anger had suddenly evaporated.

And then she'd realized the car was coming too fast. She'd turned around to try to wave Alex down.

And then the blur.

The car rushing toward her, swerving away at the last minute, then only a series of sounds.

A shriek of skidding tires—

A scraping noise—

A crash—

And then the awful sound of Alex screaming her name, cut off by the horrible crunching of the car hurtling into the ravine.

Then nothing—just a blank, until suddenly she was back at Carolyn Evans's, and all the kids were staring at her, their faces blank and confused.

She hadn't even been able to tell them what had

happened. She'd only been able to scream Alex's name, and point toward the road.

It had been Bob Carey who had finally understood and called the police.

And then there had been more confusion.

People scrambling out of the pool, grabbing clothes, streaming out of the house.

Most of them running down the road.

A few cars starting.

And Carolyn Evans, her eyes more furious than frightened, glaring at her.

"It's your fault," Carolyn had accused. "It's all your fault, and now I'm going to be in trouble."

Lisa had gazed at her: what was she talking about?

"My *parents*," Carolyn had wailed. "They'll find out, and ground me for the rest of the summer."

And then Kate Lewis was beside her, pulling her away.

Suddenly she was back on Hacienda Drive, and the night was filled with sirens, and flashing lights, and people everywhere, asking her questions, staring down into the ravine. . . .

It had seemed to go on forever.

Finally there was that awful moment when the stretcher had appeared, and she'd seen Alex—

Except it hadn't been Alex.

It had only been a shape covered by a blanket.

She'd only been able to look for a second, then Kate had twisted her around, and she hadn't seen any more.

Now a voice penetrated the haze.

"Lisa? Lisa Cochran?"

She looked up, nodding mutely. A policeman was looking at her, but he didn't seem to be mad at her.

"We need to get you out of here," the policeman said. "We have to take you down to the Medical Center." He held out a hand. "Can you stand up?"

"I . . . I . . . ." Lisa struggled to rise, then sank back to the ground. Strong hands slid under her arms and lifted her up. A minute later she was in the back seat of a police car. A few yards away she saw another police car, and a policeman talking to some of her friends.

But they didn't know what had happened. Only she knew.

Lisa buried her face in her hands, sobbing.

The speaker on the wall of the emergency room crackled to life once again.

"This is Unit One," the anonymous voice droned. "We'll be there in another thirty seconds. And we have an identification on the victim." Suddenly the voice cracked, losing its professional tone. "It's Alex . . . Alex Lonsdale."

Marsh stared at the speaker, willing himself to have heard the words wrong. Then he gazed around the room, and knew by the shock on everyone's face, and by the way they were returning his gaze, that he had not heard wrong. He groped behind him for a chair, found one, and lowered himself into it.

"No," he whispered. "Not Alex. Anyone but Alex . . ."

"Call Frank Mallory," Barbara Fannon told one of the orderlies, immediately taking charge. "He's next on call. His number's on the Rolodex." She moved around the desk and put a hand on Marshall Lonsdale's shoulder. "Maybe it's a mistake, Marsh," she said, though she knew that the ambulance crew wouldn't have identified Alex if they weren't absolutely sure.

Marsh shook his head and then raised his agonized eyes. "How am I going to tell her?" he asked, his voice dazed. "How am I going to tell Ellen? She . . . she had a feeling . . . she told me . . . she wanted to come with me tonight—"

"Come on." Barbara assumed her most authoritative tone, the one she always used with people she knew were close to breaking. Outside, the sound of the approaching ambulance disturbed the night. "We're getting you out of here." When Marsh failed to respond, she took him by the hand and drew him to his feet. "I'm taking you to your office."

"No!" Marsh protested as the approaching siren grew louder. "Alex is my son—"

"Which is exactly why you won't be here when they bring him in. We'll have Frank Mallory here as soon as possible, and until he gets here, Benny Cohen knows what to do."

Marsh looked dazed. "Benny's only an intern—"

Barbara began steering him out of the emergency room as the siren fell silent and headlights glared momentarily through the glass doors of the emergency entrance. "Benny's the best intern we've ever had. You told me so yourself."

Then, as the emergency-room doors opened and the gurney bearing Alex Lonsdale's nearly lifeless body was pushed inside, she forced Marsh Lonsdale into the corridor.

"Go to your office," she told him. "Go to your office and mix yourself a drink from the bottle you and Frank nip at every time you deliver a baby. I can take care of everything else, but right now I can't take care of you. Understand?"

Marsh swallowed, then nodded. "I'll call Ellen—"

"You'll do no such thing," Barbara cut in. "You'll fix a drink, drink it, and wait. I'll be there in five minutes, and by then we'll know something about how he is. Now, go!" She gave Marsh a gentle shove, then disappeared back into the emergency room.

Marsh paused a moment, trying to sort out his thoughts.

He knew that Barbara was right.

With a shambling gait, feeling suddenly helpless, he started down the hall toward his office.

In the little house behind the old mission, across the street from the graveyard, María Torres dropped the blind on the front window back into place, then shuffled slowly into the bedroom and eased her aged body into bed.

She was tired from the long walk home, and tonight it had been particularly exhausting.

Unwilling to be seen by anyone that night, María had been forced to make her way down the canyon by way of the path that wound through the underbrush a few feet below the level of the road. Each time she had heard the wailing of a siren and seen headlights flashing on the road above, she had huddled close to the ground, waiting until the car had passed before once more making her slow progress toward home.

But now it was all right.

She was home, and no one had seen her, and her job was safe.

Tonight she had no trouble. Tonight it was the *gringos* who had the trouble.

To María Torres, what had happened on the road near the hacienda tonight was nothing less than a blessing from the saints. All her life, she had spent many hours each week praying that destruction would come to the *gringos*. Tonight, she knew, was one of the nights the saints had chosen to answer those prayers.

Tomorrow, or the next day, she would find out who had been in the car that had plunged over the edge of the ravine, and remember to go to church and light a candle to whichever saint had, in answer to her prayers, abandoned one of his namesakes this evening. Her candles were not much, she knew, but they were something, and the souls of her ancestors would appreciate them.

Silence finally fell over La Paloma. For the rest of the night, María Torres slept in peace.

Benny Cohen carefully peeled away the towel that had been wrapped around Alex Lonsdale's head, and stared at the gaping wound on the boy's skull.

He's dead, Benny thought. He may still be breathing, but he's dead.

CHAPTER FOUR

Ellen Lonsdale knew her premonition had come true as soon as she opened the front door and saw Carol Cochran standing on the porch, a handkerchief clutched in her left hand, her eyes rimmed with red.

"It happened, didn't it?" she whispered.

Carol's head moved in a barely perceptible nod. "It's Alex," she whispered. "He . . . he was alone in the car . . ."

"Alone?" Ellen echoed. Where had Lisa been? Hadn't she been with Alex? But her questions went unspoken as she tried to concentrate on what Carol was saying.

"He's at the Center," Carol told her, stepping into the house and closing the door behind her. "I'll take you."

For a moment Ellen felt as if she might collapse. Then, with an oddly detached calmness, she picked her purse up from the table in the entry hall and automatically opened it to check its contents. Satisfied that everything was there, she walked past Carol and opened the front door. "Is he dead?" she asked.

"No," Carol replied, her voice catching. "He's not dead, Ellen."

"But it's bad, isn't it?"

"I don't know. I don't think anyone does."

Silently the two women got into the Cochrans' car and Carol started the engine. As she was backing down the Lonsdales' driveway, Ellen asked the question that was still lurking in her mind. "Why wasn't Lisa with him?"

"I don't know that. We got a call from the police. They said to meet them at the Center, that they were taking Lisa there. I thought . . . Oh, God, never mind what I thought. Anyway, Lisa's all right, but Alex—his car went off the road up near the old hacienda. Carolyn was having a party."

"He said he wouldn't go to any parties," Ellen said numbly, her body slumped against the car door. "He promised—" She broke off her own thought, and remained silent for several seconds as her mind suddenly began to shift gears. *I can't fall apart. I can't give in to what I'm feeling. I have to be strong. For Alex, I have to be strong.* She consciously straightened herself in the car seat. "Well, it doesn't matter what he promised, does it?" she asked. "The only thing that matters is that he be all right." She turned to gaze searchingly at Carol, and when she spoke, her voice was stronger. "If you knew how bad it was, you'd tell me, wouldn't you?"

Carol moved her hand off the steering wheel to give Ellen's arm a quick squeeze. "Of course I would. And I'm not going to tell you not to worry, either."

As Carol drove, Ellen tried to make herself concentrate on anything but what might have happened to Alex. She gazed out the window, forcing her mind to focus only on what her eyes were taking in.

"It's a pretty town," she said suddenly.

"What?" Carol Cochran asked, taken aback by Ellen's odd statement.

"I was just looking at it," Ellen went on. "I haven't really done that for a long time. I drive around it all the

time, but it's been years since I really paid attention to
what it looks like. And a lot of it hasn't really changed
since we were children."

"No," Carol said slowly, still not sure where Ellen's
thoughts were leading. "I don't suppose it has."

Ellen uttered a sound that was partly a hollow chuckle,
partly a sob. "Do you think I'm crazy, talking about
how pretty La Paloma is? Well, I'm not. Anyway, I
don't think I am. But I'm having a feeling, and if I let
myself think about *that*, then I *will* go crazy."

"Do you want to tell me what it is?"

There was another long silence, and when she spoke
again, Ellen's voice had gone strangely flat. "He's dead,"
she stated. "I have the most awful feeling that Alex is
dead. But he isn't dead. I . . . I won't *let* him be dead!"

Ellen stared at the knot of people in the emergency
waiting room. She recognized most of the faces, though
for some reason her mind refused to put names to
them. Except for a few.

Lisa Cochran.

She was sitting on a couch, huddled close to her
father, and a policeman was talking to her. Lisa saw her
and immediately stood up and started toward her.

"I'm sorry," she blurted. "Oh, Mrs. Lonsdale, I'm so
sorry. I didn't mean to—"

"What happened?" Ellen asked, her voice dull.

"I . . . I'm not sure," Lisa stammered. "We had a
fight—well, sort of a fight, and I decided to walk home.
And Alex must have been coming after me. But he was
driving too fast, and . . ." She went on, blurting out the
story of what had happened, while Ellen listened, but
only half-heard. Around them, the rest of the people in
the waiting room fell silent.

"It was my fault," Lisa finished. "It was all my fault."

Ellen laid a gentle hand on Lisa's cheek, then kissed
her. "No," she said quietly. "It wasn't your fault. You
weren't in the car, and it wasn't your fault."

She turned away to find Barbara Fannon at her elbow. "Where is he?" she asked. "Where's Alex?"

"He's in the O.R. Frank and Benny are working on him. Marsh is in his office." She took Ellen's arm and began guiding her out of the waiting room.

When she came into his office, Marsh was sitting behind his desk, a glass in front of him, staring at nothing. His gaze shifted, and he stood up, came around the desk, and put his arms around her.

"You were right," he whispered, his voice strangling on the words. "Oh, God, Ellen, you were right."

"Is he dead?" Ellen asked.

Marsh drew back sharply, as if the words had been a physical blow. "Who told you that?"

Ellen's face paled. "No one. I just . . . I just have a feeling, that's all."

"Well, that one isn't true," Marsh told her. "He's alive."

Ellen hesitated; then: "If he's alive, why don't I feel it?"

Marsh shook his head. "I don't know. But he's not dead. He's seriously injured, but he's not dead."

Time seemed to stand still as Ellen gazed deep into her husband's eyes. At last she quietly repeated Marsh's words. "He's not dead. He's not dead. He won't die." Then, despite her determination to be strong, her tears began to flow.

In the operating room, Frank Mallory carefully withdrew the last visible fragment of shattered skull from the tissue of Alex's brain. He glanced up at the monitors.

By rights, the boy should be dead.

And yet, there on the monitors was the evidence that he was not.

There was a pulse—weak and erratic, but there.

And he was breathing, albeit with the aid of a respirator.

His broken left arm was in a temporary splint, and

the worst of his facial lacerations had been stitched just
enough to stop the bleeding.

That had been the easy part.

It was his head that was the problem.

From what Mallory could see, as the car tumbled
down the ravine, Alex's head must have smashed against
a rock, crushing the left parietal plate and damaging the
frontal plate. Pieces of both bones had broken away,
embedding themselves in Alex's brain, and it was these
splinters that Mallory had been carefully removing.
Then, with all the skill he could muster, he had worked
the fractured pieces as nearly into their normal posi-
tions as possible. Now he was applying what could only
be temporary bandages—bandages intended to bind
Alex's wounds only until the electroencephalogram went
totally flat and the boy would be declared dead.

"What do you think?" Benny Cohen asked.

"Right now, I'm trying not to think," Mallory replied. "All I'm doing is putting the pieces back together, and I'm sorry to say I'm not at all sure I can do
it."

"He's not gonna make it?"

"I'm not saying that, either," Mallory rasped, unable
to admit his true thoughts. "He's made it this far, hasn't
he?"

Benny nodded. "With a lot of help. But without the
respirator, he'd be gone."

"A lot of people need respirators. That's why they
were invented."

"But most people only need them temporarily. He's
going to need it the rest of his life."

Frank Mallory glowered at the young intern, then
softened. Cohen, after all, hadn't known Alex Lonsdale
since the day the boy was born, nor had Cohen yet lost
a patient. When he did, maybe he'd realize how much
it hurt to see someone die and know there's nothing
you can do about it. But Alex had survived the first
emergency procedures, and there was still the possibil-

ity that he might live. "Let's get him into the ICU, then start setting up for X rays and a CAT scan."

Ten minutes later, still drying his hands with a white towel, Mallory walked into Marshall Lonsdale's office. Both Marsh and Ellen struggled wearily to their feet.

"He's still alive, and in the ICU," Mallory told them, gesturing for them both to sit down again. "But it's bad, Marsh. Real bad."

"Tell me," Marsh replied, his voice toneless.

Mallory shrugged. "I can't tell you all of it yet—you know that. But there's brain damage, and it looks extensive."

Ellen stiffened, but said nothing.

"We're setting up right now for every test we can give him. But it's going to be tough, because he's on a respirator and a cardiostimulator." Then, as Marsh and Ellen listened, he described Alex's injuries, using the dispassionate, factual tone he had learned in medical school, in order to keep himself under control. When he was done, it was Ellen who spoke.

"What can we do?"

Mallory shook his head. "Nothing, for the moment. Try to stabilize him, and try to find out how bad the damage is. We should know sometime early in the morning. Maybe by six."

"I see," Ellen murmured. Then: "Can I see him?"

Frank Mallory's eyes flicked toward Marsh, who nodded. "Of course you can," Mallory said. "You can sit with him all night, if you want to. It can't hurt, and it might help. You never know what people in his condition know or don't know, but if somehow he knows you're there . . . well, it can't hurt, can it?"

Barbara Fannon glanced up at the clock on the wall and was surprised to see that it was nearly five in the morning. To her, it seemed as if it couldn't have been more than an hour since the ambulance arrived with Alex.

There had been so much to do.

There had been all the tests that needed to be set up, and it had fallen to Barbara to coordinate the testing so that Alex was subjected to the least amount of movement possible. Not only had she coordinated the X rays and CAT scan, but everything else Frank Mallory had requested. And, as far as Barbara could determine, he hadn't forgotten anything: he'd ordered ultrasound imaging and a cerebrospinal tap, as well as an arteriograph and an EEG. The only thing he'd left out was a pneumoencephalograph, and Barbara knew the only reason he'd skipped it was that Alex would have had to be put in a vertical position to carry it out. In his present condition, that simply wasn't feasible. It had taken Barbara nearly an hour simply to contact all the technicians necessary and get them to the Center. And then, of course, there had been the people in the waiting room.

They had thinned out after the first couple of hours, when Barbara had finally told them that there would be no more news that night—Alex was undergoing a series of tests, but the results would be unavailable for an indefinite period.

Now, at five o'clock, she could at last go home. Everything that needed to be done, or could be done, was finished, and she realized she was bone weary. All she had to do was check the waiting room, and she could go. She pushed the door open, expecting the room to be empty.

It wasn't.

Sitting on the couch in the far corner was Lisa Cochran, her parents flanking her. She was dry-eyed now, and sitting straight up, her hands folded quietly in her lap. Barbara hesitated, then went into the waiting room, letting the door swing shut behind her.

"Can I get you anything?" she asked. "Some coffee, maybe?"

Lisa shook her head, but said nothing.

"If you can think of a way to convince her to come home with us, that might help," Carol said, rising to

her feet, stretching, and offering the tired nurse a re-
signed smile.

"I can't, Mama," Lisa whispered. "What if he wakes
up and asks for me?"

Barbara crossed the room and sat next to the girl.
"He's not going to wake up tonight, Lisa."

Lisa regarded her with bloodshot eyes. "Is . . . is he
going to wake up at all?"

Barbara knew it wasn't her place to talk to anyone
about Alex Lonsdale's condition, but she also knew
exactly who Lisa was, and how Alex felt about her. God
knew he'd spent enough time perched on the edge of
Barbara's desk telling her how wonderful Lisa was. And
after watching her through the last several hours, Barbara was convinced that Alex was right. She sighed
heavily. "I don't know," she said carefully; then, when
Lisa's eyes turned suddenly frightened, she went on: "I
said I don't know. That doesn't mean he's not going to
wake up. All it means is that I don't know, and no one
else does either."

"If he wakes up, will that mean he's going to be all
right?"

Barbara shrugged. "We don't know that, either. All
we can do is wait and see."

"Then I'll wait," Lisa said.

"You could go home and try to get some sleep,"
Barbara suggested. "I promise I'll arrange for someone
to call you if anything happens. Anything at all."

Lisa rubbed at her eyes, then shook her head. "No,"
she said. "I want to be here. Just in case." She looked
at the nurse beseechingly. "He *might* wake up."

Barbara started to speak, then changed her mind.
She's right, she decided. He damned well might wake
up. And as she absorbed the thought, she realized that
she, like most of the staff at the clinic, had only been
going through the motions of administering to Alex.

For all of them, all the trained medical people who
had seen injuries like Alex's before, it was a hopeless
case. You did what you could, tried not to overlook any

measure, no matter how drastic, that might save the life, but deep inside you prepared yourself for the fact that the patient wasn't going to make it.

And at the end of your shift, you went home.

But Lisa Cochran wasn't going home, and Barbara Fannon decided she wasn't going home either, even though her shift had ended long ago. Coming to that decision, she stood up. "Come on," she said.

The Cochrans looked at her uncertainly, but followed her down the hall. Without knocking, she opened the door to Marshall Lonsdale's office and led them inside. "If we're all going to stay, we might as well be as comfortable as possible."

"This is Marsh's office," Jim Cochran said.

"Nobody else's."

"Should we be here?"

"You're his friends, aren't you? It's been a long night, and it's going to be an even longer one. I was going home, but if you can stick this out, so can I. But not out there." She lowered the lights a little, and closed the blinds to the windows. "Make yourselves comfortable while I go find some coffee. If you want something stronger, you might poke around the office while I'm gone. I've heard rumors that sometimes there's a bottle in here."

Jim eyed the nurse. "Any rumors about just where it might be?"

"No," Barbara replied. Then, as she left the office, she spoke once more. "But if I were you, I'd start looking in the credenza. Bottom right."

Ellen Lonsdale sat in a straight-backed chair that had been pulled close to Alex's bed, her right hand resting gently on his. He lay as he had been placed, on his back, the cast on his left arm suspended slightly above the mattress, his limp right arm extended parallel to his body. His face, covered with the respirator mask and a mass of bandages, was barely visible, and totally unrecognizable. Around him was an array of equipment that Ellen couldn't begin to comprehend. All she knew was that the monitors and machinery were somehow keeping her son alive.

She had been there for nearly five hours now. The sky outside the window was beginning to brighten, and she shifted slightly in her chair, not as a reaction to the stiffness that had long ago taken over her body, but so that she could get a clearer look at Alex's eyes.

For some reason, she kept thinking they should be open.

The night had been filled with odd thoughts like that.

Several times she had found herself feeling surprise that the respirator was still operating.

Once, when they brought Alex back from one of the tests—she couldn't remember which one—she had been shocked at the warmth of his hand when she touched it.

She knew what the odd feelings were about.

Despite what she had been told—despite her own inner resolve—she still had the horrible feeling that Alex was dead.

Several times she had found herself studying the monitors, wondering why they were still registering life signs in Alex.

Since he was dead, the graphic displays of his heart-beat and breathing should be flat.

She kept reminding herself that he wasn't dead, that he was only asleep.

Except he wasn't asleep.

He was in a coma, and despite what everyone kept saying, he wasn't going to come out of it.

Abstractly she already understood that it wasn't a matter of waiting to see what would happen. It was a matter of deciding when to remove the respirator and let Alex go.

She didn't know how long that thought had been in her mind, but she knew she was beginning to get used to the reality of it. Sometime today, or perhaps tomorrow, after all the test results had been studied and analyzed, she and Marsh were going to have to make

the most difficult decision of their lives, and she wasn't
at all sure either of them would be up to it.

If Alex's brain was, indeed, dead, they were going to
have to accept that keeping Alex alive the way he was
was cruel.

Cruel to Alex.

She stared again at all the machinery, and momentarily wondered why it had ever been invented.

Why couldn't they just let people die?

And yet, she realized with sudden clarity, even though
she understood the reality of Alex's situation, she would
never simply let him die.

If she were going to, she would have done it already.
During the last two hours there had been plenty of
opportunities. All she would have had to do was turn off
the respirator. Alarms would have gone off, but she could
have dealt with that. And it wouldn't have taken long—
only a minute or two.

But she hadn't done it. Instead, she'd simply sat
there battling her feelings of despair, strengthening her
resolve not to let him die, and whispering encouraging
words to Alex as she held his hand.

And even though part of her still insisted that Alex
was already dead, the other part of her, the part that
was determined that he should live, was growing stronger
by the hour.

Suddenly the door opened, and Barbara Fannon
stepped into the room, closing the door behind her.

"Ellen? It's eight o'clock—you've been here all night."

Ellen turned her head. "I know."

"Marsh is in Frank's office. They have the test results. They're waiting for you."

Ellen thought about it for a moment, then slowly
shook her head. "No," she said at last. "I'll stay here
with Alex. Marsh will tell me what I need to know."

Barbara hesitated, then nodded. "I'll tell them," she
said, then let herself out of the room, leaving Ellen
alone with her son.

*   *   *

"It's bad," Frank Mallory said. "About as bad as it can get, I'm afraid."

"Let's see." Marsh's whole body felt drained from the shock and exhaustion of the last hours, but for some reason his mind was perfectly clear. Slowly and deliberately he began going over the results of all the tests and examinations that had been administered to Alex during the long night.

Mallory was right—it was very bad.

The damage to Alex's brain was extensive. Bone fragments seemed to be everywhere, driven deep into the cortex. The cerebrum showed the heaviest damage, much of it apparently centered in the temporal lobe. But nothing seemed to have escaped injury—the parietal and frontal lobes showed extensive injury as well.

"I'm not an expert at this," Marsh said, though both he and Mallory were well aware that many of the ramifications of Alex's injuries were obvious.

Mallory decided to take the direct approach. "If he lives at all, he won't be able to walk or talk, and it's doubtful that he'll be able to hear. He may be able to see—the occipital lobe seems to have suffered the least amount of damage. But all that's almost beside the point. It's highly doubtful if he'll be aware of anything going on around him, or even be aware of himself. And that's if he wakes up."

"I don't believe that," Marsh replied, fixing Mallory with cold eyes.

"Don't, or won't?" Mallory countered gently.

"It doesn't make any difference," Marsh replied. "Everything's going to be done for Alex that is humanly possible."

"That goes without saying, Marsh," Frank Mallory said, his voice reflecting the pain Marsh's words had caused. "You know there isn't anyone here who wouldn't do his best for Alex."

If Marshall heard him, he ignored him. "I want you to start by getting hold of Torres, down in Palo Alto."

"Torres?" Mallory repeated. "Raymond Torres?"

"Is there anyone else who can help Alex?"

Mallory fell silent as he thought about the man to whom Marsh was considering turning over his son.

Raymond Torres had grown up in La Paloma, and though there was little question in anyone's mind of the man's brilliance, there were, and always had been, many questions about the man himself. He had left La Paloma long ago, remaining in Palo Alto after medical school, returning to La Paloma only to see his mother— old María Torres. And even his visits to her were rare. There was a feeling in La Paloma that Torres resented his mother, that she was little more to him than a constant reminder of his past, and that, if there was one thing Torres would like to ignore, it was his past. In La Paloma he was primarily regarded as a curiosity: the boy from behind the mission who had somehow made good.

Beyond La Paloma, he had become, over the years, something of an enigma within the medical community. To his supporters, his aloofness was a result only of the fact that he devoted nearly every waking hour to his research into the functioning of the human brain, while his detractors attributed that same aloofness to intellectual arrogance.

But for all the questions about him, Raymond Torres had succeeded in becoming one of the country's foremost authorities on the structure and functioning of the human brain. In recent years, the thrust of his research had changed slightly, and his primary interest had become reconstuctive brain surgery.

"But isn't most of his work experimental?" Mallory asked now. "I don't think a lot of it has even been tried on human beings yet."

Marshall Lonsdale's desperation was reflected in his eyes. "Raymond Torres knows more about the human brain than anybody else alive. And some of the reconstruction work he's done is just this side of incredible. I'd say it *was* incredible if I hadn't seen the results myself. I want him to work on Alex."

"Marsh—"

But Marsh was on his feet, his eyes fixed on the pile of X rays, CAT scans, lab results, graphs, and other documentation pertaining to the damage his son's brain had sustained. "He's still alive, Frank," he said. "And as long as he's alive, I have to try to help him. I can't just leave him alone—you can see what he'll be like as well as I can. He'll be a vegetable, Frank. My God, you told me so yourself just now. Nothing can hurt him anymore, Frank. All Torres can do is help. Call him for me. Tell him what's happened, and that I want to talk to him. Just talk to him, that's all. Just get me in to see him."

When Frank Mallory still hesitated, Marshall Lonsdale spoke once more. "Alex is all I have, Frank. I can't just let him die."

When he was alone, Frank Mallory picked up the phone and dialed the number of Raymond Torres's office in Palo Alto, twenty miles away. After talking to him for thirty minutes, he finally convinced Torres to see Marsh Lonsdale and look at Alex's case.

The doctor made no promises, but he agreed to talk, and to look.

Privately, Frank half-hoped Torres would turn Marsh down.

CHAPTER FIVE

Exhaustion was overtaking Marsh, and he was beginning to feel that the situation was hopeless. He'd been in Raymond Torres's offices for most of the day, and for most of the day he'd been by himself. Not that it hadn't been interesting; it had, despite the overriding fear for his son's life that had never left his consciousness since the moment he had arrived that morning.

He'd stared at the Institute through bleary eyes. The building itself was a bastard—it had obviously started out as a home, and an imposing one. But from the central core of the mansion—for a mansion it had been—two wings had spread, and no attempt had been made to make them architecturally compatible with the original structure. Instead, they were sleekly functional, in stark contrast with the Georgian massiveness of the core. The buildings were surrounded by a sprawling lawn dotted with trees, and only a neat brass plaque mounted on the face of a large rock near the street identified the structure: INSTITUTE FOR THE HUMAN BRAIN.

Inside, a receptionist had led him immediately to Raymond Torres's office, where he'd turned all of Alex's records over to the surgeon himself, who, without so much as glancing at them, had given them to an assistant. When the assistant had disappeared, Torres had offered him a chair, then spent what Marsh thought was an unnecessarily long time lighting his pipe.

It took Marsh only a few seconds to decide that there was nothing of Torres's scientific reputation in either his manner or his bearing. He was tall, and his chiseled features were carefully framed by prematurely graying hair in a manner that seemed to Marsh more suitable for a movie star than a scientist. The star image was further enhanced by the perfectly cut tan silk suit Torres wore, and the cool casualness of his posture. For all his fine credentials, the first impression Raymond Torres gave his visitor was that of a society doctor more interested in the practice of golf than in the practice of medicine.

Nor was Marsh's instinctive dislike of the man alleviated by the fact that once the pipe was lit, the meeting had lasted only long enough for Torres to tell him that there would be no decision made until his staff had been able to analyze Alex's case, and that the analysis would take most of the day.

"I'll wait," Marsh had said. From behind his desk, Raymond Torres had shrugged with apparent disinterest. "As you wish, but I could just as easily call you when I've come to a decision."

Marsh had shaken his head. "No. I have to be here. Alex is my only child. There's . . . well, there's just nowhere else for me to go."

Torres had risen from his chair in a manner that Marsh found almost offensively dismissive. "As I said, as you wish. But you'll have to excuse me—I have a great deal to do this morning."

Marsh had stared at the man in stunned disbelief. "You're not even interested in hearing about the case?"

"It's all in the records, isn't it?" Torres had countered.

"*Alex* isn't in the records, Dr. Torres," Marsh had replied, his voice trembling with the effort to control his anger. Torres seemed to consider his words for a moment, but didn't reseat himself, and when he finally replied, his voice was cool.

"I'm a research man, Dr. Lonsdale. I'm a research man because, as I discovered long ago, I don't have much of a bedside manner. There are those, I know, who don't think I relate to people very well. Frankly, I don't care. I'm interested in helping people, not in coddling them. And I don't have to know the details of your son's life in order to help him. I don't care who he is, or what he's like, or what the details of his accident were. All I care about are the details of his injuries, so that I can make a reasonable judgment about whether or not I can help him. In other words, everything I need to know about your boy should be in his records. If there is anything missing, I—or someone on my staff—will know, and do whatever has to be done to rectify the matter. If you want to spend the rest of the day here, just in case we need you, I have no objection. Frankly, I doubt we'll need you. If we need anybody, it will be the patient's attending physician."

"Frank Mallory."

"Whoever." Torres shrugged disinterestedly. "But feel free to stay. We have a comfortable lounge, and you'll certainly find plenty to read." Suddenly he smiled. "All of it, of course, having to do with our work. One thing I insist on is that the lounge be well stocked with every article and monograph I've ever written."

Offended as he was by the man's open pride in himself, Marsh managed to keep silent, for without Torres, he knew there was no hope for Alex at all. And by two o'clock that afternoon he'd become totally convinced that whatever Raymond Torres lacked in personal warmth, he more than made up for in professional expertise.

The articles he'd read—and he'd read at least thirty of them, forcing himself to maintain his concentration through the interminable hours—covered a wide field of interest. Torres had not only made himself an expert on the structure of the brain, but he had also become a leading theorist on the functioning of the brain as well. In dozens of articles, Torres had described cases in which he'd found methods with which to circumvent damaged areas of a brain, and utilize other, healthy areas to take over the functions of the traumatized tissue. And through it all ran one constant theme—that the mysteries of the human brain were, indeed, solvable, but that the potentialities of the brain were only just being discovered. Indeed, he'd summed it up in a few sentences that had particularly intrigued Marsh:

The backup systems of the brain appear to me to be almost limitless. Long ago, we discovered that if a portion of the brain fails, another portion of the same brain can sometimes take over the function of the failed portion. It is almost as if each area of the brain not only knows what every other area does, but can perform that work itself if it really has to. The problem, then, seems to be one of convincing a damaged brain not to give up, and, further, of making it aware of its own problems so that it may redistribute its work load among its healthy components.

Marsh had read and reread that article several times when the receptionist suddenly appeared, smiling warmly at him.

"Dr. Lonsdale? Dr. Torres will see you now." He put the journal aside and followed the neat young woman back to Torres's office. Nodding a greeting, Torres beckoned him to a chair near his desk. In another chair, already seated, was Frank Mallory.

"Frank? What are you doing here?"

"I asked him to come," Torres replied. "There are some things I have to review with him."

"But Alex—"

"He's stable, Marsh," Frank told him. "There haven't been any changes in his condition for several hours. Benny's there, and a nurse is always in the room."

"If we may proceed," Torres interrupted. He turned toward a television screen on a table next to his desk. The screen displayed a high-resolution photograph of a human brain.

"It's not what you think it is," Torres said. Startled, both Marsh Lonsdale and Frank Mallory glanced toward Torres.

"I beg your pardon?" Frank asked.

"It's not a photograph. It's a computer-generated graphic representation of Alexander Lonsdale's brain." He paused a beat; then: "Before the accident."

Mallory's gaze shifted back to the screen. "Here's what happened," he heard Torres's voice say. "Or, more exactly, here's a reconstruction of what happened." He typed some instructions into the keyboard in front of him, and suddenly the image on the monitor began to move, turning upside down. Then, at the bottom of the screen, another shape came into view. As the three of them watched, the image of the brain came into contact with the other object, and suddenly began to distort. It was, Marsh realized, just like watching a movie of someone's head being smashed against a sharp rock.

In slow motion, he could see the skull crack, then splinter and begin to cave in.

Beneath the skull, brain tissue gave way, part of it crushed, part of it torn. Fragments of skull broke away, lacerating the brain further. Frank Mallory and Raymond Torres watched in silence, but Marsh was unable to stifle a groan of empathic pain. Suddenly it was over, and the brain was once again right-side-up. And then, as Torres tapped more instructions into the computer, the image changed again.

"Christ," Mallory whispered. "That's not possible."

"What is it?" Torres demanded.

"It's Alex's head," Mallory breathed. Marsh, his face

ashen, gazed at Mallory, but the other man's eyes remained fixed on the screen. "It's his head," Mallory breathed. "And it looks just the way it did when they brought him into the hospital. But . . . how?"

"We'll get to that," Torres replied. Then: "Dr. Mallory, I want you to concentrate on that image very hard. This is very important. How close is that picture to what you saw when they brought the patient in?" He held up a cautioning hand. "Don't answer right away, please. Examine it carefully. If you need me to, I can rotate the image so you can see it from other angles. But I need to know how exact it is."

For two long minutes, as Marsh looked on in agonized silence, Mallory examined the image, asking Torres to turn it first in one direction, then in another. At last he nodded. "As far as I can tell, it's perfect. If there are any flaws, I can't see them."

"All right. Now, the next part should be easier for you. Don't say anything, just watch, and if there's anything that doesn't look as you remember it, tell me."

As they watched, the image came to life once more. A forceps appeared and began removing fragments of bone from the brain. Then the forceps was gone, and a probe appeared. The probe moved, and a small bit of brain tissue tore loose. Mallory winced.

It went on and on, in agonizing detail. For each fragment of bone that was removed from the wound, a new wound was inflicted on Alex's brain. And then, after what seemed an aeon, it was over.

Frank Mallory was staring at an exact image of Alex's brain after he'd finished cleaning his wounds.

"Well?" Torres's voice asked.

Mallory heard his own voice shake as he spoke. "Why did you show me that? Just to prove my incompetence?"

"Don't be ridiculous," Torres snapped. "Aside from the fact that I don't need to waste my time with such a thing, you're not an incompetent. In fact, you did as good a job under the circumstances as could have been expected. What I need to know is whether that reconstruction was accurate."

Mallory chewed his lip, then nodded. "I'm afraid so. I'm sorry—I was doing my best."

"Don't be sorry," Torres remarked coldly. "Just think about it."

"It's accurate," Mallory assured him. "Now, can you tell us how you did it?"

"*I* didn't do it," Torres replied. "A computer did it all. For the last"—he glanced at the clock on his desk—"six hours, we've been feeding the computer information. Much of it the results of the CAT scan your lab did in La Paloma. Fortunately, that was a good job too. But our computer goes a lot further than yours. Your machinery can display any aspect of the brain, from any angle, in two dimensions. Ours is much more sophisticated," he went on, and suddenly his eyes, so cool and aloof until now, took on a glowing intensity. "Once it had all the data, it was able to reconstruct everything that happened to Alexander Lonsdale's brain from the first impact to the time of the CAT scan. For ourselves, an educated guess would have been the best we could do. We would have been able to extrapolate the approximate shape of the traumatizing instrument, and the probable angle from which it struck. And that would have been about all. But the wounds are extensive, and the computer is designed to handle a great many variables simultaneously. According to the computer, what you just saw is 99.624 percent accurate, given that the input was accurate. That's why I wanted you to look at the reconstruction. If there were any basic errors in the data, they would have been magnified by the extrapolation process to the point where you'd have seen something significantly in error. But you didn't, so we can assume that what we saw is what happened."

While Mallory sat in silence, Marsh voiced the question that was in both their minds. "Why is that important? It seems to me that what comes next is what we should be concerned with."

"Exactly," Torres agreed. "Now, watch carefully. What you're about to see is going to be at high speed, but it's what we think we can do for Alexander."

"Everyone calls him Alex," Marsh interjected.

Torres's brows arched slightly. "Very well. Alex. It makes no difference what we call him." He ignored the flash of anger in Marsh's eyes, and his fingers once more flew over the keyboard. The picture began to change again. As the two doctors from La Paloma watched in fascination, layers of brain tissue were peeled back. Certain tissue was removed entirely; some was simply maneuvered back into place. The chaos of the wound began to take on a semblance of order, and then, slowly, the mending process began, beginning deep within the medulla and proceeding outward through the various lobes of the brain. At last it was over, and the image on the screen was once again filled with the recognizable shape of a human brain. Certain areas, however, had taken on various shades of red, and Marsh's frown reflected his puzzlement.

"Those are the areas that are no longer functional," Torres told him before he could ask his question. "The pale pink ones are deep within the brain, the bright red ones on the surface. The gradations, I think, are obvious."

Mallory glanced at Marsh, whose attention seemed totally absorbed by the image on the screen. Finally he turned to Torres, his fingers interlaced beneath his chin. "What you've shown us is pure science fiction, Dr. Torres," he said. "You can't cut that deep, and make repairs that extensive, without killing the patient. Beyond that, it appears to me that what you're proposing to do is to reconstruct Alex's brain, even to the extent of repairing nerve cells. Frankly, I don't believe you or anyone else can do that."

Torres chuckled. "And, of course, you're right. I can't do that, nor can anybody else. Unfortunately, I'm much too large, and my hands are much too clumsy. Which is why Alexan—*Alex*," he corrected himself, "is going to have to be brought here." He switched off the monitor and rose from his chair. "Come with me. I want to show you something."

They left Torres's office and walked down a corridor that led to the west wing of the building. A security guard looked up at them as they passed, then, recognizing Torres, went back to gazing at the television monitor at his desk. Finally they turned into a scrub room, beyond which was an operating room. Wordlessly Torres stood aside and let the two others precede him through the double doors.

In the center of the room was an operating table, and against one wall was the customary array of O.R. equipment—all the support systems and monitors that both Marsh and Frank Mallory were used to. The rest of the room was taken up with an array of equipment the likes of which neither of them had ever seen before.

"It's a computerized microsurgical robot," Torres explained. "In the simplest terms possible, all it does is reduce the actions of the surgeon—in this case, me—down from increments of millimeters into increments of millimicrons. It incorporates an electron microscope, and a computer program that makes the program you just saw look like simple addition in comparison to advanced calculus. In a way," he went on, the pride in his voice belying his words, "with the development of this machine, I've reduced myself from being a brain surgeon to being little more than a technician. The microscope looks at the problems, and then the computer analyzes them and determines the solutions. Finally it tells me what to attach to what, and I make the movements relative to an enlarged model of the tissue. The robot reduces my motions and performs the procedures on the real tissue. And it works. Physically, that machine and I can repair much of the damage done to Alex Lonsdale's brain."

Marsh studied the equipment for several minutes, then turned to face Torres once again. When he spoke, his voice clearly reflected the uncertainty he was feeling. "What are the chances of Alex surviving the operation?"

Torres's expression turned grim. "Let's go back to my office. The computer can tell us that, too."

No one spoke again until they were back in the old core building, with the door to Torres's office closed behind them. Marsh and Frank Mallory took their seats, and Torres switched the computer back on. Quickly he began entering a series of instructions, and then the monitor flashed into life:

	SURGERY PERFORMED	SURGERY NOT PERFORMED
PROBABILITY OF SURVIVAL PAST ONE WEEK	90%	10%
PROBABILITY OF REGAINING CONSCIOUSNESS	50%	.02%
PROBABILITY OF PARTIAL RECOVERY	20%	0%
PROBABILITY OF TOTAL RECOVERY	0%	0%

Marsh and Mallory studied the chart, then, still staring at the screen, Marsh asked the first question that came to mind.

"What does partial recovery mean, exactly?"

"For starters, that he'll be able to breathe on his own, and that he'll be both cognizant of what is going on around him and able to communicate with the world beyond his own body. To me, anything less is no recovery at all. Though such a patient may be technically conscious, I still consider him to be in a state of coma. I find it inhuman to keep people alive under such circumstances, and I don't believe that simply because such people can't communicate their suffering, they are therefore *not* suffering. For me, such a life would be unbearable, even for a few days."

Marsh struggled to control the inner rage he was feeling at this cool man who was able to discuss Alex so dispassionately. And yet, deep down, he wasn't at all sure he disagreed with Torres. Then he heard Frank Mallory asking another question.

"And full recovery?"

"Exactly what the words say," Torres replied. "In this case, full recovery is simply not possible. Too much tissue has been destroyed. No matter how successful the surgery might be, there will never be total healing. He might, however—and I want to stress the word 'might'—recover what anyone would consider a remarkable number of his faculties. He might walk, talk, think, see, hear, and feel. Or he could recover any combination of those abilities."

"And you, I assume, are willing to perform the surgery?"

Torres shrugged. "I'm afraid I don't like the odds," he said. "I'm a man who doesn't like to fail."

Marsh felt a knot forming in his stomach. "Fail?" he whispered. "Dr. Torres, you're talking about my son. Without you, he'll die. We're not talking success or failure. We're talking life or death."

"I didn't say I wouldn't do it," Torres replied. "In fact, under certain conditions, I will do it."

Marsh's relief was apparent in his sigh, and he allowed himself to slump in his chair. "Anything," he whispered. "Anything at all."

But Frank Mallory was suddenly uneasy. "What are those circumstances?" he asked.

"Very simple. That I be given complete control over the case for as long as I deem necessary, and that I be absolved of any responsibility for any of the consequences of either the surgery or the convalescent period." Marsh started to interrupt, but Torres pressed on. "And by convalescent period, I mean until such time as I—and only I—discharge the patient." He reached into a drawer of his desk and withdrew a multipage document, which he handed to Marsh. "This is the agreement that you and the boy's mother will sign. You may read it if you want to—in fact I think you should—but not so much as a comma of it can be changed. Either you sign it or you don't. If you do, and your wife does, bring the boy here as soon as possible. The longer you wait, the riskier the surgery will be. As I'm sure you know, patients in your son's condition rarely get stronger—if anything, they get weaker." He rose from his chair, indicating his dismissal. "I'm sorry this has taken so long, but I'm afraid there was no choice. Even my computers need time to work."

Mallory rose to his feet. "If the Lonsdales decide to go ahead, when will you do the surgery, and how long will it take?"

"I'll do it tomorrow," Torres replied. "And it will take at least eighteen hours, with fifteen people working. And don't forget," he added, turning to Marsh. "The odds are eighty percent that we'll fail, at least to some extent. I'm sorry, but I don't believe in lying to people."

He opened the door, held it for Marsh and Frank, then closed it as soon as they had stepped through.

Raymond Torres sat alone for a long time after showing the two doctors from La Paloma out of his office.

La Paloma.

Odd that this case—the most challenging case he'd ever been given the opportunity to work on—should not only come from the town he'd grown up in but also involve someone he'd known all his life.

He wondered if Ellen Lonsdale would even remember who he was. Or, more to the point, who he'd been.

Probably not.

In La Paloma, as in most of California during those years of his childhood, he and all the other descendants of the old Californios had been regarded as just more Mexicans, to be ignored at best, and despised at worst.

And in return, his friends had despised the *gringos* even more than they were despised themselves.

Raymond Torres could still remember the long nights in the little kitchen, when his grandmother listened to the indignities his mother and her sisters had suffered at the hands of their various employers, then talked, as she always did, of the old days before even she had been born, when the Meléndez y Ruiz family had owned the hacienda, and the Californios were preeminent. Back then, it had been the families of Torres and Ortiz, Rodríguez and Flores who had lived in the big white houses on the trail up to the hacienda. Over and over, his grandmother had told the legend of the massacre at the hacienda, and the carnage that followed as one by one the old families were driven from their homes, and slowly reduced to the level of *peones*. But things would change, his grandmother had insisted. All they and their friends had to do was maintain their hatred and wait for the day when the son of Don Roberto de Meléndez y Ruiz would return and drive the *gringos* away from the lands and homes they had stolen.

Raymond had listened to it all, and known it was all useless. His grandmother's tales were no more than legends, and her certainty of future vengeance no more solid than the ghost on which her hopes depended. When she had finally died, he'd thought it might end, but instead, his mother had taken up the litany. Even now, the old legends and hatreds seemed to be all she lived for.

But there would be no revenge, and there would be no driving away of the *gringos*, at least not for Raymond Torres. For himself, he had taken another path, ignoring the slights of the *gringos* and closing his ears to the hatreds of his friends and their plans for someday avenging their ancestors.

For Raymond Torres, vengeance would be simple. He would acquire a *gringo* education and become as superior to the *gringos* as they thought they were to him. But his superiority would be real, not imagined.

Now, finally, the day had come when *they* needed *him*.

And he would help them, despite the fury he would face from his mother.

He would help them, because he had long ago decided that all the years of having been dismissed as being unworthy of the *gringos*' attention would best be avenged by the simple act of forcing them to realize that they had been wrong; that he had always been their equal. He'd always been their equal, though he'd never had their power.

Now, because of an accident on the very site of the ancient massacre, that power had come into his hands.

The skill he would need he had acquired over long years of hard work. Now he would combine that skill with the power they would give him to rebuild Alex Lonsdale into something far more than he had been before his accident.

Slowly and carefully he began making the preparations to rebuild Alex Lonsdale's mind.

In the demonstration of his own genius, he would have his own revenge.

"But why can't he do it here?" Ellen asked. Several hours of fitful sleep had eased the exhaustion she had felt that morning, but she still found it impossible to absorb every word Marsh had spoken. Patiently Marsh explained it once again.

"It's the equipment. It's extensive, and it's all built into his O.R. It simply can't be moved, at least not quickly, and not into our facility. We just don't have the space."

"But can Alex survive it?"

This time it was Frank who answered her question. "We don't know," he said. "I think he can. His pulse is weak, but it's steady, and the respirator can go in the ambulance with him. There's a mobile ICU in Palo Alto, and we can use that."

There was a silence, then Marsh spoke, his voice quiet but urgent. "You have to decide, Ellen. This waiver needs both our signatures."

Ellen gazed at her husband a moment, her thoughts suddenly far in the past.

Raymond Torres. Tall and good-looking, with dark, burning eyes, but no one anyone would ever consider going out with. And he'd been smart, too. In fact, he'd been the smartest person in her class. But strange, in a way she'd never quite understood, nor even, for that matter, cared about understanding. He'd always acted as though he was better than anyone, and never had any friends, either of his own race or of hers. And now, suddenly, the life of her son depended on him.

"What's he like?" she suddenly asked.

Marsh looked at her curiously. "Does it matter?"

Ellen hesitated, then slowly shook her head. "I don't suppose so," she replied. "But I used to know him, and he was always . . . well, I guess he seemed arrogant, and sometimes he was almost scary. None of us ever liked him."

Marsh smiled tightly. "Well, he hasn't changed. He's still arrogant, and I don't like him at all. But he might be able to save Alex."

Once more Ellen hesitated. In times past, she and Marsh used to spend hours discussing their problems, listening to each other, balancing their thoughts and feelings, weighing what was best for them. But in the last few months—or had it become years?—that easy communication had been lost. They had been too busy— Marsh with the expanding Medical Center, herself with the expanding social life that had accompanied the build- ing of the Center. What had been sacrificed, finally, was their ability to communicate with each other. Now, with Alex's life hanging in the balance, she had to come to a decision.

She made up her mind. "We don't have a choice, do we?" she asked. "We have to try." She picked up the pen and signed the waiver, which she had not bothered to read, then handed it back to Marsh. A sudden thought flashed through her mind.

If Raymond Torres thinks it will work, why won't he take responsibility for it?

Then she decided that she didn't want to know the answer to that question.

CHAPTER SIX

Carol Cochran covered the telephone's mouthpiece with her right hand and called up the stairs, "Lisa? It's for you." She waited a few seconds, and when there was no answer, she called out again: "Lisa?"

"Tell whoever it is I'm not here." Lisa's voice was muffled, and Carol paused a moment, wondering if she ought to go upstairs and insist that Lisa take the call. Then she sighed. "She says she isn't here, Kate. I'm sorry, but she just doesn't want to talk to anyone right now. I'll have her call you back, all right?"

Hanging up the phone, Carol mounted the stairs, and found Kim standing in the hall.

"Her door's locked, and she won't come out," the six-year-old reported.

"I'll take care of it, dear. Why don't you go find your father?"

"Is he lost?" Kim replied with the same look of innocence Jim always wore when he tortured her with the same kind of response.

"Just go, all right? I need to talk to your sister."

"Do I have to?" Kim begged. "I could talk to her too."

"I'm sure you could," Carol observed. "But right now I want to talk to her alone."

Kim cocked her head, her eyes narrowing inquisitively. "Are you gonna talk about Alex?"

"Possibly," Carol parried.

"Is Alex going to die?"

"I don't know," Carol replied, sticking to the policy of total honesty she'd always followed in raising her children. "But that's something we won't talk about until it happens. I hope it won't. Now, run along and find your father."

Kim, who had long since learned when she'd pushed her luck as far as it would go, headed down the stairs as Carol tapped at Lisa's door.

"Lisa? May I come in?"

There was no answer, but a moment later Carol heard a click as Lisa turned the key from the inside. The door opened a few inches, and Carol saw Lisa's retreating back as the girl returned to her bed, sprawled out on her back, and fixed her gaze on the ceiling. Carol stepped into the room and closed the door behind her.

"Do you want to talk about it?" she asked. When there was no reply, Carol crossed to the bed and sat down on the edge of it. Lisa moved slightly to one side to make more room. "Well, I want to talk about it," Carol went on. "I know what you're thinking, and you're wrong."

Lisa's tear-streaked face turned slowly toward her mother, who reached out to brush a stray hair from her brow. "It was my fault, Mom," she said, her voice bleak. "It was all my fault."

"We're not going to go over it all again," Carol told her. "I've heard the whole story too many times already. If you want to feel guilty, you can feel guilty about talking Alex into going to that party. But that's *all* you can feel guilty about. It was Alex who drank the beer, and it was Alex who was driving the car."

"But he had to swerve—"

"Only because he was driving too fast. *He* caused the accident, Lisa. Not you."

"But . . . but what if he dies?"

Carol bit her lip, then took a deep breath. "If he dies, then we will all feel very badly for a while. Ellen and Marsh will feel badly for a long time. But the world won't end, Lisa. And if Alex does die, that won't be your fault any more than the accident was your fault."

"But Carolyn Evans said—"

"Carolyn Evans is a selfish, spoiled brat, and you weren't the only one who heard her say it was all your fault. I've talked to Bob Carey and Kate Lewis tonight, and they both told me exactly what Carolyn meant. She meant that if you hadn't left the party, then Alex wouldn't have either, and that the accident might not have happened. And do you know what she was worried about? Not you, and not Alex. The only thing that concerned darling Carolyn was the fact that her party was no longer going to be her little secret. Also, as far as I know, Carolyn was the only person at the party who didn't bother to go to the Center last night. All she did was go home and try to clean up the house."

"It doesn't make any difference what she meant," Lisa said, rolling over to face the wall. "It still doesn't change the way I feel."

Carol sat silently for a few seconds, then reached out and pulled Lisa close. "I know, honey. And I suppose you're going to have to get over that feeling your own way. In the meantime, what about Alex?"

Lisa stirred suddenly, and sat up. "Alex? What about him?"

"Suppose he wakes up?"

"He *will* wake up," Lisa said. "He *has* to."

"Why? So you can stop feeling sorry for yourself? Is that why you want him to wake up? So it will make you feel better?"

Lisa's eyes widened with shock. "Mom! That's an awful thing to say—"

Carol shrugged. "Well, what else can I think?" She took Lisa's hands in her own. "Lisa, I want you to listen very carefully. There's a chance that Alex may survive all this, and there's a chance he may wake up. But if he does, he's going to be in bad shape, and he's going to need all the help he can get. His parents won't be enough. He's going to need his friends, too, and he's going to need you. But if you're spending all your energy feeling guilty and sorry for yourself, you're not going to be much good to him, are you?"

Lisa looked dazed. "But what can I do?"

"None of us will know that till the time comes. But for starters, you could try pulling yourself together." She hesitated for a moment, then went on. "Alex is going to be operated on tomorrow." Lisa's eyes reflected her surprise, but before she could say anything, Carol went on. "I know you're going to want to be there—we all want to be there—but you're not going to sit on a sofa and cry. If anyone's going to do that, it's going to be Ellen, and I suspect *she* won't do that either. It's going to be a long operation, and Alex might not make it through. But if you want to be there, both your father and I expect you to behave like the girl we hope we raised."

There was a long silence; then the slightest trace of a smile appeared at the corners of Lisa's mouth. "You mean keep my chin up?" she asked in a tiny voice.

Carol nodded. "And remember that it's Alex who's in trouble, not you. Whatever happens tomorrow, or next week, or whenever, your life will go on. If Alex comes through this, he's not going to have a lot of time to spend cheering you up." She stood up, and forced a grin she didn't truly feel. "The ball's in your court, kid. Play it."

Forty minutes later, Lisa Cochran came downstairs. She was wearing one of her father's old white shirts and a pair of jeans, and her hair, still wet from the shower, was wrapped in a towel. "Who all called?" she asked. Her father lowered his paper and opened his mouth. "I mean *besides* Prince Andrew and John Travolta, Dad. I already talked to them and told them it's definitely over."

"All the messages are by the phone," her mother told her. "Anything going on you want to tell us about, or shall we read it in the papers?"

"Nothing much," Lisa said. "I just thought I'd get the kids organized for tomorrow. Do you know what time they're operating on Alex?"

Jim put his paper aside, looking curiously at his older daughter. "Early," he said. "They want to start by six, I think." As Lisa started out of the room, he called her back. "Mind telling me just what you're organizing?"

"Well, everyone's going to want to go down there, but there's no point in having everyone show up at once. I'm just going to sort of get them spaced out."

"Most of them already are," Jim commented.

Lisa ignored him. "Tomorrow's Sunday, so nobody has to go to school or anything. We might as well all help out."

Carol frowned uncertainly. "I hope there's not going to be a mob like there was last night—"

"I'll tell them not to stay very long. And I'm going to ask Kate if she'll just sort of hang around, in case anybody needs anything."

Now Jim was shaking his head. "Lisa, honey, I know you want to do the right thing, but—"

"It's all right," Carol interrupted. "But, Lisa? Can I make a suggestion? Why don't you call Ellen and see what she thinks? She might prefer it if you just kept everybody away, at least until we know what's happening."

Lisa's face fell, and she groaned. "Why didn't I think of that?"

" 'Cause you're an idiot," Kim said, abandoning the

drawing she'd been working on to scramble into her father's lap. "Isn't she an idiot, Daddy?"

"It takes one to know one."

"Daddy! You're s'posed to be on my side."

"I guess I forgot." Jim snuggled the little girl in, then turned back to Lisa. "Got any plans for your sister?" he asked mildly. "If you really want to do some organizing, why don't you line up your friends to take care of Kim?"

"I want to go with you!" Kim immediately objected.

"That's what you say now," Jim told her. "That's not what you'll say tomorrow. And don't argue with me—I'm bigger than you are, and can pound you into the ground." Kim giggled, but closed her mouth. "Maybe someone could take her to a movie or something. And we'll need a baby-sitter after dinner."

Lisa's eyes clouded. "Won't it be all over by then?"

Carol and Jim exchanged a glance, then Jim spoke. "I talked to Marsh earlier," he said. "He told me the operation will take at least eighteen hours. It's not going to be any party, honey."

Lisa paled slightly, and fought down the tears that were welling in her eyes. When she spoke, though, her voice was steady. "I know it's not a party, Dad," she said softly. "I just want to do whatever I can to help."

"Your mother can—"

"No! I can, and I will. I'll take care of Kim, and see to it that there's no mob scene. I'll be all right, Dad. Just let me do this my way, all right?"

When she was gone, and they could hear her murmuring into the telephone, Jim turned to Carol. "What happened up there?" he asked.

"I think she just grew up, Jim. Anyway, she's sure trying."

There was a silence, then Kim squirmed in her father's lap, twisting around to look up at him. "Do I have to go to the movies with her dumb old friends?" she demanded.

"If you do, I'll bet they'll let you choose the movie,"

Jim replied. Somewhat mollified, Kim settled down again.

"I hope Alex gets better soon," she said. "I *like* Alex."

"We all do," Carol told her. "And he *will* get better, if we all pray a lot."

And, she added to herself, if Raymond Torres really knows what he's doing.

As Carol Cochran entertained that thought, Raymond Torres himself was making his final rounds of the evening.

Not, of course, that they were really rounds, for Alex Lonsdale was his only patient. He stopped first in Alex's room, just across the hall from the operating complex. The night nurse glanced up from the book she was reading. "Nothing, doctor," she said as Torres scanned the monitors that were tracking Alex's vital functions. "No change from an hour ago."

Torres nodded, and gazed thoughtfully at the boy in the bed.

Looks like his mother. The thought drifted through his mind, followed by a sudden flood of unbidden memories from a past he thought could no longer hurt him. Along with his memories of Ellen Lonsdale came memories of three other girls, and as their faces came into focus in his mind's eye, he felt himself begin to tremble.

Forget it, he told himself. *It was long ago, and it's all over now. It doesn't matter.* With an effort of will, he forced himself to concentrate on the motionless form of Alex Lonsdale. He leaned over and carefully opened one of the boy's eyes, checked the pupil, then closed the eye again. There had been no reaction to the sudden incursion of light. Not a good sign.

"All right," he said. "I'm sleeping here tonight, in the room over my office. If anything happens—anything at all—I want to be awakened at once."

"Of course, doctor," the nurse replied. Not that he need have said anything—the first rule for staff working under Torres was made very clear at the time they were hired: "If anything happens, let Dr. Torres know at once." And everyone at the Institute adhered to the rule, quickly learning to suspend his own judgment. So tonight, if Alex Lonsdale so much as twitched, an instrument would record it, and Raymond Torres would be notified immediately. As Torres left the room, the nurse went back to her book.

Torres crossed the corridor and went into the scrub room, his eyes noting instantly that everything necessary for tomorrow's scrub was already there—gowns, gloves, masks, everything. And it would all be checked at least twice more during the night. He proceeded into the O.R. itself, where six technicians were going over every piece of equipment in the room, running test after test, rechecking their own work, then having it verified by two other technicians. They would continue working throughout the night, searching for anything that could possibly fail, and replacing it. They would leave only when it was time for the sterilization process to begin, an hour before the operation was scheduled.

Satisfied, he moved on down the corridor to what had long ago become known as the Rehearsal Hall. It was a large room, housing several desks, each of which held a computer terminal. It was here that every operation carried out at the Institute was rehearsed.

Tonight, all the desks were occupied, and all the terminals glowed brightly in the soft light of the Rehearsal Hall. The technicians at the monitors, using the model of Alex's brain that had been generated earlier that day, were going over the operation step by step, searching for bugs in the program that the computer itself, using its own model, had generated.

They didn't expect to find any bugs, for they had long ago discovered that programs generated by computers are much more accurate than programs written by men.

Except that there was also the possibility that somewhere in the system there was a sleeper.

"Sleeper" was their term for a bug that had never been found. The defect might not even be in the program they were using. It could have been in a program that had been used to write another program, that had, in turn, been used to generate still a third program. They all knew, from bitter experience, that the bug could suddenly pop up and destroy everything.

Or, worse, it could simply inject a tiny error into the program, creating a new sleeper.

In this case, that would be a wrong connection in Alex Lonsdale's mind, which could lead to anything.

Or nothing.

Or Alex's death.

Torres moved silently through the room, concentrating first on one monitor, then on another. All of what he saw was familiar; he would see it all again tomorrow.

Except that tomorrow wouldn't be a rehearsal. Tomorrow his fingers would be on the robot's controls, and as he followed the program, making the connections inside Alex's brain, there would be no turning back. Whatever he did tomorrow, Alex Lonsdale would live with for the rest of his life.

Or die with.

One of the technicians leaned back and stretched.

"Problems?" Torres asked.

The technician shook his head. "Looks perfect so far."

"How many times have you been through it?"

"Five."

"It's a beginning," Torres said. He wished they had months to keep rerunning the program, but they didn't. So even in the morning, they wouldn't be sure there were no bugs. That, indeed, was the worst thing about bugs—sometimes they didn't show up for years. The only way to find them was to keep running and rerunning a program, hoping that if something was going to go wrong it would go wrong early on. But this time, they simply didn't have time—they would have to trust that the program was perfect.

Yet as he moved toward the little bedroom above his office that was always kept ready for him, one thought kept going through Torres's mind: Nothing is ever perfect.

Something always goes wrong.

He pushed the thought away. Not this time. This time, everything had to be perfect. And only he would ever know what that perfection really was.

At five o'clock the next morning, Ellen and Marshall Lonsdale arrived in Palo Alto. It was still dark, but all over the Institute for the Human Brain, lights glowed brightly, and people seemed to be everywhere. They were shown into the same lounge where Marsh had spent most of the previous day, and offered coffee and Danishes.

"Can we see Alex?" Ellen asked.

The receptionist smiled sympathetically. "I'm sorry. He's already being prepped." Ellen carefully kept her expression impassive, but the other woman could clearly see the pain in her eyes. "I really am sorry, Mrs. Lonsdale, but it's one of Doctor's rules. Once the prepping starts, we always keep the patient totally isolated. Doctor's a fanatic about keeping everything sterile."

Suddenly the door opened, and a friendly voice filled the room. "Why do they always have to have operations at dawn?" Valerie Benson asked of no one in particular. "Do they think it's a war or something?" She crossed the room and gave Ellen a quick hug. "It's going to be all right," she whispered. "I don't get up this early unless I know nothing can possibly go wrong, and here I am. So you might as well stop worrying right now. Alex is going to be fine."

Ellen couldn't resist smiling at Valerie, who was a notorious late-riser. Indeed, Valerie sometimes claimed that the real reason she'd divorced her husband was that demanding breakfast by nine A.M. was the worst sort of mental cruelty. But here she was, as always, coming through in the pinch, and looking as if she'd been up for hours.

"You didn't have to come," Ellen told her.

"Of course I did," Valerie said. "If I hadn't, everybody would have talked about it for years. Is Marty here yet?"

"I don't know if she's even coming. And it's so early—"

"Nonsense," Valerie snorted. "Must be nearly noon." She gave Marsh a quick kiss on the cheek. "Everything okay?" she asked, her voice dropping.

"They won't even let us see Alex before the operation," Marsh replied, making no attempt to hide the anger he was feeling. Valerie nodded knowingly.

"I've always said Raymond Torres is impossible. Brilliant, yes. But impossible."

Ellen's eyes clouded. "If he can save Alex, I don't care how impossible he is."

"Of course you don't, darling," Valerie assured her. "None of us does. Besides, maybe he's changed over the last twenty years. My God, if I had any brains, I'd marry him! This is some place, isn't it? Is it all his?"

"Val," Ellen interrupted. "You can slow down. You don't have to distract us—we're going to get through this."

Valerie's bright smile faded, and she sat down abruptly, reaching into her purse and pulling out a handkerchief. She sniffled, wiped her eyes, then determinedly put the handkerchief away. "I'm sorry," she said. "It's just that the thought of anything happening to Alex . . . Oh, Ellen, I'm just so sorry about all of this. Is there anything I can do?"

Ellen shook her head. "Nothing. Just stay with me, Val. Having you and Marty Lewis and Carol here is going to be the most important thing." To know that her friends would be here to support her, to try to comfort her, would help.

The longest day of her life had just begun.

CHAPTER SEVEN

When the lounge door opened just after ten-thirty that evening, neither Ellen nor Marsh paid much attention. People had been in and out all day, some staying only a few minutes, others remaining for an hour or two. But now only her closest friends were still there: the Cochrans, Marty Lewis, and Valerie Benson. Only Cynthia Evans had not come.

Slowly she realized that someone was standing in front of her, had spoken to her. She looked up into the face of a stranger.

"Mrs. Lonsdale? I'm Susan Parker—the night person. Dr. Torres wants to see you and your husband in his office."

Ellen glanced at Marsh, who was already on his feet, his hand extended to her. Suddenly she felt disoriented—she'd thought it was going to take until midnight. Unless . . . She closed her mind to the thought that Alex must, at last, have died. "It's over?" she managed. "He's finished?"

Then she was in Torres's office, and the doctor was gazing at her from the chair behind his desk. He stood up, and came around to offer her his hand. "Hello, Ellen," he said quietly.

Her first fleeting thought was that he was even more handsome than she'd remembered him. Hesitantly she took his hand and squeezed it briefly, then, still clutching his hand, she gazed into his eyes. "Alex," she whispered. "Is he—?"

"He's alive," Torres said, his voice reflecting the exhaustion he was feeling, while his eyes revealed his triumph. "He's out of the O.R., and he's off the respirator. He's breathing by himself, and his pulse is strong."

Ellen's legs buckled, and Marsh eased her into a chair. "Is he awake?" she heard her husband ask. When Torres's head shook negatively, her heart sank.

"But it doesn't mean much," Torres said. "The soonest we want him to wake up is tomorrow morning."

"Then you don't know if the operation is a success." Marsh Lonsdale's voice was flat.

Again Torres shook his head, and rubbed his eyes with his fists. "We'll know tomorrow morning, when— if—he wakes up. But things look good." He offered them a twisted smile. "Coming from me, that's something. You know what I consider success and what I consider failure. And I can tell you right now that if Alex dies in the next week, it won't be from his brain problems. It will be from complications—pneumonia, some kind of viral infection, that sort of thing. I intend to see that that doesn't happen."

"Can . . . can we see him?" Ellen asked.

Torres nodded. "But only for a minute, and only through the window. For the time being, I don't want anyone in that room except members of my staff." Marsh seemed about to say something, but Torres ignored him. "I'm sorry, but that includes you. What you can do is take a look at him—Susan will take you over there—and then go home and get some sleep. Tomorrow morning's going to tell the tale, and I want you to be here. If he wakes up, I'm going to want to try to determine if he can recognize people."

"Us," Ellen breathed.

"Exactly." Torres stood up. "Now, if you'll excuse me, I'm going up to bed."

Ellen struggled to her feet, and reached out to grasp Torres's hand once again. "Thank you, Raymond," she whispered. "I . . . I don't know what to say. I didn't believe . . . I couldn't—"

Torres abruptly withdrew his hand from hers. "Don't thank me, Ellen," he said. "Not yet. There's still a good chance that your son will never wake up." Then he was gone, leaving Ellen to stare after him, her face ashen.

"It's just him," Marsh told her. "It's just his way of telling us not to get our hopes too high."

"But he said—"

"He said Alex is alive, and breathing by himself. And that's all he said." He began guiding her toward the door. "Let's go take a look at him, then go home."

Silently Susan Parker led them into the west wing and down the long corridor past the O.R. She stopped at a window, and the Lonsdales gazed through the glass into a large room. In its center stood a hospital bed, its guardrails up. Around the bed was an array of monitors, each of them attached to some part of Alex's body.

His head, though swathed with bandages, seemed to bristle with tiny wires.

But there was no respirator, and even from beyond the window they could see his chest rising and falling in the deep, even rhythm of sleep. A glance at one of the monitors told Marsh that Alex's pulse was now as strong and regular as his breathing.

"He's going to come out of it," he said softly. Next to him, Ellen squeezed his hand tightly.

"I know," she replied. "I can feel it. He did it, Marsh. Raymond gave us back our son." Then: "But what's he going to be like? He won't be the same, will he?"

"No," Marsh said slowly, "he won't be. But he'll still be Alex."

There was a soft beeping sound, and the nurse whose sole duty was to watch Alex Lonsdale glanced quickly up, scanning the monitors with a practiced eye, then noting the exact time.

Nine-forty-six A.M.

She pressed the buzzer on the control panel, then went to the bed to lean over Alex, concentrating on his eyes.

The beeping sounded again, and this time she saw its cause. She picked up the phone and pressed two buttons. On the first ring, someone picked it up.

"Torres. What is it?"

"Rapid-eye movement, doctor. He may be dreaming, or—"

"Or he may be waking up. I'll be right down." The phone went dead in her hand and the nurse's attention went back to Alex.

Once more, the beeping began, and the occasional faint twitching in Alex Lonsdale's eyelids increased to an erratic flutter.

Hazily he became vaguely aware of himself. Things were happening around him.

There were sounds, and faint images, but none of it meant anything.

Like watching a movie, but run so fast you couldn't see any of it.

And darkness. Darkness all around him, and no sense of being at all. Then, slowly, he began to feel himself. There was more than the darkness, more than the indistinct sounds and images.

A dream.

He was having a dream.

But what was it about? He tried to focus his mind. If it was a dream, where was he? Why wasn't he part of it?

The darkness began to recede a little, and the sounds and images faded away.

Not a dream. Real. He was real.

He.

What did "he" mean?

"He" was a word, and he should know what it meant. There should be a name attached to it, but there wasn't.

The word had no meaning.

Then slowly "he" faded into "me."

"Me." "Me" became "I."

I am me. He is me.

Who?

Alexander James Lonsdale.

The meaning of those little words came back into his mind.

He began to remember.

But there were only fragments, and most of them didn't make any sense. He was going somewhere. Where? A dance. There had been a dance. Picture it.

If you want to remember something, picture it.

Nothing.

Going somewhere.

Car. He was in a car, and he was driving. But where?

Nothing. No image came to mind, no street name.

Picture something—anything.

But nothing came, and for a moment he was sure that all he would ever know was his name. There was nothing else in his mind. Nothing but that great dark void. Then more names came into his mind.

Marshall Lonsdale.

Ellen Smith Lonsdale.

Parents. They were his parents. Then, very slowly, the blackness surrounding him faded into a faint glow.

He opened his eyes to blinding brightness, then closed them again.

"He's awake." The words meant something, and he understood what they meant.

He opened his eyes again. The brightness faded, and

blurred images began to form. Then, slowly, his eyes focused,

Certain images clicked in his mind, things he'd seen before, and suddenly he knew where he was. He was in a hospital.

A hospital was where his father worked. His father was a doctor. His eyes moved again, and he saw a face.

His father?

He didn't know. He opened his mouth.

"Wh-who . . . are . . . you?"

"Dr. Torres," a voice said. "Dr. Raymond Torres." There was a silence, then the voice spoke again. "Who are you?"

He lay quiet for a few seconds, then, once more, spoke, the words distorted, but clear enough to be understood. "Lonsdale. Alexander James Lonsdale."

"Good," the man whose name was Dr. Torres told him. "That's very good. Now, do you know where you are?"

"H-hob . . ." Alex fell silent, then carefully tried it again. "Hos . . . pi . . . tal," he said.

"That's right. Do you know why you're in the hospital?"

Alex lapsed into silence again, his mind trying to grasp the meaning of the question. Then, in a rush, it came to him.

"Ha-hacienda," he whispered. "Car."

"Good," Dr. Torres said softly. "Don't try to say anything else right now. Just lie there. Everything's going to be all right. Do you understand?"

"Y-yes."

The image of the doctor disappeared from his vision, and was replaced by another face that he didn't recognize. He closed his eyes.

Ellen and Marsh rose anxiously to their feet as Torres walked into his office a few minutes later.

"He's awake," he told them. "And he can speak."

"He . . . he actually said something?" Ellen asked,

her voice alive with hope for the first time since the accident. "It wasn't just sounds?"

Torres seated himself at his desk, his demeanor, as always, perfectly composed. "Better than just saying something. The first thing he did was ask me who I was. Then he told me his name. And he knows what happened."

Marshall Lonsdale felt his heart pounding, and suddenly a vision leapt into his mind. It was the chart of probabilities he'd seen two days earlier. Partial recovery had been only a twenty-percent chance. Full recovery had been zero percent. But Alex could hear, and he could speak, and apparently he could think. Then he realized that Torres was still speaking, and forced himself to concentrate on the doctor's words.

". . . but you have to realize that he might not recognize you."

"Why not?" Ellen asked. Then: "Oh, God. He . . . he isn't blind, is he?"

"Absolutely not," Torres assured her. His eyes fixed on her, and Ellen felt a small shiver run through her. There was a quality of strength in his eyes that had not been there twenty years ago. Where once his eyes had smoldered in a way that she used to find frightening, now they burned with a reassuring self-confidence. Whatever Raymond Torres told her, she was suddenly certain, would be the absolute truth. And if Alex could be healed, Raymond Torres was the one man who could heal him. In his presence, the overriding fear she had fallen victim to since the moment she heard of Alex's accident began to ebb away. She found herself concentrating on his words with an intensity she had never felt before.

"At this point there's no way of knowing what he will remember and what he won't. He could remember your names, but have no memory at all of what you look like. Or just the opposite. You might be familiar to him, but he won't remember exactly who you are. So when you see him, be very careful. If he doesn't recognize you, don't be upset, or at least try not to let him know that you're upset."

"The fact that he's alive, and that he's conscious, is enough," Ellen breathed. Then, though she knew she could never truly express what she was feeling, she went on. "How can I thank you?" she asked. "How can I ever thank you for what you've done?"

"By accepting Alex in whatever condition he is now in," Torres replied, ignoring the emotion in Ellen's words.

"But you said—"

"I know what I said. You must understand that Alex will undoubtedly have a lot of limitations from now on, and you must learn to deal with them. That may not be a simple task."

"I know," Ellen said. "I don't expect it to be. But whatever Alex's needs are, I know we'll be able to meet them. You've given us back Alex's life, Raymond. You . . . well, you've worked a miracle."

Torres rose to his feet. "Let's go see him. I'll take you in myself, and I'd like to do it one at a time. I don't want to give him too much to cope with."

"Of course," Marsh agreed. They started toward the west wing and paused outside Alex's room. Through the window, nothing seemed to have changed. "Does it matter which of us goes in first?" he asked.

"I'd rather you went first," Torres replied. "You're a doctor, and you'll be less likely to have any kind of reaction to whatever might happen."

The Lonsdales exchanged a glance, and Ellen managed to conceal her disappointment. "Go on," she said. "I'll be fine."

Torres opened the door, and the two men stepped inside. Ellen watched as Marsh approached the bed, stopping when he was next to Alex.

Alex's eyes opened again, and he recognized Dr. Torres. On the other side of him was someone else.

"Who . . . are . . . you?"

There was a slight pause, and then the stranger spoke. "I'm your father, Alex."

"Father?" Alex echoed. His eyes fixed on the man, and he searched his memory. Suddenly the face that had been strange was familiar. "Dad," he said. Then, again: "Dad."

He saw his father's eyes fill with tears, then heard him say, "How are you, son?"

Alex searched his mind for the right word. "H-hurt," he whispered. "I hurt, but not . . . not too bad." A phrase leapt into his mind. "Looks like we're going to live after all."

He watched as his father and Dr. Torres glanced at each other, then back down at him. His father was smiling now. "Of course you are, son," he heard his father say in an oddly choked voice. "Of course you are."

Alex closed his eyes and listened to the sound of footsteps moving away from the bed. The room was silent; then there were more footsteps, and he knew people were once again standing by the bed. Dr. Torres, and someone else. He opened his eyes and peered upward. A face seemed to hang in the air, framed by dark wavy hair.

"Hello . . . Mom," he whispered.

"Alex," she whispered back. "Oh, Alex, you're going to be fine. You're going to be just fine."

"Fine," he echoed. "Just fine." Then, exhausted, he let himself drift back into sleep.

"You can spend the day here if you want to," Torres told them when they were back in his office. "But you won't be allowed to see Alex again until tomorrow."

"Tomorrow?" Marsh asked. "But why? What if he wakes up? What if he asks for us?"

"He won't wake up again," Torres replied. "I'm going to look at him once more, and then give him a sedative."

Marsh's eyes suddenly clouded. "A sedative? He just came out of a coma. You don't give that kind of patient a sedative—you try to keep them awake."

Torres's face seemed cut from stone. "I don't believe I asked for your advice or your opinions, Dr. Lonsdale," he said.

"But—"

"Nor am I interested in hearing them," Torres went on, ignoring the interruption. "Frankly, I don't have time to listen to what you have to say, and I'd just as soon you kept whatever thoughts you might have to yourself. Alex is my patient, and I have my own methods. I made that clear day before yesterday. Now, if you'll excuse me." He opened the door in his habitual gesture of dismissal.

"But he's our son," Marsh protested. "Surely we can—"

"No, Marsh," Ellen interrupted. "We'll do whatever Raymond wants us to do."

Marsh gazed at his wife in silence for a moment, his jaw tightening with anger. But her obvious anguish washed his rage away, and when he turned back to Torres, he had regained his composure. "I'm sorry—I was out of line." He offered Raymond Torres a crooked smile. "From now on I'll try to remember that I'm not the doctor here. I've dealt with enough worried parents to know how difficult they can be."

Torres's demeanor thawed only slightly. "Thank you," he replied. "I'm afraid I have few patients, and no patience, but I do know what I'm doing. Now, if you'll excuse me, I want to get back to Alex."

But as Ellen led him toward the lounge, Marsh's anger surged back. "I've never heard of such a thing—he as much as told us he doesn't want us around!"

"Apparently he doesn't," Ellen agreed.

"But I'm Alex's father, dammit!"

Exhaustion threatening to overwhelm her, Ellen regarded her husband with oddly detached curiosity. Wasn't he even pleased with what Raymond Torres had accomplished? "He's Alex's doctor," she said. "And without him, we wouldn't even have Alex anymore. We owe

Raymond Alex's life, Marsh, and I don't intend to forget that."

"Raymond," Marsh repeated. "Since when are you on a first-name basis with him?"

Ellen gazed at him in puzzlement. "Why wouldn't I be?"

"I'm not," Marsh countered.

Her confusion deepened. What on earth was the matter with him? And suddenly the answer came to her. "Marsh, are you jealous of him?"

"Of course not," Marsh replied, too quickly. "I just don't like the man, that's all."

"Well, I'm sorry," Ellen said, a distinct chill in her voice. "But he did save our son's life, and even if you don't like him, you should be grateful to him."

Her words struck home, and once again Marsh's anger evaporated. "I am," he said quietly. "And you were right back there. He *did* perform a miracle, and it's one I couldn't have performed myself. Maybe I *am* a little jealous." He slipped his arms around her. "Promise me you won't fall in love with him?"

For just a moment, Ellen wasn't sure if he was joking or not, but then she smiled and gave him a quick kiss. "I promise. Now, let's tell everyone the good news."

They stepped into the lounge to find Carol and Lisa Cochran pacing anxiously. "Is it true?" Lisa asked eagerly. "Is he really awake?"

Ellen gathered Lisa into her arms and hugged her. "It's true," she said. "He woke up, and he can talk, and he recognized me."

"Thank God," Carol breathed. "The girl at the desk told us, but we could hardly believe it."

"And," Marsh told her, "we've just been thrown out. Don't ask me why, but Torres wants to put him to sleep again, and says we can't see him until tomorrow."

Carol stared at him with incredulous eyes. "You're kidding, of course."

"I wish I were," Marsh replied. "I think it's crazy, but around here, I'm not the doctor. Let's get out of

here and go home. I don't know about you, but I didn't
get much sleep last night, and I don't think Ellen got
any."

As they stepped out into the bright sunlight of the
May morning, Ellen paused and looked around as if
seeing her surroundings for the first time. "It's beautiful, isn't it?" she asked. "The grounds, and the building—
it's just lovely!"

Carol Cochran grinned at her. "This morning, anything would look lovely to you!"

For the first time since Alex's accident, a truly happy
smile covered Ellen's face. "And why shouldn't it?" she
asked. "Everything's going to be fine. I just know it!"
Impulsively she hugged Lisa close. "We've got him
back!" she cried. "We've got him back, and he's going
to be all right."

"Alex?" Raymond Torres waited for a moment, then
spoke again. "Alex, can you hear me?"

Alex's eyes fluttered for a second, then opened, but
he said nothing.

"Alex, do you think you can answer a couple of
questions?"

Alex struggled for the right words, then spoke carefully: "I don't know. I'll try."

"Good. That's all I want you to do. Now, try to think,
Alex. Do you know why you didn't recognize your
father?"

There was a long silence; then: "After he told me he
was my father, I knew who he was."

"But when you first saw him, Alex, did he look
familiar?"

"No."

"Not at all?"

"I . . . I don't know."

"But you recognized your mother, didn't you?"

"Yes."

"So she *did* look familiar?"

"No."

Torres frowned. "Then how did you recognize her?"

Alex fell silent for a moment, then spoke again, his words strained, as if he weren't sure he was using the right ones.

"I . . . I thought she had to be my mother if he was my father. I thought about it, and decided that if my father was here, then my mother was here too. After I decided she was my mother, she started to look familiar."

"So you didn't recognize either of them until you knew who they were?"

"No."

"All right. Now, I'm going to give you something that's going to put you to sleep, and when you wake up again, I'll come to see you." He slid a hypodermic needle under the skin of Alex's right arm and pressed the plunger. As he swabbed the puncture with a wad of cotton soaked with alcohol, he asked Alex if the needle had hurt.

"No."

"Did you feel it at all?"

"Yes."

"What did it feel like?"

"I . . . I don't know," Alex said.

"All right," Torres told him. "Go to sleep now, Alex, and I'll see you later."

Alex closed his eyes, and Torres watched him for a moment, then stepped to the monitors at the head of the bed and made some adjustments. Before leaving the room, he checked Alex once more.

Alex's eyelids were twitching rapidly. Torres wished there were a way to know exactly what was happening inside the boy's mind.

But there were still some mysteries that even he hadn't yet unraveled.

PART TWO

CHAPTER EIGHT

Alex glanced at the clock on Raymond Torres's desk, and, as he always did, Torres took careful note of the action.

"Two more hours," he said. "Getting excited?"

Alex shrugged. "Curious, I guess."

Torres placed his pen on the desk and leaned back in his chair. "If I were you, I think I'd be excited. You're finally going home after three months—it seems to me that should be exciting."

"Except I'm not really going home, am I?" Alex asked, his voice as expressionless as his eyes. "I mean, Mom and Dad have moved, so I'll be going to a house I've never lived in before."

"Do you wish you were going back to the house you grew up in?"

Alex hesitated, then shook his head. "I guess it doesn't matter where I go, since I don't remember the old house anyway."

"You don't have any feelings about it at all?"

"No." Alex uttered the single word with no expression whatsoever.

And that, Torres silently reminded himself, was the crux of the matter. Alex had no feelings, no emotions. That was not to say that Alex's recovery had not been remarkable; indeed, it was very little short of miraculous. The boy could walk and talk, see, hear, and touch. But he seemed not to be able to feel at all.

Even the news that he was being released from the Institute had elicited no emotional response from him. Rather, he'd accepted the news with the same detachment with which he now accepted everything. And that, Torres knew, was the one factor that kept the medical world from viewing the operation as a complete success.

"What about going back to La Paloma?" Torres pressed.

Alex shifted in his chair and started to cross his legs. On the second try, his left ankle came to rest on his right knee.

"I . . . I guess I wonder what it will be like," he finally said. "I keep wondering if I'll recognize anything, or if it's all going to be like it was when I first woke up."

"You've remembered a lot since then," Torres replied.

Alex shrugged indifferently. "But I keep wondering if I really remember anything, or if I'm just learning things all over again."

"Not possible," Torres stated flatly. "It has to be recovery—nobody could learn things as fast as you have. And don't forget that when you first woke up, you spoke. You hadn't forgotten language."

"There were a lot of words I didn't understand," Alex reminded him. "And sometimes there still are." He stood up and took a shaky step, paused, then took another.

"Take it easy, Alex," Torres told him. "Don't demand too much of yourself. It's all going to take time. And speaking of time, I think we'd better get started." He waited while Alex swiveled his chair around so both of them were facing the screen that had been set up in a corner of the large office. When Alex was ready, Torres switched off the lights. A picture flashed on the screen.

"What is it?" Torres asked.

Alex didn't hesitate so much as a second. "An amoeba."

"Right. When did you take biology?"

"Last year. It was Mr. Landry's class."

"Can you tell me what Mr. Landry looked like?"

Alex thought a minute, but nothing came. "No."

"All right. What about your grade?"

"An A. But that was easy—I always got A's in science."

Torres said nothing, and changed the slide.

"That's the *Mona Lisa*," Alex said promptly. "Leonardo da Vinci."

"Good enough. Is there another name for it?"

"*La Gioconda.*"

The pictures changed again and again, and each time Alex correctly identified the image on the screen. Finally the slide show ended, and Torres turned the lights back on. "Well? What do you think?"

Alex shrugged. "I could have learned most of that stuff since I've been here," he said. "All I've been doing is reading."

"What about your grades? Did you read them here, too?"

"No. But Mom told me. I don't really remember much of anything about any of my classes. Just names of teachers and that kind of thing. But I don't *see* anything. Know what I mean?"

Torres nodded, and rifled through some of his notes. "Having problems visualizing things? No mental images?"

Alex nodded.

"But you don't have problems visualizing things you've seen since the accident?"

"No. That's easy. And sometimes, when I see something, it seems familiar, but I can't quite put it together. Then, when someone tells me what it is, it's almost like I remember it, but not quite. It's hard to describe."

"Sort of like *déjà vu*?"

Alex knit his brows, then shook his head. "Isn't that where you think what's happening now has happened before?"

"Exactly."

"It's not like that at all." Alex searched his mind, trying to find the right words to describe the strange sensations he had sometimes. "They're like half-memories," he finally said. "It's like sometimes I see something, and I think I remember it, but I really don't."

"But that's just it," Torres told him. "I think you *do* remember, but your brain isn't healed yet. You've had a lot of damage to your brain, Alex. I was able to put it back together again, but I couldn't do it perfectly. So there are a lot of connections that aren't there yet. It's as though part of your brain knows where the data it's looking for are stored, but can't get there. But it doesn't stop trying, and sometimes—and I think this will happen more and more—it finds a new route, and gets what it's after. But it's a little different. Not the data itself—just the way you remember it. I think you'll have more and more of those half-memories over the next few months. In time, as your brain finds and establishes new paths through itself, it'll happen less and less. And eventually, everything left in your mind after the accident will become accessible again." A buzzer sounded. Torres picked up the phone and spoke for a moment, then hung up. "Your parents are here," he told Alex. "Why don't you go over to the lab, and I'll have a talk with them? And when you're done, that's it. We check you out, and you only have to come back for a couple of hours a day."

Alex got to his feet and started toward the door in the shambling gait that, most of the time, got him where he wanted to go. He was still unsteady, but he hadn't actually lost his footing for a week, and each day he was doing better. Still, he wasn't allowed to attempt stairs without someone there to help him, and he used a cane whenever he wanted to go more than a few yards. But it was coming back to him.

The door opened just before Alex got to it, and his parents stepped inside. He stopped short, leaning his weight on the cane, and bent his head to kiss his mother's cheek as she gave him a hug. Then he shook his father's hand, and started out of the office.

"Alex?" Ellen asked. "Where are you going?"

"My tests, Mom," Alex replied, his voice flat. "Then we can go home, I guess." He turned away, and shambled out of the room. Ellen, her brows furrowed, watched him go, then stood perfectly still for several long moments. When at last she spoke, she still faced the door.

"I'm not sure I'm going to be able to stand this, Raymond," she said, her voice trembling. "He isn't changing, is he? He doesn't really care if he goes home or not."

"Sit down, Ellen." Torres gestured the Lonsdales toward the sofa, but remained standing himself, preferring to roam the room while he brought them up to date on Alex's progress.

"So that's it," he finished thirty minutes later. "Physically and intellectually, he's doing better than we could possibly have hoped for."

"But still no emotions," Ellen said, her voice dull. Then she sighed, and forced a smile. "I'm sorry," she said. "I've got to learn not to expect miracles, don't I?"

"We've already had the miracle," Torres replied. "And I'm not through yet. But I think you have to face the fact that Alex is probably never going to be the same as he was before."

"I don't expect him to be," Marsh said evenly, determined that today he would keep his dislike of Torres under control. "I'll be honest—I never expected him to come as far as he has."

Torres shook his head. "Some of it may be deceiving. There are still enormous gaps in his memory, and when he leaves here, he may become completely disoriented.

He says he doesn't remember what La Paloma looks like, or how to get to his house."

"We'll get him there," Marsh said. "Anyway, we'll try," he added, grinning ruefully. "I'm afraid I still go to the old place a couple of times a week. But I'm getting better."

Torres didn't respond to Marsh's grin. "Actually, I think Alex could get you there himself. We gave him a map, and after he studied it, I asked him to tell me how to get home from here. He didn't miss a turn. But he says he doesn't have any idea of what any of it looks like. He simply can't get a mental image of anything he hasn't actually seen since the accident."

"Is that possible?" Ellen asked.

"Possible, but unlikely." He told them what he'd told Alex earlier, then, finally, sat down behind his desk. "Which brings us, finally, to the problem of his personality, or lack of it."

Marsh and Ellen exchanged a glance—it was Alex's altered personality that had, during the last few weeks, become their primary concern. Steadfastly Ellen had insisted that Alex's strange passivity was only temporary, that once he had recovered physically from his injuries, Raymond Torres would begin working to restore his personality. Marsh, on the other hand, had tried to prepare her for the possibility that Alex's personality might never recover, that the emotional center of his brain might very well be irrevocably damaged.

"No," Ellen had insisted over and over again. "It's just a matter of time. Raymond will help him. We just have to trust him, that's all."

Futilely Marsh had pointed out that Torres was a surgeon, not a psychologist, but it had done no good. Through the end of spring and the long summer that followed, Ellen's faith in Torres's abilities had only grown stronger, while at the same time, Marsh's own dislike of the man had increased proportionately. On the surface, Marsh pretended that his animosity toward Torres was based solely on the man's arrogance, but privately he was all too aware that he was, indeed, jealous of Torres. More and more, Torres was taking over the role of father to his son, and adviser and confidant to his wife. And there was nothing he could do about it—he owed the man Alex's very life.

"I'm afraid Alex has what we call a flat personality," he heard Torres saying.

"I know the term," he said, abandoning his previous resolve and making no attempt to keep his voice free of sarcasm.

"I don't doubt it," Torres replied coldly. "But I'm going to explain it anyway." He turned to Ellen. "It's very common in this kind of case," he went on. "Often, when there is brain damage—even much less brain damage than Alex suffered—the emotional structure of the victim is the slowest to recover. Sometimes the damage results in what is called a labile personality, in which the patient tends to exhibit inappropriate emotions—such as laughing uncontrollably at things that don't appear funny to others, or suddenly bursting into tears for no apparent reason. Or, as in Alex's case, the personality simply goes flat. There seems to be little emotional reaction to anything. Over a long period of time, the personality may be partially rebuilt, but there is rarely a full recovery. And that, I'm afraid, may easily be the case with Alex. From what we've seen so far, it appears that the permanent damage in him is going to be to his personality."

There was a silence. Then: "I told you at the outset that there was no chance for a complete recovery."

"But of course he *will* recover," Ellen said, and Marsh felt a slight chill at the determination in her voice, and the faith in her eyes as she gazed at Raymond Torres. "He has you to help him." Torres nodded, but made no reply. "All I have to know," Ellen went on, "is how to help him. Should I go ahead and put my arms around him, even though he just stands there? Should I *try* to elicit emotional responses in him?"

Again Torres nodded. "Of course you should. And

frankly, I don't think you'll be able to resist trying. But I've worked with Alex all summer, and I can tell you there are times when it will be very frustrating. You'll want him to be as excited about his progress as you are, and it just won't happen. Or perhaps it's just that he hasn't learned how to express his feelings yet. We'll just have to wait and see."

Ellen nodded, and smiled triumphantly at Marsh. "Is there anything else we should expect?" she asked.

"I don't know. Expect anything and nothing. Just don't be surprised at anything. Alex's mind is still healing, and all kinds of things might happen during that process. The most important thing for you to do is keep track of what happens. I want you to keep notes, and bring them with you every day. I don't care what's in the notes—I want to know when his behavior seems normal, and when it doesn't. I particularly want to know what, if anything, makes him laugh or cry. Or even smile."

"Don't worry," Ellen assured him. "I'll get him smiling again."

"I hope so," Torres replied. "But try not to worry about it too much if it doesn't happen. And keep in mind that while he doesn't smile, he doesn't frown, either."

Marsh silently wondered if Torres had intended that to be a comforting thought. If he had, he'd failed totally.

In the lab, Alex began to come up from the anesthesia that was always administered to him during the daily tests, and, as always, slowly became aware of the strange and fleeting images that filled his mind. As always, the images were unidentifiable; as always, they were accompanied by an incomprehensible stream of something that was almost, but not quite, like sound.

Then he came fully awake, and the images and sounds faded away. He opened his eyes.

"How do you feel?" the technician asked. His name was Peter Bloch, but other than that, Alex didn't know much about him. Nor, for that matter, was he curious to know anything about him. To Alex, Peter was simply one more part of the Institute.

"Okay," he said. Then: "How come I always see and hear things just before I wake up?"

Peter frowned. "What kind of things?"

"I don't know. It's like a flickering I can't quite see, and there's a sort of squeaky, rasping sound."

Peter began disconnecting the monitors from the tiny wires that emerged, almost like hairs, from the metal plate that had replaced part of Alex's left parietal bone, and the scalp that had been drawn across to cover it. "What about pain?"

"No. There's no pain."

"Anything at all? Do you feel anything, or smell anything? Taste anything?"

"No."

"Well, I'm not sure," Peter told him. "I know that during the tests, some of these electrodes are constantly stimulating your brain, then measuring its responses. That's why we have to put you to sleep. We're giving your brain artificial stimuli, and if you were awake, it could be pretty unpleasant. You might feel like we'd burned your hand, or cut your arm, or you might smell or taste something pretty awful. It sounds like you're just waking up too early, and responding to visual and otic stimuli—seeing and hearing things that aren't there at all."

Alex got up from the table and pulled his shirt on, then sat still, waiting for the last of the anesthesia to wear off. "Shall I tell Dr. Torres about it?"

Peter Bloch shrugged. "If you want. I'll make a note of it, and tomorrow we'll hold off on flushing you out with oxygen for a few more minutes."

"That's okay," Alex replied. "It doesn't bother me."

Peter offered him an uncertain grin. "Does *anything* ever bother you?"

Alex thought a moment, then shook his head. "No." He tucked in his shirt and carefully put his feet on the floor, then took his cane in his right hand and began making his slow way to the door.

Peter Bloch watched him go, and his grin faded away. He began closing up the lab, shutting down the equipment that had been in use almost constantly over the last three months. For himself, he was glad Alex Lonsdale was going home. The work load, since Alex had arrived, had been nearly intolerable, and Torres had never let up on the staff for a moment.

Besides, Peter realized as he took off his lab jacket and hunched into his favorite khaki windbreaker, he didn't like Alex Lonsdale.

True, what Torres had accomplished with Alex would probably make some kind of medical history, but Peter wasn't impressed. To him, it didn't matter how well Alex was doing.

The kid was a zombie.

Marsh drove north out of Palo Alto, staying on Middlefield Road until he came to La Paloma Drive, where he turned left to start up into the hills. Every few minutes he glanced over at Alex, who sat impassively in the passenger seat next to him, while from the back seat Ellen kept up a steady stream of chatter:

"Do you remember what's just around the next curve? We're almost to La Paloma, and things will start looking familiar to you."

Alex pictured the map he'd studied. "The county park," he said. "Hillside Park."

"You remember!" Ellen exclaimed.

"It was on the map Dr. Torres gave me," Alex corrected her. They came around the bend in the road, and Marsh slowed the car. "Stop," Alex suddenly said.

Marsh braked the car, and followed Alex's gaze. In the distance, there was a group of children playing on a swing set, while two teenage boys tossed a Frisbee back and forth.

"What is it, Alex?" Marsh asked.

Alex's eyes seemed to be fixed on the children on the swings.

"I always wanted to do that when I was little," he said.

Marsh chuckled. "You not only wanted to, you nearly drove us crazy." His voice took on a singsong tone as he mimicked a child's voice. " 'More! More! Don't want to go home. Want to swing!' That's why I finally hung one in the backyard at the old house. It was either that or spend every free minute I had bringing you out here."

Alex turned and gazed at his father, his eyes steady. "I don't remember that at all," he said.

In the rearview mirror, Marsh saw Ellen's worried eyes, and wondered if either of them would be able to stand seeing their son's memory wiped clean of every experience they had all shared. "Do you want to swing now?" he asked.

Alex hesitated, then shook his head. "Let's go home," he said. "Maybe I'll remember our house when I see it."

They drove into La Paloma, and Alex began examining the town he'd lived in all his life. But it was as if he'd never seen it before. Nothing was familiar, nothing he saw triggered any memories.

And then they came to the Square.

Marsh bore right to follow the traffic pattern three-quarters of the way around before turning right once again into Hacienda Drive. Alex's eyes, he noted, were no longer staring out toward the front of the car. Instead, he was leaning forward slightly, so he could look across Marsh's chest and see into the Square.

"Remembering something?" he asked quietly.

"The tree . . ." Alex said. "There's something about the tree." As he stared at the giant oak that dominated the Square, Alex was certain it looked familiar. And yet, something was wrong. The tree looked right, but nothing else did.

"The chain," he said softly. "I don't remember the chain, or the grass."

In the back seat, Ellen nodded, sure she understood

what was happening. "It hasn't been there a long time," she said. "When you were little, the tree was there, but there wasn't anything around it."

"A rope," Alex suddenly said. "There was a rope."

Ellen's heart began to pound. "Yes! There was a rope with a tire on it! You and your friends used to play on it when you were little!"

But the image that had flashed into Alex's mind wasn't of a tire at all.

It was the image of a man, and the man had been hanging at the end of the rope.

He wondered if he ought to tell his parents what he'd remembered, but decided he'd better not. The image was too strange, and if he talked about it, his parents might think he, too, was strange.

For some reason—a reason he didn't understand—it was important that people not think he was strange.

Marsh pulled into the driveway, and Alex gazed at the house.

And suddenly he remembered it.

But it, like the oak tree, didn't look quite right either. He stared at the house for a long time.

From the driveway, all he could see was a long expanse of white stucco, broken at regular intervals by deeply recessed windows, each framed with a pair of heavy shutters. There were two stories, topped by a gently sloping red tile roof, and on the north side there was a garden, enclosed by walls which were entirely covered with vines.

It was the vines that were wrong. The garden wall, like the house itself, should be plain white stucco, with decorative tiles implanted in it every six feet or so. And the vines should be small, and climbing on trellises.

He sat still, trying to remember what the inside looked like, but no matter how he searched his memory, there was nothing.

He stared at the chimney that rose from the roof. If there was a chimney, there was a fireplace. He tried to picture a fireplace, but the only one he could visualize was the one in the lobby of the Institute.

He got out of the car, and with his parents following behind him, approached the house. When he came to the wide steps leading up to the garden gate, he felt his father's hand on his elbow.

"I can do it," he said.

"But Dr. Torres told us—" his mother began. Alex cut her off.

"I know what he said. Just stay behind me, in case I trip. I can do it."

Carefully he put his right foot on the first step, then, supporting himself with the cane, cautiously began to bring his left foot up toward the second step. He swayed for a moment, then felt his father's hands steadying him.

"Thank you," he said. Then: "I have to try again. Help me get back down, please."

"You don't have to try right now, darling," Ellen assured him. "Don't you want to go in?"

Alex shook his head. "I have to go up and down the steps by myself. I have to be able to take care of myself. Dr. Torres says it's important."

"Can't it wait?" Marsh asked. "We could get you settled in, then come back out."

"No," Alex replied. "I have to learn it now."

Fifteen minutes later Alex slowly but steadily ascended the three steps that led up to the gate, then turned to come back down. Ellen tried to put her arms around him, but he turned away, his face impassive. "All right," he said. "Let's go in."

As she followed him into the garden, across the tiled patio and into the house itself, Ellen hoped he'd turned away before he saw the tears that, just for a moment, she had been unable to hold back.

Alex gazed around the room that was filled with all the possessions he'd had since he was a child. Oddly, the room itself seemed vaguely familiar, as if sometime, long ago, he'd been in it. But its furnishings meant nothing to him. Against one wall was a desk, and he opened the top drawer to stare at the contents. Some pens and pencils, and a notebook. He picked up the notebook and glanced at its contents.

Notes for a geometry class.

The name of the teacher came instantly to mind: Mrs. Hendricks.

What did Mrs. Hendricks look like?

No image.

He began reading the notes. At the end of the notebook there was a theorem, but he'd never finished the proof of it. He sat down at the desk and picked up a pencil. Writing slowly, his handwriting still shaky, he began entering a series of premises and corollaries in the notebook. Two minutes later, he'd proved the theorem.

But he still couldn't remember what Mrs. Hendricks looked like.

He began scanning the books on the shelf above the desk, his eyes finally coming to rest on a large volume bound in red Leatherette. When he looked at the cover, he saw that it was emblazoned with a cartoon figure of a bird, and the title: *The Cardinal*. He opened it.

It was his high-school annual from last year. Taking the book with him, he went to his bed, stretched out, and began paging slowly through it.

An hour later, when his mother tapped softly at the door, then stuck her head inside to ask him if he wanted anything, he knew what Mrs. Hendricks looked like, and Mr. Landry. If he saw them, he would recognize them.

He would recognize all his friends, all the people Lisa Cochran had told him about each day when she came to visit him at the Institute.

He would recognize them, and be able to match their names to their faces.

But he wouldn't know anything about them.

All of it was still a blank.

He would have to start all over again. He put the book aside and looked up at his mother.

"I don't remember any of it," he said at last. "I thought I recognized the house, and even this room, but I couldn't have, could I?"

"Why not?" Ellen asked.

"Because I thought I remembered the garden wall without vines. But the vines have always been there, haven't they?"

"Why do you say that?"

"I looked at the roots and the branches. They look like they've been there forever."

Ellen nodded. "They have. The wall's been covered with morning glory as long as I can remember. That's one of the reasons I always wanted this house—I love the vines."

Alex nodded. "So I couldn't have remembered. And this room seemed sort of familiar, but it's just a room. And I don't remember any of my things. None of them at all."

Ellen sat on the bed next to him, and put her arms around him. "I know," she said. "We were all hoping you'd remember, but Raymond told us you probably wouldn't. And you mustn't worry about it."

"I won't," Alex said. "I'll just start over, that's all."

"Yes," Ellen replied. "We'll start over. And you'll remember. It will be slow, but it'll come back."

It won't, Alex thought. It won't ever come back. I'll just have to act like it does.

One thing he had learned in the last three months was that when he pretended to remember things, people seemed to be happy with him.

As he followed his mother out to the family room a few minutes later, he wondered what happiness felt like—or if he'd ever feel it himself.

CHAPTER NINE

The Monday after Labor Day was the kind of California September morning that belies any hint of a coming change of season. The morning fog had burned off by seven, and as Marsh Lonsdale dropped Alex off in front of the Cochrans' house, the heat was already building.

"Sure you don't want me to take you both to school?"

"I want to walk," Alex replied. "Dr. Torres says I should walk as much as I can."

"Dr. Torres says a lot about everything," Marsh commented. "That doesn't mean you have to do everything he says."

Alex opened the car door and got out, then put his cane in the back seat. When he looked up, his father was watching him with disapproval. "Did Dr. Torres tell you not to use the cane anymore?"

Alex shook his head. "No. I just think it would be better if I stopped using it, that's all."

His father's hard expression dissolved into a smile. "Good for you," he said. Then: "You okay with going back to school?"

Alex nodded. "I think so."

"It's not too late to change your mind. If you want, we can get a tutor up from Stanford, at least for the first semester . . ."

"No," Alex said. "I want to go to school. I might remember a lot, once I'm there."

"You're already remembering a lot," Marsh replied. "I just don't think you should push yourself too hard. You . . . well, you don't have to remember everything that happened before the accident."

"But I do," Alex replied. "If I'm going to get really well, I have to remember everything." He slammed the car door and started toward the Cochrans' front porch, then turned to wave to his father, who waved back, then pulled away from the curb. Only when the car had disappeared around the corner did Alex start once again toward the house, idly wondering if his father knew he'd lied to him.

Since he'd come home, Alex had learned to lie a lot.

He pressed the doorbell, waited, then pressed it again. Even though the Cochrans had told him over and over again that he should simply let himself into their house as he used to, he hadn't yet done it.

Nor did he have any memory of ever having let himself into their house.

Their house, like the one next door where he knew he'd spent most of his life, had rung no bells in his head, elicited no memories whatsoever. But he'd been careful not to say so. Instead, when he'd walked into the Cochrans' house for the first time after leaving the Institute, he'd scanned the rooms carefully, trying to memorize everything in them. Then, when he was sure he had it all firmly fixed in his mind, he'd said that he thought he remembered a picture upstairs—one of himself and Lisa, when they were five or six years old.

Everyone had been pleased. And since then, after he'd relearned something he was sure he'd known before, and discovered as much as he could about its past, he would experiment with "remembering."

It worked well. Last week, while looking for a pen in his parents' desk, he had found a repair bill for the car. He'd studied it carefully, then, as they were driving to the Cochrans' that evening, and passed the shop where the car had been fixed, he'd turned to his father.

"Didn't they work on the car last year?" he'd asked.

"They sure did," his father had replied. Then: "Do you remember what they did to it?"

Alex pretended to ponder the question. "Transmission?" he asked.

His father had sighed, then smiled at him in the rearview mirror. "Right. It's coming back, isn't it?"

"A little bit," Alex had said. "Maybe a little bit."

But, of course, it wasn't.

The front door opened, and Lisa was smiling at him. He carefully returned the smile. "Ready?"

"Who's ever ready for the first day of school?" Lisa replied. "Do I look all right?"

Alex took in her jeans and white blouse, and nodded gravely. "Did you always wear clothes like that to school?"

"Everybody does." She called a good-bye over her shoulder, and a moment later the two of them set out toward La Paloma High.

As they walked through the town, Alex kept asking Lisa an endless series of questions about who lived in which house, the stores they passed, and the people who spoke to them. Lisa patiently answered his questions, then began testing his memory, even though she knew that Alex never seemed to forget anything she told him.

"Who lives in the blue house on Carmel Street?"

"The Jamesons."

"What about the old house at the corner of Monterey?"

"Miss Thorpe," Alex replied. Then he added, "She used to be a witch."

Lisa glanced at him out of the corner of her eye, wondering if he was teasing her, even though she knew he wasn't. Since he'd come home, Alex never teased anybody. "She wasn't *really* a witch," she said. "We just always *thought* she was when we were little."

Alex stopped walking. "If she wasn't one, why did we think she was?"

Lisa wondered what to tell him. He seemed to have forgotten everything about his childhood, including what it had been like to be a child. How could she explain to him how much fun it used to be to scare themselves half to death with speculations on what old Miss Thorpe might be doing behind her heavily curtained windows, or what she might do to them if she ever caught them in her yard? For Alex never seemed to imagine anything anymore. He always wanted to know what things were, and who was who, but it didn't seem to matter to him, and he didn't seem, really, to care. In fact, though she'd told no one of her feelings, Lisa was glad that school was finally starting and she could legitimately spend less time with Alex.

"I don't know," she said at last. "We just thought she was a witch, that's all. Now, come on, or we'll be late."

Alex moved uncertainly around the campus of La Paloma High School. Deep in the recesses of his mind, he had a faint feeling of having been here before, but nothing seemed to be quite right.

The school was built around a quadrangle, with a fountain at its center, and from the fountain, some of the campus seemed familiar.

And yet, the picture in his mind seemed incomplete. It was as if he could remember only parts of the campus; other areas were totally strange.

Still, it was a memory.

He looked at his program card, and when the first bell sounded, he started toward the building that housed what would be his homeroom that year.

It was in one of the buildings he had no memory of, but he had no problem in locating the room. Just before the second bell rang, he stepped into the classroom, and started toward an empty seat next to Lisa Cochran.

Before he could sit down, the teacher, whom he recognized from the picture in the yearbook as Mr. Hamlin, told him that he was to report to the dean of boys. He looked questioningly at Lisa, but she only shook her head and shrugged. Silently he left the classroom and went to the Administration Building.

As soon as he was inside, he knew that he was in familiar territory. As he glanced around, the walnut wainscoting seemed to strike a chord in him, and he stopped for a moment to take in the details of the lobby.

To the left, where it felt as though it should be, was a large glass-fronted office. Through the glass, he could see a long counter, and beyond it, several secretaries sitting at desks, typing.

Straight ahead, and off to the right, two corridors ran at right angles to each other, and without thinking, Alex turned right and went into the second office on the left.

A nurse looked up at him. "May I help you?"

Alex stopped short. "I'm looking for Mr. Eisenberg's office. But this isn't it, is it?"

The nurse smiled and shook her head. "It's in the other wing. First door on the right."

"Thank you," Alex said. He left the nurse's office and started back toward the main foyer.

Something, though, was wrong. When he had come into the building, he had recognized everything, and known exactly where the dean's office was. Yet it wasn't there.

Apparently he hadn't remembered after all.

Still, as he made his way into what really was the dean's office, he had the distinct feeling that he *had* remembered, and when the dean's secretary glanced up and smiled at him, he decided he knew what had happened.

"How do you like the new office?" he asked.

The smile faded from the secretary's face. "New office?" she asked. "What are you talking about, Alex?"

Alex swallowed. "Wasn't Mr. Eisenberg's office where the nurse is this year?"

The secretary hesitated, then shook her head. "It's been right here for as long as I've been here," she said. Then she smiled again. "You can go right in, and don't worry. You're not in any trouble."

He passed the desk and knocked at the inner door, as he had always knocked at Dr. Torres's door before going inside.

"Come in," a voice called from within. He opened the door and stepped through. As with everyone else who had been pictured in the yearbook in his bedroom, he recognized the face and knew the man's name, but had no memory of ever having met him before. Whatever his flash of remembrance had been about, it was over now.

Dan Eisenberg unfolded his large frame from the chair behind his desk to offer Alex his hand. "Alex! It's great to see you again."

"It's nice to see you, too, sir," Alex replied, hesitating only a second before grasping Eisenberg's hand in a firm shake. A moment later, the dean indicated the chair next to his desk.

"Sorry to have to call you in on the first day of school," he said, "but I'm afraid a little problem has come up."

Alex's face remained impassive. "Miss Jennings said I wasn't in trouble—"

"And you aren't," Eisenberg reassured him "But I did take the liberty of talking to Dr. Torres last week, and he suggested that perhaps we might want to give you a couple of tests." He looked for a reaction from Alex, but saw none. "Do you have any idea what the tests might be for?"

"To see how much I've forgotten," Alex said, and Eisenberg had the distinct feeling that Alex wasn't making a guess, but already knew about the tests.

"Right. I take it Dr. Torres told you about them."

"No. But it makes sense, doesn't it? I mean, you don't know which class I should be in if you don't know how much I remember."

"Exactly." Eisenberg picked up a packet of standard form tests. "Do you remember these?" Alex shook his head. "They're the same tests you took at the beginning of last year, and would have taken again in the spring, except . . ." His voice trailed off, and he looked uncomfortable.

"Except for the accident," Alex finished for him. "I don't mind talking about it, but I don't remember it too well, either. Just that it happened."

Eisenberg nodded. "Dr. Torres tells us there are still a lot of gaps in your memory—"

"I've been studying all summer," Alex broke in. "My dad wants me to be in the accelerated class this year."

Which is certainly not going to happen, Eisenberg thought. From what Torres had told him of Alex's case, he knew it was far more likely that Alex would have to start all over again with the school's most basic courses. "We'll just have to see, won't we?" he asked, trying to keep his pessimism out of his voice. "Anyway, if you feel up to it, I'd like you to take the tests today."

"All right."

Ten minutes later Alex sat in an empty classroom while Eisenberg's secretary explained the testing system and the time limits. "And don't worry if you don't finish them," she said as she set the time clock for the first of the battery of eight tests. "You're not expected to finish all of them. Ready?" Alex nodded. "Begin."

Alex opened the first of the booklets and began marking down his answers.

Dan Eisenberg looked up from the report he was working on, his smile fading when he saw the look of disappointment in his secretary's eyes. A glance at his watch told him Alex had begun the tests only an hour and a half ago. "What's happened, Marge? Couldn't he do it?"

The young woman shook her head sorrowfully. "I don't think he even tried," she said. "He just . . . well, he just started marking answers randomly."

"But you told him how they're scored, didn't you? Right minus wrong?"

Marge nodded. "And I asked him again each time he handed me one of his answer sheets. He said he understood how it was scored, and that he was finished."

"How many did he do?"

Marge hesitated; then: "All of them."

The dean's brows arched skeptically. "All of them?" he repeated. Then, after Marge had nodded once more: "But that's impossible. Those tests are supposed to take all day, and even then, no one's supposed to finish them."

"I know. So he must have simply gone down the sheets, marking in his answers. I'm not really sure there's any point in scoring it." Still, she handed the stack of answer sheets to Dan, and he slid the first one under the template.

Behind each tiny slot in the template, there was a neat black mark. Dan frowned, then shook his head. Wordlessly he matched the rest of the answer sheets to their templates. Finally he leaned back, a smile playing around the corners of his mouth.

"Cute," he said. "Real cute." The smile spread into a grin. "He's still working on them, isn't he?"

Now it was Marge Jennings who frowned. "What are you talking about?"

"I'm talking about you," Dan said, chuckling. "You came in early and dummied up this set of answer sheets, didn't you? Well, you went too far. Did you really expect me to buy this?"

"Buy what?" Marge asked. She stepped around the desk and repeated the process of checking the answer sheets. "My God," she breathed.

Dan looked up at her, fully expecting to see her eyes twinkling as she still tried to get him to fall for her joke.

And then, slowly, he began to realize it was not a joke at all.

Alex Lonsdale had completed the tests, and his scores were perfect.

"Get Torres on the phone," Dan told his secretary.

Marge Jennings returned to her office, where Alex sat quietly on a sofa, leafing through a magazine. He looked up at her for a moment, then returned to his reading.

"Alex?"

"Yes?" Alex laid the magazine aside.

"Did you . . . well, did anyone show you a copy of those tests? I mean, since you took them last year?"

Alex thought a moment, then shook his head. "No. At least not since the accident."

"I see," Marge said softly.

But, of course, she didn't see at all.

Ellen glanced nervously at the clock, and once more regretted having allowed Cynthia Evans to set up an appointment for her to interview María Torres. Not, of course, that she didn't need a housekeeper; she did. A few months ago, before the accident, she would have felt no hesitation about hiring María Torres. But now things were different, and despite all of Cynthia's arguments, she still felt strange about asking the mother of Alex's doctor to vacuum her floors and do her laundry. Still, it would only be two days a week, and she knew María was going to need the work: starting next month, Cynthia herself was going to have full-time, live-in help.

But right now, María was late, and Ellen herself was due for what Marsh always referred to, with a hint of what Ellen considered to be slightly sexist overtones, as "lunch with the girls." Of course, part of it was her own fault, for try as she would, she still hadn't been able to train herself to think of her friends as "women": they had known each other since childhood, and they would be, forever, "girls," at least in Ellen's mind.

Except Marty Lewis, who had long since stopped being a girl in any sense of the word. Ellen often wondered if Alan Lewis's alcoholism had anything to do with the changes that had come over Marty in the last few years.

Of course it had. If Alan hadn't turned into a drunk, Marty would have been just like the rest of them— staying home, raising her kids, and taking care of her husband. But for Marty, things had been different. Alan couldn't hold a job, so Marty had taken over the support of the family, and made a success of it, too, while Alan drifted from treatment program to treatment program, sobering up and working for a while, but only a while. Sooner or later, he would begin drinking again, and the spiral would start over again. And Marty, finally, had accepted it. She'd talked of divorce a few years ago, but in the end had simply taken over the burdens of the family. At the fairly regular lunches the four of them—Carol Cochran and Valerie Benson were the other two—enjoyed, Marty's main conversation was about her job, and how much she liked it.

"Working's *fun!*" she would insist. "In fact, it's a lot better this way. I never was much good at the domestic scene, and now that Kate's growing up, I don't even feel I'm robbing her of anything. And I don't have to get terrified every time Alan starts drinking anymore. Do you know what it was like? He'd start drinking, and I'd start saving, because I always knew that it would only be a matter of months before he was going to be out of a job again." Then she'd smile ruefully. "I suppose I should have left him years ago, but I still love him. So I put up with him, and hope that every binge will be the last one."

And, of course, there was Valerie Benson, who, three years ago, actually *had* divorced her husband. "Dumbest thing I ever did," was now Val's characteristically blunt summation of the divorce. "I can't even remember what he used to do that made me think I couldn't stand it anymore. I had this idea that if I only got rid of

George, life would be wonderful. So I got rid of him, and you know what? Nothing changed. Not one damn thing. Except now I don't have George to blame things on, so, in a way, I suppose I'm a better person." Then she'd roll her eyes: "Lord, how I loathe those words. I'm sick of being a better person. I'd rather be married and miserable."

Ellen glanced at the clock once more, and realized that if María didn't arrive within the next five minutes, she was going to have to choose between waiting for María and going to lunch. Not that the interview would take long—María had been a fixture in La Paloma all of Ellen's life, and all Ellen really had to do was explain to the old woman what she wanted done, then leave the house in María's hands.

Lunch, however, was something else. This would be the group's first lunch since Alex's accident, and she was sure that Alex would be the main topic of conversation.

Alex, and Raymond Torres.

And, she readily admitted to herself, she was looking forward to the lunch, looking forward to spending even a few hours relaxing with her friends.

It had been a long summer. Once the decision had finally been made that Alex could go back to school, Ellen had begun looking forward to this day. This morning, after Alex and Marsh had left, she had treated herself to a leisurely hour of pure relaxation, and then spent two full hours getting herself ready for today's lunch. She was determined that Alex wasn't going to be the only topic of conversation that day, nor was Raymond Torres. Instead, she was going to encourage the others to talk about themselves rather than the Lonsdales' problems. It would be wonderful to laugh and chat with old friends as if nothing had changed.

The doorbell and the telephone rang simultaneously, and Ellen called out to María to let herself in as she picked up the receiver. Then, when the voice at the other end of the wire identified itself as Dan Eisenberg, her heart sank, and she waved María Torres into the living room as she focused her attention on the telephone.

"What's happened?" she asked, wearily setting her purse back on the table.

"I'm not sure," Eisenberg replied. "But I'd like you to come down to the school this afternoon."

"This afternoon?" Ellen asked, relief flooding through her. "Then it isn't an emergency?"

There was a momentary silence. When Eisenberg spoke again, his voice was apologetic. "I'm sorry," he said. "I should have told you right away that Alex is all right. It's just that we gave him some tests this morning, and I'd like to go over the results with you. Both you and Dr. Lonsdale, actually. Would two o'clock be all right?"

"Fine with me," Ellen told him. "I'll have to call my husband, but I imagine it will be fine with him too." She paused; then: "Where Alex is concerned, he tends to make time, even if he hasn't got it."

"Then I'll see you both at two," Eisenberg replied. He was about to hang up when Ellen stopped him.

"Mr. Eisenberg? The tests. Did Alex do all right on them?"

There was a slight hesitation before Eisenberg spoke. "He did very well, Mrs. Lonsdale," he said. "Very well indeed."

A moment later, as Ellen turned her attention to María Torres, she decided to put Dan Eisenberg's words, and the tone in which he'd spoken them, out of her mind. If she didn't, the feeling she had of something amiss would ruin the lunch for her, and she was determined that that wouldn't happen.

María, dressed as always in black, her skirt reaching almost to the floor, still hovered near the door, a worn shawl wrapped around her stooped shoulders, despite the heat of the summerlike day. Her eyes were fixed on the floor. "I am sorry, *señora*," she said softly. "I am very late."

The abject sorrow evident in the old woman's entire

being dissolved Ellen's impatience. "It's all right," she said gently. "I don't really need to interview you anyway, do I?" Without waiting for a reply, she began giving María hurried instructions. "All the cleaning things are in the laundry room behind the kitchen, but if you'll just try to get some vacuuming done today, that's all I really need. Then we can go over the rest of it on Saturday. All right?"

"Sí, señora," María muttered, and as she started toward the kitchen, Ellen hurriedly threw on a coat, picked up her purse, and left the house.

The moment she was gone, María's back straightened and her glittering old eyes began taking in every detail of the Lonsdales' house. She prowled the rooms slowly, examining every possession of the *gringo* family whose son had been saved by Ramón.

Better if Ramón had let him die, as all the *gringos* should die. And it would happen someday, María was sure. It was all she thought about now, as she spent her days wandering through La Paloma, cleaning the old houses for the *ladrones*.

The thieves.

That's what they all were, and even if Ramón didn't understand it, she did.

But she would go on cleaning for them, go on looking after the houses that rightfully belonged to her people, until Alejandro returned to avenge the death of his parents and sisters, and all his descendants could finally return to their rightful homes.

And the time of vengeance was coming. She could feel it, deep in her old bones.

At last she came into the boy's room, and suddenly she knew. Alejandro was here. Soon, *la venganza* would begin.

For Ellen, the lunch she had so looked forward to had been a disaster. As she'd expected, the conversation had revolved around Raymond Torres and Alex, but she had found herself totally distracted with worry over what the dean might have to tell her after lunch. And now, though she'd listened carefully, it still didn't make sense. "I'm sorry," she said, "but I still don't understand exactly what it all means."

She and Marsh had been in Dan Eisenberg's office for nearly an hour, and thirty minutes ago Raymond Torres, too, had arrived. But Ellen still felt as confused as ever—it all seemed quite impossible.

"It means Alex is finally using his brain," Marsh told her. "It's not so difficult. We've seen the results of the tests. His scores were perfect!"

"But how can that be?" Ellen argued. "I know he's been studying all summer, and I know he has a good memory, but *this*"—she picked up the math-testing booklet—"how could he have even done the calculations? He simply didn't have the time, did he?" She dropped the test back on Eisenberg's desk and turned to Torres. If anyone could make her understand, he could. "Explain it to me again," she said, and as his intense eyes met hers, she began to relax, and concentrate.

Torres spread his hands and pressed his fingers together thoughtfully. "It's very simple," he said in the slightly patronizing tone that never failed to infuriate Marsh. "Alex's brain works differently from the way it did before. It's a matter of compensation. If a person loses one sense, his others become sharper. The same kind of thing has happened to Alex. His brain has compensated for the damage to its emotional centers by sharpening its intellectual centers."

"I understand that," Ellen agreed. "At least, I understand the theory. What I don't understand is what it means. I want to know what it means for Alex."

"I'm not sure anyone can tell you that, Mrs. Lonsdale," Dan Eisenberg replied.

"Nor does it matter," Torres pronounced. "With Alex we are no longer at a point where we can do anything about his abilities, or his responses. I've done what can be done. From now on, all I can do is observe Alex—"

"Like a laboratory animal?" Marsh broke in. Torres regarded him with cold eyes.

"If you wish," he said.

"For God's sake, Torres, Alex is my son." Marsh turned to Ellen. "All this means for Alex is that he is a remarkably intelligent young man. In fact," he went on, his attention now shifting to Dan Eisenberg, "I suspect there probably isn't much this school can do for him anymore. Is that right?"

Eisenberg reluctantly nodded his agreement.

"Then it seems to me that perhaps we should take him down to Stanford next week and see if we can get him into some sort of special program."

"I won't agree to that," Torres interrupted. "Alex is brilliant, yes. But brilliance isn't enough. If he were my son—"

"Which he's not," Marsh replied, his smile gone.

"Which he's not," Torres agreed. "But if he *were*, I would keep him right here in La Paloma, and let him reestablish all his old friendships and old patterns of behavior. Somewhere, there might be a trigger, and when he stumbles across that trigger, his mind may fully reopen, and the past will come back to him."

"And what about his intellect?" Marsh demanded. "Suddenly I have a very brilliant son, Dr. Torres—"

"Which, I gather," Torres interrupted in a voice as cool as Marsh's own, "is something you have always wanted."

"Everyone hopes his children will be brilliant," Marsh countered.

"And Alex *is* brilliant, Dr. Lonsdale," Torres replied. "But keeping him here for another year isn't going to affect that. I should imagine that the school can design a course of study for him that will keep his mind active and challenged. But there is another side to Alex—the emotional side—and if he has any chance to recover in that area, I think we have an obligation to give him that chance."

"Of course we do," Ellen agreed. "And Marsh knows

it as well as we do." She turned to her husband. "Don't you?"

Marsh was silent for a long time. Torres's words, he knew, made sense. Alex *should* stay home. But he couldn't just go on letting Torres run his life, and the lives of his wife and son.

"I think," he said at last, "that perhaps we ought to talk to Alex about it."

"I agree," Torres replied, rising to his feet. "But not for at least a week. I want to think about this for a while, and then I'll decide what's best for Alex." He glanced at his watch, then offered Eisenberg his hand. "I'm afraid I have another meeting. If you need me for anything, you have my number." With nothing more than a nod to either Marsh or Ellen, he left the dean's office.

Alex lay on his bed staring at the ceiling.

Something was wrong, but he had no idea what it might be, or what he ought to do about it.

All he knew was that something was wrong with him. He was no longer the same as he had been before the accident, and for some reason his parents were upset about it. At least, his mother was upset. His father seemed pleased.

They had told him about the test results as they drove him home that afternoon, and at first he hadn't understood what all the fuss was about. He could have told them he'd correctly answered all the questions before they even checked. The questions had been easy, and didn't really involve anything like thinking. In fact, he'd thought they must be testing his memory rather than his ability to think, because all the tests had involved were a series of facts and calculations, and if you had a good memory and knew the right equations, there wasn't anything to them.

But now they were saying he was brilliant, and his father wanted him to go into a special program down in Palo Alto. From what he'd heard in the car, though, he didn't think that was going to happen. Dr. Torres would see to it that he stayed home.

And that, he decided, was fine with him. All day, he'd been trying to figure out what had happened at school that morning—why he had remembered some things so clearly, other things incorrectly, and still others not at all.

He was sure it had something to do with the damage his brain had suffered, and yet that didn't make sense to him. He could understand how parts of his memory could have been destroyed, but that wouldn't account for the things he had remembered incorrectly. He should, he was sure, either remember things or not remember them. But memories shouldn't have simply changed, unless there was a reason.

The thing to do, he decided, was start keeping track of the things he remembered, and how he remembered them, and see if there was a pattern to the things he remembered incorrectly.

If there was, he might be able to figure out what was wrong with him.

And then, there was María Torres.

She had been in his room when he got home that afternoon, and when he had first seen her, he'd thought he recognized her. It had only been a fleeting moment, and a sharp pain had shot through his head, and then it was over. A moment later he realized that what he'd recognized was not her face, but her eyes. She had the same eyes that Dr. Torres had: almost black eyes that seemed to peer right inside you.

She'd smiled at him, and nodded her head, then quickly left him alone in his room.

By now he should have forgotten the incident, except for the pain in his head.

The pain itself was gone now, but the memory of it was still etched sharply in his mind.

CHAPTER TEN

Lisa Cochran's face set into an expression of stubbornness that Kate Lewis had long ago come to realize meant that the argument was over—Lisa would, in the end, have her way. And, as usual, Kate knew Lisa was right. Still, she didn't want to give in too easily.

"But what if he won't go?" she asked.

"He'll go," Lisa insisted. "I can talk him into it. I've always been able to talk Alex into anything."

"That was before," Kate reminded her. "Ever since he's come home, he's . . . well, he's just different, that's all. Most of the time he acts like he doesn't even like us anymore."

Lisa sighed. Over and over again she'd tried to explain to Kate and Bob that Alex *did* still like them—and all his other friends too—but that right now he was just incapable of showing his feelings. Kate and Bob, however, had remained unconvinced.

"If we're going to go up to San Francisco," Bob repeated for the third time that afternoon, "I want to go

141

with people I can have fun with. All Alex ever does anymore is ask questions. He's like a little kid."

The three of them were sitting in their favorite hangout, Jake's Place, which served pizza and video games. While the games had long since lost their novelty, the kids still came for the pizza, which wasn't very good, but was cheap. And Jake didn't mind if they came in right after school and sat around all afternoon, nursing a Coke and talking. Today, gathered around a table with a Pac-Man unit in its top, they had been talking a long time as Lisa tried to convince Bob and Kate that they should take Alex along to San Francisco day after tomorrow. Jake, they knew, had been listening to them casually, but, as always, hadn't tried to offer them any advice. That, too, was one of the reasons they hung out here. Suddenly, however, he appeared by their table and leaned over.

"Better make up your minds," he told them. "Alex just came in."

Kate and Bob looked up guiltily as Lisa waved to Alex. "Over here!" Alex hesitated only a second before coming over to slide into the seat next to Lisa.

"Hi. I looked for you after school, but you didn't wait. What's going on?"

Lisa glanced at Kate and Bob, then decided to end their argument immediately. "We're talking about going up to the City on Saturday. Want to go with us?"

Alex frowned. "The city? What city?"

"San Francisco," Lisa replied, ignoring the roll of Bob Carey's eyes. "Everybody calls it that. Want to go with us?"

"I'll have to ask my folks."

"No, you don't," Lisa told him. "If you tell your folks, they'll tell my folks and Kate's folks, and they'll all say no. We're just going to go."

Bob Carey suddenly reached into his pocket, pulled out a quarter, and began playing Pac-Man. Lisa, sure he was doing it only to avoid talking to Alex, glared at him, but he ignored her. Alex, however, didn't seem to notice the slight. His eyes were fastened on the little yellow man that scooted through the maze under Bob's control.

"What's it do?" he asked, and Lisa immediately knew it was yet one more thing of which he had no memory. Patiently she began explaining the object of the game as Alex kept watching while Bob played. In less than two minutes, the game was over.

"Want me to show you how to do it?" Alex asked. Bob looked at him with skeptical curiosity.

"You? You're even worse at this than me."

Alex slipped a quarter in the slot, and began playing, maneuvering the little man around the maze, always just out of reach of the hungry goblins that chased him. But when the goblins suddenly turned blue, Alex turned on them, gobbling them up one after the other. He cleared board after board, never losing a man, racking up an array of fruit, and an enormous score.

After ten minutes, he took his hands off the controls. Instantly, Pac-Man was gobbled up, and a new one appeared. Alex ignored it, and in a few seconds it, too, was devoured. "It's easy," he said. "There's a pattern, and all you have to do is remember the pattern. Then you know where all the goblins are going to go."

Bob shifted in his chair. "How come you could never do that before?" he asked.

Alex frowned, then shrugged. "I don't know," he admitted.

"And I don't care," Lisa declared. "What about going to the City? Do you want to go with us, or not?"

Alex considered it a moment, then nodded his head. "Okay. What time?"

"We'll tell our folks we're going to the beach in Santa Cruz," Lisa said. "I'll even pack us a lunch. That way we can leave early, and we won't have to be back until dinnertime."

"What if we get caught?" Kate asked.

"How can we get caught?" Bob countered. Then, his eyes fixed on Alex, he added, "Unless someone tells."

"Don't worry," Lisa assured him. "Nobody's going to tell."

Kate drained the last of the warm Coke that had been sitting in front of her most of the afternoon, and stood up. "I've got to get home. Mom'll kill me if I haven't got dinner started when she gets home from work."

"You want us to come along?" Lisa asked. Though none of the kids talked about it much, they all knew about Mr. Lewis's drinking problem. Kate shook her head. "Dad's still sort of okay, but I think he'll have to go back to the hospital next week. Right now he's at the stage where he just sits in front of the TV all the time, drinking beer. I wish Mom would just kick him out."

"No, you don't," Bob Carey said.

"I do too!" Kate flared. "All he does is talk about what he's going to do, but he never does anything except get drunk. If I could, I'd move out!"

"But he's still your father—"

"So what? He's a drunk, and everybody knows it!"

Her eyes brimming with sudden tears, Kate turned and hurried out of Jake's Place, Bob right behind her. "Pay the check, will you, Alex?" Bob called back over his shoulder.

When they were alone, Lisa grinned at Alex. "Do you have any money?" she asked. "Or do I get stuck with the check again?"

"Why should I pay it?" Alex asked, bewildered. "I didn't eat anything."

"Alex! I was only kidding!"

"Well, why *should* I pay it?" Alex insisted.

Lisa tried to keep the exasperation she was feeling out of her voice. "Alex," she said carefully, "nobody expects you to pay the check. But Bob was in a hurry, and he'll pay you back tomorrow. You and Bob have always done that."

Alex's eyes fixed steadily on her. "I don't remember that."

"You don't remember anything," Lisa replied, her voice edged with anger. "So I'm telling you. Now, why don't you just give Jake some money, and we'll get out of here?" Then, when Alex still hesitated, she sighed. "Oh, never mind. I'll do it myself." She paid the check, and started toward the door. "You coming?"

Alex stood up and followed her out into the afternoon sunshine. They started walking toward the Cochrans', and after a few minutes of silence, Lisa finally took Alex's hand in her own. "I'm sorry," she said. "I shouldn't have gotten mad."

"That's okay." Alex dropped her hand, and kept walking.

"You mad at me?" Lisa asked.

"No."

"Is something else wrong?"

Alex shrugged, then shook his head.

"Then how come you don't want to hold hands?" Lisa ventured.

Alex said nothing, but wondered silently why holding hands seemed so important to her.

Apparently it was yet something else he didn't remember. Feeling nothing, he ignored her outstretched hand.

Carol Cochran climbed the stairs to Lisa's room, and found her daughter stretched out on the bed staring at the ceiling as the thundering music of her favorite rock group seemed to make the walls shake. Carol went to the stereo and turned the volume down, then perched on the edge of the bed.

"Want to tell me what's wrong, or is it too big a secret?"

"Nothing's wrong," Lisa replied. "I was just listening to my records."

"For three solid hours," Carol told her. "And it's been the same record, over and over, which is driving your father crazy."

Lisa rolled over onto her side and propped her head up on one hand. "It's Alex. He's . . . well, he's just so different. Sometimes he's almost spooky. He takes everything so seriously, you can't even joke with him anymore."

Carol nodded. "I know. I guess you just have to be patient. He might get over it."

Lisa sat up. "But what if he doesn't? Mom, what's happening is terrible."

"Terrible?" Carol repeated.

"It's the other kids," Lisa told her. "They're starting to talk about him. They say all he ever does is ask questions like a little kid."

"We know what that's all about," Carol replied.

Lisa nodded. "I know. But it still doesn't make it any easier."

"For whom?"

Lisa seemed startled by the question, then flopped onto her back again. "For me," she whispered. Then: "I just get so tired of trying to explain him to everyone all the time. And it's not just that, anyway," she added, her voice suddenly defiant.

"Then what is it?"

"I'm not sure he likes me anymore. He . . . he never seems to want to hold hands with me, or kiss me, or anything. He's just . . . oh, Mom, he just seems so cold."

"I know about that, too," Carol sighed. "But it's not just you, honey. He's that way with everyone."

"Well, that doesn't make it any easier."

"No, it doesn't." Carol shook her head, considering what to tell her daughter. Lisa sat against the headboard, drawing her knees up to her chest and wrapping her arms around her legs, as her mother continued. "I'm going to go right on treating Alex the way I always have, and try not to let my feelings get hurt if he doesn't respond the way he used to," she said. "And he may never respond the way he used to. It's a function of the accident. In a way, Alex is crippled now. But he's still Alex, and he's still my best friends' son. If they can get through this, and Alex can get through this, so can I."

"And so can I?" Lisa asked, but Carol shook her head.

"I don't know. I don't even know if you should try. You're only sixteen, and there's no reason at all that you should have to spend your time explaining Alex to anyone or trying to deal with his new personality. There are lots of other boys in La Paloma, and there's no reason why you shouldn't date them."

"But I can't just dump Alex," Lisa protested.

"I'm not saying you should," Carol replied. "All I'm saying is that you have to make certain decisions based on what's best for you. If it's too difficult for you to go on spending so much time with Alex, then you shouldn't do it. And you shouldn't feel badly about it, either."

Lisa's eyes filled with tears. "But I *do* feel bad," she said. "And I don't even know why. I don't know if I don't like him anymore, or if I'm just hurt because I'm not sure he still likes me. And I don't know if I'm getting tired of having to defend him all the time, or if I'm mad at everybody else for not understanding him. Mom, I just don't know what to do!"

"Then don't do anything," Carol told her. "Just take it all day by day, and see what happens. In time, it will all work out."

Lisa nodded, then got up from the bed and went to the stereo, where she changed the record. Then, with her back to her mother, she said, "What if it doesn't work out, Mom? What if Alex never changes? What's going to happen to him?"

Carol rose to her feet and pulled her daughter close. "I don't know," she said. "But in the end, it really isn't your problem, is it? It's Alex's problem, and his parents' problem. It's only yours if you make it yours, and you don't have to. Do you understand that?"

Lisa nodded. "I guess so," she said. She wiped her eyes, and forced a smile. "And I'll be all right," she said. "I guess I was just feeling sorry for myself."

"And for Alex," Carol added. "I know how much you want to help him and how bad it feels not to be able

to." She started toward the door. "But there is one
thing you can do," she added before she left the room.
"Turn that awful music down, so at least your sister can
get some sleep. Good night."

" 'Night, Mom." As the door closed, Lisa plugged in
her headset, and the room fell silent as the music from
the stereo poured directly into her ears.

Alex lay awake late into the night, pondering what
had happened at Jake's Place and on the way home
afterward. He knew he'd made a mistake, but he still
couldn't quite figure it out.

Lisa had wanted to hold hands with him, and even
though he didn't understand why, he should have gone
ahead and done it anyway. And she had been mad at
him, which was another thing he didn't understand.

There was so much that just didn't make any sense.

At the beginning of the week, there had been the
strange memories, and the odd pain that had gone
through his head when he'd first seen María Torres.

And beyond those things, which he was sure he
would eventually figure out, there were the other things,
the concepts he was beginning to feel certain he would
never understand.

Love.

That was something he couldn't get any kind of grasp
on. His mother was always telling him that she loved
him, and he didn't really doubt that she did.

The trouble was, he didn't understand what love was.
He'd looked it up, and read that it was a feeling of
affection.

But, as he had slowly come to understand as he read
more, apparently he didn't have feelings.

It was something he was only beginning to be aware
of, and he didn't know whether he should talk to Dr.
Torres about it or not. All he knew so far was that
things seemed to happen to other people that didn't
happen to him.

Things like anger.

He knew Lisa had been angry at him this afternoon, and he knew it was a feeling that she got when he did something she didn't approve of.

But what did it *feel* like?

He thought, from what he'd read, that it must be like pain, only it affected the mind instead of the body. But what was it like?

He was beginning to suspect he'd never know, for every day he was becoming more and more aware that something had, indeed, gone wrong, and that he was no longer like other people.

But he was supposed to be like other people. That was the whole idea of Dr. Torres's operation—to make him the way he'd been before.

The problem was that he couldn't remember how he'd been before. If he could remember, it would be easy. He could *act* as though he was the same, and then people wouldn't know he was different.

He was already doing some of it.

He'd learned to hug his mother, and kiss her, and whenever he did that, she seemed to like it.

He'd decided not to act on any of the things he seemed to remember until he'd determined if his memory of them was correct.

And after this afternoon, he'd remember to hold Lisa's hand when they were walking together, and to pay a check if Bob Carey asked him to.

But what about other people? Were there other people he used to borrow money from and loan money to?

Tomorrow, when he saw Lisa, he'd ask her.

No, he decided, he wouldn't ask her. He couldn't keep asking everybody questions all the time.

He'd seen the look on Bob Carey's face when he'd asked Lisa what city she was talking about, and he knew what it meant, even though it hadn't bothered him.

Still, Bob Carey thought he was stupid, even though he wasn't. In fact, after the tests on Monday, he knew he was just the opposite. If anything, he was a lot smarter than everybody else.

He got out of bed and went to the family room. In the bookcase next to the fireplace, there was an *Encyclopaedia Britannica*. He switched on a lamp, then pulled Volume VIII of the Micropaedia off the shelf. A few minutes later, he began reading every article in the encyclopedia that referred to San Francisco.

By the time they got there, he would be able to tell them more about the city than they knew themselves. And, he decided, he would know his way around.

Tomorrow—Friday—he would find a map of San Francisco, and memorize it by the next morning.

Memorizing things was easy.

Figuring out what was expected of him, and then doing it, was not so easy.

But he would do it.

He didn't know how long it would take, but he knew that if he watched carefully, and remembered everything he saw, sooner or later he would be able to act just like everybody else.

But he still wouldn't feel anything.

And that, he decided, was all right. If he could learn to act as though he felt things, it would be good enough.

Already he'd learned that it didn't matter what he was or wasn't.

The only thing that really mattered was what people *thought* you were.

He closed the book and put it back on the shelf, then turned around to see his father standing in the doorway.

"Alex? Are you all right?"

"I was just looking something up," Alex replied.

"Do you know what time it is?"

Alex glanced at the big clock in the corner. "Three-thirty."

"How come you're not asleep?"

"I just got to thinking about something, so I decided to look it up. I'll go back to bed now." He started out of the room, but his father stopped him with a hand on his shoulder.

"Is something bothering you, son?"

Alex hesitated, wondering if maybe he should try to explain to his father how different he was from other people, and that he thought something might be wrong with his brain, then decided against it. If anyone would understand, it would be Dr. Torres. "I'm fine, Dad. Really."

Marsh dropped into his favorite chair, and looked at Alex critically. Certainly the boy *looked* fine, except for his too-bland expression. "Then I think maybe you and I ought to talk about your future, before Torres decides it for us," he suggested.

Alex listened in silence while Marsh repeated his idea of sending Alex into an advanced program at Stanford. As he talked, Marsh kept his eyes on his son, trying to see what effect his words might be having on the boy.

Apparently there was none.

Alex's expression never changed, and Marsh suddenly had the uneasy feeling that Alex wasn't even hearing him. "Well?" he asked at last. "What do you think?"

Alex was silent for a moment, then stood up. "I'll have to talk to Dr. Torres about it," he said. He started out of the room. "Good night, Dad."

For a moment, all Marsh could do was stare at his son's retreating back. And then, like a breaking storm, fury swept over him. "*Alex!*" The single word echoed through the house. Instantly Alex stopped and turned around.

"Dad?"

"What the hell is going on with you?" Marsh demanded. He could feel blood pounding in his veins, and his fists clutched into tight knots at his side. "Did you even hear me? Do you have any idea of what I was saying to you?"

Alex nodded silently, then, as his father's furious eyes remained fixed on him, began repeating Marsh's words back to him.

"Stop that!" Marsh roared. "Goddammit, just stop it!"

Obediently Alex fell back into silence.

Marsh stood still, forcing his mind to concentrate on the soft ticking of the grandfather clock in the corner, willing his rage to ease. A moment later he became vaguely aware that Ellen, too, was in the room now, her face pale, her frightened eyes darting from him to Alex, then back again.

"Marsh?" she asked uncertainly. "Marsh, what's going on?" When Marsh, still trembling with anger, made no reply, she turned to her son. "Alex?"

"I don't know," Alex replied. "He was talking about me going to college, and I said I'd talk to Dr. Torres about it. Then he started yelling at me."

"Go to bed," Ellen told him. She gave him a quick hug, then gently eased him toward the hall. "Go on. I'll take care of your father." When Alex was gone, she turned to Marsh, her eyes damp. When she spoke, her voice was a bleak reflection of the pain she was feeling, not just for her son, but for her husband too. "You can't do this," she whispered. "You know he's not well yet. What do you expect from him?"

Marsh, his anger spent, sagged onto the couch and buried his face in his hands.

"I'm sorry, honey," he said softly. "It's only that talking to him just now was like talking to a brick wall. And then all he said was that he'd talk to Torres about it. Torres!" he repeated bitterly, then gazed up at her, his face suddenly haggard. "I'm his father, Ellen," he said in a voice breaking with pain. "But for all the reaction I get from him, I might as well not even exist."

Ellen took a deep breath, then slowly let it out. "I know," she said at last. "A lot of the time I feel exactly the same way. But we have to get him through it, Marsh. We can't just send him off somewhere. He can barely deal with the people he's known all his life—how would he ever be able to deal with total strangers?"

"But he's so bright . . ." Marsh whispered.

Ellen nodded. "I know. But he's not well yet. Raymond—" She broke off suddenly, sensing her husband's animosity toward the man who had saved Alex's life. "Dr. Torres," she began again, "is helping him, and we have to help him too. And we have to be patient with him, no matter how hard it is." She hesitated, then went on. "Sometimes . . . well, sometimes the only way I can deal with it is to remember that whatever I'm going through, what Alex is going through must be ten times worse."

Marsh put his arms around his wife and pulled her close. "I know," he said. "I know you're right, but I just can't help myself sometimes." A rueful smile twisted his face. "I guess there's a good reason why doctors should never treat their own family, isn't there? Lord knows, my bedside manner deserted me tonight." His arms fell away from Ellen as he stood up. "I'd better go apologize to him."

But when he entered Alex's room, his son was sound asleep. As far as he could see, even his rage hadn't affected the boy. Still, he laid his hand gently on Alex's cheek. "I'm sorry, son," he whispered. "I'm sorry about everything."

Alex rolled over, unconsciously brushing his father's hand away.

CHAPTER ELEVEN

At a few minutes past nine on Saturday morning, Bob Carey maneuvered his father's Volvo into the left lane of the Bayshore Freeway, and three minutes later they left Palo Alto behind. Alex sat quietly in the back seat next to Lisa, his ears taking in the chatter of his three friends while his eyes remained glued to the world outside the car. None of it looked familiar, but he studied the road signs carefully as they passed through Redwood City, San Carlos, and San Mateo, then began skirting the edge of the bay. His eyes took in everything, and he was sure that on the return trip that afternoon, even though he would be seeing it all from the other direction, all of it would be familiar.

Then, a little north of the airport, Bob veered off the freeway and started inland.

"Where are we going?" Kate Lewis asked. "We want to go all the way into the City!"

"We're going to the BART station in Daly City," Bob told her.

"BART?" Kate groaned. "Who wants to ride the subway?"

"I do," Bob told her. "I *like* the subway, and besides, I'm not going to drive Dad's car in the City. All I need is to have to try to explain how I smashed a fender on Nob Hill when I was supposed to be in Santa Cruz. I'd wind up grounded lower than Carolyn Evans was."

Kate started to protest further, but Lisa backed Bob up. "He's right," she said. "I had to argue with my folks for half an hour to keep from having to bring Kim along, and if we get caught now, we'll all be in trouble. Besides, I like BART too. It'll be fun!"

Forty minutes later, they emerged from the BART station, and Alex gazed around him, knowing immediately where he was. Yesterday he'd found a tour guide to San Francisco in the La Paloma bookstore, then spent last night studying it. The city around him looked exactly like the pictures in the guidebook. "Let's ride the cable car out to Fisherman's Wharf," he suggested.

Lisa stared at him with surprised eyes. "How did you know it goes there?" she asked.

Alex hesitated, then pointed to the cable car that was just coasting onto the turntable at Powell and Market. On its end was a sign that read "Powell & Mason" and, below that, "Fisherman's Wharf."

They wandered around the wharf, then started back toward the downtown area, through North Beach on Columbus, then turning south on Grant to go into Chinatown. People milled around them, and suddenly Alex stopped dead in his tracks. Lisa turned to him, but he seemed unaware of her. His eyes were gazing intently at the faces of the people around him.

"Alex, what is it?" she asked. All morning, he'd seemed fine. He'd asked a few questions, but not nearly as many as usual, and he'd always seemed to know exactly where he was and where they were going. Once, in fact, he'd even told them where a street they were looking for was, then, when asked how he knew, admitted to having memorized all the street signs while they

rode the cable car. But now he seemed totally baffled.
"Alex, what's wrong?" Lisa asked again.

"These people," Alex said. "What are they? They
don't look like us."

"Oh, Jeez," Bob Carey groaned.

"They're Chinese," Lisa said, keeping her voice as
low as she could, and silencing Bob with a glare. "And
stop staring at them, Alex. You're being rude."

"Chinese," Alex repeated. He started walking again,
but his eyes kept wandering over the Oriental faces
around him. "The Chinese built the railroads," he suddenly said. Then: "The railroad barons, Collis P. Hunt-
ington and Leland Stanford, brought them in by the
thousands. Now San Francisco has one of the biggest
Chinese populations outside of China."

Lisa stared at Alex for a moment; then suddenly she
knew. "A tour book," she said. "You read a tour book,
didn't you?"

Alex nodded. "I didn't want to spend all day asking
you questions," he said. "I know you don't like that. So
I studied."

Bob Carey's eyes narrowed suspiciously. "You studied? You read a whole guidebook just because we were
coming up here for a day?"

Again Alex nodded.

"But who can remember all that stuff? Who even
cares? For Christ's sake, Alex, all we're doing is mess-
ing around."

"Well, I think it's neat," Kate told her boyfriend.
Then she turned to Alex. "Did you really memorize all
the streets while we were on the cable car?"

"I didn't have to," Alex admitted. "I got a map, too. I
memorized it."

"Bullshit!" Bob's eyes were suddenly angry. "Where's
the mission?" he demanded.

Alex hesitated a moment; then: "Sixteenth and Dolores. It's on the corner, and there's a park in the same
block."

"Well?" Kate asked Bob. "Is he right?"

"I don't know," Bob admitted, his face reddening. "Who even cares where the mission is?"

"I do," Lisa said, reaching out to squeeze Alex's hand. "How do we get there?"

"Go down to Market, then up to Dolores, and left on Dolores."

"Then let's go."

The little mission with its adjoining cemetery and garden was exactly where Alex had said it would be, crouching on the corner almost defensively, as if it knew it was no more than a relic from the city's long-forgotten past. The city, indeed, had even taken away its original name—San Francisco de Asís. Now it was called Mission Dolores, and it seemed to have taken on the very sadness its name implied.

"Want to go in?" Lisa asked of no one in particular.

"What for?" Bob groaned. "Haven't we all seen enough missions? They used to drag us off to one every year!"

"Well, what about Alex?" Lisa argued. "I bet he doesn't remember ever seeing a mission before. And did you ever see *this* mission? Come on."

Following Lisa, they went into the little church, then out into the garden, and suddenly the city beyond the garden walls might as well have disappeared, for within the little space occupied by the mission, there was no trace of the modern world.

The garden, still kept neatly trimmed after nearly two hundred years, was in the last stages of its summer bloom. Here and there dead leaves had already fallen to the ground, dotting the pathways with bright gold. Off in the far corner, they could see the old cemetery. "Over there," Alex said softly. "Let's go over there."

The quietness of his voice caught Lisa's attention, and she turned to look into Alex's eyes. For the first time since the accident, there seemed to be life in them. "What is it, Alex?" she asked. "You're remembering something, aren't you?"

"I don't know," Alex whispered. He was walking slowly along one of the paths now, but his eyes remained fixed on the weathered headstones of the graveyard.

"The graveyard?" Lisa asked. "Do you remember the graveyard?"

Alex's mind was whirling, and he barely heard Lisa's question. Images were flickering, and there were sounds. But nothing was clear, except that the images and sounds were connected with this place. Trembling slightly, he kept walking.

"What's wrong with him?" Kate asked, her voice worried. "He looks weird."

"I think he's remembering something," Lisa replied.

"We'd better go with him," Bob added, but Lisa shook her head.

"I'll go," she told them. "You guys wait for us, okay?"

Kate nodded mutely, and as Alex stepped into the tiny fenced cemetery, Lisa hurried after him.

The images had begun coming into focus as soon as he'd entered the cemetery. His heart was pounding, and he felt out of breath, as if he'd been running for a long time. He scanned the little graveyard, and his eyes came to rest on a small stone near the wall.

In his mind, there were images of people.

Women dressed in black, their faces framed by white cowls, their feet clad in sandals.

Nuns.

In his mind's eye he saw a group of nuns clustering around a boy, and the boy was himself.

But he was different somehow.

His hair was darker, and his skin had an olive complexion to it.

And he was crying.

Unconsciously Alex moved closer to the headstone that had triggered the strange images, and the images seemed to move with him. Then he was standing at the grave, gazing down at the inscription that was still barely legible in the worn granite:

Fernando Meléndez y Ruiz
1802–1850

A word flashed into his mind, and he repeated it out loud. "*¡Tío!*" As he uttered the word, a stab of pain knifed through his brain, then was gone.

And then voices began whispering to him—the voices of the nuns, though the images of them had already faded away.

"*Él está muerto.*" He is dead.

And then there was another voice—a man's voice—whispering to him out of the depths of his memory. "*¡Venganza . . . venganza!*"

He stood very still, his eyes brimming with unfamiliar tears, his pulse throbbing. The voice went on, whispering to him in Spanish, but only the one word registered on his mind: "*Venganza.*"

His tears overflowed, and a sob choked his throat. Then, as the strange words pounded in his head, he gave in to the sudden unfamiliar rush of emotion.

Time seemed to stand still, and he felt a kind of pain he couldn't remember having ever felt before. Pain of the heart, and of the soul.

The pain seared at him, and then he became aware of a hand tugging at him, slowly penetrating the chaos in his mind.

"Alex?" a voice said. "Alex, what's wrong? What is it?"

Alex pointed to the grave, sobbing brokenly, and Lisa, after a moment of utter confusion, began to understand what must have happened. She had listened carefully that day last month before Alex came home from the hospital, and she could still remember the words.

"He could start laughing or crying at any time," Alex's mother had told her. "Dr. Torres says it won't matter if something is funny or sad. It's just that it's possible that there will be misconnections in his brain, and he could react inappropriately to something. Or he could simply overreact."

And that, Lisa was certain, was exactly what was happening now. Alex was overreacting to an ancient grave.

But why?

He had remembered something, she had been sure of it. And now he was staring at the grave, tears streaming down his face, uncontrollable sobs racking his body. Gently she tried to pull him away as a priest appeared from the back of the church and looked at them quizzically.

"Something wrong?"

"No," Lisa quickly replied. "Everything's all right. It . . ." She floundered for a moment, trying to think of an explanation for Alex's behavior, but her mind had suddenly gone blank. "Come *on*, Alex," she whispered. "Let's get out of here."

Half-dragging Alex, she edged her way past the priest, then out of the graveyard. Once back in the garden, she put her arms around Alex and squeezed him. "It's all right, Alex," she whispered. "It was only an old grave. Nothing to cry about."

Slowly Alex's sobs began to subside, and he made himself listen to Lisa's words.

Only a grave. But it hadn't been only a grave. He had recognized the grave, as he had recognized the cemetery itself. What he had just experienced, he had experienced before.

The memories were clear in his mind now. He could remember having been in that cemetery, having looked down at the grave, having listened to the nuns telling him his uncle was dead.

His uncle.

As far as Alex knew, he had no uncle.

And certainly he wouldn't remember an uncle who had died in 1850.

But it was all so clear, just as clear as the memory he'd had at school last week. Clear, but impossible.

He took a deep breath, and his last sob released its grip on his throat. Lisa found a handkerchief in her bag and handed it to him. He blew his nose. "What happened?" she asked.

Alex shrugged, but his mind was whirling. It didn't make any sense, and if he told her what had happened, she would think he was crazy. But he had to tell her something. "I'm not sure," he said. "I . . . I remembered something, but I'm not sure what. But it was like I was here before, and something terrible happened. But I can't remember what."

Lisa frowned. "*Were* you ever here before? Maybe something did happen here."

Then, before Alex could say anything else, Bob and Kate moved toward them, their expressions a mixture of worry and uneasiness.

"What happened?" Kate asked. "Are you okay, Alex?"

Alex nodded. "I just remembered something, and it made me cry. Dr. Torres said it might happen, but I didn't really think it would." Lisa looked at him sharply, but said nothing. If he didn't want to tell them what had really happened, she wouldn't either. "Maybe it's a good sign," he said, making himself smile. "Maybe it means I'm getting better."

Kate and Lisa exchanged a glance, each of them realizing what might have to happen. Finally Kate voiced the thought.

"Are you going to tell your folks about it?"

"He can't," Bob said. "If he does, then all our folks will find out what we did, and we'll *all* be in trouble."

"But what if it's important?" Lisa asked. "What if it means something?"

"Why can't he just say it happened at the beach?" Bob suggested. "Besides, what's the big deal about crying in a graveyard? Isn't that what you're supposed to do?"

"I didn't say it was a big deal," Lisa replied. "All I said was that it might mean something, and if it does, none of us should worry about getting into trouble. I just think Alex should tell his folks exactly what happened."

"Well, I think we should vote on it," Bob said. "And I vote he doesn't tell." He looked expectantly at Kate Lewis, whose eyes reflected her uncertainty. Finally she made up her mind, looking away from Bob.

"Lisa's right," she said. "He should tell. And I think we should go home right now."

"I don't," Alex suddenly said. The other three looked at him, puzzled. "I think I should call Dr. Torres and tell him what happened. Maybe he'll want me to stay here."

"Stay here?" Lisa asked. "Why?"

"Maybe something else will happen."

Bob Carey stared at him. "What are you, some kind of a nut? I'm not gonna waste the rest of the day waiting for you to freak out again!"

"Bob Carey, that's just gross!" Lisa said, her voice quivering with anger. "Can't you ever think of anybody but yourself? Why don't you just go away? We can get home without you. Come on!" She grabbed Alex by the hand and began walking quickly toward the church door. Kate hesitated, then started after them.

"Kate—" Bob called, but his girlfriend whirled around and cut his words off.

"Can't you ever think about anybody but yourself? Just once?" She turned and ran to catch up with Lisa and Alex.

They found a phone booth half a block away, and Alex studied the instructions carefully before placing his call. On the second try, he managed to get through to the Institute. While Lisa and Kate fidgeted on the sidewalk outside the booth, he tried to explain to Torres exactly what had happened. When he was finished, Torres was silent for a few seconds, then asked, "Alex, are you sure you remembered that cemetery?"

"I think so," Alex said. "Do you think I should stay here? Do you think I might remember something else?"

"No," Torres said immediately. "I think one experience like that is enough for one day. I want you to go home right away. I'll call your mother and explain what happened."

"She's gonna be pretty mad," Alex replied. "I . . . well, I told her we were going to the beach. She thinks I'm in Santa Cruz."

"I see." There was another silence, and then Torres spoke once more. "Alex, when you lied to your parents about where you were going today, did you know you were doing the wrong thing?"

Alex thought for a few seconds. "No," he said finally. "I just knew that if I told them where we were going, they wouldn't let me go. None of our folks would have."

"All right," Torres said. "We'll talk about all this on Monday. In the meantime, I'll fix things with your mother so you don't get into any trouble. But I don't see how I can do anything for your friends."

"That's okay," Alex said. He was about to say goodbye when Torres's voice came over the wire once more.

"Alex, do you care if your friends get into trouble?"

Alex thought about it, and knew that he was supposed to say yes, because part of having friends was caring what happened to them. But he also knew he shouldn't lie to Dr. Torres. "No," he said. Then: "I don't really care about anybody."

"I see," Torres replied, his voice barely audible. Then: "Well, we can talk about that, too. And I'll see you tomorrow, Alex. We won't wait 'til Monday."

Alex hung up the phone and stepped out of the booth. Kate and Lisa were staring anxiously at him, and a few feet away, Bob Carey stood uncertainly watching them all.

"He wants me to go home," Alex said. "He'll call my mom and tell her what happened." He fell silent, then decided what he should say. "I'll try to get my mom to make it all right with your folks too."

Lisa smiled at him, while Kate Lewis looked suddenly worried. "How are we supposed to get home?" she asked.

"I'll take you," Bob Carey offered. He stepped closer, his eyes fixed on the sidewalk at his feet. Then he hesitantly offered Alex his hand. "I'm sorry about what I said back there. It's just that . . . Aw, shit, Alex, you're just different now, and I don't know what to do. So I just get pissed off."

Alex tried to figure out what he should say, but couldn't remember being apologized to before. "That's okay," he finally replied. "I don't know what to do either, most of the time."

"But at least you don't get pissed off about it, and if anybody has a right to get pissed, I guess you do." Bob grinned, and Alex decided he'd chosen the right words.

"Maybe I will sometime," he offered. "Maybe sometime I'll get really pissed off."

There was a moment of startled silence while his three friends wondered what his words meant. Then the four of them started home.

Marsh Lonsdale hung up the phone. "Well, that's done," he said, "even though I still don't approve of it."

"But, Marsh," Ellen argued, "you talked to Raymond yourself."

"I know," Marsh replied, sighing. "But the whole idea of four kids getting off scot-free after going someplace they knew perfectly well they shouldn't go, and lying about it to boot, just rubs me the wrong way."

"Alex didn't know he shouldn't go to San Francisco—"

"But he knew he shouldn't lie," Marsh said, turning to Alex. "Didn't you?" he demanded.

Alex shook his head. "But I know now," he offered. "I won't do it again."

"And Alex is right," Ellen added. "It isn't fair for the other kids to be punished, and him not. And besides, if they hadn't decided to break all the rules and go up to the City, Alex might not have had this breakthrough."

Breakthrough, Marsh thought. Why was bursting into

tears in a graveyard a breakthrough? And yet, when he'd talked to Torres that afternoon, the specialist had assured him that it was, even though Marsh had suggested that it might be simply a new symptom of the damage that still existed in Alex's mind. Still, Marsh was not yet ready to accept Torres's assessment. "And what if it's not a breakthrough?" he asked, then held up his hand to forestall Ellen's interruption. "Don't. I know what Torres said. But I also know that I've never been to Mission Dolores, and I don't think Alex has either. Did you ever take him up there?"

"No, I don't think I did," Ellen admitted. Then she sighed heavily. "Oh, all right, I *know* I didn't. I've never been there either. But I think you might consider the possibility that Alex went there with someone else. His grandparents, for instance."

"I've already called my parents," Marsh told her. "Neither of them can remember ever taking Alex there."

"All right, maybe it was my folks who took him there. For that matter, it could have been anybody." She searched her mind, looking for something—anything—that might explain what had happened to Alex. Then she remembered. "One of his school classes went to San Francisco on a field trip once! Maybe *they* went to the mission. But if Alex remembers it, he remembers it. And I don't see why you can't simply accept that."

"Because it just doesn't make sense. Why, of all the places Alex has been—that we *know* he's been—would he remember a place that as far as either one of us knows, he's never been to at all? I'm sorry, but I just don't think it adds up." He turned back to Alex. "Are you *sure* you really remembered being there before?"

Alex nodded. "As soon as I saw it, I knew I'd seen it before."

"That could have been *déjà vu*," Marsh suggested. "That happens all the time to everyone. We've talked about it with Dr. Torres."

"I know," Alex agreed. "But this was different. When

I went in, I didn't even look around. I just went right into the cemetery, to the grave. And then I started crying."

"All right," Marsh said. He reached over and squeezed Alex's shoulder. "I guess the fact that you cried is really what's important anyway, isn't it?"

Alex hesitated, then nodded. But what about the words he'd heard? Were they important too? Should he have told his parents about seeing the nuns and hearing the voices? No, he decided, not until he'd talked to Dr. Torres about it. "Is it okay if I go to bed now?" he asked, slipping away from his father's touch.

Marsh glanced at the clock. It was only a quarter to ten, and he knew Alex was seldom in bed before eleven. "So early?"

"I'm gonna read for a while."

He shrugged helplessly. "If you want to."

Alex hesitated, then leaned down to kiss his mother. "Good night."

" 'Night, darling," Ellen replied. She watched her son leave the family room, then turned her gaze to Marsh, and immediately knew that the discussion of what had happened that day was not yet over. "All right," she said tiredly. "What is it?"

But Marsh shook his head. "No," he said. "I'm not going to talk about it anymore." Suddenly he grinned, though there was no humor in it. "I guess I've just suddenly fallen victim to a feeling, and I don't like it."

Ellen sat down on the couch next to him and slipped her hand into his. "Tell me," she said. "You know I won't laugh at you—I won't even argue with you. I've had too many feelings myself."

Marsh considered for a moment, then made up his mind. "All right," he said. "I just feel that something's wrong. I can't quite put my finger on it, because I keep telling myself that what I'm feeling is a result of the accident, and the brain surgery, and the fact that I'm not too crazy about the eminent Dr. Torres. But no matter how much I tell myself that, I still have a feeling that there's more. That Alex has changed somehow, and that it's *more* than the brain damage."

"But everything that's happened is consistent with the damage and the surgery," Ellen replied, keeping her voice as neutral as possible and choosing her words carefully. "Alex *is* different, but he's still Alex."

Marsh sighed. "That's just it," he said. "He's different, all right, but I keep getting the feeling that he's *not* Alex."

No, Ellen thought to herself. That's not it at all. You just can't stand the idea that Raymond Torres did something you couldn't have done yourself. Aloud, though, she was careful to give Marsh no clue as to what she'd been thinking. Instead, she smiled at him encouragingly.

"Just wait," she said. "We've had several miracles already. Maybe we're about to have another one."

As she went to bed that night, she decided that when she took Alex down for the special meeting Raymond had asked for tomorrow morning, she'd have a private talk with the doctor.

A talk about Marsh, not Alex.

For María Torres, sleep would not come that night. For hours she tossed in her bed, then finally rose tiredly to her feet, put on her frayed bathrobe, and went into her tiny living room to light a candle under the image of the Blessed Mother. She prayed silently for a while—a silent prayer of thanksgiving that at last the saints were listening to her entreaties, and answering her.

She was sure the answers were coming now, for she had been in the Lonsdales' house all afternoon. She had listened as they talked to their son and heard his story of what had happened at the mission in San Francisco, and like all the *gringos*, they had barely been aware of her presence.

To them, she was nobody, only someone who came in now and then to clean up after them.

But they would find out who she was, now that the

saints were listening to her, and had sent Alejandro
back at last.

And Alejandro knew her now, and he would listen to
her when she spoke to him.

She let the little candle burn out, then crept back to
her bed, knowing that sleep would finally come.

She hoped the *gringos*, too, would sleep well tonight.
Soon there would be no sleep for them at all.

CHAPTER TWELVE

"How come Peter isn't here?" Alex asked. He was lying on the examining table, his eyes closed, while Raymond Torres himself began the task of attaching the electrodes to his skull.

"Sunday," Torres replied. "Even *my* staff insists on a day or two off each week."

"But not you?"

"I try, but every now and then I have to make an exception. You qualify as an exception."

Alex nodded, his eyes still closed. "Because of how I scored on the tests."

There was a short silence, and Alex opened his eyes. Torres was at the control panel, adjusting a myriad of dials. Finally he turned back to Alex. "Partly," he said. "But frankly, I'm more interested in what happened in San Francisco yesterday, and at school on Monday morning."

"It seems like I'm getting some of my memory back, doesn't it?"

Torres shrugged. "That's what we're going to try to

find out. And we're also going to try to find out if there's any significance to the fact that even what little you have remembered seems to be faulty."

"But the dean's office used to be where the nurse's office is now," Alex protested. "Mom just told us so."

"True. But apparently it was moved long before you ever went to La Paloma High. So why—and how—did you remember where it used to be, instead of where it is? Even more important, why did you remember Mission Dolores, when you apparently have never been there?"

"But I *could* have been there," Alex suggested. "Maybe yesterday wasn't the first day I sneaked off to San Francisco."

"Fine," Torres agreed. "Let's assume that's the case. Now tell me why you remembered a grave that's over a hundred years old, and thought it was your uncle's grave? You have no uncles, let alone one who's been dead since 1850."

"Well, why did I?"

Torres's brows arched. "According to those exams you took last week, you're smart enough to know better than to ask that question before these tests."

"Maybe I'm not smart," Alex suggested. "Maybe I'm just good at remembering things."

"Which would make you some kind of *idiot savant*," Torres replied. "And the fact that you just suggested it is pretty good proof that you're more than that." He slid a pair of diskettes into the twin drives of the master monitor, then began preparing a hypodermic. "Peter tells me you woke up early a couple of times," he said, his voice studiedly casual. "How come you never mentioned it?"

"It didn't seem important."

"Can you tell me what it was like?"

Carefully Alex explained the sensations he'd had when coming up from the anesthesia that always accompanied the tests. "But it wasn't unpleasant," he finished. "In fact, it was interesting. None of it made any sense, but

I always had the feeling that if I could only slow it down, it *would* make sense." He hesitated, then spoke again. "Why do I have to be asleep when you test my brain?"

"Peter already explained that," Torres replied. He swabbed Alex's arm with alcohol, then plunged the needle into his arm.

Alex winced slightly, then relaxed. "But if it got bad—if I started hurting or something—you could stop the tests, couldn't you?"

"I could, but I won't," Torres told him. "Besides, if you were awake, the very fact that you'd be thinking during the examination would have an effect on the results. In order for the tests to be valid, your brain has to be at rest when they're administered."

Thirty seconds later, Alex's eyes closed and his breathing became deep and slow. Checking all the monitors one more time, Torres left the room.

In his office, Torres leaned back in his desk chair and began methodically packing his pipe with tobacco. As he carried out the ritual of lighting the pipe, his eyes kept flicking toward the monitor that showed what was happening in the examining room. All, as he had expected, was as it should be, and he would have a full hour alone with Ellen Lonsdale. "I presume you're going to tell me why your husband isn't here this morning?"

Ellen shifted in her chair and nervously crossed her legs, unconsciously tugging at her skirt as she did so. "He's . . . well, I'm afraid we're having a little trouble."

"That doesn't surprise me," Torres commented, concentrating on his pipe rather than Ellen. "I don't mean this as anything against your husband, but a lot of doctors have a great deal of difficulty in dealing with me. In fact," he added, his hypnotic eyes fixing directly on her, "a lot of people have always had difficulty dealing with me." The barest hint of a smile crossed

Torres's face. "I'm talking about the fact that I was always considered something of an oddball."

Ellen forced a smile, though she knew his words carried a certain truth. "Whatever you might have been in high school is all over now," she offered. "You were just so bright we were all terrified of you!"

"And, apparently, people still are," Torres replied dryly. "At least your husband seems to be."

"I'm not sure terrified is the right word—" Ellen began.

"Then what would you suggest?" Torres countered. "Frightened? Insecure? Jealous?" He brushed the words aside with an impatient gesture, and his voice grew hard. "Whatever it is—and I assure you it's of no consequence to me—it has to stop. For Alex's sake."

So this was what it was all about. Ellen sighed in relief. "I know. In fact, that's exactly what I wanted to talk to you about today. Raymond, I'm starting to worry about Marsh. This thing with Alex's intellect . . . Well, I hate to say I'm afraid he's going to get fixated on it, but I guess that's exactly what I *am* afraid of!"

"And," Torres added, "you're afraid that he might decide that I have served my purpose. Is that correct?"

Ellen nodded unhappily.

"Well, then we'll just have to see that that doesn't happen, won't we?" Torres smiled at her, and suddenly Ellen felt reassured. There was a strength to the man, a determination to do whatever must be done, that made her feel that whatever happened, he would be able to deal with it. She felt herself begin to relax under his steady gaze.

"Is there anything I can do?"

Torres shrugged, seeming unconcerned. "Until he actually suggests removing Alex from my care, I don't see that either you or I need to do anything. But if the time comes, you can be sure that I will deal with your husband."

Your husband. Ellen repeated the words to herself, and tried to remember if Raymond had ever used Marsh's first name. To the best of her memory, he hadn't. Was there a reason for that? Or was it just Raymond's way?

Suddenly she realized how little she actually knew about Raymond Torres. Practically nothing, really. A thought drifted into her mind: did he feel as strange about his mother working for her as she did? "Raymond, may I ask you a question that has nothing to do with Alex at all?"

Torres frowned slightly, then shrugged. "You can ask me anything, but I might not choose to answer."

Ellen felt herself flush red. "Of course," she said. "It . . . well, it's about your mother. You know, she's working for me now, and—"

"For you?" Torres broke in. Suddenly he put his pipe on the desk and leaned forward, his eyes blazing with interest. "When did that start?"

Ellen gasped with embarrassment. "Oh, God, what have I done? I was sure you'd know."

"No," Torres replied, shaking his head. Then he picked up his pipe and drew deeply on it. "And don't worry," he added. "There is a lot about my mother that I don't know. Frankly, we don't see each other that much, and we don't agree on much, either. For instance, we don't agree on her working."

"Oh, Lord," Ellen groaned. "I'm sorry. I should never have hired her, should I? I didn't really think it was right, but when Cynthia absolutely insisted, I . . . well, I . . ." She fell silent, acutely aware that she had begun babbling.

"Cynthia," Torres repeated, his expression darkening. "Well, Cynthia's always had her way, hasn't she? Whatever Cynthia wanted, she always got, and whatever she didn't want, she always managed to keep well away from her."

Himself, Ellen suddenly thought. *He's talking about himself. He always wanted to go out with Cynthia, and she'd never give him the time of day.* But was he still holding an old grudge? Surely he wasn't, not after twenty years. And then he was smiling again, and the awkward moment had passed.

"As for Mother, no, I didn't know she was working for you, but it doesn't matter. I'm quite capable of supporting her, but she'll have none of it. I'm afraid," he added, his brows arching, "that my mother doesn't quite approve of me. She's very much of the old country, despite the fact that she was born here, as were her parents and grandparents. She has yet to forgive me for my own success. So she supports herself by doing what she's always done, and whom she works for is no concern of mine. If it helps, I think I'd rather have her working for you than for someone else. At least I can count on you to treat her decently."

"I can't imagine anyone not—" Ellen began, but Torres cut her off with a wave of his hand.

"I'm sure everyone treats her fine. But she tends to imagine things, and sees slights where none are meant. Now, why don't we get back to Alex?"

Though Ellen would have liked to talk more of María, the force of Raymond Torres's personality engulfed her, and a moment later, as Torres wished, they were once more deeply involved in the possible meanings of Alex's experiences in San Francisco.

Alex opened his eyes and gazed at the monitors that surrounded him. The tests were over, and today, as he came up from the sedative, there had been none of the strange sounds and images that he had experienced before. He started to move, then remembered the restraints that held him in place so that he couldn't accidentally disturb the labyrinth of wires that were attached to his skull.

He heard the door open, and a few seconds later the doctor was gazing down at him. "How do you feel?"

"Okay," Alex replied. Then, as Torres began detaching him from the machinery: "Did you find out anything?"

"Not yet," Torres replied. "I'll have to spend some time analyzing the data. But there's something I want you to do. I want you to start wandering around La Paloma, just looking at things."

"I've done that," Alex said. As the last of the wires came free, Torres released the restraints, and Alex sat up, stretching. "I've done that a lot with Lisa Cochran."

Torres shook his head. "I want you to do it alone," he said. "I want you just to wander around, and let your eyes take things in. Don't study things, don't look for anything in particular. Just let your eyes see, and your mind react. Do you think you can do that?"

"I guess so. But why?"

"Call it an experiment," Torres replied. "Let's just see what happens, shall we? Something, somewhere in La Paloma, might trigger another memory, and maybe a pattern will emerge."

As his mother drove him home, Alex tried to figure out what kind of pattern Torres might be looking for, but could think of nothing.

All he could do, he realized, was follow Torres's instructions and see what happened.

After Alex and Ellen left, Raymond Torres sat at his desk for a long time, studying the results of the tests Alex had just taken. Today, for the first time, the tests had been only that, and nothing more.

No new data had been fed into Alex's mind, no new attempts had been made to fill his empty memory.

Instead, the electrical impulses that had been sent racing through his brain had been searching for something that Torres knew had to be there.

Somewhere, deep in the recesses of Alex's brain, there had to be a misconnection.

It was, as far as Torres could see, the only explanation for what had happened to Alex in San Francisco: somehow, during the long hours of the surgery, a mistake had been made, and the result was that Alex had had an emotional response.

He had cried.

Raymond Torres had never intended that Alex have an emotional response again.

Emotions—feelings—were not part of his plan.

CHAPTER THIRTEEN

"Well, I don't give a damn what Ellen Lonsdale and Carol Cochran say, I say that Kate's grounded for the next two weeks!" Alan Lewis rose shakily to his feet, an empty glass in his hand, and started toward the cupboard where he kept his liquor. "Don't you think you've had enough?" Marty Lewis asked, carefully keeping her voice level. "It's not even noon yet."

"Not even noon yet," Alan sneered in the mocking singsong voice he always took on when his drinking was becoming serious. "For Christ's sake, Mart, it's Sunday. Even you don't have to go to work today."

"At least I go to work all week," Marty replied, and then immediately wished she could retrieve her words. But it was too late.

"Oh, back to that, are we?" Alan asked, wheeling around to fix her with eyes bleary from too much liquor and not enough sleep. "Well, for your information, it just happens that the kind of job I'm qualified for doesn't grow on trees. I'm not like you—I can't just wander out

someday and come home with a job. 'Course, when I
do come home with a job, it pays about ten times what
yours does, but that doesn't count, does it?"

Marty took a deep breath, then let it out slowly.
"Alan, I'm sorry I said that. It wasn't fair. And we're
not talking about jobs anyway. We're talking about
Kate."

"Thass what I was talking about," Alan agreed, his
voice starting to slur. "You're the one who changed the
subject." He grinned inanely, and poured several shots
of bourbon into his glass, then maneuvered back to the
kitchen table. "But I don't give a damn what we talk
about. The subject of our darling daughter is closed.
She's grounded, and thass that."

"No," Marty said, "that is not that. As long as you're
drunk, any decisions about Kate will be made by me."

"Oh, ho, ho! My, aren't we the high-and-mighty one?
Well, let me tell you something, wife of mine! As long
as I'm in this house, I'll decide what's best for my
daughter."

Marty dropped any effort to cover her anger. "At the
rate you're going, you won't be in this house in two
more hours! And if you don't pull yourself together, we
won't even be able to keep this house!"

Alan lurched to his feet and towered over his wife.
"Are you threatening me?"

As his hand rose above his head, a third voice filled
the kitchen.

"If you hit her, I'll kill you, Daddy."

Both the elder Lewises turned to see Kate standing
in the kitchen doorway, her face streaked with tears but
her eyes blazing with anger.

"Kate, I told you I'd take care of this—" Marty began, but Alan cut in, his voice quavering.

"Kill me? You'll kill me? Nobody kills their daddy . . ."

"You're not my father," Kate said, struggling to hold
back her tears. "My father wouldn't drink like you do."

Alan lurched toward her, but Marty grabbed his arm,
holding him back. "Leave us alone, Kate," she said.

"Just go over to Bob's or something. Just for a few hours. I'll get all this straightened out."

Kate gazed steadily at her father, but when she spoke, her words were for her mother. "Will you send him back to the hospital?"

"I . . . I don't know . . ." Marty faltered, even though she already knew that the binge had gone on too long, and there was no other choice. Alan had switched from beer to bourbon on Friday afternoon, and all day yesterday, while Kate had been gone, he'd been steadily drinking. All day, and then all night. "I'll do whatever has to be done. Just leave us alone. Please?"

"Mom, let me help you," Kate pleaded, but Marty shook her head.

"No! I'll take care of this! Just give me a few hours, and when you get back, everything will be fine."

Kate started to protest again, then changed her mind. After the last five years, she knew the last thing her mother needed during one of her father's binges was an argument from her. "All right," she said. "I'll go. But I'll call before I come back, and if he's not gone, I won't come home."

"You won't even leave!" Alan Lewis suddenly roared. "You take one step out of this house, young lady, and you'll regret it!"

Kate ignored him, and walked out into the patio, letting the screen door slam behind her. A moment later she slammed the patio gate as well, and hurried away down the street, her hands clenched into fists as she tried to control her churning emotions.

In the kitchen, Alan Lewis glared drunkenly at his wife. "Well, this is a fine fuckin' mess you've made," he muttered. "A man's wife shouldn't turn his little girl against him."

"I didn't," Marty hissed. "And she's not against you. She loves you very much, except when you get like this. And so do I."

"If you loved me—"

"Stop it, Alan!" Marty's voice rose to a shout. "Just

stop it! None of this is my fault, and none of it is Kate's. It's your fault, Alan! Do you hear me? Your fault!" She stormed out of the kitchen and upstairs to the bedroom her husband had never appeared in last night, shutting the door behind her and locking it.

She had to get control of herself. Right now, shouting at him would accomplish nothing. She had to calm herself down and deal with the situation.

He'd be upstairs in a minute, pounding on the door and alternately begging her forgiveness and threatening her. And she'd have to get through it all once more, and try to talk him into letting her drive him to the hospital in Palo Alto to check himself into the alcoholism unit. Or, if worse came to worst, call them herself, and have them come for Alan with an ambulance. That, though, had only happened once, and she prayed it wouldn't happen again.

She went into the bathroom and washed her face with cold water. Any second now, he'd be at the door, and the argument would begin. Only this time, it wouldn't be about Kate. Kate, at least, would be out of it. Now it would be the drinking again.

Five minutes went by, and nothing happened.

Finally Marty opened the bedroom door and stepped out to the landing at the top of the stairs. From below, there was only silence. "Alan?" she called.

There was no answer.

She started down the stairs, pausing at the bottom to call her husband once more. When there was still no answer, she headed for the kitchen. Perhaps he'd passed out.

The kitchen was empty.

Oh, God, Marty groaned to herself. Now what? She poured herself a cup of coffee from the pot she always kept hot on the stove in the hopes that Alan would choose it over alcohol, and tried to figure out what to do.

At least he hadn't taken his car. If he had, she'd have

heard him pulling out of the garage. Still, she checked the garage anyway. Both cars were still there.

Maybe she should call the police. No. If he'd taken his car, she would have, but as long as he was on foot, he couldn't hurt anyone. In fact, one of the La Paloma police would probably pick him up within the hour anyway.

Would they bring him home, or take him to the hospital? Or maybe even to jail?

Marty decided she didn't really care. Yesterday, last night, and this morning had been just too exhausting. It was time for Alan to clean up his own messes. She'd call no one, and do nothing about finding him, at least until this evening. Then, if he still wasn't home, she'd start looking.

Her decision made, she began cleaning up the kitchen, starting with Alan's liquor. She drained the half tumbler of bourbon into the sink, then began taking the bottles off the cupboard shelf.

One by one, she emptied them, too, into the drain, and threw the bottles in the trash basket by the back door.

Thirty minutes later, when the kitchen was spotless, she started on the rest of the house.

Alex wandered through the village, doing his best to follow Raymond Torres's instructions to keep his eyes open and his mind clear. But so far, nothing had happened. The village seemed familiar now, and everything seemed to be in the right place, and surrounded by the right things. After an hour, he stopped in a complex of little shops that specialized in the expensive items that so intrigued the computer people in town.

In one window there was a small glass sphere that seemed to have nothing in it but water. Then, when he looked closer, he realized that there were tiny shrimp swimming in the water, and a little bit of seaweed. It was, according to the card next to it, a fully balanced and self-contained ecosystem that would live on in the sealed globe for years, needing only light to survive. He watched it for a few minutes, fascinated, and then a thought came into his head.

It's like my brain. Sealed up, with no way to get at what's inside. A moment later he turned away and continued up La Paloma Drive until he came to the Square.

He stopped to gaze at the giant oak, and found himself wondering if he'd ever climbed the tree, or carved his initials in its trunk, or tied a swing to its lower branches. But if he had, the memories were gone now.

And then, very slowly, things began to change. His eyes fixed on the base of the tree, and everything around him seemed to fade away, almost as if the coastal fog had drifted down from the hillsides and swallowed up everything except himself and the tree.

Once again, as at the mission in San Francisco, images began to come into his mind, and something he had only vaguely remembered when he came home from the Institute was suddenly clearly visible.

There was a rope hanging from the lowest limb of the tree, and at the end of the rope, a body hung.

Whose body?

Around the body, men on horseback were laughing.

And then a sudden pain lashed through his brain, and the whispering began, as it had begun in the cemetery at the mission in San Francisco.

The words were in Spanish, but he understood them clearly.

"They take our land and our homes. They take our lives. Venganza . . . venganza . . ."

The words droned on and on in his mind, and then, finally, Alex turned away from the ancient oak.

Standing a few yards away, staring at him, was María Torres. His eyes met hers, and then she turned and began walking toward the tiny plaza a few blocks away.

As the strange mists gathered closer around him, Alex followed the old woman.

*   *   *

The plaza had changed, but as Alex sat on a rough-hewn bench, María Torres whispering beside him in the Spanish he now clearly understood, it seemed to him that the plaza had always looked this way.

The mission church stood forty yards away, its white-washed walls glistening brightly in the sunlight. Brown-cassocked priests, their feet clad in sandals, made their way in and out of the sanctuary, and in the shade of the building, three Indians lounged on the ground.

Set at right angles to the church, the little mission school stood with its doors and windows open to the fresh air, and in the schoolyard five children were playing while a black-habited nun looked on, her hands modestly concealed under the voluminous material of her sleeves.

On the other side of the plaza there was a small store, its wood construction in odd contrast to the substantial adobe of the mission buildings. As Alex watched, a woman came out, and though she looked directly at him, seemed not to see him.

He began to listen as María whispered to him of the church and of the brightly painted images of the saints that lined its walls.

Then María began whispering to him of La Paloma and of the people who had built the village and loved it.

"But there were others," she went on. "Others came, and took it all away. Go, Alejandro. Go into the church and see how it was. See what once was here."

As if in a dream, he rose from the bench and crossed the plaza, then stepped through the doors of the sanctuary. There was a coolness inside the church, and the light from two stained-glass windows, one above the door, the other above the altar, danced colorfully on the walls. In niches all around the sanctuary stood the saints María had told him of, and he went to one of them and looked up into the martyred eyes of the statue. He lit a candle for the saint, then turned and

once more left the church. Across the plaza, still sitting
on the bench, María Torres smiled at him and nodded.

Without a word being spoken, Alex turned, left the
plaza, and began walking through the dusty paths of the
village, the whispering voices in his head guiding his
feet.

Marty Lewis woke up and listened for the normal
morning sounds of the house. Then, slowly, she came
to the realization that it was not morning at all, and that
the house was empty.

A nap.

After Alan had left, and she'd cleaned up the house,
she'd decided to take a nap.

She rolled over on the bed and stared at the clock.
Two-thirty. She had been asleep for almost three hours.
Groaning tiredly, she rose to her feet and went to the
window, where she stared out for a moment into the
hills behind the house, and wondered if Alan were up
there somewhere, sleeping off his bender. Possibly so.

Or he might have walked into the village and be
sitting right now at one of the bars, adding fuel to the
fires of his rage.

But he wasn't at the Medical Center. If he were, she
would have heard from them by now.

She slipped into a housecoat and went downstairs,
wondering once more if she should call the police, and
once more deciding against it. Without a car, there was
little harm Alan could do.

She poured the last of the morning's coffee, thick
with having been heated too long, down the drain, and
began preparing a fresh pot.

When Alan came home—*if* Alan came home—he was
going to be in need of coffee.

She was just about to begin measuring the coffee into
the filter when she heard the back gate suddenly open,
then close again. Relief flooded through her.

He'd come back.

She went on with her measuring, sure that before she was done the door would open and she would hear Alan's voice apologizing once again for his drunkenness and pleading with her for forgiveness.

But nothing happened.

She finished setting up the coffee maker, turned it on, and, as it began to drip, went to the back door.

Two minutes later, her heart pounding in her throat, she knew what was going to happen to her, and knew there was nothing she could do about it.

Alex blinked, and looked around him. He was sitting on a bench in the plaza, staring across at the village hall and at the black-clad figure of María Torres disappearing down the side street toward the little cemetery and her home.

A thought flitted through his mind: *She looks like a nun. An old Spanish nun.*

Suddenly he became aware of someone waving to him from the steps of the library, and though he wasn't quite sure who it was, he waved back.

But how had he gotten to the plaza?

The last thing he remembered, he'd been at the Square looking at the old oak tree and trying to remember if he'd ever played in it when he was a boy.

And now he was in the plaza, two blocks away.

But he was tired, as if he'd walked a couple of miles, much of it uphill.

He glanced at his watch. It was a quarter past three. The last time he had looked, only a few minutes ago, it was one-thirty.

Almost two hours had gone by, and he had no memory of it. As he started home, his mind began working at the problem. Hours, he knew, didn't simply disappear. If he thought about it long enough, he knew, he would figure out what had happened during those hours, and know why he didn't remember them.

* * *

The back door slammed, and Marsh looked up from the medical journal he was reading in time to see Alex come in from the kitchen. "Hi!"

Alex stopped, then turned toward Marsh. "Hi," he replied.

"Where you been?"

Alex shrugged. "Nowhere."

Marsh offered his son a smile. "Funny, that's exactly where I always was when I was your age."

Alex made no response, and slowly the smile faded away from Marsh's face as Alex silently left the room, drifting upstairs toward his own room. A few months ago, before the accident, Alex's eyes would have lit up, and he would have asked where, exactly, nowhere was, and then they would have been off, the conversation quickly devolving into total nonsense on the subject of the exact location of nowhere and just precisely what one was doing when one was doing nothing in the middle of nowhere.

Now there was nothing in his eyes.

For Marsh, Alex's eyes had become symbolic of all the changes that had come over him since the accident.

The old Alex had had eyes full of life, and Marsh had always been able to read his son's mood with one glance.

But now his eyes showed nothing. When he looked into them, all he saw was a reflection of himself. And yet, he had no sense that Alex was trying to hide anything. Rather, it was as if there was nothing there; as if the flatness of his personality had become visible in his eyes.

The eyes, Marsh remembered, had sometimes been referred to as the windows to the soul. And if that was true, then Alex had no soul. Marsh felt chilled by the thought, then tried to banish it from his mind.

But all afternoon, the thought kept coming back to him.

Perhaps Ellen's feeling on that awful night in May had been right after all. Perhaps Raymond Torres had not saved him at all.

Perhaps in a way Alex was truly dead.

CHAPTER FOURTEEN

Kate Lewis listened to the hollow ringing of the phone long past the time when she knew it was going to go unanswered. For the fourth time in the last hour, she told herself that her mother must have taken her father to the hospital. But if she had, why hadn't she left a message on the answering machine? Why hadn't the answering machine even been turned on? Worried, she hung up the phone at the back of Jake's and returned to the table she and Bob Carey had been occupying throughout the long Sunday afternoon.

"Still nothing?" Bob asked as Kate slid back into the booth.

Kate tried to force a casual shrug, but failed. "I don't know what to do. I want to go home, but Mom said to call first."

"You've been calling all afternoon," Bob pointed out. "Why don't we go up there, and if they're still fighting, we can leave again. We don't even have to go in. But I'll bet she took him to the hospital." He reached across the table and squeezed Kate's hand reassuringly. "Look, if he was as drunk as you said he was, she was probably so busy getting him out of the house and into the car that she didn't have time to turn on the machine."

Kate nodded reluctantly, though she was still unconvinced. Always before, her mother had left a message for her, or if her father was really bad, not even tried to take him to the hospital. Instead, she'd called an ambulance.

And this morning, her father had been really bad. Still, she couldn't just go on sitting around Jake's. "Okay," she said at last.

Ten minutes later they pulled into the Lewises' driveway, and Bob shut off the engine of his Porsche. They stared first at the open garage door and the two cars that still sat inside it. Then they turned their attention toward the house.

"Well, at least they're not fighting," Kate said, but made no move to get out of the car.

"Maybe she called an ambulance, and went with it," Bob suggested.

Kate shook her head. "She would have followed it, so she wouldn't have to call someone for a ride home."

"You want to stay here while I go see if they're home?" Bob asked.

Kate considered a moment, then shook her head. Her hand trembling, she opened the door of the Porsche and got out. With Bob behind her, she started up the walk to the front door.

When she found it unlocked, she breathed a sigh of relief. One thing she was absolutely certain of—her mother would never leave the house unlocked. She pushed the door open and stepped inside.

"Mom? I'm home!" she called out. An empty silence hung over the house, and Kate's heart began beating faster. "Mom?" she called again, louder this time. She glanced nervously at Bob. "Something's wrong," she whispered. "If the door's unlocked, Mom should be here."

"Maybe she's upstairs," Bob suggested. "You want me to go look?"

Kate nodded silently, and Bob started up the stairs. A moment later he was back. "Nobody up there " he told her. "Let's look in the kitchen."

"No," Kate said. Then, her voice quavering, she spoke again. "Let's call the police."

"The police?" Bob echoed. "Why?"

"Because I'm scared," Kate said, no longer trying to control the fear in her voice. "Something's wrong, and I don't want to go into the kitchen!"

"Aw, come on, Kate," Bob told her, starting down the hall toward the closed kitchen door. "Nothing's wrong at all. She probably just called an ambulance and—" He fell silent as he pushed open the kitchen door. "Oh, God," he whispered. For just a moment he stood perfectly still. Then he stepped back and let the door swing closed. He turned unsteadily around, his face ashen. "Kate," he whispered. "Your mom—I think . . . She looks like she's dead."

Kate stared at him for a moment while the words slowly registered in her mind. Then, without thinking, she started down the hall, pushing her way past Bob and into the kitchen. Wildly, she scanned the room, and then found what she was looking for.

Her knees buckled, and she sank sobbing to the floor.

Roscoe Finnerty glanced up at Tom Jackson. "You okay?"

Jackson nodded. "I can handle it." He stared at Marty Lewis's body for a moment, trying to get a handle on what he was feeling. It wasn't at all like last spring, when he'd almost fallen apart at the sight of Alex Lonsdale's broken body trapped in the wreckage of the Mustang. No, this was different. Except for the look on her face, and the pallor of her skin, this woman could be sleeping. He knelt and pressed his finger to her neck.

She wasn't sleeping.

"What do you think?" he asked, getting to his feet once more.

"Until I talk to the kids, I don't think anything." A siren sounded, and a few seconds later an ambulance pulled into the driveway. Two medics came into the room and repeated the procedure Finnerty and Jackson had gone through when they'd arrived a few minutes earlier. "Don't move her," Finnerty told them. "Just make sure she's dead, then don't do anything till the detectives get up here. Tom, you get outside and make sure none of the rubberneckers try to come inside, and I'll have a talk with the kids."

Finnerty left the kitchen and went back to the living room, where he found Kate Lewis and Bob Carey still sitting on the sofa where he'd left them, Kate sobbing softly while Bob tried to comfort her.

"How's she doing?" Finnerty asked. Bob looked dazedly up at him.

"How do you *think* she's doing?" he demanded, his voice cracking. "Her mom's . . . her mom's . . ." And then he fell silent as his own emotions overcame him and he choked back a sob.

"It's all right," Finnerty told him. "Just try to take it easy." He searched his memory; then it came to him. "You're Bob Carey, aren't you?"

Bob nodded, and seemed to calm down a little.

"Have you called your folks yet? Do they know what's happened?" Bob shook his head. "Okay. I'll call them and have them come over here. Then I'd like to talk to you. Will that be okay?"

"Nothing happened," Bob said. "We just came over here, found her, and called the cops."

Finnerty patted the boy on the shoulder. "Okay. We'll get the details in a little while." He found the phone and the phone book, and spent the next five minutes assuring Dave Carey that his son was all right. Then he went back to the living room.

Slowly he pieced together the story. The longer he

listened, the more he was sure he knew what had happened. It was a story he'd heard over and over during his years as a cop, but this was the first time in his experience that the story had ever ended in death. Only when Dave Carey arrived did Finnerty return to the kitchen.

Two detectives were there, and Finnerty watched in silence as they went over the room, methodically looking for clues as to what might have happened there.

"How's it look?" he asked when Bill Ryan finally nodded to him.

Ryan shrugged. "Without talking to anybody, I'd say it was premeditated, and pretty cold. No signs of a fight, no signs of forced entry, no signs of rape."

"If what the kids say is true, it was the husband. He was drunk, and they were having an argument when the girl left this morning. In fact, that's why she left— her father was pissed at her, and her mother was trying to get him to lay off. The girl thinks her mother was going to try to get her father into detox today."

"And he didn't want to go."

"Right."

Suddenly the back door opened, and Tom Jackson appeared, his right arm supporting a bleary-eyed man whose hands were trembling and whose face was drawn. Without being told, Finnerty knew immediately who he was.

"Mr. Lewis?"

Alan Lewis nodded mutely, his eyes fastened on the sheet-covered form on the floor. "Oh, God," he whispered.

"Read him his rights," Ryan said. "Let's see if we can get a confession right now."

"I still can't believe it," Carol Cochran sighed. "I just can't believe that Alan would have killed Marty, no matter how drunk he was."

It was a little after nine, and the Cochrans had been at the Lonsdales' since six-thirty. All through a dispirited dinner which had gone all but untouched, the Cochrans and the Lonsdales had been discussing what had happened in La Paloma that day. Now, as they sat in the still only partially furnished living room, with Lisa and Alex upstairs and Kim asleep in the guest room, the discussion threatened to go on right through the evening.

"Can't we talk about something else?" Ellen wondered, although she knew the answer. All over La Paloma, there was only one thing being talked about tonight: did Alan Lewis kill his wife, or did someone else?

"Don't ever underestimate what a drunk can do," Marsh Lonsdale told Carol, ignoring his wife's question.

"But Alan was always a harmless drunk. My God, Marsh, Alan's not very effectual when he's sober. And when he's drunk, all he does is pass out."

"Hardly," Jim Cochran observed. "Last time I played golf with him, he wrapped his putter around a tree, and took a swing at me when I suggested maybe he ought to lay off the sauce."

"That's still a far cry from killing your wife," Carol insisted.

"But there weren't any signs of a struggle," Marsh reminded her. "As far as the police can tell, Marty knew whoever killed her."

Carol shook her head dismissively. "Marty knew everybody in town, just like all the rest of us. Besides, she always felt safe in that house, although God alone knows why." Her eyes scanned the Lonsdales' living room, and she shuddered slightly. "I'm sorry, but these old places always give me the willies."

"Carol!"

"Honey, Ellen and I have been friends long enough so I don't have to lie to her. Besides, I told her when she first started looking at this place that if she didn't do something drastic to it within six months, I'd never visit her again. I mean, just look at it—it looks like some kind of monastery or something. I always feel that there

ought to be chanting going on in the background. And
what about the windows? All covered up with wrought
iron—like a prison!" Suddenly running out of steam,
she fell into a slightly embarrassed silence, then grinned
crookedly at Ellen. "Well, it's what I think."

"And in a way, you're right," Ellen agreed. "Except
that I happen to like all those things you hate. But I
don't see what it has to do with Marty."

"It's just that she always said that old fortress made
her feel safe, and look what happened to her."

"Honey," Jim protested, "murders can happen anywhere. It didn't matter where the house was, or what it
looked like."

Once more, Carol sighed. "I know. And I also know
it looks as though Alan must have done it. But I don't
care. I just don't think that's the way it happened at
all."

Suddenly Lisa appeared in the wide archway that
separated the living room from the foyer, and the four
adults fell guiltily silent.

"Are you still talking about Mrs. Lewis?" Lisa asked
uncertainly. Her mother hesitated, then nodded. "Can
I . . . well, is it all right if I sit down here and listen?"

"I thought you and Alex were listening to some
records—"

"I don't want to," Lisa said, and the sharpness in her
voice made the Lonsdales and the Cochrans exchange a
curious glance. It was Ellen who finally spoke.

"Lisa, did something happen up there? Did you and
Alex have a fight about something?" Lisa hesitated,
then shook her head, but it seemed to Ellen the girl
was holding something back. "Tell us what happened,"
she urged. "Whatever it is, it can't be so bad that you
can't tell us about it. *Did* you two have a fight?"

"With Alex?" Lisa suddenly blurted. "How can you
have a fight with Alex? He doesn't care about anything,
so he won't fight about anything!" Suddenly she was
crying. "Oh, I'm sorry. I shouldn't say that but—"

"But it's true," Marsh said softly. He got up and went

to Lisa, putting his arms around her. "It's okay, Lisa. We all know what Alex is like, and how frustrating it is. Now, tell us what happened."

Somewhat mollified, Lisa sat down and dabbed at her eyes with her father's handkerchief. "We were listening to records, and I wanted to talk about Mrs. Lewis, but Alex wouldn't. I mean, he'd talk, but all he'd say were weird things. It's like he doesn't care what happened to her, or who did it. He . . . he doesn't even care that she's dead." Her eyes fixed on her mother. "Mom, he said he never even met Mrs. Lewis, and even if he had, it wouldn't matter. He said everybody dies, and it doesn't make any difference how." Burying her face in her handkerchief, she began sobbing quietly.

There was a long silence in the room. Carol Cochran moved over to sit next to her daughter, while Marsh, his expression cold, gave his wife a long look. "It . . . it doesn't mean anything—" Ellen began, but he cut her off.

"No matter what it means, he doesn't need to say things like that. He's smart enough to keep his mouth shut sometimes." He turned and started toward the foyer and the stairs.

"Marsh, leave him alone," Ellen protested, but it was too late. All of them could hear the echo of his feet tramping up the stairs. Ellen, her voice trembling, turned back to Lisa. "Really, Lisa," she said again, "it doesn't mean anything. . . ."

Marsh walked into Alex's room without knocking, his breath coming in short, angry rasps, and found his son lying on the bed, a book propped against his drawn-up knees. From the stereo, the precise notes of *Eine Kleine Nachtmusik* echoed off the bare walls. Alex glanced up at his father, then put the book aside.

"Are the Cochrans gone?"

"No, they're not," Marsh grated. "No thanks to you. What the hell did you say to Lisa?" Then, before Alex could answer, he went on, his voice icily cold. "Never

mind. I know what you said. What I want to know is
why you said it. She's down there crying, and I can't
say that I blame her."

"Crying? How come?"

Marsh stared at Alex's serene face. Was it possible
the boy really didn't know? And then, as he made a
conscious effort to bring his breath under control, he
realized that it was, indeed, quite possible that Alex
didn't know what effect his words would have on Lisa.

"Because of what you said," he replied. "About Mrs.
Lewis, and about dying."

Alex shrugged. "I didn't know Mrs. Lewis. Lisa wanted
to talk about her, but how could I? If you don't know
someone, you can't talk about them, can you?"

"It wasn't just that, Alex," Marsh said. "It was what
you said about dying. That everybody dies, and that it
doesn't matter how they die."

"But it's true, isn't it?" Alex countered. "Everybody
does die. And if everybody dies, why should it be a big
deal?"

"Alex, Marty Lewis was murdered."

Alex nodded, but then said, "But she's still dead,
isn't she?"

Marsh took a deep breath, and when he spoke, he
chose his words carefully. "Alex, there are some things you
have to understand, even though they don't have any
meaning to you right now. They have to do with feelings and emotions."

"I know about emotions," Alex replied. "I just don't
know what they feel like."

"Exactly. But other people do know, and you used to
know. And someday, when you're all well again, you'll
feel them too. But in the meantime, you have to be
careful, because you can hurt people's feelings by what
you say."

"Even if you tell them the truth?" Alex asked.

"Even if you tell them the truth. You have to remember that right now, you don't know the full truth about
everything. For instance, you don't know that you can

hurt people mentally as well as physically. And that's how you hurt Lisa. You hurt her feelings. She cares a great deal about you, and you made her feel as though you don't care about anything."

Alex said nothing. Watching him, Marsh couldn't see whether the boy was thinking about his words or not. And then, once again, Alex spoke.

"Dad, I don't think I do care about anything. Not the way other people do, anyway. Isn't that what's still wrong with me? Isn't that why Dr. Torres says I'll never get well? Because I don't have all those feelings and emotions that other people have, and I never will?"

The hopelessness of Alex's words was only reinforced by the tonelessness of his voice. Suddenly Marsh wanted to reach out and hold Alex as he'd held him when he was a baby. And yet he knew it would do no good. It wouldn't make Alex feel more secure or more loved, for Alex didn't feel insecure, and didn't feel unloved.

He felt nothing. And there was nothing Marsh could do about it.

"That's right," he said quietly. "That's exactly what's wrong, and I don't know how to fix it." He reached out and squeezed Alex's shoulder, though he knew the gesture was much more for himself than for Alex. "I wish I could fix it, son. I wish I could help you be the way you used to be, but I can't."

"It's all right, Dad," Alex replied. "I don't hurt, and I don't remember what I used to be like."

Marsh tried to swallow the lump that had formed in his throat. "It's okay, son," he managed to say. "I know how hard everything is for you, and I know how hard you're trying. And we'll get you through all this. I promise. Some way, we'll get you through." Then, unwilling to let Alex see him cry, Marsh left the room, pulling the door closed behind him.

Ten minutes later, when he had his emotions back under control, he went downstairs.

"He's sorry," he told Lisa and her parents. "He says he's sorry about what he said, and he didn't really mean it." But a few minutes later, as the Cochrans left, he wondered if anyone had believed his words.

Alex woke up, and for a moment didn't realize where he was. And then, as the walls of his room came into focus, so also did the dream that had awakened him.

He remembered the details, which were as clear in his mind as if he had just experienced them, yet there was no beginning to the dream.

He was just there, in a house very much like the one he lived in, with white plaster walls and a tile floor in the kitchen. He was talking to a woman, and even though he didn't know the woman, did not recognize her face, he knew it was Martha Lewis.

And then there was a sound outside, and Mrs. Lewis went to the back door, where she spoke to someone. She opened the door and let the other person in.

For a moment Alex thought the other person was himself, but then he realized that although the boy resembled him, his skin was darker, and his eyes were almost as black as his hair. And he was angry, though he was trying not to show it.

Mrs. Lewis, too, seemed to think the other boy was Alex, and she was ignoring Alex now, talking only to the other boy, and calling him Alex.

She offered the boy a Coke, and the boy took it. But then, after he'd taken only a couple sips of the Coke, he set it down on the table and abruptly stood up.

Muttering softly, his eyes blazing with fury, he started toward Mrs. Lewis, and began killing her.

Alex remained still in the corner of the kitchen, his eyes glued to the scene that was being played out a few feet away.

He could feel the pain in Mrs. Lewis's neck as the dark-skinned boy's fingers tightened around it.

And he could feel the terror in her soul as she began to realize she was going to die.

But he could do nothing except stand where he was, helplessly watching, for as he endured the pain Mrs.

Lewis was feeling, he was also enduring the pain of the thought that kept repeating itself in his brain.

It's me. The boy who is killing her is me.

And now, fully awake, the thought stayed with him, as did the memory of the feelings he'd had during the killing he'd watched.

Feelings. Emotions.

Pity for Mrs. Lewis, anger toward the boy, fear of what might happen after the murder was done.

Then, just as Mrs. Lewis died and Alex woke up, the emotions were gone. But the memory of them remained. The memory, and the image of the killing, and the words the boy had spoken as he killed.

Alex got out of bed and went downstairs. In the back of the third volume of the dictionary, he found the translation of the words the boy had repeated over and over again.

Venganza . . . vengeance.

Ladrones . . . thieves.

Asesinos . . . murderers.

But vengeance for what?

Who were the thieves and murderers?

None of it made any sense to him, and even though he'd recognized her in his dream, Alex still couldn't remember ever meeting Martha Lewis.

Nor did he know Spanish.

Then the boy in the dream couldn't have been him.

It was just a dream.

He put the dictionary back on the shelf, then took himself back to bed.

But the next morning, when he opened up the La Paloma *Herald*, he stared at the picture of Martha Lewis for a long time.

It was, without any question, the woman he had seen in his dream.

CHAPTER FIFTEEN

On the morning of Martha Lewis's funeral, Ellen Lonsdale woke early. She lay in bed staring out the window at the cloudless California sky. It was not, she decided, the right kind of day for a funeral. On this, of all mornings, the coastal fog should have been hanging over the hills above La Paloma, reaching with damp fingers down into the village below. Beside her, Marsh stirred, then opened one eye.

"You don't have to get up yet," Ellen told him. "It's still early, but I couldn't sleep."

Marsh came fully awake, and propped himself up on one elbow. He reached out a tentative finger to touch the flesh of Ellen's arm, but she shrank away from him, threw back the covers, and got out of bed.

"Do you want to talk about it?" he asked, though he knew full well that she didn't. If she wanted to talk to anybody, it would be Raymond Torres. Increasingly he was feeling more and more cut off from both his wife and his son.

As Marsh had expected, Ellen shook her head. "I'm just not sure how much more I can cope with," she said, then forced a smile. "But I will," she went on.

"Maybe you shouldn't," Marsh suggested. "Maybe you and I should just take off for a while, and see if we can find each other again."

Ellen stopped dressing to face Marsh with incredulous eyes. "Go away? How on earth can we do that? What about Alex? What about Kate Lewis? Who's going to take care of them?"

Marsh shrugged; then he, too, got out of bed. "Valerie Benson's been taking care of Kate, and she can go right on doing it. Hell, at least it gives her something better to do than whine about how she never should have gotten a divorce."

"That's a cruel thing to say—"

"It's not cruel, honey," Marsh interrupted. "It's true, and you know it. As for Alex, he's quite capable of taking care of himself, even if he isn't like he used to be. But you and I are having a problem, whether we want to face it or not." For a split second Marsh wondered why it was all going to come out now, and if he should try to hold his feelings in. But he knew he couldn't. "Did you know you don't talk to me anymore? For three days now, you've barely said a word, and before that, all you were doing was telling me what Raymond Torres had to say about how we should run our lives. Not just Alex's life, but ours too."

"There's no difference," Ellen said. "Right now, Alex's life *is* our life, and Raymond knows what's best."

"Raymond Torres is a brain surgeon, and a damned fine one. But he's not a shrink or a minister—or even God Almighty—even though he's trying to act as though he is."

"He saved Alex's life—"

"Did he?" Marsh asked. He shook his head sadly. "Sometimes I wonder if he saved Alex, or if he stole him. Can't you see what's happening, Ellen? Alex isn't ours anymore, and neither are you. You both belong to

Raymond Torres now, and I'm not sure that isn't exactly what he wants."

Ellen sank onto the foot of the bed and put her hands over her ears, as if by shutting out the sound of Marsh's voice she could shut out the words he'd spoken as well. She looked up at him beseechingly. "Don't do this to me, Marsh," she pleaded. "I have to do what I   nk is best, don't I?"

She looked so close to tears, so defeated, that Marsh felt his bitterness drain away. He knelt beside his wife and took her hands, cold and limp, in his own. "I don't know," he said quietly. "I don't know what any of us has to do anymore. All I know is that I love you, and I love Alex, and I want us to be a family again."

Ellen was silent for a moment, then slowly nodded. "I know," she said at last. "But I just keep wondering what's coming next."

"Nothing's next," Marsh replied. "There's no connection between Alex and Marty Lewis. What happened to Alex was an accident. Marty Lewis was murdered, and unless Alan can come up with something better than 'I don't remember anything,' I'd say he's going to be tried for it, and found guilty."

Ellen nodded glumly. "But I keep having a feeling that there's more to it than that. I keep getting this strange feeling that there's some kind of curse hanging over us."

"That," Marsh told her, "is the silliest thing I've heard in months. There's no such thing as curses, Ellen. What's happening to us is life. It's as simple as that."

But it's not, Ellen thought as she finished dressing, then went downstairs to begin fixing breakfast. In life, you raise your family and enjoy your friends. Everything is ordinary. But Alex isn't ordinary, and someone killing Marty isn't ordinary, and getting up every morning and wondering if you're going to get through the day isn't ordinary.

She glanced at the clock. In another five minutes

Marsh would be down, and a few minutes later, Alex, too, would appear. That, at least, was ordinary, and she would concentrate on that. In her mind, she began to make a list of things she could do that would make her life seem as unexceptional and routine as it once had been, but by the time Marsh and Alex appeared, she had come up with nothing. She poured them each a cup of coffee, and kissed Alex on the cheek.

He made no response, and, as always, a pang of disappointment twisted at her stomach.

She mixed up a can of frozen orange juice and poured a glass for her husband and one for her son. It was then that she noticed that Alex was dressed for school, not for Marty Lewis's funeral.

"Honey, you're going to have to change your clothes. You can't wear those to the funeral."

"I decided I'm not going," Alex said, draining his glass of orange juice in one long gulp.

Marsh glanced up from the front page of the paper. "Of course you're going," he said.

"Alex, you *have* to go," Ellen protested. "Marty was one of my best friends, and Kate's always been a friend of yours."

"But it's stupid. I didn't even know Kate's mother. Why should I go to her funeral? It doesn't mean anything to me."

Ellen, too stunned by Alex's words to respond, slid the muffins under the broiler, and reminded herself of what Raymond Torres had told her over and over again: Don't get upset. Deal with Alex on his own level, a level that has nothing to do with feelings. She searched her mind, trying to find something that would reach him.

There was so little, now.

More and more, she was realizing that relationships—Alex's as well as her own and everyone else's—were based on feelings: on love, on anger, on pity, on all the emotions that she'd always taken for granted, and that Alex no longer had. And slowly, all his relationships were disappearing. But how could she stop it? Her thoughts were interrupted by Marsh's voice. She turned to see him staring angrily at Alex.

"Does it make any difference that we'd like you to go?" she heard him ask. "That it would mean a lot to us for you to be there with us?" He sat back, his arms folded across his chest, and Ellen knew he was going to say no more until Alex came up with some kind of answer to his question.

Alex sat still at the table, analyzing what his father had just said.

He'd made a mistake, just as he'd made a mistake with Lisa the other night. He could see from the look on his father's face that he was angry, and now he had to figure out why.

And yet, in his mind, he knew why.

He'd hurt his mother's feelings, so his father was angry.

He was starting to understand feelings, ever since the dream he'd had about Mrs. Lewis. He could still remember how he'd felt in the dream, even though he'd felt nothing since. At least he now had the memory of a feeling. It was a beginning.

"I'm sorry," he said quietly, knowing the words were what his father wanted to hear. "I guess I wasn't thinking."

"I guess you weren't," his father agreed. "Now, I suggest you get yourself upstairs and into your suit, and when you go to that funeral—which you will do—I will expect you to act as if you care about what happened to Marty Lewis. Clear?"

"Yes, sir," Alex said. He rose from the table and left the kitchen. But as he started up the stairs, he could hear his parents' raised voices, and though the words were indistinct, he knew what they were talking about.

They were talking about him, about how strange he was.

That, he knew, was what a lot of people talked about now.

He knew what happened when he came into a room.

People who had been talking suddenly stopped, and their eyes fixed on him.

Other people simply looked away.

Not, of course, that it bothered him. The only thing that bothered him was the dream he'd had, but he still hadn't figured out what it meant, except that it seemed that if he had feelings in his dreams, he should, sooner or later, have them when he was awake, too. And when he did, he'd be like everyone else.

Unless, of course, he really had killed Mrs. Lewis.

Maybe, after all, there was a reason to go to the funeral. Maybe if he actually saw her body, he'd remember whether or not he had killed her.

Alex stepped through the gate of the little cemetery, and immediately knew that something was wrong.

It was happening again.

He had a clear memory of this place, and now it no longer looked as it should have.

The walls were old and worn, and the lawn—the soft grass that the priests always tended so well—was gone. In its place was barren earth, covered only in small patches by tiny clumps of crabgrass.

The tombstones, too, didn't look right. There were too many of them, and they, like the walls, seemed to have worn away so he could barely read the names on them. Nor were there flowers on the graves, as there always had been before.

He gazed at the faces of the people around him. None of them were familiar.

All of them were strangers, and none of them belonged here.

Then the now-familiar pain slashed through his brain, and the voices started, whispering in his ears.

"Ladrones . . . asesinos . . ."

Suddenly he had an urge to turn around and run

away. Run from the pain in his head, and the voices, and the memories.

He felt a hand on his arm, and tried to pull away, but the grip tightened, and the touch of strong fingers gouging into his flesh suddenly cut through the voices.

"Alex," he heard his father whisper. "Alex, what's wrong?"

Alex shook his head, and glanced around. His mother was looking at him worriedly. A few feet away he recognized Lisa Cochran with her parents. He scanned the rest of the crowd: Kate Lewis stood next to the flower-covered coffin, with Valerie Benson at her side. Over by the wall, he recognized the Evanses.

"Alex?" he heard his father say again.

"Nothing, Dad," Alex whispered back. "I'm okay."

"You're sure?"

Alex nodded. "I just . . . I just thought I remembered something, that's all. But it's gone now."

His father's grip relaxed, and once more Alex let his eyes wander over the cemetery.

The voices were silent now, and the cemetery suddenly seemed right again.

And why had he thought about priests?

He gazed up at the village hall that had once been a mission, and wondered how long it had been since there had been priests here. Certainly there hadn't been any since he was born.

Then why had he remembered priests tending the cemetery?

And why had all the faces of the people looked strange to him?

The words that had been whispered in the depths of his mind came back to him.

"Thieves . . . murderers . . ."

The words from his dream. All that was happening was that he was remembering the words from his dream. But deep in his mind, he knew that it was more. The words had meaning, and the dream had meaning, and all of it was more than dreams and false memories.

All of it, some way, was real, but he couldn't think about it now. There were too many people here, and he could feel them watching him. He had to act as if nothing was wrong.

He forced himself to concentrate on the funeral then, focusing on the coffin next to the grave.

And then, once more, he heard his father's voice.

"What the hell is that son of a bitch doing here?"

He followed his father's eyes. A few yards away, standing alone, he saw Raymond Torres.

He nodded, and Torres nodded back.

He's watching me, Alex suddenly thought. He didn't come here for the funeral at all. He came here to watch me.

Deep in his mind, at the very edges of his consciousness, Alex felt a sudden flicker of emotion.

It was so quick, and so unfamiliar, that he almost didn't recognize it. But it was there, and it wasn't a dream. Something deep inside him was coming alive again—and it was fear.

"How are you, Alex?" Raymond Torres's hand extended. Alex took it, as he knew he was expected to. The funeral had ended an hour ago, and most of the people who had been there were gathered in Valerie Benson's patio, talking quietly, and searching for the right words to say to Kate. Alex had been sitting alone, staring at a small fishpond and the waterfall that fed it, when Torres had approached.

"Okay," he said, feeling the doctor's sharp eyes on him.

"Something happened at the cemetery, didn't it?"

Alex hesitated, then nodded. "It . . . well, it was sort of like what happened up in San Francisco."

Torres nodded. "I see. And something happened here, too." A statement, not a question.

Alex hesitated, then nodded. "The same thing. I came in, and for a minute I thought I recognized the house, but it's different than I remember it. It's the

fishpond. The whole patio looked familiar, except the
fishpond. I just don't remember it at all."

"Maybe it's new."

"It doesn't look new," Alex replied. "Besides, I asked
Mrs. Benson about it, and she said it's always been
here."

Again Torres nodded. "I think you'd better come
down tomorrow, and we'll talk about it."

Suddenly his father appeared at his side. Alex felt his
father's arm fall over his shoulders, but made no move
to pull away. "He'll be going to school tomorrow," he
heard his father say.

Torres shrugged. "After school's fine."

Marsh hesitated. Every instinct in him was telling
him to inform Torres that he wouldn't be bringing Alex
to him at all anymore.

But not here. He nodded curtly, making a mental
note to clear his schedule tomorrow so that he could
take Alex to Palo Alto himself. "That will be fine." And
tomorrow afternoon, he added to himself, you and I
will have our last conversation. Keeping his arm around
Alex's shoulder, he started to draw his son away from
Torres, but Torres spoke again.

"Before you make any decisions, I'd like to suggest
that you read the waiver you signed very carefully."
Then Torres himself turned and strode out of the patio.
A moment later, a car engine roared to life, and tires
squealed as Torres shot down the road.

As he drove out of La Paloma, Raymond Torres wondered if it had been a mistake to go to Martha Lewis's
funeral after all. He hadn't really intended to go. It had
been years since he was part of La Paloma, and he
knew that he would be something of an intruder there.

And that, of course, was exactly what had happened.
He'd arrived, and recognized many of the faces, but
most of the people hadn't even acknowledged his presence. It was just as his mother had told him it would be

when he stopped to see her before going into the cemetery.

"*Loco*," she had said. "You are my son, but you are *loco*. You think they want you there? Just because you have a fancy degree, and a fancy hospital all your own, you think they will accept you? Then go! Go let them treat you the way they always did. You think they've changed? *Gringos* never change. Oh, they won't say anything! They'll be polite. But see if any of them invite you to their homes." Her eyes had flashed with fury, and her body had quivered with the pent-up anger of the years. "Their homes!" she had spit. "The homes they stole from our ancestors!"

"That was generations ago, Mama," he had protested. "It's all forgotten. None of these people had anything to do with what happened a hundred years ago. And I grew up with Marty."

"Grew up with her," the old woman had scoffed. "*Sí*, you grew up with her, and went to school with her. But did she ever speak to you? Did she ever treat you like a human being?" María Torres's eyes had narrowed shrewdly. "It's not for her you go to the funeral. It's something else. What, Ramón?"

Under his mother's penetrating gaze, Raymond Torres found his carefully maintained self-confidence slipping away. How did she know? How did she know that his interest in the funeral went beyond the mere paying of respects to the memory of someone he'd known long ago? Did she know that deep in his heart he wanted to see the pain in the eyes of Martha Lewis's friends, see the bewilderment on Cynthia Evans's face, see all of them suffering as he'd suffered so many years ago? No, he decided, she couldn't know all that, and he would never admit it to her.

"It's Alex," he had finally told her. "I want to see what happens to him at the funeral." He told her about Alex's experience in San Francisco, and the old woman nodded knowingly.

"You don't know whose grave that was?" she asked.

"Don Roberto had a brother. His name was Fernando, and he was a priest."

"Are you suggesting that Alex Lonsdale saw a ghost?" he asked, his voice betraying his disbelief in his mother's faith.

The old woman's eyes glittered. "Do not be so quick to scoff. There are legends about Don Roberto's family."

"Among our people, there are legends about everything," Torres replied dryly. "In fact, that's about all we've got left."

"No," María had replied. "We have something else. We have our pride, too. Except for you. For you, pride was never enough. You wanted more—you wanted what the *gringos* have, even if it meant becoming one of them to get it. And now you have tried, and you have failed. Look at you, with your fancy cars, and your fancy clothes, and *gringo* education. But do they accept you? No. And they never will."

And so he had left the little house he had been born in. His mother had been right. He had felt out of place at the funeral, even though he knew almost everyone there.

But he was right to have gone.

Something *had* happened to Alex Lonsdale. For a few moments, before his father had grasped his arm, Alex's whole demeanor had changed.

His eyes had come to life, and he had seemed to be listening to something.

But what?

Raymond Torres thought about it all the way back to Palo Alto. When he reached the Institute, he went directly to his office and began going over the records of Alex's case once more.

Somewhere, something had gone wrong. Alex was showing more signs of emotional behavior.

If it went too far, it would destroy everything, including Alex himself.

CHAPTER SIXTEEN

Alex stood in the middle of the plaza, waiting for the pain to strike his brain, and the strange memories that didn't fit with the real world to begin churning through his mind. He gazed intently at the old buildings that fronted on the plaza, searching for the unfamiliar details that he had expected to find in them. But nothing struck a chord. The buildings merely looked as they had always looked—a village hall that had once been a mission church, and a library that had once been a school.

No voices whispered in his head, and no pain racked his mind. It was all as it had been throughout his lifetime.

When he was at last certain that nothing in the plaza or the buildings around it was going to trigger something in his mind, he walked slowly into the library and approached the desk. Arlette Pringle, who had been librarian in La Paloma for thirty years, raised her brows reprovingly.

"Did someone declare a holiday without telling me, Alex?"

Alex shook his head. "I went to Mrs. Lewis's funeral this morning. And this afternoon . . . well, there's some things I need to look up, and the school library can't help me."

"I see." Arlette Pringle tried to figure out whether Alex had just told her a very smooth lie—and after thirty years of dealing with the children of La Paloma as well as their parents, she thought she'd heard them all—or if he really was working on a school project and was here with the blessing of his teachers. Then she decided it really didn't matter at all. So few of the kids came to the library anymore that a young face was welcome under any circumstances. "Can I help you find anything?"

"The town," Alex said. "Are there any books about the history of La Paloma? I mean, all the way back, when the fathers first came?"

Arlette Pringle immediately nodded, and opened the locked case behind her desk. She pulled out a leather-bound volume and handed it to him. "If it's the old history you're after, this is it. But it was printed almost forty years ago. If you need anything more up-to-date, I'm afraid you're out of luck."

Alex glanced at the cover of the thin oversized book, then opened it to study the first page. Superimposed over an ink drawing of the plaza was the title: *La Paloma: The Dove of the Peninsula*. On the next page was a table of contents, and after scanning it, Alex knew he'd found what he was looking for. "Can I check this out?"

Miss Pringle shook her head. "I'm sorry, but it's the only copy we have, and it can't be replaced. I even made Cynthia Evans sit right here every time she had to refer to it for the hacienda." When Alex looked puzzled, Arlette Pringle suddenly remembered what she'd been told about Alex's memory. "For the restoration," she went on. "In fact, after you read about it, you might want to go up to the Evanses' and see what they've done. On the outside, at least, it's exactly as it used to be." The front door opened, and Arlette instinctively glanced toward it. "If you have any questions, I'll be here," she finished, then turned to the new arrival as Alex settled himself at one of the heavy oak tables that graced the single large room of the library.

The book, as he paged through it, proved to be primarily a collection of old pictures of the early days of La Paloma, accompanied by a sketchy narrative of the history of the town, beginning with the arrival of the Franciscan fathers in 1775, the Mexican land grants to the Californios in the 1820's, and the effect of the Treaty of Hidalgo Guadalupe in 1848. An entire chapter dealt with the story of Roberto Meléndez y Ruiz, who was hanged after attempting to assassinate an American major general. After the hanging, his family abandoned their hacienda in the hills above La Paloma and fled back to Mexico, while the rest of the Californios quickly sold their homes to the Americans, and followed.

The rest of the book was devoted to detailed drawings of the mission, the hacienda, and the homes of the Californios. It was the drawings that commanded Alex's attention.

There was page after page of floor plans and elevations of all the old houses that still stood in and around the village. For many of them, there were accompanying photographs as well, showing how the houses had been altered and modified over the years.

Near the end of the book, Alex found his own house, and stared at the old drawings for a long time. Little had changed over the years—of all the houses in La Paloma, the Lonsdales' alone seemed to have survived in its original condition.

Except for the wall around the garden.

In the detailed drawings of the house that had been done by one of the priests shortly after the mission had lost its lands to the Californios, the patio wall was shown in great detail, complete with intricately tiled insets at regular intervals along its main expanse. Between the insets, set with equal precision, were small, well-clipped vines, espaliered on small trellises. Alex studied the picture carefully.

It was exactly as he had thought the wall should look when his parents had first brought him home from the Institute. But in the photograph of the same wall, taken forty-odd years ago, the vines had long since grown wild, covering the wall with a tangle of vegetation that completely obliterated the insets.

On the next page, he found Valerie Benson's house. It bore little resemblance to what it had once been. Over the years, it had twice burned, and both times, during the rebuilding, walls had been moved and roof lines changed. The only thing that had not been altered beyond recognition was the patio, but even that had not completely survived the remodeling.

In 1927, a fishpond, fed by a waterfall, had been added.

Once again Alex studied the old drawing and the more recent photograph.

Once again it was the old drawing that looked right to him, that depicted the patio as he'd thought he remembered it only that morning.

He closed the book, and sat still for several minutes, trying to find an answer to the puzzle that was forming in his mind. At last he stood up and carried the volume over to Arlette Pringle's desk. The librarian took it from him and carefully slid it back into its position in the locked cabinet behind her desk.

"Miss Pringle?" Alex asked. "Is there any way to tell when the last time I looked at that book was?"

Arlette Pringle pursed her lips. "Why, Alex, what on earth would you want to know that for?"

"I . . . well, I don't remember so many things, but some of the things in that book look kind of familiar. And I just thought it might help if I could find out when the last time I looked at it was."

"Well, I don't know," Miss Pringle mused, wondering if it was worth her while to dig through the old records of the locked cabinet. Then, remembering once more what had happened to Alex only a few months ago, she made up her mind. "Of course," she said. "If it were in the open stacks, it would be impossible, but I keep records of every book that goes in and out of that cabinet. Let's have a look." From the bottom drawer of her desk she took a thick ledger and began flipping through its pages. A minute later she smiled bleakly at Alex. "I'm sorry, Alex. According to my records, you've never seen that book before. In fact, nobody but Cynthia Evans has looked at it for the last five years, and before that, you and your friends were all so young I wouldn't have let you touch it anyway."

Alex frowned, then wordlessly turned and left the library. He walked home slowly, lost in thought. As he approached his house he finally made up his mind, and, though he was already tired, trudged on up Hacienda Drive.

He stopped once to rest, at the curve where only a few months ago his car had crashed through the safety barrier and plunged into the canyon below. He stayed there for nearly half an hour, searching his mind for memories of the crash.

He knew what had happened: he'd been told the details many times since he'd awakened in the hospital. There had been a party, and he and Lisa had had a quarrel, and she had left. A few minutes later he'd gone after her, but he'd been driving too fast, and had to swerve to avoid hitting her. And that was when he'd gone off the road.

But something seemed to be missing. Deep in his mind, he was sure there was one more image—a fleeting glimpse of something he couldn't quite grasp—that was the real reason for his accident.

Somehow, he knew that there was more to it than avoiding Lisa. There had been something else—someone else—whom he had also swerved to avoid.

But who? He couldn't bring the image into focus, couldn't quite identify it.

Struggling to his feet, he went on toward the Evanses' mansion and the hills beyond.

Marsh Lonsdale sat in the records office of the Medical Center and punched angrily at the keys of the computer. The screen sat like a Cyclops on the desk in front of him. There were times, of course, when he thanked all the various gods he could think of for the computer system that had been put in the Center five years earlier, but there were times—and this was one of them—when he wished that the microprocessor had never been invented.

"You have to have a special degree just to operate this damned thing," he muttered. From the file cabinet, Barbara Fannon smiled sympathetically.

"It doesn't respond to cursing," she told him. "Why don't you tell me what you're looking for, and I'll pull it up for you." Gently nudging him aside, she sat down and put her fingers on the keyboard.

"Alex," Marsh said. "All I want is the medical records for my own son, and this damned machine won't give them to me."

"Don't be silly," Barbara told him. "You just have to ask it politely, in terms it understands." She tapped at the keyboard for a few moments, and the screen came to life. "There you are. Just push this button, and it will scroll right on down, from the day he was born until the last time he was here." She stood up, relinquishing the chair to Marsh once again, and went back to her filing.

Marsh began scrolling through the record, paying little attention to anything until he suddenly came to the end of the file. The last entry was for a routine checkup that Alex had undergone the previous April. He gazed irritably at the screen for a moment, then glared at Barbara Fannon's back. "Are we really five months behind in the records?"

"I beg your pardon?"

"I asked if we're really five months behind in the records," Marsh repeated. "This is September, and the last entry in Alex's file is for his checkup in April. That's five months."

"That's ridiculous," Barbara replied. "We haven't even been twenty-four hours behind in the last three years. Usually everything that happens to a patient is in the records within two or three hours. Let me see." She bent over Marsh's shoulder and began tapping on the keyboard once more, but this time nothing happened. The record simply came to an abrupt end.

"See?"

"I see that something's wrong, and it could be any number of things. Now, why don't you just go back to your office and get back to administering this place, and I'll figure out what's happened to Alex's records. If I can't get them out of the computer, I'll bring you the originals from downstairs, but that will take a while. All right?"

Reluctantly Marsh got up and started out of the office, but Barbara Fannon stopped him. "Marsh, is something wrong? With Alex, I mean?"

"I don't know," Marsh replied. "I just have a bad feeling about him, and I don't like Torres. I want to go over his records and see exactly what was done, that's all."

"All right," Barbara Fannon sighed. "Then at least I know what I'm looking for. I'll have something for you as soon as possible."

But an hour later, when she came into his office, her expression was both puzzled and worried. "I can't find them," she said.

Marsh looked up from the report he was revising. "They're not in the computer?"

"Worse than that," Barbara replied, seating herself in the chair opposite Marsh and handing him a file folder. "They aren't here at all."

Frowning, Marsh opened the folder, which had Alex's

name neatly typed at the top. Inside was a single sheet of paper, with one sentence typed on it:

Contents of this file transferred to the Institute for the Human Brain, by authority of Marshall Lonsdale, M.D., Director.

Marsh's frown deepened. "What the hell does this mean?"

Barbara shrugged. "I assume it means that you sent all the records relating to the accident to Palo Alto, and they never came back."

Marsh reached over and pressed a key on the intercom. "Frank, can you come in here?" A moment later Frank Mallory came into the office, and Marsh handed him the sheet of paper. "Do you know anything about this?"

Mallory glanced at it, then shrugged. "Sure. All the records went to Palo Alto. Torres needed them."

"But why didn't they come back? And why didn't we keep copies?"

Now Mallory, too, was frowning. "I . . . well, I guess I thought they had. They should have been here months ago, along with copies of what was done down there. It's all part of Alex's medical history."

"Exactly," Marsh agreed. "But apparently they didn't. Barbara, would you mind getting on the phone and calling down there? Find out what's going on, and why those records never came back."

When they were alone, Frank Mallory studied Marsh for a moment. "Why the sudden upset, Marsh?" he asked. "Is something going on with Alex that I don't know about?"

"I don't know," Marsh admitted. "It's just something I can't quite put my finger on. I'm worried about him."

"And you don't like Raymond Torres."

"I've never said I did," Marsh replied, unable to keep a defensive tone out of his voice. "But it's more than that. Torres is acting more and more as though he owns Alex, and Alex . . . well, I guess I'm just worried about him."

"What about Ellen? Is she worried too?"

Marsh shrugged helplessly. "I wish she were. Unfortunately, she thinks Torres is the miracle man of the century. But she also thinks there's a curse on La Paloma, or some such thing."

Mallory's eyes widened in disbelief. "A curse? Oh, come on, Marsh, not Ellen—"

"I know," Marsh sighed. "And I don't think she really believes it herself. She was just upset this morning. What with Marty Lewis being killed so soon after Alex's accident—"

"Which events have no connection whatsoever," Mallory pointed out.

"I told her that," Marsh agreed. "And when she thinks about it, I'm sure she'll realize it's true. But what's really bugging me is Torres's attitude." He told Mallory about the conversation he'd had with Torres after the funeral. "And all he did was suggest that I read the release we signed."

"And have you? I mean, since the night you signed it?"

Before Marsh could reply, the door opened, and Barbara Fannon stepped into the office, another file folder in her hand. One look at her face told Marsh that something was wrong.

"What is it? What did they say?"

Barbara shook her head, as if even she couldn't believe what she'd been told. "They said they have all the records and that they won't be returning them. They won't even be returning *our* records, let alone forwarding copies of their own!"

"That's impossible," Marsh said. "They can't do that—"

"They . . . they said they can, Marsh," Barbara replied, her voice so low the two men had to strain to hear her. "They said the instructions and authorizations are very clear in the release you signed before the operation."

"I don't believe it," Marsh declared. "Let's take a look at that release."

Silently Barbara handed him the folder. "I thought you'd want to see it," she said. "I . . . well, I already read it."

Marsh scanned the document, then went back and reread the whole thing very carefully. When he was done, he handed it to Frank Mallory.

"It won't hold up," Mallory said when he, too, had read every word of the agreement Marsh and Ellen had made with the Institute for the Human Brain. "There isn't a court in the country that would uphold all this. My God, according to this, the man isn't accountable to anybody. He doesn't have to release any records, describe any procedures—nothing. And he can do anything he wants with Alex for as long as he wants. According to this, you've even given him custody of Alex. Why the hell did you sign it in the first place?" At the look on Marsh's face, he immediately regretted his words. "Sorry, Marsh," he mumbled, "that was out of line."

"Was it?" Marsh asked, his voice hollow. "I wonder. I should have read it—Lord knows Torres told me to enough times. But I guess I thought it was a standard release."

"It's about as far from standard as anything I've ever seen," Mallory said. "I think we'd better get a lawyer on this right away."

Marsh nodded. "But I'm not sure what good it'll do. Even if a lawyer can get it broken, it'll take months, if not years. Besides," he added, "even if I'd read it thoroughly, I would have signed it."

"But it seems to me the circumstances constitute duress of the worst kind," Mallory said. "It was either sign or let Alex die, for God's sake! What else could you do?"

"More to the point, what do I do now?" Marsh asked.

An uncomfortable silence fell over the room, as all three of its occupants realized the position Marsh was in. Without the records, they had no idea of what had been done to Alex, but that was the least of it.

The first thought that had flashed through all their minds was simply to remove Alex from the area. But that, of course, was impossible now.

Besides not knowing what procedures had been used to save Alex's life, they also had no idea of what treatment might still be in progress, and what the ramifications of ending that treatment might be.

It was a trap, and there seemed to be no way out.

Alex sat on the hillside, the afternoon sun warming his back even though the offshore breeze was already starting to bring the cool sea air inland. He was staring down at the hacienda, and in his memory, images were once again beginning to flash.

He seemed to remember horses filling the courtyard, then riding away toward the village.

He remembered people—his people—walking slowly away from the hacienda, carrying small bundles.

And he remembered three people who remained in the courtyard long after all the others were gone. In his memory, he couldn't see their faces clearly, but he knew who they were.

They were his family.

Then the faintly remembered voices began in his head, one voice standing out from all the others.

"We are not afraid to die . . . we will not leave our land . . ."

But they *had* left. The book had said they fled to Mexico.

"It will do you no good to kill us . . . my son will find you, and he will kill you . . ."

The words echoed in Alex's head. He stood up and began walking up the hillside, and then, when he was near the top, he plunged into a tangle of scrub oak, and a moment later began digging. The earth, packed hard after nearly a century and a half, resisted, but in the end gave way.

Two feet below the surface, Alex found the ancient skeletons. He hunched low to the ground, staring at the three skulls, their hollow eye sockets seeming to plead with him; then he slowly reburied them. When the job was finished, he began walking once again, staying high on the hillside, but always keeping the hacienda in his view. The memories were coming clearer now, and images of what had happened there flashed brightly in his mind.

The walls—the whitewashed walls—were stained with crimson, and the bodies, crumpled and torn, lay still in the dust.

And then, as he moved around to the east, the images began to fade, and soon were gone altogether.

The images were gone, but the memories remained.

Finally he came back down into the village.

Lisa Cochran looked up when the bell on Jake's door clattered noisily, and waved to Alex as he walked into the pizza parlor. He hesitated, then joined Lisa and Bob Carey at the table they were sharing.

"How come you weren't in school this afternoon?"

"I went to the library," Alex replied. "There was some stuff I wanted to look up."

"So you just went?" Bob asked. "Jeez, Alex, didn't you even ask anyone if it was all right? They'll mark you down for a cut."

Alex shrugged. "It doesn't matter."

Lisa looked at Alex sharply. "Alex, is something wrong?"

Again Alex shrugged, then glanced from Lisa to Bob. "Can I . . . well, can I ask you guys a question without you thinking I'm nuts?"

Bob Carey rolled his eyes and stood up. "Ask Lisa," he said. "I gotta get out of here—I promised Kate I'd come by on my way home and give her the homework assignments."

"When's she coming back to school?" Lisa asked.

"Search me," Bob replied. Then he lowered his voice.

"Did you hear anything about her not coming back at all?"

Lisa shook her head. "Who'd you hear that from?"

"Carolyn Evans. She said she didn't think Kate would come back to school until after they try her dad, and if he gets convicted, she doesn't think Kate will come back at all."

Lisa groaned. "And you believed her? Carolyn Evans? Oh, come on, Bob. Even if Mr. Lewis did do it, nobody's going to hold it against Kate!"

"I don't know," Bob replied. "Sometimes people can get really weird." Then, after shooting a meaningful look toward Alex, he left.

"I don't believe it!" Lisa cried when he was gone. "I swear to God, Alex, sometimes people make me so mad. Carolyn Evans spreading gossip like that, and Bob looking at you like you're some kind of nut—"

"Maybe I am," Alex said, and Lisa, her mouth still open, stared at him for a moment.

"What?"

"I said, maybe I am a nut."

"Oh, come on, Alex. You're not crazy—you just don't remember a lot of things."

"I know," Alex replied. "But I'm starting to remember some things, and they're really strange. I mean, they're things I couldn't possibly remember, because they happened before I was even born."

"Like what?" Lisa asked. She started to fidget with a straw that lay dripping Coke on the Formica tabletop. She wasn't at all sure she wanted to know.

"I'm not sure," Alex said. "It's just images, and words, and things that don't look quite right. But I don't know what it all means."

"Maybe it doesn't mean anything. Maybe it's just all in your brain. You know, from the accident?"

Alex hesitated, then nodded. "Maybe you're right." But in his own mind, he wasn't so sure. The memories had seemed too real to be figments of his imagination.

Suddenly Lisa looked up at him. "Alex, do you think Mr. Lewis killed Mrs. Lewis?"

Alex hesitated, then shrugged. "How should I know?"

"Well, none of us *knows*," Lisa replied. "But what do you think?"

Suddenly Alex remembered his dream from the night Kate's mother had died.

"I don't think he did it," he said. "I think someone else did it." He hesitated. "And I think it's going to happen again."

Lisa stared at him, then stood up. "That's an awful thing to say," she whispered, her eyes furious. "If you're trying to convince me you're nuts, you've just done it. Nobody but a crazy person would say something like that!" Picking up her books and her bag, she hurried out into the street, letting the door slam shut behind her.

Alex, his eyes empty, watched her go.

CHAPTER SEVENTEEN

Ellen listened quietly as her husband once again recited the terms of the release they'd signed before Alex's operation. Even after more than an hour's discussion, she was still certain he was overreacting. "Marsh, you're being absolutely paranoid," she said when he at last fell silent. "I don't care what you think Raymond Torres is up to, because you're wrong. Raymond isn't up to anything. He's Alex's doctor, and whatever he's doing is in Alex's best interests."

"Then why won't he let us see the records?" Marsh demanded, and Ellen could only shake her head wearily.

"I don't know. But I'm sure there's an explanation, and it seems to me the person you should be talking to is Raymond, not me."

Marsh had been standing next to the fireplace, leaning on the mantel, but now he wheeled around to face his wife. He hadn't gotten through to her at all. No matter what he told her—about the wall of secrecy Torres had erected around Alex's case, about the terms of the release, in which they'd given Torres full legal custody of Alex—she still remained steadfast in her defense of the man. To her, it came down to only one thing—Torres had saved Alex's life.

"Besides, what does it matter?" he heard her asking. "Why are the records so important? The point is that whatever he did, it worked!" Suddenly the calm façade she had been maintaining slipped, and her voice took on a bitter edge. "I should think you'd be grateful! You always said Alex was brilliant—gifted, even—and now Raymond's proved it."

"But there's more to it than that. For Christ's sake, Ellen. Don't you even *see* Alex anymore? He's like a machine! He doesn't feel anything. Not for any*one* or any*thing*. He's . . . well, in some ways he's just like your precious Raymond Torres. And it's not changing."

Ellen's eyes flashed with sudden anger. Though she knew that what she was about to say would only widen the chasm between them, she didn't try to hold the words back. "So that's what it's all about! I knew it! I knew when this whole thing started that it had nothing to do with the release. It's Raymond, isn't it? In the end, it all comes down to the same thing. You're jealous, Marsh. He did what you couldn't do, and you can't stand it."

Marsh stood silently for a moment, then nodded briefly. "It started out that way," he admitted, moving away from the fireplace to flop into his favorite easy chair. "I'm not going to pretend it didn't. But something's wrong, Ellen. The more I think about it, the less I understand it. How is it possible that Alex could have made such a phenomenal recovery intellectually, and physically, and show no progress at all emotionally?"

"I'm sure there's an explanation—" Ellen began.

"Oh, there is!" Marsh interrupted. He rose to his feet again and began nervously pacing the room. "And it's all in the records that Torres won't let us see."

Ellen sighed and stood up. "This is getting us nowhere. All we're doing is going in circles. I'm sure

Raymond has his reasons for keeping the records closed, and I'm sure they're valid. As for the rest of it—the terms of the release . . ." She hesitated, then plunged on. "Well, I'm afraid that's a problem you're going to have to deal with yourself."

"You mean you can accept those terms?" Marsh asked, his voice heavy with disbelief.

Ellen nodded. "I'm sure they're there to protect Alex, and I'm sure Raymond will explain them to me. In fact, he started to the other day."

"The other day?" Marsh asked. "What are you talking about?"

"I talked to him," Ellen replied. "When you were going to pull Alex out of school and send him down to Stanford, I talked to Raymond about it. I was . . . well, I was afraid you might ignore his advice. At any rate, he assured me that I had nothing to worry about. He said . . . well, he said that if you tried to do something, he could deal with you."

Marsh felt dazed. "*Deal* with me? He actually said that?"

Ellen nodded, but said nothing.

"And that didn't faze you at all, that as far as he's concerned, I'm simply someone to be *dealt* with?"

Ellen was silent for several long seconds. "No," she said at last. "In fact, it made me feel relieved."

The words struck Marsh with the force of a physical blow. He sank back into his chair as Ellen rose and quietly left the room.

Alex had long since stopped listening to the argument that was going on downstairs, tuning out his parents' voices as he immersed himself in the book he'd picked up at the library after he left Jake's.

When he'd come in for the second time, Arlette Pringle had immediately turned to the locked case, but Alex had stopped her.

"I need some medical books," he'd told her.

"Medical books? But doesn't your father have any?"

"I need new ones," Alex went on. "I need something about the brain."

"The human brain?"

Alex nodded. "Do you have anything?"

Arlette Pringle removed her glasses and thoughtfully chewed on an earpiece while she ran over the library's medical collection in her mind. "Not much that's really technical," she said at last. "But there's one new one we just got in." She rose from her desk and went to the small shelf labeled "Current Nonfiction." "Here it is. *The Brain*. Think that's specialized enough for you?"

Alex thumbed through the book, nodding. "I think so," he replied. "I'll tell you tomorrow. Can I check this out?"

Arlette led him back to the desk and showed him the process of checking out a book. "If this doesn't seem familiar," she said dryly, "I can tell you why. You were never much of a one for books."

"Then I guess that's something different about me, too," Alex replied, thinking: And maybe the reason why is in here.

Since dinner, while his parents had been arguing, he'd scanned the entire book, and reread Chapter 7, the chapter dealing with learning and memory, two more times. And the more he read, the more puzzled he became.

From what he'd read, what was happening to him seemed to be impossible.

He was about to begin the chapter for the third time, sure that he must have missed something, when there was a soft tap at the door. A second later his mother stuck her head in.

"Hi."

"Hi, Mom." He glanced up from the book. "You and Dad still fighting?"

Ellen studied her son carefully, searching for any sign that the angry words she and Marsh had just exchanged might have upset Alex, but his expression was as bland as always, and his question had been asked in the same tone he might have used had he been interested in the time of day. "No," she said. "But it wasn't really a fight, honey. We were just discussing Dr. Torres, that's all."

Alex frowned thoughtfully; then: "Dad doesn't like him, does he?"

"No," Ellen agreed, "he doesn't. But it doesn't matter. The only thing that matters is that you keep getting better."

"But what if I'm not getting better?"

Ellen stepped into the room and closed Alex's door behind her, then came to sit on the end of the bed. "But you are getting better."

"Am I?"

"Of course you are. You're starting to remember things, aren't you?"

"I don't know," Alex replied. "Sometimes I think I am, but the memories don't always make sense. It's like . . . I remember things that I couldn't possibly remember."

"What do you mean?"

Alex tried to explain some of the things that had happened, but carefully made no mention of the voices that sometimes whispered inside his head. He wouldn't mention those until he understood them. Ellen listened carefully as he talked, and when he was done, she smiled reassuringly.

"But it's all very simple. Obviously you saw the book before."

"Miss Pringle says I didn't."

"Arlette Pringle's memory isn't as good as she likes people to think it is," Ellen replied. "And anyway, even if you didn't ever see that copy of the book, you certainly might have seen it somewhere else. At your grandparents', for instance."

"My grandparents? But I don't even remember them. How could I remember something I saw at their house, without remembering them or their house either?"

"We'll ask Dr. Torres. But it seems to me that your

memory must be coming back, even if it's just scraps. Instead of worrying about what you're remembering, I think you ought to be trying to remember more." For the first time her eyes fell on the book Alex had been reading, and she picked it up, studying the immensely enlarged brain cell on the cover for a moment. "Why are you reading this?"

"I thought maybe if I knew more about the brain, I might be able to figure out what's happening to me," Alex replied.

"And are you?"

"I don't know yet. I'm going to have to do a lot more studying."

Ellen put the book down and took Alex's hands. Though he made no response, neither did he immediately draw away from her. "Honey, the only thing that matters is that you're getting better. It doesn't matter why or how. Don't you see that?"

Alex shook his head. "The thing is, I'm not sure I *am* getting better, and I want to know. It just seems . . . well, I just think it's important that I know what's happening in my brain."

Ellen squeezed his hands, then let them go and stood up. "Well, I'm not going to tell you not to study, and Lord knows your father won't either. But don't stay up all night, okay?" Alex nodded and picked up his book. When Ellen leaned down to kiss him good night, he returned the gesture.

But as his mother left the room, Alex wondered why she always kissed him, and what she felt when she did. For his own part, he felt nothing. . . .

Marsh was still in his easy chair, staring morosely into the cold fireplace, when Alex came into the living room an hour later. "Dad?"

Marsh looked up, blinking tiredly. "I thought you'd gone to bed."

"I've been studying, but I need to talk to you. I've

been reading about the brain," Alex began, "and there's some things I don't understand."

"So you thought you'd ask the family doctor?" He gestured toward the sofa. "I'm not sure I can help you, but I'll try. What's the problem?"

"I need to know how bad the damage was to my brain," Alex said. Then he shook his head. "No, that's not really it. I guess what I need to know is how deep the damage went. I'm not too worried about the cortex itself. I think that's all right."

The tiredness suddenly drained out of Marsh as he stared at Alex. "You think that's all right?" he echoed. "After reading for a couple of hours, you think the cortex is all right?"

Alex nodded, and if his father's skeptical tone affected him at all, he gave no sign. "It seems as though there must have been damage a lot deeper, but there are some things that don't seem to make any sense."

"For instance?" Marsh asked.

"The amygdala," Alex said, and Marsh stared at him. He searched his mind, and eventually associated the word with a small almond-shaped organ deep within the brain, nearly surrounded by the hippocampus. If he'd ever known its exact function, he'd long since forgotten.

"I know where it is," he said. "But what about it?"

"It seems like mine must have been damaged, but I don't see how that's possible."

Marsh leaned forward, his elbows resting on his knees. "I'm not following you," he said. "Why do you say the amygdala must have been injured?"

"Well, according to this book, what's been happening to me seems like it must be associated with the amygdala. I don't seem to have any emotions, and we know what happened to my memory. But now I'm starting to remember things, except that the way I remember them isn't the way they are, but the way they used to be."

Marsh nodded, though he wasn't exactly sure where

Alex was going. "All right. And what do you think that means?"

"Well, it seems that I'm having imaginary memories. I'm remembering things that I couldn't remember."

"Maybe," Marsh cautioned him. "Or maybe your memories are just twisted a bit."

"I've thought of that," Alex said. "But I don't think so. I keep remembering things as they were long before I was even born, so I must only be imagining that I'm remembering them."

"And what does that have to do with the amygdala?"

"Well, it says in the book I read that the amygdala may be the part of the brain that mediates rearrangement of memory images, and that seems to be what's happening to me. As though the images are getting rearranged, and then coming out as real memories when they're not."

Marsh's brows arched skeptically. "And it seems to *me* as though you're jumping to a pretty farfetched conclusion."

"But there's something else," Alex went on. "According to this book, the amygdala also handles emotional memories. And I don't have any of those at all. No emotions, and no memories of emotions."

With a force of will, Marsh kept his expression impassive. "Go on."

Alex shrugged. "That's it. Given the combination of no emotions or memories of emotions, and the imaginary memories, the conclusion is that my amygdala must have been damaged."

"If you read that book right, and if its information is correct—which is a big if, considering how little is actually known about the brain—then I suppose your conclusion is probably right."

"Then I should be dead," Alex stated.

Marsh said nothing, knowing all too well that what his son was positing was absolutely true.

"It's too deep," Alex went on, his voice as steady as if he were discussing the weather. "In order to damage the amygdala, practically everything else would have to be destroyed first: the frontal lobe, the parietal lobe, the hippocampus, the corpus callosum, the cingulate gyrus, and probably the thalamus and the pineal gland too. Dad, if all that happened to me, I should be dead, or at least a vegetable. I shouldn't be conscious, let alone walking, talking, seeing, hearing, and everything else I'm doing."

Marsh nodded, but still said nothing. Again, everything Alex had said was true.

"I want to know what happened, Dad. I want to know how badly my brain was damaged, and how Dr. Torres fixed it. And I want to know why part of my brain is doing so well, and other parts aren't working at all."

Marsh leaned back in his chair, closing his eyes for a moment as he tried to decide what to say to his son. At last, though, he made his decision. Alex might as well know the truth. "I can't tell you," he said. "In fact, I got curious about the same things, and today I tried to pull your records out of our computer. They aren't there anymore. Dr. Torres has all the information pertaining to what happened to you in his own files, and for some reason he doesn't want me or anyone else to see it."

Now it was Alex who fell silent as he turned his father's words over in his mind. When he finally spoke, his eyes met his father's squarely. "It means something's wrong, doesn't it?"

Marsh kept his voice deliberately neutral. "Your mother doesn't think so. She thinks everything is fine, and Torres is simply protecting the privacy of his records."

Alex shook his head. "If that's what she thinks, then she's wrong."

"Or maybe we're wrong," Marsh suggested. He kept his eyes on Alex, searching for any sort of emotional reaction from the boy. So far, there was none. Alex was only shaking his head.

"No, we're not wrong. If I'm alive, then what's happening to me shouldn't be happening. And I *am* alive. So something's wrong, and I have to find out what."

"*We* have to find out," Marsh said softly. He rose to his feet and went to put his hand on Alex's shoulder. "Alex?" he said quietly. The boy looked up at him. "Alex, are you scared?"

Alex was silent for a moment, then shook his head. "No. I'm not scared. I'm just curious."

"Well, *I'm* scared," Marsh admitted.

"Then you're lucky," Alex said quietly. "I keep wishing I was scared, not just curious . . . I wish I was terrified."

Alex sat alone in his first class the next morning. He had known something was wrong from the moment he had stopped by the Cochrans' to walk to school with Lisa, and discovered that she had already left. It was Kim who had told him.

"She thinks you're crazy," the little girl had said, gazing up at Alex with her large and trusting blue eyes. "She says she doesn't want to go out with you anymore. But she's dumb." And then Carol Cochran had appeared, and sent Kim back into the house.

"I'm sorry, Alex," she told him. "She'll get over it. It's just that you scared her yesterday when you told her you thought whoever killed Marty Lewis was still loose."

"I didn't mean to scare her," Alex said. "All she did was ask me if I thought Mr. Lewis did it, and I said I didn't."

"I know what you said," Carol sighed. "And I'm sure Lisa will get over it. But this morning she just wanted to go to school by herself. I'm sorry."

"It's okay," Alex had replied. He'd said good-bye to Lisa's mother, then continued on his way to school. But he wasn't surprised when no one spoke to him, and he wasn't surprised when the classroom fell silent when he came in.

Nor was he surprised to see that there was no empty seat next to Lisa.

He wasn't surprised, but neither was he hurt.

He simply made up his mind that in the future he would be more careful what he said to people, so they wouldn't think he was crazy.

He listened to the first few words of the teacher's history lecture, but then tuned him out, as he had tuned his parents out the night before. All the material the teacher was talking about was in the textbook, and Alex had read it three days earlier.

The entire contents of the history text were now imprinted on his memory. If he'd been asked to, he could have written the book down word for word.

Besides, what concerned Alex that morning was not the history text, but the book about the brain that he had borrowed from the library. In his mind he began going over the problem he had discussed with his father the night before, looking for the answer. Somewhere, he was certain, he had made a mistake. Either he had misread the book, or the book was wrong.

Or there was a third possibility, and it was that third possibility that he spent the rest of the day considering.

The idea came to him late in the afternoon.

His last class had been a study hall, and he'd decided not to bother with it. Instead, he'd wandered around the campus, trying once more to find something that jogged one of his dormant memories to life. But it was useless. Nothing jarred his memory, and more and more, everything he saw was now familiar. Each day, there was less and less in La Paloma that he had not refamiliarized himself with.

He was wandering through the science wing when someone called his name. He stopped and glanced through the open door of one of the labs. At the desk, he recognized Paul Landry.

"Hello, Mr. Landry."

"Come on in, Alex."

Alex stepped into the lab and glanced around.

"Recognize any of it?" Landry asked. Alex hesitated, then shook his head. "Not even that?"

Landry was pointing toward a wooden box with a glass top covering a table near the blackboard. "What is it?" Alex asked.

"Take a look. You don't remember it at all?"

Alex gazed at the crude construction. "Should I?"

"You built it," Landry said. "Last year. It was your project, and you finished it just before the accident."

Alex walked over to examine the plywood construction. It was a simple maze, but apparently he'd made each piece separately, so that the maze could be easily and quickly changed into a myriad of different patterns. "What was I doing?"

"Figure it out," Landry challenged. "From what Eisenberg tells me, it shouldn't take you more than a minute."

Alex glanced at his watch, then went back to the box. At one end was a runway leading to a cage containing three rats, and at the other was a food dispenser. Built into the front of the box was a timer. Forty-five seconds later, Alex nodded. "It must have been a retraining project. I must have wanted to be able to time the rate at which the rats learned each new configuration of the maze. But it looks pretty simpleminded."

"That's not what you thought last year. You thought it was pretty sophisticated."

Alex shrugged disinterestedly, then lifted the gate that allowed the rats to run into the maze. One by one, with no mistakes, they made their way directly to the food and began eating. "How come it's still here?"

Landry shrugged. "I guess I just thought you might want it. And since I was teaching summer school this year, it wasn't any trouble to keep it."

It was then, as he watched the rats, that the idea suddenly came into Alex's mind. "What about the rats?" he asked. "Are they mine too?"

When Landry nodded, Alex removed the glass and picked up one of the large white rats. It wriggled for a moment, then relaxed when Alex put it back in its cage. A minute later, the other two had joined the first. "Can I take them home?" Alex asked.

"Just the rats? What about the box?"

"I don't need it," Alex replied. "It doesn't look like it's worth anything. But I'll take the rats home."

Landry hesitated. "Mind telling me why?"

"I have an idea," Alex said. "I want to try an experiment with them, that's all."

There was something in Alex's tone that struck Landry as strange, and then he realized what it was. There was nothing about Alex of his former openness and eagerness to please. Now he was cold, and, though he hated to use the word, arrogant.

"It's fine with me," he finally said. "Like I said, they're your rats. But if you don't want the box, leave it there. You may think it's pretty simpleminded—which, incidentally, it is—but it still demonstrates a few things. I've been using it for my class." He grinned. "And I've also been telling my kids that this project would have earned the brilliant Alex Lonsdale a genuine C-minus. Even last year, you could have done better work than that, Alex."

"Maybe so," Alex replied, picking up the rat cage and heading toward the door. "And maybe I would have, if you'd been a better teacher."

Then he was gone, and Paul Landry was left alone, trying to reconcile the Alex he'd just talked to with the Alex he'd known the year before. He couldn't, for there was simply no comparison. The Alex he'd known last year had disappeared without a trace. In his place was someone else, and Landry was grateful that whoever he was, he wasn't in his class this year. Before he left that day, he took Alex's project and threw it into the dumpster.

CHAPTER EIGHTEEN

The kitchen door slammed, and despite herself, Ellen jumped. "Alex?" she called. "Is that you? Do you know what time it—" And then, as Alex came into the living room, she fell silent, her eyes fixed on the cage he held in his right hand. "What on earth have you got there?"

"Rats," Alex told her. "The ones from my science project last year. Mr. Landry still had them."

Ellen eyed the little creatures with revulsion. "You're not going to keep them, are you?"

"I've figured out an experiment," Alex told her. "They'll be gone in a couple of days."

"Good. Now, let's go, or we'll be late. In fact," she added, her eyes moving to the clock, "we already are. And you know how Dr. Torres feels about punctuality."

Alex started toward the stairs. "Dad and I aren't sure I ought to keep going to Dr. Torres."

Ellen, in the midst of struggling into a light coat, froze. "Alex, what are you talking about?"

Alex's face remained impassive as he regarded her.

"Dad and I had a talk last night, and we think maybe something's wrong with me."

"I don't understand," Ellen breathed, although she was afraid she understood all too well. She and Marsh had barely spoken to each other this morning, and today he had, for the first time in her memory, failed to call her even once. And now, apparently, he was going to use Alex as a pawn in their battle. Except that she wasn't going to tolerate it, particularly when she knew that in the end, the loser would not be her, but Alex himself.

"I've been doing some reading," she heard Alex saying.

"Stop!" Ellen said, her voice sharper than she'd intended. "I don't care what you've been reading, and I don't care what your father and you have decided. You're still a patient of Raymond Torres's, and you have an appointment for this afternoon, which you're going to keep, whether you want to or not."

Alex hesitated only a split second before he nodded. "Can I at least take this up to my room?" he asked, raising the cage.

"No. Leave it outside on the patio."

As they drove down to Palo Alto, neither of them spoke.

"I thought your husband was coming today, Ellen." Raymond Torres remained seated behind his desk, but gestured to the two chairs that Ellen and Alex normally occupied.

"He's not," Ellen replied. "And I think we'd better talk about it." Her eyes shifted slightly toward Alex. Torres immediately picked up her message.

"I don't think the lab's quite ready for you yet," he told Alex. "Why don't you wait in Peter's office while he sets up?"

Wordlessly Alex left Torres's office, and when he was gone, Ellen finally sat down and began telling the doctor what had happened between herself and her husband the night before. "And now," she finished, "he's apparently convinced Alex that something's wrong, too."

Torres's fingers drummed on the desktop for a moment, then began the elaborate ritual of packing and lighting his pipe. Only when the first thick cloud of smoke had begun drifting toward the ceiling did he speak.

"The problem, of course, is that he's right," he finally observed. "In fact, today I was going to tell him that I want to check Alex back into the Institute."

Ellen suddenly felt numb. "What . . . what do you mean?" she stammered. "I thought . . . well, I thought everything was going very well."

"Of course you would," Torres said. "And for the most part, it is. But there's something going on that I don't quite understand." His head turned slightly, and his gaze fixed on Ellen. "So Alex will come back here until I know what's happening, and have decided what to do about it."

Ellen closed her eyes for a moment, as if by the action she could shut out the thoughts that were suddenly crowding in on her. How could she handle Marsh now? If she left Alex at the Institute, as she knew Raymond was going to insist upon, what could she say to Marsh? That he'd been right, that something was, indeed, wrong with Alex, and that she'd left him with a doctor who had apparently made a mistake? But then she realized that that wasn't what Torres had said. All he'd said was that something was wrong.

"Can you tell me just exactly what's wrong?" she asked, unable to control the trembling in her voice.

"Nothing too serious," Torres assured her, his voice soothing while his eyes remained locked to hers. "In fact, perhaps nothing at all. But until I know just what it is, I'll want Alex here."

Ellen found herself nervously twisting her wedding ring, knowing that if he insisted, she would inevitably give in. "I don't know if Alex will agree to that," she said so softly the words were almost whispered.

"But Alex doesn't have anything to say about it, does he?" Torres pointed out. "Nor, for that matter, does your husband." Then, when Ellen still hesitated, he spoke once more. "Ellen, you know that what I'm doing is in Alex's best interests."

Ellen hesitated only slightly before nodding. "But can't it wait a day?" she pleaded. "Can't I at least have a day to try to convince Marsh? If I go home without Alex this afternoon, I hate even to think what he might do."

Raymond Torres turned it over in his mind, briefly reviewing once again what his lawyer had told him only that morning: "Yes, in the long run the release will probably hold up. But don't forget that Marshall Lonsdale is not only the boy's father, but a doctor as well. He'll be able to get an injunction, and keep the boy until the issue is decided in the courts. And by then, it'll be too late. I know you hate it, Raymond, but in this instance, I suggest you try to negotiate. If you don't try to take the boy, perhaps they'll give him to you."

"All right," he said. "For today, I'll just take some tests, but tomorrow I want you to bring Alex back. You have twenty-four hours to convince your husband."

Alex had been in Peter Bloch's office next door to the test lab for almost five minutes before he saw the stack of orders on the technician's desk.

On the top of the stack, he found Torres's neatly typed orders relating to himself. He scanned the single page, trying to translate the various abbreviations in his mind, but none of it meant anything to him.

And then his eyes fell onto a line near the bottom of the page: "Anesthesia: SPTL."

He stared at the four letters for several seconds, then his eyes moved to the old IBM Selectric II that sat on the desk's return. The idea formed in his head instantly, and almost as quickly, he made up his mind. He inserted the page into the carriage, and carefully lined up the letters with the red guidemarks on the cardholder. Thirty seconds later he was finished, and the line near the bottom of the page was changed.

"Anesthesia: NONE."

When Peter Bloch came in a few minutes later, Alex was sitting in a chair next to the door, thumbing through a catalog of lab equipment. Out of the corner of his eye, he watched the technician go to the desk and pick up the thin stack of orders.

"Hunh," Bloch grunted. "Finally talked him into it, did you?"

Alex looked up, laying the catalog aside. "Talked him into what?"

Bloch made a sour face, then shrugged. "Never mind. But if you don't like what happens today, don't blame me. Blame yourself and Dr. Brilliant. Come on, let's get started."

Twenty minutes later Alex was strapped securely to the table, and the electrodes had all been connected to his skull. "Hope you don't decide you want to change your mind," Bloch said. "I don't have any idea what's going to happen to you, but I can practically guarantee you it isn't going to be pleasant." Leaving Alex's side, he stepped to the panel and began adjusting its myriad controls.

The first thing Alex noticed was a strange odor in the room. At first it was like vanilla, sweet and pleasant, but slowly it began mutating into something else. The sweetness faded away, and was replaced by an acrid odor, and Alex's first thought was that something in the lab must be burning. Then the smoky scent turned sour, and Alex's nostrils suddenly seemed to fill with the stench of rotting garbage.

It's in my mind, Alex told himself. It's all in my mind, and I'm not really smelling anything.

And then the sounds began, and with them the physical sensations.

The room was heating up, and he could feel himself beginning to sweat as a shrill screaming noise cut through his eardrums and slashed into his mind.

The heat increased, and suddenly centered in his groin.

A hot poker.

Someone was pressing into his genitalia with a white-hot poker.

He could smell the sickly sweetness of burning flesh, and he writhed helplessly against the bonds that held him to the table.

The sound in his mind was his own voice screaming in agony.

The burning stopped, and he was suddenly cold. Slowly, reluctantly, he opened his eyes, but saw nothing except the blinding whiteness of snowflakes swirling around him, while the wind whistled and moaned in his ears.

Suddenly there was pressure on his left leg.

It was gentle at first, as if something were there, touching him every few seconds.

Then, its yellow eyes glaring at him through the blizzard, its fangs dripping saliva, he saw the face of the wolf.

The image disappeared, and as the beast's hungry snarl drifted high over the wailings of the wind, he felt its jaws close on his leg.

His flesh was being torn to shreds, and in the strength of the wolf's jaws, his bones gave way. His lower leg went numb, but he could sense his blood spurting from the severed artery below his knee.

All around him, the blizzard shrieked.

Suddenly the sounds began fading away, and with it the pain. The blinding whiteness of the blizzard began taking on tinges of color, and soon he was surrounded by a sea of soft blue. He felt the warm waters laving his skin, and a cool breeze wafted over his face.

He floated peacefully, rocked gently by the motion of the water, and then began to feel something else in the back reaches of his mind.

It was indistinct at first, but as he began to focus on it, it became clearer.

Energy.

It was as if pure energy were flowing directly into his mind.

And then it stopped, and the cool breezes died out. The waters around him were no longer moving, and the blueness in front of his eyes gave way slowly until he was once more staring at the ceiling of the laboratory. Peter Bloch loomed over him.

"I almost shut you down," the technician said. "You started screaming, and twisting around until I was afraid you were going to hurt yourself."

Alex said nothing for a moment, but kept his eyes anchored steadily on the lamp above his head as he fixed everything that had happened in his memory.

"Nothing happened," he said at last.

"Horseshit," Peter Bloch replied. "You damned near went crazy! What the hell's Torres trying to prove now?"

"Nothing," Alex repeated. "Nothing happened to me, and he's not trying to prove anything."

Bloch shook his head doubtfully. "Maybe nothing happened, but I'll bet you thought something was happening. Want to tell me about it?"

Alex's eyes finally shifted to the lab technician. "Don't you know?"

"You think Torres tells me anything?" Peter countered. "I know we're stimulating your brain. But what it's all about, I don't know."

"But that *is* what it's about," Alex said quietly. "It's about what gets into my brain, and how my brain reacts." Then his expression twisted into a strange smile. "Except that it's not my brain anymore, is it?" When Peter Bloch made no answer, Alex answered his own question.

"It's not my brain anymore. Ever since I woke up from the operation, it's been Dr. Torres's brain."

Raymond Torres wordlessly took Alex's test reports from Peter Bloch's hands and began flipping through them. He frowned slightly, then the frown deepened into a scowl.

"You must have made a mistake," he said finally, tossing the thin sheaf of papers onto the desk as he faced his head technician. "None of these results make any sense at all. These are what you'd get from a brain that was awake, not asleep."

"Then there's no mistake," Bloch replied, his face set into a mask of forced unconcern. As always when dealing with Raymond Torres, he would have preferred to roll the test results up tight and shove them down the man's arrogant throat. But the money was too good and the work too light to throw it away over something as trivial as his dislike of his employer, who, he noticed, was now glowering at him.

"What do you mean, no mistake? Are you telling me that Alex Lonsdale was awake during this?"

Peter Bloch felt as if the floor had just tilted. "Of course he was," he said as forcefully as he could, though he was suddenly certain he knew exactly what had happened. "You wrote the order yourself."

"Indeed I did," Torres replied. "And I have a copy of it right here." He opened his bottom desk drawer and pulled out a sheet of pink paper, which he silently handed to Bloch. There, near the bottom of the page, were the words: "Anesthesia: SPTL."

Once more, Peter pictured Alex Lonsdale, his face impassive, sitting thumbing through a catalog.

And watching him.

How long had he been there? Apparently, long enough.

"I thought . . . I thought it was highly unusual, sir," he mumbled.

"Unusual?" Torres demanded, his voice crackling with harsh sarcasm. "You thought it was unusual to put a patient out with Sodium Pentothal while inducing hallucinations in his brain?"

"No, sir," the technician muttered, thoroughly cowed.

"I thought it was unusual *not* to. I should . . . well, I should have called."

Torres was fairly trembling with rage now. "What, exactly, are you talking about?"

Exactly three minutes and twenty-two seconds later, when Bloch had returned to his office, Torres knew. His eyes fixed on the altered anesthesia prescription for several long seconds, then shifted slowly to the technician.

"And you didn't think you ought to call me about this?" he asked, his voice deceptively low.

"I . . . well, the kid told me a long time ago he wanted to take the test without the Pentothal. I thought he'd finally talked you into letting him try."

Raymond Torres rose to his feet, and leaned across the desk so that his face was close to Peter Bloch's. When he spoke, he made no attempt to keep his fury under control. "Talked me into it?" he shouted. "We never even discussed such a thing! Do you have any idea of exactly what goes on in those tests?"

"Yes, sir," Peter Bloch managed.

"Yes, sir," Torres mimicked, his tone icy. "We deliberately induce pain, Mr. Bloch. We induce physical pain, and mental pain, and of the worst sort. The only thing that makes it tolerable at all is that the patient is unconscious. Without the anesthetic, we are at risk of driving a patient insane."

"He's . . . he seems to be all right," Bloch stammered, but Torres froze him with a look.

"And perhaps he is," Torres agreed. "But *if* he is, it is only because the boy has no emotions. Or, as you have so inelegantly put it in the past, because he's a 'zombie.' "

Bloch flinched, but stood his ground. "I was going to shut it off," he insisted. "I was watching him carefully, and if it looked like it was getting too bad, I was going to shut it off in spite of your orders."

"Not good enough," Torres replied. "If you had any questions about those orders, you should have called me immediately. You didn't. Well, perhaps you will do this: go to your lab and begin packing anything that is personally yours. Then you will wait there for a security guard to come and escort you out of the building. Your check will be sent to you. Is that clear?"

"Sir—"

"Is that clear?" Torres repeated, his voice rising to drown out the other man.

"Yes, sir," Bloch whispered. A moment later he was gone, and Raymond Torres seated himself once more, then waited until his breathing had returned to its normal rhythm before picking up the sheaf of test results.

Perhaps, he reflected, it will be all right after all. The boy hadn't cracked under the battering his brain had absorbed. With any luck at all, Alex's brain had been so busy dealing with the chaos of stimulation that he hadn't consciously noticed what else had been happening.

Or had he?

CHAPTER NINETEEN

"But he didn't say what was wrong, did he?" Marsh asked. He folded his napkin precisely—a gesture Ellen immediately recognized as a sign that his mind was irrevocably made up—and placed it on the table next to his coffee cup.

"That's why he wants Alex back," Ellen said for the third time. Why, she wondered, couldn't Marsh understand that there was nothing sinister in Raymond's wanting Alex to come back to the Institute for a few days? "Besides," she went on, "if he thought it was anything serious, he wouldn't have let Alex come home with me this afternoon. He could have just kept him there."

"And I would have had an injunction by tomorrow morning," Marsh pointed out. "Which I'm sure he knows. In spite of that release, I'm still his father, and unless he tells us the details of the surgery, and tells us exactly what he thinks has gone wrong, Alex doesn't go back there again." He pushed his chair back and stood up, and though Ellen wanted to argue with him further, she knew it was useless. She would just have to do what she knew was best for Alex, and deal with Marsh after she'd done it. As Marsh left the dining room, she began clearing the dishes from the table and loading them into the dishwasher.

Marsh found Alex in his room. He was at his desk, one of Marsh's medical texts in front of him, opened to the anatomy of the human brain, while one of the white rats poked inquisitively around among the clutter that surrounded the book.

"Anything I can help you with?"

Alex looked up. "I don't think so."

"Try me," Marsh challenged. When Alex still hesitated, he picked up the rat and scratched it around its ears. The little animal wriggled with pleasure. "Mind telling me what you're going to use to dissect this little fellow's brain with?"

Alex's eyes met his father's. "How did you know?"

"I may not be a genius," Marsh replied, "but last night you told me that considering the damage that was done to your brain, you ought to be dead. Now I find you studying the anatomy of the brain, and white rats are not exactly unheard of as subjects for dissection."

"All right," Alex said. "I want to see what happens to the rat if I cut as far into its brain as Dr. Torres had to cut into mine."

"You mean you want to see if it dies," Marsh replied. His son nodded. "Then I think we'd better go down to the Center, and I think you'd better let me help you."

"You mean you will?" Alex asked.

"If I don't, your rats won't survive the first cut."

When they came downstairs a few minutes later, Ellen glanced at them from her place at the kitchen sink, then, seeing the rat cage, smiled appreciatively. "Well, at least we agree that the house is no place for those things," she offered, hoping to break the tension that had spoiled dinner.

"We're taking them down to the lab," Marsh told

her. "And we may hang around awhile, if anything interesting's going on."

Ellen frowned. "Interesting? What could be interesting in the lab at this hour? There won't even be anyone there."

"We'll be there," Marsh replied. Then, while Ellen wondered what was going on, her husband and son disappeared into the patio. A moment later she heard the gate slam closed.

The fluorescent lamps over the lab table cast a shadowless light, and as Marsh prepared to inject the anesthesia into the rat's vein, he suddenly wondered if the creature somehow knew what was about to happen. Its little eyes seemed wary, and he could feel it trembling in his hand. He glanced at Alex, who stood at the other side of the table, looking on impassively. "It won't survive this, you know," Marsh told his son.

"I know," Alex replied in the emotionless voice Marsh knew he would never get used to. "Go ahead."

Marsh slid the needle under the rat's skin and pressed the plunger. The rat struggled for a few seconds, then gradually went limp, and Marsh began fastening it to the dissecting board. When he was done, he studied the illustration he'd found in one of the lab books, then deftly used a scalpel to cut the skin away from the rat's skull, starting just behind the left eye and slicing neatly around to the opposite position behind the right eye, then folding the loose flap of skin forward. Then, using a tiny saw, he began removing the top of the skull itself. He worked slowly. When he was done, the rat's brain lay exposed to the light, but its heartbeat and breathing were still unaffected.

"This probably isn't going to work," Marsh said. "We should have much smaller tools, and proportionally, much more of a rat's brain than a human's is used to keep its vital functions going."

"Then let's just cut away a little bit at a time, and see how deep we can go."

Marsh hesitated, then nodded. Using the smallest scalpel he had been able to find, he began peeling away the cortex of the rat's brain.

An hour later, all three of the rats were dead. In none of them had Marsh succeeded in reaching the inner structures of the brain before their heartbeats had ceased.

"But they didn't have to die," he pointed out. "I could have gone in with a probe, and destroyed part of the limbic system without doing much damage to anything else."

Alex shook his head. "It wouldn't have meant anything, Dad. When you cut away their brains the way Torres had to cut away mine, the rats died. So why didn't I?"

"I don't know," Marsh confessed. "All I know is that you didn't die."

Alex was silent for a long time, staring at the three small corpses on the lab table. "Maybe I did," he said at last. "Maybe I'm really dead."

Valerie Benson looked up from her knitting. Across the room, Kate Lewis was curled up on the sofa, her eyes on the television set, but Valerie was almost sure she wasn't watching the program.

"Want to talk about it?" she asked. Kate's eyes remained on the television.

"Talk about what?"

"Everything that's bothering you."

"Nothing's bothering me," Kate replied. "I'm okay."

"No," Valerie replied, "you're not okay." She put her knitting aside, then got up and turned off the television set. "Are you planning to go back to school tomorrow?"

"I . . . I don't know."

I should have had children, Valerie thought. If I'd had children of my own, I'd know what to do. Or would she? Would she really know what to say to a teenage girl whose father had killed her mother? What was there to say? And yet, Kate couldn't just go on sitting in front of the television set all day and all evening, moping.

"Well, I think it's time you went back," Valerie ventured. Then, sure she knew what was really going on in Kate's mind, she went on: "What happened wasn't your fault, Kate, and none of the kids are going to hold it against you."

Kate turned to stare at Valerie. "Is that what you think?" she asked. "That I'm afraid of what the kids might think?"

"Isn't it?"

Kate slowly shook her head. "Everybody knew all about Dad," she said so quietly Valerie had to strain to hear her. "I always talked about what a drunk he is so no one else could do it first."

Valerie went to the sofa and sat close to Kate. "That couldn't have been easy."

"It was better than having everybody gossip." Her eyes met Valerie's for the first time. "But he didn't kill Mom," she said. "I don't care how it looks, and I don't care if he doesn't remember what happened after I left. All I know is they used to fight every time he got drunk, but he never hit her. He yelled at her, and sometimes he threatened her, but he never hit her. In the end, he always let her take him to the hospital."

"Then you should be out with your friends, letting them know exactly what you think."

Kate shook her head silently, and her eyes filled with tears. "I . . . I'm scared," she whispered.

"Scared? Scared of what?"

"I'm afraid of what might happen if I leave. I'm afraid I might come back and find you . . . find you . . ." Unable to say the words, Kate began sobbing softly, and Valerie held her close.

"Oh, honey, you don't have to worry about me. What on earth could happen to me?"

"But someone killed Mom," Kate sobbed. "She was by herself, and someone came in and . . . and . . ."

Your father killed her, Valerie thought, but she knew

she wouldn't say it out loud. If Kate didn't want to believe the evidence, she wouldn't try to force her to, at least not yet. But after the trial, after Alan Lewis was convicted . . . She cut the thought off, telling herself that she should at least try to keep an open mind. "No one's going to do anything to me," she said. "I've been living by myself in this house for five years now, and there's never been any trouble at all. And I'm not going to let you become a prisoner here." She stood up briskly, went to pick up the telephone that sat on the table next to her chair, and brought it to the coffee table in front of the sofa. "Now you call Bob Carey and tell him you want to go out for a pizza or something."

Kate hesitated. "I can't do that—"

"Of course you can," Valerie told her. "He comes by every day and drops off your homework, doesn't he? So why wouldn't he want to take you out?" She picked up the phone. "What's his number?"

Kate blurted it out before she could think, and Valerie promptly punched the numbers. When Bob himself answered, she said only, "I have someone here who wants to talk to you," and handed the phone to Kate. Kate sniffled, but took the phone.

Forty-five minutes later, Valerie stood at the front door. "And no matter what she says, I don't want her back a minute before eleven," she told Bob Carey. "She's been cooped up too long, and she needs a good time." When Bob's car had disappeared down the hill, she closed the door, then went back to her knitting.

Ellen was about to call the Medical Center when she heard the patio gate slam once more. Then the door opened, and her husband and son came in. She dropped the receiver back on the hook just as the dial tone switched over to the angry whine of a forgotten phone, and didn't try to conceal the irritation she was feeling. "You might have told me how long you were going to be gone. What on earth have you been doing?"

"Killing rats," Alex said.

Ellen paled slightly, and her eyes moved to her husband. "Marsh, what's he talking about?"

"I'll tell you later," Marsh replied, but the look on Ellen's face told him that she was going to demand an explanation right now. He sighed, and hung his jacket in the armoire that stood opposite the front door. "We were dissecting their brains, to see how much damage they could sustain before they died."

Ellen's stomach turned queasy, and she had to struggle to keep her voice steady. "You killed them?" she asked. "You killed those three helpless creatures?"

Marsh nodded. "Honey, you know perfectly well that rats die in laboratories every day. And there was something both Alex and I wanted to know." He stepped past Ellen and moved into the living room, then glanced at Alex. "Why don't you make yourself scarce?" he asked. Then he smiled tiredly. "I have a feeling your mother and I are about to have another fight." Alex started toward the stairs, but Marsh stopped him, fishing in his pocket for his car keys. "Why don't you go find some of your friends?" he asked, tossing the keys to his son.

Ellen, watching, felt a chill go through her. Something had happened between her husband and her son. She was certain that an alliance had somehow formed between them that she was not a part of. A moment later, when Alex spoke again, she knew she was right.

"You mean do what we were talking about?" he asked, and Marsh nodded. And then something happened that Ellen hadn't seen since the night of the prom last spring.

Alex smiled.

It was a tentative smile, and it didn't last long, but it was still a smile. And then he was gone.

Ellen stared after him, then slowly turned to Marsh, her anger evaporating.

"Did you see that?" she breathed. "Marsh, he smiled. He actually smiled!"

Marsh nodded. "But it doesn't mean anything," he

said. "At least it doesn't mean anything yet." Slowly he tried to explain the conversation he and Alex had had on the way home, and what they had decided Alex should do.

"So you see, the smile didn't really mean anything at all," he finished fifteen minutes later. "He doesn't feel anything, Ellen, and he knows it, which is making it even worse. He told me he's starting to wonder if he's even human anymore. But he said he can mimic emotions if he wants to, or at least mimic emotional reactions. And that's what he did. He intellectually figured out that he should be happy that he gets to go out for the evening and use my car, and he knows that when people are happy, they smile. So he smiled. He didn't feel the smile, and there was nothing spontaneous about it. It was like an actor performing a role."

The growing chill Ellen had been feeling as Marsh talked turned into a shudder. "Why?" she whispered. "Why should he want to do such a thing?"

"He said people are beginning to think he's crazy," Marsh replied. "And he doesn't want that to happen. He said he doesn't want to be locked up until he knows what's wrong with him."

"Locked up?" The room seemed to be spinning, and for a moment Ellen thought she might faint. "Who would lock him up?"

"But isn't that what happens to crazy people?" Marsh asked. "You have to look at it from his point of view. He knows we love him, and he knows we care for him, but he doesn't know what that means. All he knows is what he's read, and he's read about mental institutions." His voice suddenly broke. "Hell," he muttered. "He reads damned near everything, and remembers it all. But he just doesn't know what anything means."

María Torres shifted the heavy weight of her shopping bag from her right hand to her left, then sighed and lowered it to the sidewalk for a moment.

Ramón had promised to come that evening and take

her shopping, but then he'd telephoned and said he wasn't coming. Something had come up with his patient, and he had to stay in his office. His patient, she thought bitterly. His patient was Alejandro, and there was nothing wrong with the boy. But Ramón couldn't see that, not for all his schooling. Ramón had forgotten. Forgotten so much. But someday he would understand. Someday soon, Ramón would know that all the hatreds she had carefully nursed in him were still there. But for now, he still pretended to be a *gringo*.

And tonight, the shopping still had to be done, even though she was tired after working all day, so she'd walked the five blocks to the store, which wasn't too bad. It was the five blocks home, with the full shopping bag, that was the hard part. Her arms aching with arthritis, she picked up the bag and was about to continue on her way when a car pulled up to the curb next to her. She glanced at it with little interest, then looked again as she recognized the driver.

It was the boy.

And he was returning her gaze, his eyes studying her. He knew who she was, and the saints—her saints—had sent him. It was an omen: though Ramón had not come to her tonight, Alejandro had. She stepped forward, and bent down to put her head through the open window of the car.

"*Vámos,*" she whispered, her rheumy eyes glowing. "*Vámos a matar.*"

The words echoed in Alex's ears, and he understood them. *We go to kill.* Deep in his mind, a memory stirred and the mists began gathering around him once again. He reached across the front seat and pushed the door open. María Torres settled herself into the seat beside him, and pulled the door closed. As the old woman whispered to him, he put the car in gear and started slowly up into the hills above the town.

Fifteen minutes later, he parked the car, still listening to the words María was whispering in his ears. And then he was alone, and María Torres was walking slowly away from the car, her bag of groceries clutched close to her breast.

Only when she had finally disappeared around a bend in the road did Alex, too, leave the car, and step through the gate into Valerie Benson's patio.

In the dark recesses of his throbbing brain, the familiar voices took up María's ancient litany . . .

Venganza . . . venganza . . .

Vaguely he became aware of another sound, and turned to see a woman standing framed in the light of an open doorway.

"Alex?" Valerie Benson asked. "Alex, are you all right?"

She'd heard the gate open, and waited for the doorbell to ring. When it hadn't, she'd gone to the door and pressed her eye to the peephole. There, standing in the patio, she'd seen Alex Lonsdale, and opened the door. But when she'd spoken, he hadn't replied, so she'd stepped outside and called to him.

Now he was looking at her, but she still wasn't sure he'd heard her words.

"Alex, what is it? Has something happened?"

"*Ladrones,*" Alex whispered. "*Asesinos . . .*"

Valerie frowned, and stepped back, uneasy. What was he talking about? Thieves? Murderers? It sounded like the ravings of a paranoiac.

"K-Kate's not here," she stammered, backing toward the front door. "If you're looking for her, she's gone out."

She was inside and the door was halfway closed when Alex hurled himself forward, his weight slamming into the door, sending Valerie sprawling to the floor while the door itself smashed back against the wall.

Valerie tried to scramble away across the red quarry tile of the foyer, but it was too late.

Alex's fingers closed around her neck, and he began to squeeze.

"*Venganza . . .*" he muttered once more. And then again, as Valerie Benson died: "*Venganza . . .*"

* * *

Alex stepped through the door of Jake's and glanced around. In the booth in the far corner, he saw Kate Lewis and Bob Carey sitting with Lisa Cochran and a couple of other kids. Carefully composing his features into a smile, he crossed the room.

"Hi. Is it a private party, or can anybody join?"

The six occupants of the booth fell silent. Alex saw the uneasy glances that passed between them, but he kept his smile carefully in place. Finally Bob Carey shrugged and squeezed closer to Kate to make room at the end of the booth. Still no one said anything. When the silence was finally broken, it was Lisa, announcing that she had to go home.

Alex carefully changed his expression, letting his smile dissolve into a look of disappointment. "But I just got here," he said.

Lisa hesitated, her eyes fixing suspiciously on Alex. "I didn't think you'd care if I stayed or not," she said. "In fact, none of us thought you cared about anything anymore."

Alex nodded, and hoped that when he spoke his voice would have the right inflection. "I know," he said. "But I think things are starting to change. I think . . ." He dropped his eyes to the table, as he'd seen other people do when they seemed to be having trouble saying something. "I think I'm starting to feel things again." Then, making himself stammer slightly, he went on. "I . . . well, I really like you guys, and I'm sorry if I hurt your feelings."

Once again the rest of the kids glanced at each other, their self-consciousness only worsening at Alex's words.

It was Bob Carey who broke the embarrassed silence. "Hey, come on. Don't go all weird on us the other way now."

And suddenly everything was all right again, and Alex knew he'd won.

They'd believed his performance.

But slowly, as the conversation went on, he began to

wonder, for Lisa Cochran still seemed to be avoiding talking to him.

Lisa herself was not about to tell him that she was wondering exactly what he was up to.

Long ago, before the accident, she'd heard Alex stammer and seen him look away when he was talking about his feelings.

And always, when he did that, he'd blushed.

This time, everything had been fine except for that one thing.

This time, Alex hadn't blushed.

CHAPTER TWENTY

"Come in with me."

Bob Carey couldn't see Kate's face in the darkness, but the tremor in her voice revealed that she was frightened. His eyes moved past her silhouette, focusing on the house beyond. Everything, he thought, looked normal. Except for the gate.

The patio gate stood open, and both he and Kate clearly remembered closing it when they had left earlier in the evening.

"Nothing's wrong," he assured her, trying to make his voice sound more confident than he was actually feeling. "Maybe we didn't really latch it."

"We did," Kate breathed. "I know we did."

Bob got out of the car and went around to open the other door for Kate, but instead of getting out, she only gazed past him at the ominously open gate. "Maybe . . . maybe we ought to call the police," she whispered.

"Just because the gate's open?" Bob asked with a bravado he wasn't feeling. "They'd think we were nuts."

"No they wouldn't," Kate argued. "Not after . . ."
She fell silent, unable to finish the thought.

Bob wavered, telling himself once more that the
open gate meant nothing. The wind could have done it,
or Mrs. Benson might have gone out herself and left
the gate open. In fact, she might not even be home.

He made up his mind.

"Stay here," he told Kate. "I'll go see."

He went through the open gate into the patio and
looked around. The lights flanking the front door were
on, and the white walls of the patio reflected their glow
so that even the shadowed areas of the little garden
were clearly visible. Nothing seemed to be amiss, and
yet as he stood in the patio, he sensed that something
was wrong.

Bob told himself the growing uneasiness he felt was
only in his imagination. As soon as he rang the bell,
Mrs. Benson would come to the door and everything
would be all right.

But when he rang the bell, Mrs. Benson did not
come to the door. Bob rang the bell once more, waited,
then tried the door. It was locked. Slowly he backed
away from the door, then hurried to the car.

"She's not here," he told Kate a few seconds later.
"She must have gone somewhere." But even as he
spoke the words, he knew they weren't true. He started
the car.

"Where are we going?"

"We're going to call the police, just like you wanted
to. It doesn't feel right in there."

Fifteen minutes later they were back. Bob parked his
Porsche behind the squad car, then got out and went to
the patio gate.

"Stay in your car," one of the cops at the front door
told him. "If there's a creep in here, I don't want to
have to worry about you." Only when Bob had disappeared did Roscoe Finnerty reach out and press the
bell a second time, as Bob himself had done only a few
minutes earlier. "She probably just took off somewhere,"

he told Tom Jackson, "but with these two, I guess we can't blame them for being nervous." When there was still no answer, Finnerty moved to a window and shone his flashlight through into the foyer. "Shit," he said softly, and Tom Jackson immediately felt his stomach knot.

"She there?" he asked.

Finnerty nodded. "On the floor, just like the other one. And if there's any blood, I don't see it. Take a look."

Tom Jackson dutifully stepped to the window and peered into the foyer. "Maybe she's just unconscious," he suggested.

"Maybe she is," Finnerty replied, but both men knew that neither of them believed it. "Go ask the Lewis girl if she's got a key, but don't tell her what we've seen. And when you ask for the key, see how she reacts."

Jackson frowned. "You don't think—"

"I don't know what I think," Finnerty growled. "But I sure as hell know Alan Lewis didn't do this one, and I keep thinking about the shit that came down in Marin a few years back when that girl and her boyfriend killed her folks, then went out and partied all night. So you just go see if she has a key, and keep your eyes open."

"Is she all right?" Kate asked when Jackson approached the car.

"Don't even know if she's here," Jackson lied. "Do you have a key? We want to take a look around."

Kate fumbled in her purse for a moment, then silently handed Jackson a single key on a ring. "Stay here," Jackson ordered. He started back to the house, wondering what he was supposed to have been looking for. Whatever it was, he hadn't seen it—all he'd seen were two kids who'd had a horrible experience only a few days ago, and were now very frightened.

"Well?"

Jackson shrugged. "She just gave me the key when I asked for it. Asked if the Benson woman's okay."

"What'd you say?"

"I lied. Figured we should both be there when we tell them."

Finnerty nodded, and slid the key into the lock, then pushed the door open and led his partner into the silent house. One look at Valerie Benson's open eyes and grimace of frozen terror told him she was dead. He called the station and told the duty officer what had happened, then rejoined Jackson. "Might as well tell them."

From then on, the long night took on a feeling of eerie familiarity, as Finnerty replayed the scene he'd gone through less than a week earlier when the same two kids had found the body of Martha Lewis.

The dusty road wound steadily up the hill, and Alex looked neither to the left nor to the right. He knew every inch of these hills, for he'd ridden over them with his father ever since he was a little boy. Now, though, he walked, for along with his father's land, the *gringos* had taken the horses as well. Indeed, they'd taken everything, even his name.

Still, he hadn't left La Paloma—would never leave La Paloma until finally the *gringos* had paid with their lives for the lives they had taken.

He came to a house, opened the gate, and stepped through into the patio. Not too long ago he'd been in this patio as an honored guest, with his parents and his sisters, attending a *fiesta*. Now he was here for another reason.

For a few *centavos*, the new owners would let him take care of the plants in their patio. Idly he wondered what they would do if they knew who he really was.

As he worked, he kept a watchful eye on the house, and one by one the people left, until he knew that the woman was alone. Then he went to the front door, lifted the heavy knocker, and let it fall back against its plate. The door opened, and the woman stood in the cool gloom of the foyer, looking at him uncertainly.

He reached out and put his hands around her neck.

As he began squeezing her life away, he felt her terror, felt all the emotions that racked her spirit. He felt her die, and began to sweat. . . .

He woke up with a start, and sat up. The dream ended, but Alex could still see the face of the woman he'd strangled, and his body was damp with the memory of fear.

And he knew the woman in the dream.

It was Valerie Benson.

But who was he?

The memory of the dream was clear in his mind, and he went over it piece by piece.

The road hadn't been paved. It had been a dirt road, and yet it hadn't seemed strange to him.

And he didn't have a name.

They'd stolen his name.

He knew who "they" were, just as he knew why he'd strangled Valerie Benson.

His parents were dead, and he was taking vengeance on the people who had killed them.

But it still made no sense, for his parents were asleep in their room down the hall.

Or were they?

More and more, the line between what was real and what was not was becoming indistinct.

More and more the odd memories of things that couldn't be were becoming more real than the unfamiliar world he lived in.

Perhaps, that very night, he had killed his parents, and now had no memory of it. He glanced at the clock by the bed; the fluorescent hands read eleven-thirty. He had been in bed only half an hour. There hadn't been enough time for him to go to sleep, then wake up, kill his parents, go back to sleep, then dream about it.

He went back over the evening, step by step, and all of it was perfectly clear in his memory, except for one brief moment. He'd parked across the street from Jake's when María Torres had spoken to him.

Spoken to him in Spanish.

The next thing he remembered was going into Jake's, and that, too, was very clear: he'd gotten out of the car, locked it, and walked from the parking lot into the pizza place.

The parking lot.

He distinctly remembered parking his car on the street across from the pizza parlor, but he also remembered entering Jake's from the parking lot, which was next to the restaurant.

The two memories were in direct conflict, but were equally as strong. There must, therefore, have been two events involved. He must have gone to Jake's twice.

He was still trying to make sense out of his memories, and tie them to the dream, when he heard the wailing of a siren in the distance. Then there was another sound, as the telephone began to ring.

Alex got out of bed and put on his robe, then went down the hall to his parents' room. Though their voices were muffled by the closed door, he could still make out the words.

"They don't know," he heard his father say. "All they know is that they're bringing her in, and that they think she's a DOA."

"If you're going down there, I'm going with you," his mother replied. "And don't try to argue with me. Valerie and I have been friends all our lives. I want to be there."

"Honey, neither of us is going anywhere. I'm not on call tonight, remember? They called because they knew Valerie was a friend of ours."

Slowly Alex backed away from the closed door and returned to his own room.

Valerie. He searched his memory, hoping there was another Valerie there, but there wasn't. It had to be Valerie Benson, and she was dead.

Then, though he had no conscious memory of it at all, he knew why he had arrived at Jake's twice.

He'd gone there once, and then left. After María Torres had spoken to him in Spanish, he'd driven away and gone to Valerie Benson's house, and he'd killed her. Then he'd gone back to Jake's, and sat down at the table with Kate and Bob and Lisa, and talked for a while.

And then he'd come home and gone to bed and dreamed about what he'd done.

But he still didn't know why.

His parents were still alive, and he'd hardly even known Valerie Benson. He had no reason to kill her.

And yet he had.

He got back in bed, and lay for a while staring up at the ceiling in the darkness. Somewhere in his mind he was sure there were answers, and if he thought about the problem long enough, he would figure out what those answers were.

He heard a door open and close, then footsteps in the hall. It was his mother. He heard her going downstairs, then, a little later, he heard his father following her.

For a few minutes he toyed with the idea of going downstairs himself, and telling them about his dream, and that he was sure he'd killed Valerie Benson, and probably Mrs. Lewis too. But then he rejected the whole idea. Unless he could tell them why he'd killed the two women, they surely wouldn't believe he'd done it.

Instead, they'd just think he was crazy.

Alex turned over and pulled the covers snugly around him. He let his mind run free.

And, as he was sure they would, the connections began to come together, and he began to understand what was happening to him.

A few minutes later, he was sound asleep. Through the rest of the night his sleep was undisturbed.

"I'm telling you, Tom, the kids did it," Roscoe Finnerty said as he and Jackson sat in the police station the next morning.

Neither of them had had any sleep, and all Tom Jackson really wanted to do was go home and go to bed, but if Finnerty wanted to talk—and Finnerty usually

did—the least he could do was listen. In fact, with
Finnerty, listening was all he really had to do, since
Finnerty was as capable of posing the questions as he
was of coming up with the answers.

"Lookit," Finnerty was saying now. "We got two
killings, same M.O. And we got the same two kids
discovering both bodies. What could be simpler? And
don't tell me there's no previous record of trouble with
these kids. They were both up at that bash last spring,
when the Lonsdale kid smashed up his car, and they
were both drunk—"

"Now, wait a minute, Roscoe," Jackson interrupted.
"Let's at least be fair. Did you give any of those kids a
test?"

"Well, no, but—"

"Then don't tell me you're going to stand up in court
and tell a judge they were drunk, 'cause you ain't! Now,
why don't we just go home and let the plainclothes guys
do their job?"

Finnerty stared at his partner over the edge of his
coffee cup for several long seconds. "You think we
ought to just forget it?"

Jackson sighed, and stretched his tired muscles. "I'm
not saying to forget it. I'm just saying we've got a job to
do, and I think we oughta do it, and not butt in where
we aren't invited."

"And leave that poor drunken slob locked up for
something he obviously didn't do."

"Whoa up, buddy!" Jackson said, deciding that enough
was enough. "You forgetting that the two events might
not be connected at all? That we just might have two
different perps here?"

"Oh, sure. Both of them apparently let into the house
by the victims, and both of them strangled. And both of
them discovered by the same girl, who happens to live
in the houses where the crimes are committed. You ask
me, that's just a bit too much."

"So what are you suggesting?" Jackson asked, knowing full well that whatever it was, it wasn't going to involve going home and going to bed.

"For openers, I think we might have a talk with the other kids that were down at Jake's last night, and see if they noticed anything funny about their friends."

Her eyes puffy from lack of sleep, Carol Cochran stared at the two policemen on the front porch, then glanced at her watch. Though it was a few minutes past seven, it felt much earlier. But despite her exhaustion, she was sure she knew why they were here.

"It's about Valerie Benson, isn't it?" she asked.

The two officers exchanged a glance, then Finnerty nodded. "I'm afraid so. We . . . well, we'd like to talk to your daughter."

Carol blinked. What on earth were they talking about? What could Lisa have to do with what had happened to Valerie? "I . . . I'm sorry," she stammered, "but I don't know what you're talking about." Jim, she thought. Call Jim. He'll know what to do. As if he'd heard her thought, her husband emerged from the kitchen.

"Something wrong, honey?" she heard him ask, and managed to nod her head.

"They . . . they want to talk to Lisa . . ."

Jim Cochran stepped out onto the porch, pulling the door closed behind him. "Now, what's this all about?" he asked. As briefly as they could, Finnerty and Jackson explained why they were there.

Reluctantly Jim invited them into the living room and asked them to sit down. "If she wants to talk to you, it's all right," he said. "But she doesn't have to, you know."

"I know," Finnerty replied. "Believe me, Mr. Cochran, we don't suspect her of anything. All we want to know is if she noticed anything last night."

"I find it impossible to believe that Kate Lewis and Bob Carey would kill anyone," Jim said, his voice tight. "Let alone two people."

"I know, sir," Finnerty said. "But I'd still like to talk to your daughter, if you don't mind."

"What is it?" Carol asked when Jim came into the kitchen a moment later. Jim glanced around the room, but only his wife and older daughter were there. Kim was nowhere to be seen. "I sent Kim up to her room and told her not to come down again until I came up for her. Now, what do they want?"

"It's crazy, if you ask me," Jim replied. "For some reason, they think maybe Kate and Bob killed Valerie, and they want to talk to Lisa about what happened last night. They want to know if she noticed anything strange about either one of them."

"Oh, God," Carol groaned. She sank into a chair, her fingers suddenly twisting at the tie of her bathrobe. Lisa, her eyes wide, was shaking her head in disbelief.

"They think Kate killed Mrs. Benson?" she asked. "That's the dumbest thing I ever heard."

"I know, sweetheart," Jim said. "It doesn't seem possible, but apparently that's what they think. And you don't have to talk to them if you don't want to."

But Lisa stood up. "No," she said. "It's all right. I'll talk to them. And I'll tell them just what a dumb idea they've come up with."

She went into the living room, and the two officers rose to their feet, but before they could speak, Lisa began talking.

"Kate and Bob didn't do anything," she said. "And if you want me to say they were acting funny last night, I won't. They were acting just like they always act, except that Kate was a little quieter than usual."

"Nobody's saying anyone did anything, Lisa," Finnerty interjected. "We're just trying to find out what happened, and if the kids could have had any part in it at all."

"Well, they couldn't," Lisa replied. "And I know why you're asking questions about them. It's those kids in Marin, isn't it?"

Finnerty swallowed, and nodded.

"Well, they were creeps. They were doing drugs all the time, and drinking, and all that kind of stuff. And Bob and Kate aren't like that at all."

"Honey, take it easy," Jim Cochran said, stepping into the room and putting his arm around his daughter. "They just want to ask some questions. If you don't want to answer them, you don't have to, but don't try to keep them from doing their job."

As Lisa turned to gaze into her father's eyes, her indignation dissolved into tears. "But, Daddy, it's so awful. Why would they think Kate and Bob would do such a thing?"

"I don't know," Jim admitted. "And maybe they don't. Now, do you want to talk to them, or not?"

Lisa hesitated, then nodded, and dabbed at her eyes with the handkerchief her father handed her. "I'm sorry," she apologized. "But nothing happened last night."

"All right," Finnerty said, taking out his notebook. "Let's start with that."

Slowly Lisa reconstructed the events of the evening before. She'd gone to Jake's by herself, and, as usual, a lot of the kids had been there. Then, when Bob and Kate came in, the three of them had taken a table together, and sat sipping Cokes and talking about nothing in particular. Then Alex Lonsdale had joined them for a while, and eventually they had all left.

"And there wasn't anything odd about Kate or Bob? They didn't seem nervous, or worried, or anything?"

Lisa's eyes narrowed. "If you mean did they act like they'd just killed someone, no, they didn't. In fact, when they left, Kate even wondered if they ought to call Mrs. Benson and tell her they were on their way." Then, when she saw the two policemen exchange a glance, she spoke again. "And don't try to make anything out of that, either. Kate always called her mom if she was going to be late. She always said her mom had enough to worry about with her dad being a drunk and shouldn't have to worry about her, too."

Finnerty closed his notebook and stood up. "All right,"

he said. "I guess that's it, if you can't think of anything else—anything out of the ordinary at all."

Lisa hesitated, and once more Finnerty and Jackson exchanged a glance.

"Is there something?" Jim asked.

"I . . . I don't know," Lisa replied.

"It doesn't matter what it is," Finnerty told her, reopening his notepad.

"But it doesn't have anything to do with Kate and Bob," Lisa said.

Jackson frowned. "Then what does it have to do with? One of the other kids?"

Again Lisa hesitated, then nodded. "With . . . with Alex Lonsdale," she said.

"What about Alex?" Jim asked. "It's all right, honey. Just tell us what happened with Alex."

"Well, nothing, really," Lisa said. "Ever since the accident, he's so strange, but last night he said he was getting better, and for a while I thought he was. I mean, he was smiling, and he laughed at jokes, and he seemed almost . . . well, almost like he used to be." She fell silent, and Finnerty finally asked her what, exactly, had happened.

"I don't know," Lisa confessed. "But finally Bob started teasing Alex about something, and Alex didn't blush."

"That's all?" Finnerty asked. "The strange thing was that he *didn't blush?*"

Lisa nodded. "Alex always used to blush. In fact, some of the kids used to say things to him just to watch him get embarrassed. But last night, even though he was smiling, and laughing, and all that, he still wasn't blushing."

"I see," Finnerty said. He closed his notebook for the last time and slid his pencil back in his pocket. A few minutes later, when they were outside, he turned to Jackson. "Well, what do you think?"

"I still think we're barking up the wrong tree," Jackson replied. "But I guess we might as well have a talk with the Lonsdale boy."

"Yeah," Finnerty agreed. Then he rolled his eyes. "Kids amaze me," he said. "They spend a whole evening together, and the only odd thing the girl can remember is that her boyfriend didn't blush. Isn't that something?"

Jackson frowned. "Maybe it *is* important," he said. "Maybe it's very important."

CHAPTER TWENTY-ONE

Marsh Lonsdale sat listening as the two officers interviewed Alex about the events of the night before, but found himself concentrating much more on the manner in which his son spoke than on the words themselves. They were in the living room, gathered around the fireplace, and at the far end—huddled alone in a chair as if she wanted to divorce herself from everything—Ellen seemed not to be listening at all.

"Everything," Finnerty had said an hour ago. "We want you to tell us everything you remember about last night, just the way you remember it."

And ever since, Alex had been speaking, his voice steady and expressionless, recounting what he remembered of his activities the night before, from the time he left the house to go to Jake's, to the moment he returned. It was, Marsh realized, almost like listening to a tape recorder. Alex remembered what everyone had said, and repeated it verbatim. After the first twenty minutes, both Finnerty and Jackson had stopped taking notes, and were now simply sitting, listening. When, at last, Alex's recitation was over, there was a long silence, then Roscoe Finnerty got to his feet and went to the mantel. Resting most of his weight on the heavy oak beam that ran the width of the fireplace, he gazed curiously at Alex.

"You really remember all that?" he asked at last.

Alex nodded.

"In that kind of detail?" Finnerty mused aloud.

"His memory is remarkable," Marsh said, speaking for the first time since the interview had begun. "It seems to be a function of the brain surgery that was done after his accident. If he says he remembers all of what he just told you, then you can believe he does."

Finnerty nodded. "I'm not doubting it," he said. "I'm just amazed at the detail, that's all." He turned back to Alex. "You've told us everything that happened at Jake's, and you've told us everything everyone said. But what I want to know is if you noticed anything about Kate Lewis and Bob Carey. Did they act . . . well, *normal?*"

Alex gazed steadily at Finnerty. "I don't know," he said. "I don't really know what normal is anymore. What you're asking me to do is describe how they appeared to be feeling, but I can't do that, since I don't have feelings anymore. I had them before the accident—or at least everyone says I did—but since the accident I don't. But they acted just like they always have." Suddenly he grinned uncomfortably. "Bob was teasing me a little."

"I know," Tom Jackson said. "Your girlfriend told us about that. And she said you didn't blush."

"I don't think I can blush. I might be able to learn how, but I haven't yet."

"Learn how?" Jackson echoed blankly. "But you just *smiled.*"

Alex glanced at his father, and Marsh nodded. "I've been practicing. I'm not like other people, so I'm practicing being like other people. It seemed like I ought to grin before I admitted that Bob was teasing me, so I did."

"Okay," Finnerty said, staring at the boy and feeling chilled. "Is there anything else you remember? Anything at all?"

Alex hesitated, then shook his head. A few minutes later, Finnerty and Jackson were gone.

"Alex?" Marsh asked. "Is there something else you remember about last night that you didn't tell them?"

Once again, Alex shook his head. Everything he remembered, he'd told them about. But they hadn't asked him if he knew who killed Valerie Benson. If they had, he would have told them, though he wouldn't have been able to tell them why she died, or why Mrs. Lewis died, either. But when he'd awakened this morning, the last pieces had fallen into place, and it had all come together in his mind. He understood his brain now, and soon he would understand exactly what had happened.

He would understand what had happened, and he would know who he was.

"Why, Alex," Arlette Pringle said, her plain features lighting up with a smile, "you're becoming quite a regular here, aren't you?"

"I need some more information, Miss Pringle," Alex replied. "I need to know more about the town."

"La Paloma?" Miss Pringle asked, her voice doubtful. "I'm afraid I just don't have much. I have the book I showed you a couple of days ago, but that's about it." She shrugged ruefully. "I'm afraid not much ever happened here. Nothing worth writing about, anyway."

"But there has to be something," Alex pressed. "Something about the old days, when the town was mostly Mexican."

"Mexican," Arlette repeated, her lips pursing thoughtfully as her fingers tapped on her desktop. "I'm afraid I just don't know exactly what you want. I have some information about the Franciscan fathers, and the missions, but I'm not sure there's much that's specifically about *our* mission. La Paloma just wasn't that important."

"What about when the Americans came?"

Again Arlette shrugged. "Not that I know of. Of course, there are the old stories, but I don't pay any attention to them, and I don't think they're written down anywhere."

"What stories?"

"Oh, some of the older Chicanos in town still talk about the old days, when Don Roberto de Meléndez y Ruiz still had the hacienda, and about what happened after the treaty was signed." She leaned forward, and her voice dropped confidentially. "Supposedly there was a massacre up there."

Alex frowned slightly, as a vague memory stirred on the edges of his consciousness. "At the hacienda?"

"That's what they say. But of course, the stories have been passed down through the generations, and I don't suppose there's much truth to any of them, really. But if you really want to know about them, why don't you go see Mrs. Torres?"

"María?" Alex asked, his voice suddenly hollow. For the first time since his operation, a pang of genuine fear crashed through the barriers in his mind, and he felt himself tremble. It fit. It fit perfectly with the idea that had begun forming in his mind last night, then come to fruition this morning.

Arlette Pringle nodded. "That's right. She still lives around the corner in a little house behind the mission. You tell her I sent you, but I warn you, once she starts talking, she won't stop." She wrote an address on a slip of paper and handed it to Alex. "Now, don't believe everything she says," she cautioned as Alex was about to leave the library. "Don't forget, she's old, and she's always been very bitter. I can't say I blame her, really, but still, it's best not to put too much stock in her stories. I'm afraid a lot of them have been terribly exaggerated."

Alex left the library, and glanced at the address on the scrap of paper, then crumpled it and threw it into a trash bin. A few minutes later he was a block and a half away, his eyes fixed on a tiny frame house that seemed on the verge of falling in on itself.

Home.

The word flashed into his mind, and images of the little house tumbled over one another. He knew, with all the certainty of a lifetime of memories, that he had come home. He pushed his way through the broken gate and made his way up onto the sagging porch. He knocked at the front door, then waited. As he was about to knock again, the door opened a crack, and the ancient eyes of María Torres peered out at him.

A sigh drifted from her throat, and she opened the door wider.

"M-Mama?" Alex stammered uncertainly.

María gazed at him for a moment, then slowly shook her head. "No," she said softly. "You are not my son. You are someone else. What do you want?"

"M-Miss Pringle sent me." Alex faltered. "She said you might be able to tell me what happened here a long time ago."

There was a long silence while she seemed to consider his words. "You want to know?" she asked at last, her eyes narrowing to slits. "But you already know. You are Alejandro."

Alex frowned, suddenly certain that the familiar searing pain was about to rip through his mind and that the voices were about to start whispering to him. He could almost feel them, niggling around the edges of his consciousness. Doggedly he fought against them. "I . . . I just want to know what happened a long time ago," he managed to repeat.

María Torres fell silent once more, regarding him thoughtfully. At last she nodded. "You are Alejandro," she said again. "You should know what happened." She held the door wide, and Alex stepped through into the eerily familiar confines of a tiny living room furnished only with a threadbare couch, a sagging easy chair, and a Formica-topped table surrounded by four worn dining chairs.

All of it was exactly as it had been in his memories a few moments before.

The shades were drawn, but from one corner a color television suffused the room with an eerie light. Its sound was muted.

"For company," the old woman muttered. "I don't listen, but I watch." She lowered herself carefully into the easy chair, and Alex sat gingerly on the edge of the sofa. "What stories you want to hear?"

"The thieves," Alex said quietly. "Tell me about the thieves and the murderers."

María Torres's eyes flashed darkly in the dim light. "*Por qué?*" she demanded. "Why do you want to know now?"

"I remember things," Alex said. "I remember things that happened, and I want to know more about them."

"What things?" The old woman was leaning forward now, her eyes fixed intently on Alex.

"Fernando," Alex said. "Tío Fernando. He's buried in San Francisco, at the mission."

María's eyes widened momentarily, then she nodded, and let herself sag back in the chair once again. "*Su tío*," she muttered. "*Sí, es la verdad . . .*"

"The truth?" Alex asked. "What's the truth?"

Once again the old woman's eyes brightened. "*Habla usted español?*"

"I . . . I don't know," Alex said. "But I understood what you said."

The old lady fell silent again, and examined Alex closely through her bleary eyes. In the light of the television set, his features were indistinct, and yet, she realized, the coloring was right. His hair was dark, and his eyes were blue, just as her grandfather had told her Don Roberto's had been, and as his own had been. Making up her mind, she nodded emphatically.

"Sí," she muttered. "*Es la verdad. Don Alejando ha regresado . . .*"

"Tell me the stories," Alex said again. "Please just tell me the stories."

"They stole," María said finally. "They came and they stole our lands, and murdered our people. They went up into the canyons first, and murdered the wives of the overseers while the men were out on the land. Then they went to the hacienda and took Don Roberto away and hanged him."

Alex frowned. "The tree," he said. "They hanged him from the big tree."

"Sí," María agreed. "And then they went back to the hacienda, and they killed his family. They killed Doña María, and Isabella, and Estellita. And they would have killed Alejandro, too, if they had found him."

"Alejandro?" Alex asked.

"*El hijo,*" María Torres said softly. "The son of Don Roberto de Meléndez y Ruiz. Doña María told them she had sent him to Sonora, and they believed her. But he stayed. He hid in the mission with his uncle, who was the priest, and they fled to San Francisco. And then, when Padre Fernando died, Alejandro returned to La Paloma."

"Why?" Alex asked. "Why did he come back?"

María Torres stared at him for a long time. When she spoke, her voice was barely audible, but nonetheless her words seemed to fill the room. "*Venganza,*" she said. "He came for vengeance on the thieves and the murderers. Even when he was dying, he said he would never leave. From beyond the grave, he said. From beyond the grave, *venganza.*"

Alex emerged from the little house into the blazing sun of the September morning. He began walking through the village, pausing here and there, turning over the bits and pieces of the story María Torres had told him, examining them carefully, searching for the flaw. His mind told him that the answer he had come up with was impossible, but still the pieces of the story matched his strange memories too well. He knew, though, where he would fin the ultimate truth, and what he would do once he found it.

The phone on his desk jangled loudly. For a moment Marsh was tempted to let it ring. Then he realized the call was coming in on his private line. Only a few people knew that number, and even they used it only when it was an emergency.

"I trust you aren't going to force me to implement the provisions of the release," Raymond Torres's cold voice said.

"How did you get this number?"

"I've had this number since the moment I took on your son's case, Dr. Lonsdale. Not that it matters. The only thing that matters is that your wife was to bring Alex to me today."

"I'm afraid that won't be possible, Dr. Torres," Marsh replied. "We've discussed the matter, and it's my decision that you can do Alex no more good. I'm afraid he won't be coming back there anymore."

There was a long silence, and when Torres's voice finally came over the line again, its tone had hardened even further. "And I'm afraid that's not your decision to make, Dr. Lonsdale."

"Nonetheless," Marsh replied, "that's the decision I've made. And I wouldn't advise you to try to come and get him, or have anyone else try to come and get him either. I'm his father, Dr. Torres, and despite your release, I have some rights."

"I see," Torres said, and Marsh thought he heard a sigh come through the phone. "Very well, I'm willing to strike a compromise with you. Bring Alex down this afternoon, and I will explain to you exactly what my procedures have been up until now, and why I think it's necessary that he come back to the Institute."

"Not a chance. Until I know exactly what you've done, you won't see Alex again."

In the privacy of his office, Raymond Torres slumped tiredly behind his desk. Too many hours of too little sleep had finally taken their toll, and he knew he was no longer thinking clearly. But he also knew that letting Alex leave the Institute yesterday had been a mistake. Whatever the consequences, he had to get him back.

"Very well," he said. "What time can I expect you?"

Marsh glanced at his appointment book. "A couple of hours?"

"Fine. And after you've heard what I have to say, I'm sure you'll agree that Alex should be back here." The line went dead in Marsh's hand.

Alex paused at the garden gate, and stared at the high vine-covered wall that separated the patio from the street. Then, making up his mind, he went into the patio, then into the house. The house, as he had hoped it would be, was empty. He went to the garage and began searching through the mound of boxes that still sat, unpacked, against the back wall. Each of them was neatly marked with its contents, and it didn't take him long to find the two he was looking for.

The hedge clippers were at the bottom of the first box. As Alex worked them loose from the tangle of other tools, he wondered if he was doing the right thing. And yet, he had to know. The vines covering the garden wall were part of the pattern, and he had to see for himself if he was right.

The book, after all, might have been wrong.

The clippers in hand, he left the garage and walked down the driveway to the sidewalk. Then, working slowly and deliberately, he began cutting the vines off as close to the ground as the strength in his arms and the thickness of the trunks would allow. He worked his way slowly up the hill until the last stems had been cut; then, going the other way, he tore the thickly matted vegetation loose, letting it pile on the sidewalk at his feet. When he was done, he stepped back and looked at the wall once more.

Though it was covered with the collected dust and dirt of the years, and its whitewash had long since disappeared, the tiles remained.

The wall looked exactly as he had thought it should look when he had first come home from the Institute.

He went back into the garage and opened the second box. His father's shotgun was on top, neatly packed away in its case. He opened the case and methodically began putting the pieces together. When the gun was fully assembled, he took five shells from a half-full box of ammunition and put them in his pocket. Carrying the gun easily in the crook of his right arm, he left the garage and walked once more down the driveway, then turned to the right and started the long climb up toward the hacienda. . . .

It had been a bad morning for Ellen, and as she started up Hacienda Drive she was beginning to wonder if she was going to get through the next few days at all.

She'd spent most of the morning with Carol Cochran, and none of it had been easy. Part of the time they'd simply cried, and part of the time they'd tried to make plans for Valerie Benson's funeral. And over it all hung the question of who had killed Valerie.

And then there had been Carol's oddly phrased questions about Alex:

"But is he really getting better? I mean, Lisa keeps telling me about strange things he says."

"No, I don't really remember what"—though Ellen was quite sure she did, and simply didn't want to tell her. "But Lisa really seems very worried. In fact, I think she's just a little frightened of Alex."

Ellen had become increasingly certain that after Valerie's funeral, the Cochrans and the Lonsdales would be seeing a lot less of each other.

She came around the last curve, swinging wide to pull into the driveway, when she suddenly slammed on the brakes. Piled on the sidewalk, nearly blocking the driveway itself, lay the ruins of the masses of morning glory that had covered the patio wall only two hours ago.

"I don't believe it," she whispered aloud, though she was alone in the car. Suddenly the sound of a horn yanked her attention away from the tangle of vines, and she jerkily pulled into the driveway to make room for the car that was coming down the hill. She sat numbly behind the wheel for a moment, then got out of the car and walked back down the drive to stare once more at the mess on the sidewalk.

Who would do such a thing? It made no sense—no sense whatever. It would take years for the vines to grow back. She surveyed the wall, slowly taking in the streaked and stained expanse of plaster, and the intricate patterns of tile that were now all that broke its forbidding expanse. And then, behind her, a voice spoke. Startled, she turned to see one of the neighbors standing on the sidewalk looking glumly at the vines. Ellen's mind suddenly blanked and she had to grope for the woman's name. Then it came back to her. Sheila. Sheila Rosenberg.

"Sheila," she said. Then, her bewilderment showing in her voice: "Look at this. Just look at it!"

Sheila smiled ruefully. "That's kids," she said.

Ellen's expression suddenly hardened. "Kids? Kids did this?"

Now it was Sheila Rosenberg who seemed at a loss. "I meant leave the job half-done." She sighed. "Well, I suppose you know what you're doing, but I'm going to miss the vines, especially in the summer. The colors were always so incredible—"

"What *I'm* doing?" Ellen asked. "Sheila, what on earth are you talking about?"

Finally the smile faded from Sheila's face. "Alex," she said. "Didn't you ask him to cut the vines down?"

Alex? Ellen thought. Alex did this? But . . . but why? Once again she surveyed the wall, and this time her eyes came to rest on the tiles. "Sheila," she asked, "did you know that wall had tiles inlaid in it?"

The other woman shook her head. "Who could know? Those vines were two feet thick, at least. No one's seen the wall itself for years." Her eyes scanned the wall, and her brows furrowed speculatively. "But you know, maybe you did the right thing. If you put in smaller plants, and maybe some trellises, it could be very pretty."

"Sheila, I didn't ask Alex to cut down those vines. Are you sure it was him?"

Sheila stared at her for a moment, then nodded her head firmly. "Absolutely. Do you think I would have let a stranger do it? I saw him a couple of hours ago, and then I got busy with something else. The next time I looked, the vines were all down, and Alex was gone. I thought he must be having lunch or something."

Ellen's gaze shifted to the house. "Maybe that's what he's doing," she said, though she didn't believe it. For some reason, she was sure that Alex was not in the house. "Thanks, Sheila," she said abstractedly. "I . . . well, I guess I'd better find out what's going on." Leaving Sheila Rosenberg standing on the sidewalk, she went through the patio into the house. "Alex? Alex, are you here?"

She was still listening to the silence of the house when the phone began ringing, and she snatched the receiver off the hook and spoke without thinking. "Alex? Alex, is that you?"

There was a moment of silence, and then Marsh's voice came over the line. "Ellen, has something else happened?"

Something else? Ellen thought. My best friends are being murdered, and I don't know what's happening to my son, and you want to know if something else is wrong? At that particular moment, she decided, she hated her husband. When she spoke, though, her voice was eerily calm. "Not really," she said. "It's just that for some reason Alex cut all the vines off the patio wall."

Again there was a silence; then: "Alex is supposed to be at school."

"I know that," Ellen replied. "But apparently he isn't. Apparently he left school—if he even went—and came home and cut down the vines. And now he's gone. Don't ask me where, because I don't know."

In his office, Marsh listened more to the tone of his wife's voice than to her words, and knew that she was on the edge of coming apart.

"Take it easy," he said. "Just sit down and take it easy. I'm on my way home to get you, and then we're going down to Palo Alto."

"Palo Alto?" Ellen asked vacantly. "Why?"

"Torres has agreed to talk to us," Marsh replied. "He'll tell us what's happening to Alex."

Ellen nodded to herself. "But what about Alex?" she asked. "Shouldn't we try to find him?"

"We will," Marsh assured her. "By the time we get back from Palo Alto, he'll probably be home."

"What . . . what if he's not?"

"Then we'll find him."

Now, Ellen thought. We should find him now. But the words wouldn't come. Too much was happening, and too much was closing in on her.

And maybe, she thought, as she sat waiting for Marsh to come for her, maybe finally Raymond would be able to convince Marsh to let him help Alex.

Half a mile away, on the hill above the hacienda, Alex, too, was waiting.

He wasn't yet sure what he was waiting for, but he knew that whatever it was, he was prepared for it.

In his arms, cradled carefully against his chest, was the now loaded shotgun.

CHAPTER TWENTY-TWO

Cynthia Evans glanced nervously at her watch. She was running late, and she hated to run late. But if she hurried, she could get the shopping done, swing by the school and pick up Carolyn, and still be home in time for her three-thirty appointment with the gardener. She pulled the front door closed behind her, and moved quickly toward the BMW that stood just inside the gates to the courtyard. As she was about to get into the car, a flash of reflected sunlight caught her eyes, and she looked up onto the hillside that rose beyond the hacienda walls.

He was still sitting there, as he had been since a little past noon.

She knew who it was—it was Alex Lonsdale. She'd determined that much when she'd first seen him, then gotten her husband's binoculars to take a better look. If it had been a stranger, she would have called the police immediately, especially after what had happened to Valerie Benson last night. But to call the police on Alex was another matter. Alex—and Ellen as well—had had enough troubles lately, without her adding to them. If he wanted to sit in the hills, he probably had his reasons.

Even so, she was starting to get annoyed. When they bought the hacienda, why had they not bought the surrounding acreage as well? It was far too easy for people to climb up the hillside and gaze down over the walls, as Alex had done today, invading the privacy they had spent so much money to achieve. For a moment Cynthia was tempted to call the police anyway, and to hell with the Lonsdales' feelings. The only reason she didn't, in fact, was the time.

She was running late, and she hated to run late.

She started the BMW, put it in gear, and raced out of the courtyard and down Hacienda Drive, not even taking the time to make sure the security gates had closed behind her.

Alex watched the car disappear from sight, and knew the house was empty now. He rose to his feet and began scrambling down the hill, holding the shotgun in his left hand, using his right to steady himself on the steep slope. Five minutes later he was at the gates, staring into the courtyard.

The gates were wrong.

They should have been wooden. He remembered them as being made of massive oaken planks, held together by wide wrought-iron straps ending in immense hinges.

And the courtyard itself wasn't right, either. There should be no pool, and instead of the flagstone paving, there should only be packed earth, swept of its dust by the *peones* each day. Silently, his memories coming clearer, Alex moved through the gates, across the courtyard, and into the house.

Here, things were better. The rooms looked as he remembered them, and there was a comforting familiarity. He wandered through them slowly, until he came to the room that had been his. He had been happy when he had lived in this room, and the house had been filled with his parents and his sisters, and everyone else who lived on the hacienda.

Before the *gringos* came.

Los ladrones. Los ladrones y los asesinos.

The pain that always filled him when the memories came surged through him now, and he left the room on the second floor and continued moving through the house.

In the kitchen, nothing was right. The old fireplace was there, but the cooking kettle was gone, and there were new things that had never been there in the old days. He left the kitchen and went back to the foyer.

He stopped, frowning.

There was a new door, a door he had never seen before. He hesitated, then opened it.

There were stairs down into a cellar.

His house had never had a cellar.

Clutching the gun tighter, he descended the stairs, and gazed around him.

All along the wall, there was a mirror, and in front of the mirror, on glass shelves, were masses of bottles and glasses.

All of it wrong, all of it belonging to the thieves.

Raising the shotgun, Alex fired into the mirror.

The mirror exploded, and shards of glass flew everywhere, then the shelves of glasses and bottles collapsed on themselves. A moment later, all that was left was wreckage.

Alex turned away, and started back up the stairs. He would wait in the courtyard for the murderers, as his mother and sisters had waited before.

Now, at last, he would have his vengeance. . . .

"Darling, how would I know why Alex was up there? All he was doing was sitting, looking down at the house."

"Well, you should have called the police," Carolyn complained. "Everybody knows Alex is crazy."

Cynthia shot her daughter a reproving glance. "Carolyn, that's unkind."

"It's true," Carolyn replied. "Mom, I'm telling you—he's acting weirder and weirder all the time. And Lisa says he told her he didn't think Mr. Lewis killed Mrs. Lewis and that he thought someone else was going to get killed. And look what happened to Mrs. Benson last night."

Cynthia turned left up Hacienda Drive. "If you're trying to tell me you think Alex killed them, I don't want to hear it. Ellen Lonsdale is a friend of mine—"

"What's that got to do with anything? I don't care if she's the nicest person in the world—Alex is a fruitcake!"

"That's enough, Carolyn!"

"Aw, come on, Mom—"

"No! I'm tired of the way you talk about people, and I won't hear any more of it." Then, remembering her own impulse just before she'd left the house an hour ago, she softened. "Tell you what. You promise not to talk about him like that anymore, and I promise to call the police if he's still there when we get back. Okay?"

Carolyn shrugged elaborately, and they drove on up the ravine in silence. They came around the last curve, and as Cynthia scanned the hillside, she heard Carolyn groaning.

"Now what's wrong?"

"The gates," Carolyn said. "If I'd left them open, you'd ground me for a week."

Cynthia swore under her breath, then reminded herself that she'd only been gone an hour, and it was the middle of the afternoon. Besides, the courtyard was empty. She drove inside and got out of the car. "Well, at least we don't have to call the police," she observed, her eyes scanning the hills once more. "He's gone."

"Thieves," a soft voice hissed from the shadows of the wide loggia in front of the house. "Murderers."

Cynthia froze.

"Who . . . who's there?" she asked.

"Oh, God," she heard Carolyn whimper. "It's Alex. Mama, it's Alex."

"Quiet," Cynthia said softly. "Just don't say anything, Carolyn. Everything will be all right." Then, her voice louder: "Alex? Is that you?"

Alex stepped out of the shadows, the shotgun held firmly in his hands. "I am Alejandro," he whispered.

His face was dripping blood from a cut above his left eye, and his shirt was stained darkly from another on his shoulder, but if he felt any pain, he gave no sign. Instead he walked slowly forward.

"There," he said, gesturing with the gun toward the south wall. "Over there."

"Do as he says, Carolyn," Cynthia said softly. "Just do as he says, and everything will be all right."

"But he's crazy, Mama!"

"Hush! Just be quiet, and do as he says." She waited for what seemed like an aeon, praying that Carolyn wouldn't try to get back in the car or bolt toward the gates. Then, out of the corner of her eye, she saw her daughter begin to move slowly around the end of the car until she was standing at her side. Cynthia took the girl's hand in her own. "We'll do exactly as he says," she said again. "If we do as he says, he won't hurt us."

Slowly, keeping her eyes fixed on Alex, she began backing around, pulling Carolyn with her. "What is it, Alex?" she asked. "What do you want?"

"*Venganza*," Alex whispered. "*Venganza para mi familia.*"

"Your family, Alex?"

Alex nodded. "*Sí.*" Again he began moving forward, backing Cynthia and Carolyn Evans slowly toward the wall.

He could see the wall as it had been that day, even though they'd plastered over the damage and tried to wash away the blood of his family. But the pits from the bullets were still there, and the red stains were as

bright as they had been on the day he'd watched his
family die.

And now, the moment was finally at hand.

He wondered if the *gringa* woman would face death
with the bravery of his mother, crying out her defiance
even as the bullets cut the life out of her.

He knew she wouldn't.

She would die a *gringa's* death, begging for mercy.
Even now, he could hear her.

"Why?" she was saying. "Why are you doing this?
What have we done to you?"

What did my mother and my sisters do to deserve to
die at the hands of your men? he thought, but it was
not the time for questions.

It was the time for vengeance.

He squeezed the trigger, and the quiet of the afternoon exploded with the roar of the shotgun.

The *gringa's* face exploded before his eyes, and new
blood was added to the courtyard wall. Then, as with
his mother before her, the woman's knees gave way,
and she sank slowly to the ground as her daughter
watched, screaming.

As Alex squeezed the trigger a second time, his only
wish was that the courtyard was as it should have been,
and he could have watched as the blood of the *gringas*
disappeared into the dust of the hacienda.

José Carillo turned up Hacienda Drive, and shifted
his battered pickup truck into low gear. Listening to
the transmission's angry grinding, he hoped the truck
would last long enough for him to begin the job at the
hacienda. With the amount of money that one job would
produce, he would be able to afford a new truck. But
he was already late, and worried that he might lose the
job before he ever got it. He pressed on the gas pedal,
and the old truck coughed, then reluctantly surged
forward.

It was on the second curve that he saw the boy
coming down the road, a shotgun cradled in his arms,

his face and shirt covered with blood. He braked to a stop and called out to the boy. At first the boy hadn't seemed to hear him. Only when José called out a second time did the boy look up.

"You okay?" José asked. "Need some help?"

The boy stared at him for a moment, then shook his head and continued down the road. José watched him until he disappeared through the gate in the wall whose vines had just been torn down—something José's gardener's eyes had noticed as he'd come up the hill. Then he forced the truck back in gear.

He was already inside the courtyard before he saw the carnage that lay against the south wall.

"*Jesús, José, y María,*" he muttered. He crossed himself, then fought down the nausea in his gut as he hurried into the house to find a telephone.

Alex stared at himself in the mirror. Blood still oozed from the cut over his eye, and his shirt was growing stiff.

He'd already examined the shotgun, and knew that he'd fired three shells.

The last two were now in the chambers.

And though he had no conscious memory of it, he knew where he'd been when the voices began whispering to him and the images from the past began to flood his mind. He also knew where he'd been when it had ended.

When it began, he'd been on the hillside overlooking the hacienda, remembering María Torres's stories of the past.

And when it ended, he'd been walking away from the hacienda, and the smell of gunpowder was strong, and he was bleeding, and though his body was in pain, in his soul he felt nothing.

Nothing.

But tonight, he was sure, he would dream again, and see what he had done, and feel the pain in his soul.

But it was the last time it would happen, for now he knew why it had happened, and how to end it.

And he also knew that he, Alex, had done none of it.

Everything that had been done, had been done by Alejandro de Meléndez y Ruiz. Now all that was left was to kill Alejandro.

He changed his shirt, but didn't bother to bandage the cut on his forehead.

Picking up the shotgun, he went back downstairs and found the extra set of keys to his mother's car in the kitchen drawer.

He went out to the driveway and started the car. He shifted the gear lever into reverse, then kept his foot on the brake as a police car, its siren screaming, raced up the hill past the house.

He was sure he knew where it was going, and he was sure he knew what its occupants would find when they reached their destination. But instead of following the police car and trying to explain to the officers what he thought had happened, Alex went the other way.

His mind suddenly crystal clear, he drove down the hill, through La Paloma, and out of town. It would take him thirty minutes to reach Palo Alto.

"I'm telling you, something's wrong," Roscoe Finnerty had been saying when the phone on the kitchen wall suddenly rang, and he decided it could damned well ring until he'd finished what he was saying. "The kid said he parked across the street from Jake's. It's right here in my notes."

"And my notes say he parked in the lot next door," Tom Jackson replied. He nodded toward the phone. "And we're in your kitchen, so you can answer the phone."

"Shit," Finnerty muttered, reaching up and grabbing the receiver. "Yeah?" He listened for a few seconds, and Jackson saw the color drain from his face. "Aah, shit," he said again. Then: "Yeah, we'll go up." He hung up the phone and reluctantly met his partner's eyes. "We got two more," he said. "The chief wants us to take a look and see if it looks like the other two. From what he said, though, it doesn't. This time, it's messy."

But he hadn't counted on its being as messy as it actually was. He stood in the courtyard wondering if he should even try to take a pulse from the two corpses that lay against the wall. On one of them, the face was gone, and most of the head as well. Still, he was pretty sure he knew who it was, because the other corpse had taken the shotgun blast in the chest, and the face was still clearly recognizable.

Carolyn Evans.

The other one, judging from what Finnerty could see, had to be her mother. "Call the Center," he muttered to Jackson. "And tell them to bring bags, and not to bother with the sirens." Then he turned his attention to José Carillo, who was sitting by the pool, resolutely looking away from the corpses and the bloodstained wall they rested against.

"You know anything about this, José?" Finnerty asked, though he was almost certain he knew the answer. He'd known José for almost ten years, and the gardener was known only for three things: his industriousness and his honesty and his refusal to involve himself in violence under any circumstances.

José shook his head. "I was coming up for a job. When I got here . . ." His voice broke off, and he shook his head helplessly. "As soon as I found them, I called the police."

"Did you see anything? Anything at all?"

José started to shake his head, then hesitated.

"What is it?" Finnerty urged.

"I forgot," the gardener said. "On the way up, I saw a boy. He looked like he'd been fighting, and he was carrying a gun."

"Do you know who he was?"

The gardener shook his head again. "But I know where he went."

Finnerty stiffened. "Can you show me?"

"Down the road. It's right down the road."

Finnerty glanced toward the squad car, where Jackson was still on the radio. "Let's take your truck, José. You feel good enough to drive?"

José looked uncertain, but then climbed into the cab, and while Finnerty yelled to Jackson that he'd be right back, pressed on the starter and prayed that now, of all times, the truck wouldn't finally give up. The engine sputtered and coughed, then caught.

Half a mile down the hill, José brought the truck to a stop and pointed. "There," he said. "He went in there."

Finnerty stared at the house for several seconds. "Are you sure, José? This could be very serious."

José's head bobbed eagerly. "I'm sure. Look at the mess. They cut the vines off the wall and didn't even clean them up. I don't forget things like that. That's the house the boy went into."

Even with the vines off the wall, Finnerty recognized the Lonsdales' house. After all, it had been little more than eight hours since he'd been there himself.

He got out of the truck, and noted the empty garage. "José, I want you to go back up to the hacienda and send my partner down with the car. Then wait. Okay?"

José nodded, and maneuvered the truck through a clumsy U-turn before disappearing back up the hill. Finnerty stayed where he was, his eyes on the house, though he had a growing feeling that it was empty. A few minutes later, Jackson arrived, and at almost the same time, a woman appeared from the house across the street and a few yards down from the Lonsdales'.

"There isn't anyone there," Sheila Rosenberg volunteered. "Marsh and Ellen left two hours ago, and I saw Alex leave in Ellen's car a few minutes ago."

"Do you know where they went? The parents, I mean?"

"I'm sure I haven't a clue," Sheila replied. "I don't keep track of everything that happens in the neighborhood, you know." Then her voice dropped slightly. "Is something wrong?"

Finnerty glared at the woman, certain that she did, indeed, keep track of everything her neighbors were doing. "No," he said. If he told her the truth, she would be the first one up the hill. "We just want to get some information, that's all."

"Then you'd better call the Center," Sheila Rosenberg replied. "I'm sure they'll know where to find Marsh."

Despite Sheila Rosenberg's assertion that the house was as empty as he thought it was, Finnerty searched it anyway.

In the bedroom he was sure was Alex's, he found the blood-soaked shirt and carefully put it in a plastic bag Jackson brought from the squad car. Then he called the Medical Center.

'I know exactly where he went," Barbara Fannon told him after he'd identified himself. "He and Ellen went down to Palo Alto to talk to Dr. Torres about Alex. Apparently he's having some kind of trouble." And that, Finnerty thought grimly as Barbara Fannon searched for the number of the Institute for the Human Brain, is the understatement of the year.

Marsh felt his patience slipping rapidly away.

They had been at the Institute for almost two hours, and for the first hour and a half they had cooled their heels in the waiting room. This time, Marsh had ignored the journals, in favor of pacing the room. Ellen, however, had hardly moved at all from her place on the sofa, where she sat silently, her face pale, her hands folded in her lap.

And now, as they sat in Torres's office, they were being fed double-talk. The first thing Torres had done when he'd finally deigned to see them was show them a computer reconstruction of the operation.

It had been meaningless, as far as Marsh could tell. It had been speeded up, and the graphics on the monitor were not nearly as clear as they had been when Torres had produced the original depiction of Alex's injured brain.

"This is, of course, an operating program, not a diagnostic one," Torres had said smoothly. "What you're seeing here was never really meant for human eyes. It's a program designed to be read by a computer, and fed to a robot, and the graphics simply aren't important. In fact, they're incidental."

"And they don't mean a damned thing to me, Dr. Torres," Marsh declared. "You told me you'd explain what's happening to Alex, and so far, all you've done is dodge the issue. You now have a choice. Either get to the point, or I'm walking out of here—*with* my wife—and the next time you see us we'll all be in court. Can I make it any clearer than that?"

Before Torres could make any reply, the telephone rang. "I said I wasn't to be disturbed under any circumstances," he said as soon as he'd put the phone to his ear. He listened for a moment, then frowned and held the receiver toward Marsh. "It's for you, and I take it it's some sort of emergency."

"This is Dr. Lonsdale," Marsh said, his voice almost as impatient as Torres's had been. "What is it?"

And then he, too, listened in silence as the other person talked. When he hung up, his face was pale and his hands were trembling.

"Marsh . . ." Ellen breathed. "Marsh, what is it?"

"It's Alex," Marsh said, his voice suddenly dead. "That was Sergeant Finnerty. He says he wants to talk to Alex."

"Again?" Ellen asked, her heart suddenly pounding. "Why?"

When he answered, Marsh kept his eyes on Raymond Torres.

"He says Cynthia and Carolyn Evans are both dead, and he says he has reason to think that Alex killed them."

As Ellen gasped, Raymond Torres rose to his feet.

"If he said that, then he's a fool," Torres rasped, his normally cold eyes glittering angrily.

"But that *is* what he said," Marsh whispered. Then, as Torres sank slowly back into his chair, Marsh spoke again. "Please, Dr. Torres, tell me what you've done to my son."

"I saved him," Torres replied, but for the first time, his icy demeanor had disappeared. He met Marsh's eyes, and for a moment said nothing. Then he nodded almost imperceptibly.

"All right," he said quietly. "I'll tell you what I did. And when I'm done, you'll see why Alex couldn't have killed anyone." He fell silent for a moment, and when he spoke again, Marsh was almost sure he was speaking more to himself than to either Marsh or Ellen. "No, it's impossible. Alex couldn't have killed anyone."

Speaking slowly and carefully, he explained exactly what had been done to Alex Lonsdale.

CHAPTER TWENTY-THREE

Ellen tried to still her trembling hands as her eyes searched her husband's face for whatever truth might be written there. But Marsh's face remained stonily impassive, as it had been all through Raymond Torres's long recitation. "But . . . but what does it all mean?" she finally asked. For the last hour, at least, she had no longer been able to follow the details of what Torres had been saying, nor was she sure the details mattered. What was frightening her was the implications of what she had heard.

"It doesn't matter what it means," Marsh said, "because it's medically impossible."

"Think what you like, Dr. Lonsdale," Raymond Torres replied, "but what I've told you is the absolute truth. The fact that your son is still alive is the proof of it." He offered Marsh a smile that was little more than a twisted grimace. "The morning after the operation, I believe you made reference to a miracle. You were, I assume, thinking of a medical miracle, and I chose not to correct you. What it was, though, was a technological miracle."

"If what you're saying is actually true," Marsh said, "what you've done is no miracle at all. It's an obscenity."

Ellen's eyes filled with tears, which she made no attempt to wipe away. "But he's alive, Marsh," she protested, and then shrank back in her chair as Marsh turned to face her.

"Is he? By what criteria? Let's assume that what Torres says is true. That Alex's brain was far too extensively damaged even to attempt repairs." His eyes, flashing with anger, flicked to Torres. "That *is* what you said, isn't it?"

Torres nodded. "There was no brain activity whatever, except on the most primitive level. His heart was beating, but that was all. Without the respirator, he couldn't breathe, and as far as we could tell, he made no response to any sort of stimulation."

"In other words, he was brain dead, with no hope of recovery?"

Again Torres nodded. "Not only was his brain dead, it was physically torn beyond repair. Which is the only reason I went ahead with the techniques I used."

"Without our permission," Marsh grated.

"*With* your permission," Torres corrected. "The release clearly allowed me to use any methods I deemed necessary or fit, whether they were proven or unproven, traditional or experimental. And they worked." He hesitated, then went on. "Perhaps I made a mistake," he said. "Perhaps I should have declared Alex dead, and asked that his body be donated to science."

"But isn't that exactly what you did?" Marsh demanded. "Without, of course, the niceties of telling us what you were doing?"

Torres shook his head. "For the operation to be a complete success, I wanted there to be no question that Alex is still Alex. Had I declared him dead, what I have done would have led to certain questions I was not yet prepared to deal with."

Suddenly Ellen rose to her feet. "Stop it! Just stop it!" Her eyes moved wildly from Marsh to Raymond Torres. "You're talking about Alex as if he no longer exists!"

"In a way, Ellen," Torres replied, "that's exactly the truth. The Alex you knew doesn't exist anymore. The only Alex that is real is the one I created."

There was a sudden silence in the room, broken at last by Marsh's voice, barely more than a whisper. "That you created with *microprocessors*? I still can't believe it. It just isn't possible."

"But it is," Torres said. "And it isn't nearly as complicated as it sounds, except physically. It's the connections that are the most difficult. Finding exactly the right neurons to connect to the leads of the microprocessors themselves. Fortunately, the brain itself is an aid there. Given an opportunity, it will build its own pathways and straighten out most of the human errors by itself."

"But Alex is alive," Ellen insisted. "He's alive."

"His body is alive," Torres agreed. "And it's kept alive by seventeen separate microprocessors, each of which is programmed to maintain and monitor the various physical systems of his body. Three of those microprocessors are concerned with nothing except the endocrine system, and four more handle the nervous system. Some of the systems are less complicated than those two, and could be lumped together in a single chip with a backup. Four of the chips are strictly memory. They were the easy ones."

"Easy ones?" Ellen echoed, her voice weak.

Torres nodded. "This project has been under way for years, ever since I became interested in artificial intelligence—the concept of building a computer that can actually reason on its own, rather than simply make computations at an incredibly rapid speed. And the problem there is that despite all we know about the brain, we still have no real concept of how the process of original thought takes place. It very quickly became obvious to me that until we understood the process in the human brain, we couldn't hope to duplicate it in a machine. And yet, we want machines that can think like people."

"And you found the answer," Marsh said, his voice tight.

Torres ignored his tone. "I found the answer. It seemed to me that since we couldn't make a machine that could think like a man, perhaps we could create a man who could compute like a machine.

"A man with the memory capacity of a computer.

"The implication was obvious, and though the technology was not there ten years ago, it is today. The answer seemed to me to involve installing a high-capacity microprocessor inside the brain itself, giving the brain access to massive amounts of information, and enormous computational abilities, while the brain itself provides the reasoning circuits that are not yet feasible."

"And did you do that?" Marsh asked.

Torres hesitated, then shook his head. "The risks seemed to me to be entirely too great, and the stakes too high. I had no idea what the results might be. That's when I began work on the project of which Alex is the end result." He smiled thinly. "It's no accident that the Institute for the Human Brain is in the heart of Silicon Valley, you know. All our work is highly technical, and extremely expensive. And we have very little to show for it, despite all those articles out in the lobby." Marsh seemed about to interrupt him, but Torres held up a restraining hand. "Let me finish. As I said, my work is highly technical, and very expensive, but this is one area of the country that has an abundance of money available to just such work. And so I took my proposed solution to the problem to certain companies and venture capitalists, and managed to intrigue them to the point where they have been willing to fund my research. And what my research has been, for the last ten years, is nothing more or less than reducing the monitoring and operation of every system in the human body to language a computer can understand, and then programming that information into microprocessors."

"If it's true," Marsh breathed, "that's quite incredible."

"Not quite as incredible as it is useless," Torres replied. "At first glance, it might seem quite marvelous, with all kinds of applications, but I'm afraid that isn't the case. Usually, when a system goes bad in the human body, the dysfunction is caused by disease, not a failure of the brain. And good as my programs are, they can only function with healthy systems. What they don't need is a healthy brain.

"You see," he said quietly, "I decided years ago that I couldn't experiment on someone who had a normal life ahead of him. I was only willing to work with a hopelessly brain-damaged case—someone who would unquestionably die unless I tried installing my processors—but whose body was basically intact. And that meant that the memory and computation chips wouldn't be enough. So I spent ten years developing all the systems-maintenance programs as well."

Raymond Torres opened the top drawer of his desk and pulled out a Lucite block, which he pushed across the desk to Marsh. "If you're interested," he said, "that block contains duplicates of the processors that are in Alex's brain."

Marsh picked up the block of Lucite—only a couple of inches on a side—and gazed into the transparent plastic. Floating in the apparent emptiness were several tiny specks, each no bigger than the head of a pin. "Those," he heard Torres saying, "are the most powerful microprocessors available today. They're a new technology, which I don't pretend to understand, and they can operate perfectly on the tiny amount of current generated by the human body. Indeed, I'm told they require less electrical energy than the brain itself."

Finally, as he stared at the tiny chips held prisoner in the lucite, Marsh began to believe what Raymond Torres had been telling him, and when he finally shifted his gaze to the other doctor, his eyes were brimming with tears.

"Then Alex was right," he said, his voice unsteady. "When he told me last night that he thought maybe he hadn't really survived the operation—that maybe he really was dead—he was right."

Torres hesitated, then reluctantly nodded. "Yes," he agreed. "Certainly, in one sense, at least, Alex is dead. His body isn't dead, and his intellect isn't dead, but almost certainly, his personality is dead."

"No!" Ellen was on her feet, and she took a step toward Torres's desk. "You said he was all right! You said he was getting better!"

"And part of him is," Torres replied. "Physically and mentally, he's been getting better every day."

"But there's more," Ellen protested. "You know there's more. He . . . he's starting to remember things—"

"Which is exactly why I wanted him to come back here," Torres said smoothly. Until this moment, he had told them the truth.

Now the lies would begin.

"He's remembering things that he couldn't possibly remember at all. Some of them are things that happened—if they happened at all—long before he was born."

"But he *is* remembering things," Ellen insisted.

Torres only shook his head. "No, he's not," he said flatly. "Please listen to me, Ellen. It's very important that you understand what I'm about to tell you." Ellen looked uncertain, then lowered herself back into her chair. "There are some things you still aren't accepting, and although I know it's difficult, you have to accept them. First, Alex has no memories of what happened before his accident. All he knows is what was programmed into the memory banks I installed during the operation, together with whatever experiences he's had since then. Basically, when he woke up he had a certain amount of data that were readily accessible to him. Vocabulary, recognition of certain images—that sort of thing. Since then, he has been taking in data and processing it at the rate of a very large computer. Which is why," he went on, turning to Marsh, "he appears to have the intelligence of a genius." Torres picked up the little block of lucite and began toying with it. "What he actually has is total recall of everything he's come in contact with since the operation, plus the ability to do calculations in his head at an astonishing rate, with total accuracy, plus the very human ability to reason. Whether that makes him a genius, I don't know. Frankly, what Alex is or is not is for other people to decide, not me.

"But he has limitations, as well. The most obvious one is his lack of emotional response." For the first time that afternoon, Torres picked up his pipe, and began stuffing it with tobacco. "We know a great deal about emotions. We even know from which areas of the brain certain of them spring. Indeed, we can create some of them by stimulating certain areas of the brain. But in the end, they aren't anything I've been able to write programs for, which is why Alex is totally lacking them. And that," he added, almost incidentally, "brings us back to the reason why I've told you all this at all." As he lit his pipe, his eyes met Marsh's, and held them steadily. "If you accept the truth of what I've been telling you, then I think you'll agree that Alex is quite incapable of murder."

"I'm afraid I don't see that at all," Marsh replied. "From what you've said, it would seem to me that Alex would make the most ideal killer in the world, since he has no feelings."

"And he would," Torres agreed. "Except that murder is not part of his programming, and he's only capable of doing what he's programmed to do. Murder, as I'm sure you're aware, is most often motivated by emotions. Anger, jealousy, fear—any number of things. But they are all things of which Alex has no knowledge or experience. He's aware that emotions exist, but he's never experienced them. And without emotions, he would never find himself prey to the urge to kill."

"Unless," Marsh replied, "he were programmed to kill."

"Exactly. But even then, he would analyze the order, and unless the killing made intellectual sense to him, he would refuse the order."

Marsh tried to digest Torres's words, but found himself unable to. His mind was too filled with conflicting emotions and thoughts. He felt a numbness of the spirit that he abstractedly identified as shock. And why not? he thought. He's dead. My son is dead, and yet he's not. He's somewhere right now, walking and talking and thinking, while I sit here being told that he doesn't really exist at all, that he's nothing more than . . . He rejected the word that came to mind, then accepted it: nothing more than some kind of a machine. His eyes moved to Ellen, and he could see that she, too, was struggling with her emotions. He got to his feet and went to her, kneeling by her chair.

"He's dead, sweetheart," he whispered softly.

"No," Ellen moaned, burying her face in her hands as her body was finally racked by the sobs she had been holding back so long. "No, Marsh, he can't be dead. He can't be. . . ." He put his arms around her and held her close, gently stroking her hair. When he spoke again, it was to Raymond Torres, and his words were choked with anger and grief.

"Why?" he asked. "Why did you do this to us?"

"Because you asked me to," Torres replied. "You asked me to save his life, any way I could, and that's what I did, to the best of my ability." Then he sighed heavily, and carefully placed his pipe back on his desk. "But I did it for myself, too," he said. "I won't deny that. I had the technology, and I had the skill." His eyes met Marsh's. "Let me ask you something. If you had been in my position, would you have done what I did?"

Marsh was silent for a full minute, and he knew that Torres had asked a question for which he had no answer. When he at last spoke, his voice reflected nothing except the exhaustion he was feeling. "I don't know," he said. "I wish I could say that I wouldn't have, but I don't know." Shakily he rose to his feet, but kept his hand protectively on Ellen's shoulder. "What do we do now?"

"Find Alex," Torres replied. "We have to find him, and get him back here. Something happened yesterday, and I don't know what effect it might have had on Alex. There was . . . well, there was an error in the lab, and Alex underwent some tests without anesthesia." Briefly he described the tests, and what Alex must have experienced. "He didn't show any effects afterward, which indicates that there was no damage done, but I'd like to be sure. And there's still the problem of the memories he thinks he's having."

Marsh stiffened as he suddenly realized that for all his carefully worded explanations, Torres was still holding something back. "But he *is* having them," he said. "How can that be?"

"I don't know," Torres admitted. "And that's why I want him back here. Somewhere in his memory banks there is an error, and that error has to be corrected. What seems to be happening is that Alex is becoming increasingly involved in finding the source of those memories. *There is no source*," Torres said, and paused as his words penetrated the Lonsdales like daggers of ice. When he discovers that, I'm not sure what might happen to him."

Marsh's voice hardened once more. "It sounds to me, Dr. Torres, as if you're implying that Alex might go insane. If that has indeed happened, isn't it possible that you're entirely wrong, and Alex could, after all, have committed murder?"

"No," Torres insisted. "The word doesn't apply. Computers don't go insane. But they do stop functioning."

"A systems crash, I believe they call it," Marsh said coldly, and Torres nodded. "And in Alex's case, may I assume that would be fatal?"

Again Torres nodded, this time with obvious reluc-

tance. "I have to agree that that is quite possible, yes."
Then, seeing the look of fear and confusion on Ellen's
face, he went on: "Believe me, Ellen, Alex has done
nothing wrong. In all likelihood, I'll be able to help
him. He'll be all right."

"But he won't," Marsh said quietly, drawing Ellen to
her feet. "Dr. Torres, please don't try to hold out any
more false hope to my wife. The best thing she can do
right now is try to accept the fact that Alex died last
May. As of this moment, I do not know exactly who the
person is who looks like my son and has been living in
my house, but I do know that it is not Alex." As Ellen
began quietly sobbing once more, he led her toward
the door. "I don't know what to do now, Dr. Torres,
but you may rest assured that should Alex come home,
I will call the police and explain to them that Alex—or
whoever he is—is legally in your custody, and that any
questions they have should be directed to you. He is
not my son anymore, Dr. Torres. He hasn't been since
the day I brought him to you." He turned away, and
led Ellen out of the office.

They were halfway back to La Paloma before Ellen
finally spoke. Her voice was hoarse from her crying. "Is
he really dead, Marsh?" she asked. "Was he telling us
the truth?"

"I don't know," Marsh replied. It was the same question he'd been grappling with ever since they'd left the
Institute, and he still had no answer. "He was telling us
the truth, yes. I believe he did exactly what he says he
did. But as for Alex, I wish I could tell you. Who knows
what death really is? Legally, Alex could have been
declared dead before we ever took him down to Palo
Alto. According to the brain scans, there was no activity, and that's a legal criterion for death."

"But he was still breathing—"

"No, he wasn't. Not really. Our machines were breathing for him. And now Raymond Torres has invented
new machines, and Alex is walking and talking. But I

don't know if he's Alex. He doesn't act like Alex, and he doesn't think like Alex, and he doesn't respond like Alex. For weeks now, I've had this strange feeling that Alex wasn't there, and apparently I was right. Alex *isn't* there. All that's there is whatever Raymond Torres constructed in Alex's body."

"But it *is* Alex's body," Ellen insisted.

"But isn't that all it is?" Marsh asked, his voice reflecting the pain he was feeling. "Isn't it the part we bury when the spirit's gone? And Alex's spirit is gone, Ellen. Or if it isn't, then it's trapped so deep inside the wreckage of his brain that it will never escape."

Ellen said nothing for a long time, staring out into the gathering gloom of the evening. "Then why do I still love him?" she asked at last. "Why do I still feel that he's my son?"

"I don't know," Marsh replied. Then: "But I'm afraid I lied back there. I was angry, and I was hurt, and I didn't want to believe what I was hearing, and for a little while, I wanted Alex to be dead. And part of me is absolutely certain that he is." He fell silent, but Ellen was certain he had more to say, so she sat quietly waiting. After a few moments, as if there had been no lapse of time, Marsh went on. "But part of me says that as long as he's living and breathing, he's alive, and he's my son. I love him too, Ellen."

For the first time in months, Ellen slid across the seat and pressed close to her husband. "Oh, God, Marsh," she whispered. "What are we going to do?"

"I don't know," he confessed. "In fact, I'm not sure there's anything we can do, except wait for Alex to come home."

He didn't tell Ellen that he wasn't at all sure Alex would ever come home again.

CHAPTER TWENTY-FOUR

It was not a large house, but it was set well back from the street. Though he couldn't read the address, Alex knew he was at the right place. It had been simple, really. When he'd come into Palo Alto, he'd shut all images of La Paloma out of his mind, then concentrated on the idea of going home. After that, he'd merely followed the impulses his brain sent him at each intersection until he'd finally come to a stop in front of the Moorish-style house he was now absolutely certain belonged to Dr. Raymond Torres. He studied it for a few moments, then turned into the driveway, parking the car on the concrete apron that widened out behind the house.

From the street, the car was no longer visible.

Alex got out of the car, closed the driver's door, then opened the trunk.

He picked up the shotgun, holding it in his right hand while he used his left to slam the trunk lid. Carrying the gun almost casually, he crossed to the back door of the house and tried the knob. It was locked.

He glanced around the patio behind the house, uncertain of what he was looking for, but sure that he would recognize it when he saw it.

It was a large earthenware planter, exploding with the vivid colors of impatiens in full bloom. In the center of the planter, wrapped neatly in aluminum foil and well-hidden by the profuse foliage, he found the spare key to the house. Letting himself inside, he moved confidently through the kitchen and dining room, then down a short hall to the den.

This, he was sure, was the room in which Dr. Torres spent most of his time. There was a fireplace in one corner, and a battered desk that was in stark contrast to the gleaming sleekness of the desk Torres used at the Brain Institute. And in equal contrast to the Institute office was the clutter of the den. Everywhere were books and journals, stacked high on the desk and shoved untidily onto the shelves that lined the walls. Most were medical books and technical journals relating to Torres's work, but some were not. Resting the gun on its butt in the corner behind the door, Alex began a closer examination of the library, knowing already what he was looking for, and knowing that he would find it.

There were several old histories of California, detailing the settling of the area by the Spanish-Mexicans, and the subsequent ceding of the territory to the United States. Tucked between two thick tomes was the thin leather-bound volume, its spine intricately tooled in gold, that Alex was looking for. Handling the book carefully, he removed it from the shelf, then sat down in the worn leather chair that stood between the fireplace and the desk. He opened it to the first page, and examined the details of the illuminations that had been painstakingly worked around the ornate lettering.

It was a family tree, detailing the history of the family

of Don Roberto de Meléndez y Ruiz, his antecedents, and his descendants. Alex scanned the pages quickly until he came to the end.

The last entry was Raymond Torres, son of María and Carlos Torres.

It was through his mother, María Ruiz, that Raymond Torres traced his lineage back to Don Roberto, through Don Roberto's only surviving son, Alejandro. Below the box containing Raymond Torres's name, there was another box.

It was empty.

Alex closed the book and laid it on the hearth in front of the fireplace, then moved on to Torres's desk. Without hesitation, he pulled the bottom-right-hand drawer open, reached into its depths, and pulled out a nondescript notebook.

In the notebook, neatly penned in a precise hand, was Raymond Torres's plan for creating the son he had never fathered.

It was getting dark when Alex heard the car pull up. He retrieved the gun from the corner behind the door. When Raymond Torres entered the den a few moments later, it lay almost carelessly in Alex's lap, though his right forefinger was curled around the trigger. Torres paused in the doorway, frowning thoughtfully, then smiled.

"I don't think you'll kill me," he said. "Nor, for that matter, do I think you have killed anyone else. So why don't you put that gun down, and let us talk about what's happening to you."

"There's no need to talk," Alex replied. "I already know what happened to me. You've put computers in my brain, and you've been programming me."

"You found the notebook."

"I didn't need to find it. I knew where it was. I knew where this house was, and I knew what I'd find here."

Torres's smile faded into a slight frown. "I don't think you could have known those things."

"Of course I could," Alex replied. "Don't you understand what you've done?"

Torres closed the door, then, ignoring the gun, moved around his desk and eased himself into his chair. He regarded Alex carefully, and wondered briefly if, indeed, something had gone awry. But he rejected the idea; it was impossible. "Of course I understand," he finally said. "But I'm not sure you do. What, exactly, do you think I've done?"

"Turned me into you," Alex said softly. "Did you think I wouldn't figure it out?"

Torres ignored the question. "And how, exactly, did I do that?"

"The testing," Alex replied. "Only you weren't testing me, really. You were programming me."

"I'll agree to that," Torres replied, "since it happens to be absolutely true. Incidentally, I explained it all to your parents this afternoon."

"Did you? Did you really tell them all of it?" Alex asked. "Did you tell them that it wasn't just data you programmed in?"

Torres frowned. "But it was."

Alex shook his head. "Then you don't understand, do you?"

"I don't understand what you're talking about, no," Torres said, though he understood perfectly. For the first time, he began to feel afraid.

"Then I'll tell you. After the operation, my brain was a blank. I had the capacity to learn, because of the computers you put in my brain, but I didn't have the capacity to think."

"That's not true—"

"It *is* true," Alex insisted. "And I think you knew it, which is why you had to give me a personality as well as just enough data to look like I was . . . What? Suffering from amnesia? Was I supposed to remember things slowly, so it would look like I was recovering? But I couldn't remember anything, could I? My brain—Alex

Lonsdale's brain—was dead. So you gave me things to remember, but they were the wrong things."

"I haven't the vaguest idea what you're talking about, Alex, and neither have you," Torres declared icily.

"It's strange, really," Alex went on, ignoring Torres's words. "Some of the mistakes were so small, and yet they set me to wondering. If it had only been the oldest stuff—"

"The 'oldest stuff'?" Torres echoed archly.

"The oldest memories. The memories of the stories your mother used to tell you."

"My mother is an old woman. Sometimes she gets confused."

"No," Alex replied. "She's not confused, and neither are you. The memories served their purpose, and all the people died. You used me to kill them, and I did. And, as you wished, I had no memory of what I'd done. As soon as the killings were over, they were wiped out of my memory banks. But even if I had remembered them, I wouldn't have been able to say why I was killing. All I would have been able to do is talk about Alejandro de Meléndez y Ruiz and *venganza*. Revenge. I would have sounded crazy, wouldn't I?"

"You're sounding crazy right now," Torres said, rising to his feet.

Alex's hands tightened on the shotgun. "Sit down," he said. Torres hesitated, then sank back into his chair. "But it *was* revenge you wanted," Alex went on. "Only not revenge for what happened in 1848. Revenge for what happened twenty years ago."

"Alex, what you're saying makes no sense."

"But it does," Alex insisted. "The school. That was one of your mistakes, but only a small one. I remembered the dean's office being in the wrong place. But it wasn't the wrong place—I was just twenty years too late. When *you* were at La Paloma High, the dean's office was where the nurse's office is now."

"Which means nothing."

"True. I could have seen the same pictures of the school in my mother's yearbook that I saw in yours."

Torres's eyes flickered over the room, first to the bookshelf where his family tree rested, then to the notebook that still lay on top of his desk where Alex had left it.

Next to it, lying open, was the annual from his senior year at La Paloma High. It was open to a picture he had studied many times over the years. As he looked at it now, he felt once more the pain the people it depicted had caused him.

All four of them: Marty and Valerie and Cynthia and Ellen.

The Four Musketeers, who had inflicted wounds on him that he had nursed over the years—never allowing them to heal—until finally they had festered.

And as the wounds festered, the planning had begun, and then, when the opportunity finally came, he had executed his plan.

The memories had been carefully constructed in Alex—the memories of things he couldn't possibly remember—so that when he finally got caught, as Torres knew he eventually would, all he would be able to do was talk of ancient wrongs and the spirit of a long-dead man who had taken possession of him.

The truth would be carefully shielded, for Torres had programmed no memories in Alex of the hatred he felt toward the four women who had looked down on him so many years ago, ignored him as if he didn't exist.

Even now, he could hear his mother's voice talking about them:

"You think they even look at you, Ramón? They are *gringos* who would spit on you. They are no different than the ones who killed our family, and they will kill you too. You wait, Ramón. Pretend all you want, but in the end you will know the truth. They hate you, Ramón, as you will hate them."

And in the end, she had been right, and he had hated them as much as she did.

And now it was over. Because Raymond Torres had created Alex, he knew what Alex was going to do. Oddly, he could even accept it. "How did you figure it out?"

"With the tools you gave me," Alex replied. "I processed data. The facts were simple. From the damage done to my brain, I should have died.

"But I wasn't dead.

"The two facts didn't match, until I realized that there was one way I could make them match. I could still be alive, if something had been done to keep my body functioning in spite of the damage to my brain. And the only thing capable of doing that was a system of microprocessors performing the functions of my brain.

"But then I had to fit the memories in.

"Alex Lonsdale has no memories. None at all, because he's dead. But I was remembering things, and the answer had to be the same. What I was remembering had to have been programmed into me too, along with all the rest of the data. From there, it wasn't hard to figure out who I really am."

"My son," Torres said softly. "The son I never had."

"No," Alex replied. "I am not your son, Dr. Torres. I am you. Inside my head are all the memories you grew up with. They're not my memories, Dr. Torres. They're yours. Don't you understand?"

"It's the same thing," Torres said, but Alex shook his head.

"No. It's not the same thing, because if it were, I would be about to kill my father. But I'm you, Dr. Torres, so I guess you are about to kill yourself."

His hands steady, Alex raised the shotgun, leveled it at Raymond Torres, and squeezed the trigger. Alex watched as Raymond Torres's head was nearly torn from his body by the force of the buckshot that exploded from the gun's barrel.

As he left Torres's house, the phone began ringing, but Alex ignored it.

Getting into Torres's car—his own car, now—he started back toward La Paloma.

All of them were dead—Valerie Benson, Marty Lewis, and Cynthia Evans. All of them dead, except one.

Ellen Lonsdale was still alive.

Roscoe Finnerty carefully replaced the phone on its hook, and turned to face the Lonsdales once more.

Ellen, as she had been since they got home, was sitting on the sofa, her face pale, her hands trembling. Her eyes, reddened from weeping, blinked nervously, and she seemed to have become incapable of speech.

Marsh, on the other hand, wore a demeanor of calm that belied the inner turmoil he was feeling. Before beginning to answer Finnerty's questions, he had tried to think carefully about what he should say, but in the end he'd decided to tell the officers the truth.

First, they had asked about the gun, and Marsh had led them to the garage, and the box where he was sure his shotgun was still stored.

It was gone.

Once more, he remembered Torres's words: "Alex is totally incapable of killing anyone."

But up the street, Cynthia and Carolyn Evans had both been cut down by a shotgun, and someone matching Alex's description had been seen carrying a shotgun into this house.

Torres had been wrong.

Slowly Marsh began telling the two officers, Finnerty and Jackson, what Torres had told him only an hour or so earlier. They'd listened politely, then insisted on checking Marsh's story with Raymond Torres. When they'd called his office, they'd been told the director of the Institute had left for the day. Only after identifying themselves had they been able to obtain Torres's home phone number.

"Well, he's not there either," Finnerty said. Then: "Dr. Lonsdale, I don't want to seem to be pushing you, but I think the most important thing right now is to find

Alex. Do you have any idea where he might have gone?"

Marsh shook his head. "If he didn't go to Torres, I haven't any idea at all."

"What about friends?" Jackson asked, and again Marsh shook his head.

"He . . . well, since the accident, he doesn't really have any friends anymore." His eyes filled with tears. "I'm afraid—I'm afraid that the longer time went on, the more the kids decided that there was something wrong with Alex. Besides the obvious problems, I mean," he added.

"Okay. We're going to put a stakeout on the house," Finnerty told him. "I've already got an APB out on your wife's car, but frankly, that doesn't mean much. The odds of someone spotting it are next to none. And it seems to me that eventually, your son will come home. So we'll be out there in an unmarked car. Or, at least, someone will. Anyway, we'll be keeping an eye on this place."

Marsh nodded, but Finnerty wasn't sure he'd been listening. "Dr. Lonsdale?" he asked, and Marsh met his eyes. "I can't tell you how sorry I am about this," Finnerty went on. "I keep hoping that there's been a mistake, and that maybe your boy didn't have anything to do with this."

Marsh's head came up, and he used his handkerchief to blot away the last of the tears on his cheeks.

"It's all right, Sergeant," he said. "You're just doing your job, and I understand it." He hesitated, then went on. "And there's something else I should tell you. I . . . well, I don't think there's been a mistake. I think you should be aware that Alex may be very dangerous. Ever since the operation, he hasn't felt anything—no love, no hate, no anger, nothing. If he's started killing, for whatever reason, he probably won't stop. Nor will he care what he does."

There was a short silence while Finnerty tried to

assess Marsh Lonsdale's words. "Dr. Lonsdale," he finally asked, "would you mind telling me exactly what you're trying to say?"

"I'm trying to say that if you find Alex, I think you'd better kill him. If you don't, I suspect he won't hesitate to kill you."

Jackson and Finnerty glanced at each other. Finally, it was Jackson who spoke for both of them. "We can't do that, Dr. Lonsdale," he said quietly. "So far, it hasn't been proven that your son has done anything. For all we know, he might have been up in the hills shooting rabbits, and hurt himself some way."

"No," Marsh said, his voice almost a whisper. "No, that's not it. He did it."

"If he did, that will be for a court to decide," Jackson went on. "We'll find your son, Dr. Lonsdale. But we won't kill him."

Marsh shook his head wearily. "You don't understand, do you? That boy out there—he's not Alex. I don't know who he is, but he's not Alex. . . ."

"Okay," Finnerty said, in the gently soothing voice he'd long ago developed for situations in which he found himself dealing with someone who was less than rational. "You just take it easy for a while, Dr. Lonsdale, and we'll take care of it." He waited until Marsh had settled himself onto the sofa next to Ellen, then led Jackson out of the house. "Well? What do you think?"

"I don't know what to think."

"Neither do I," Finnerty sighed. "Neither do I."

"I don't believe any of this," Jim Cochran declared. His glance alternated between his wife and his elder daughter, neither of whom seemed willing to meet his gaze. Only Kim seemed to agree with him, and Carol had insisted she be sent up to her room five minutes ago, when it became obvious a fight was brewing. "Ellen and Marsh and Alex have been friends of ours for most of our lives. And now you don't even want me to call them?"

"I didn't say that," Carol protested, though she knew that even if she hadn't said the words, certainly that was what she had meant. "I just think we should leave them alone until we know what's happened."

"That's not you talking," Jim replied. "It's someone else."

"No!" Carol exclaimed. "After today, I just can't stand any more."

"And what about Marsh and Ellen? How do you think they feel? They're the ones whose lives are falling apart, Carol, not us."

Carol tried to close her ears to the words that were so much an echo of what she herself had said to Lisa only weeks ago. But weeks ago, no one had died.

"And what if Alex comes home?" Carol demanded. "No one knows where he is, or what he's doing, but according to Sheila Rosenberg, he murdered Cynthia and Carolyn Evans this morning, and probably murdered Marty and Valerie as well."

"We don't know that," Jim insisted. "And you both know that Sheila is the worst gossip in this town."

"Daddy!" Lisa said. "Alex didn't care about what happened to Mrs. Lewis, and he didn't think Mr. Lewis killed her. He told me so. He even said he thought someone else might get killed."

"That doesn't mean—"

"And he's been acting weirder and weirder ever since he came home. Are you going to tell me that's not true, too?"

"It's not the point," Jim insisted. "The point is that people stick by their friends, no matter what happens. And I don't accept that Alex has killed anyone."

"Then I'm afraid you're burying your head in the sand," Carol replied. "If he hasn't done anything, then where is he?"

"Anywhere," Jim said. "Who knows? He could have gone up into the hills, and had another accident."

"Daddy—"

"No," Jim said. "I've heard enough. I'm calling Marsh,

and finding out what's going on. And if they need me, I'm going up there." He left the kitchen, and a few seconds later, Carol and Lisa heard him talking on the phone.

"I don't want to go up there, Mom," Lisa said quietly, her eyes beseeching. "I'm scared of Alex."

Carol patted Lisa's hand reassuringly. "It's all right, honey. We're not going anywhere. I'm . . . well, I'm just as frightened as you are." Suddenly Jim appeared in the doorway, and Carol's attention was diverted from her daughter to her husband.

"I just talked to Marsh," Jim told them, "and he wasn't making much sense. And Ellen's not talking at all. He says she's just sitting on the sofa, and he's not sure she's even hearing what anyone says."

"Anyone?" Carol asked. "Is someone else there?"

"The police were there. They just left."

There was a silence. Carol sighed as she came to a decision. "All right," she said quietly. "If you think you have to go, we'll all go. I guess you're right—we can't just sit here and do nothing." She stood up, but Lisa remained seated where she was.

"No," she said, her eyes flooding. "I can't go."

And finally, seeing the extent of his daughter's fear, Jim relented. "It's okay, princess," he said softly. "I guess I can understand how you're feeling." His eyes moved to his wife, and he offered her a tight smile. "I guess that lets you off the hook, too."

Carol hesitated, then nodded. "I'll stay here." Guiltily, she hoped the relief she was feeling didn't show, but she was sure it did.

"I won't stay long," Jim promised. "I'll just see if there's anything I can do, and let them know they're not alone. Then I'll be back. Okay?"

Again Carol nodded, and walked with her husband to the front door, where she kissed him good-bye. "I'm sorry," she whispered. "I'm sorry I've lost my nerve, but I just have. Forgive me?"

"Always," Jim told her. Then, before he closed the

door, he spoke again. "Until I get back, don't open the door for anyone."

Then he was gone, and Carol went back to the kitchen, to wait.

CHAPTER TWENTY-FIVE

Darkness was falling as Alex made the turn off Middlefield Road, and as he started up into the hills on La Paloma Drive, he reached down and turned on the headlights of Raymond Torres's car. He wondered if he would dream about Dr. Torres tonight—if he chose to live that long—and wondered if, in whatever dreams he might have, he would feel the same emotional pain again, as he had when he dreamed about Mrs. Lewis and Mrs. Benson. With Dr. Torres, he decided, he wouldn't. Torres's death was very clear in his memory, and he felt no pain when he thought about it.

But he would dream about Mrs. Evans, and Carolyn, too, and then the pain would come.

There was, he had finally come to believe, still some little fragment of Alex Lonsdale still alive, deep within the recesses of his central brain core. It was that fragment of Alex who was having the dreams, and feeling the pain of what he had done. But when he was awake, there was none of Alex left. Only . . . who?

Did he even have a name?

Alejandro.

That was the name Dr. Torres had chosen for him, and then carefully built the memories of Alejandro into him. But the emotions that went with Alejandro's memories were Raymond Torres's, and those he had carefully left out.

It had, Alex realized, avoided confusion. When he saw the women—the women Torres hated—in the environment of Alejandro's memory, they had become other people from other times, and Alejandro had killed them.

And why not? To Alejandro, they were the wives of thieves and murderers, and as guilty of those crimes as their husbands.

But in the darkness of night, in the visions generated by the remnants of Alex Lonsdale's subconscious, they were old friends, people he had known all his life, and he mourned them.

And that had been Torres's mistake.

For his creation to have been perfect, there should have been none of Alex Lonsdale left.

Ahead of him, the headlights picked up the sign for the park that lay on the outskirts of the village. Alex pulled into the parking lot and shut off the engine.

His father had told him that when he was a boy, he'd played here often, yet he still had no memory of it. *His* only memory was Raymond Torres's memory of standing on the street, pleading with his mother to take him to the swings and push him as the other mothers were pushing their children.

"No," María Torres would mutter. "The park is not for us. It is for *los gringos*. Mira!" And she would point to the sign dedicating the park to the first American settlers who had come to La Paloma after the Treaty of Guadalupe Hidalgo had been signed. Then she would take Ramón by the hand and drag him away.

Alex got out of the car and began making his way across the empty lawn toward the swings. Tentatively he settled himself into one of them, and gave an experimental kick with his foot.

The movement had the vaguest feeling of familiarity to it, and Alex began pumping himself higher and higher. As the air rushed over his face and he felt the slight lurch in his stomach at the apex of each arc, Alex realized that this must have been what he'd done as a boy, this must be what he'd loved so much.

He stopped pumping, and let the swing slowly die until he was sitting still once again.

Then, knowing he had much to do before he went to the house on Hacienda Drive where the people who thought they were his parents lived, he left the swing and returned to his car.

He drove on into La Paloma, and turned left before he got to the Square. Two blocks further on, he came to the plaza. In the flickering lights of the gas lamps, the memories of Alejandro began creeping back to him, but Alex forced them out of his consciousness, keeping himself in the present. Only when he drove around the village hall to the mission graveyard did he let the memories come back.

Was this where they would bury him, or would they take him up into the hills above the hacienda and bury him with his mother and his sisters?

No.

They would bury him here, for they would be burying Alex, not Alejandro. Again he got out of the car, and slipped into the little graveyard. Tucked away in a dusty corner, he found the grave he was looking for.

Alejandro de Meléndez y Ruiz
1832–1926

His own grave, in a way, and already sixty years old. There were flowers on the grave, though, and Alex knew who had put them there. Old María Torres, still honoring her grandfather's memory. Alex reached down and picked one of the flowers, breathing in its fra-

grance. Then, taking the flower with him, he went back
to the car.

In the Square, he stepped over the chain around the
tree, and stood for a long time under the spreading
branches. Alejandro's memories were strong again, and
Alex let them spread through his mind.

Once more he saw his father's body swinging limply
from the hempen noose knotted around his neck, and
felt the unfamiliar sensation of tears dampening his
cheeks. He took the flower from Alejandro's grave and
laid it gently on the ground above his father's grave.
Then he turned away, knowing he'd seen the great oak
tree for the last time.

Lisa and Carol Cochran were still sitting in the friendly
brightness of the kitchen when they heard the car pull
up outside, and a door slam. Carol hesitated, then
pulled the drawn shades just far enough back to allow
her to peer out into the street. A car she didn't recognize sat by the curb, and it was too dark to see who had
gotten out of it. She dropped the shade back into position, and went to the stove, where she nervously poured
herself yet another cup of coffee. As soon as Jim had left
the house, she had given up any idea of sleeping that
night.

"Who was it, Mom?" Lisa whispered, and Carol forced
a grin that held much more confidence than she was
feeling.

"It's no one. I've never seen the car before, and I
don't think anyone's in it. Whoever it was must have
gone across the street." But even as she spoke, she had
the uncanny feeling that she was wrong, and that whoever had arrived in the car was still outside.

At that moment, the doorbell rang, its normally
friendly chime taking on an ominous tone.

"What shall we do?" Lisa asked, her voice barely
audible.

"Nothing," Carol whispered back. "We'll just sit here,
and whoever it is will go away."

The doorbell sounded again, and Lisa seemed to shrink away from the sound.

"He'll go away," Carol repeated. "If we don't answer it, he'll go away."

And then, as the bell rang for the third time, there was a pounding of feet on the stairs, and through the dining room Carol could see Kim, apparently having leapt from the third step, catching herself before crashing headlong into the door. Knowing what was about to happen, she rose to her feet. "Kim!"

But it was too late. Over her own cry, she heard Kim's exuberant voice demanding to know who was outside before she opened the door.

"Don't open it, Kim," she cried, but Kim only turned to give her an exasperated glare.

"Don't be dumb, Mommy," Kim called. "It's only Alex." She reached up and turned the knob, then pulled the door open wide.

Carrying the shotgun in his right hand, Alex stepped into the Cochrans' foyer.

"How long we going to sit here?" Jackson asked. He reached into his pocket and pulled out a cigarette, then cupped his hand over his lighter as a brief flame illuminated the dark interior of the car they had parked fifty feet up the hill from the Lonsdales'.

"As long as it takes," Finnerty growled, shifting in the seat in a vain attempt to ease the cramps in his legs. He'd been up too many hours, and exhaustion was beginning to take its toll.

"What makes you so sure the kid's going to come back here at all?"

Finnerty shrugged stiffly. "Instincts. He doesn't really have any place else to go. Besides, why shouldn't he come back here?"

Jackson glanced across at his partner, and took a deep drag on his cigarette, hoping perhaps the smoke might drive away the sleepiness that was threatening to overwhelm him. "Seems to me that if I were in his shoes, this is the last place I'd come. I think I'd be heading for Mexico right about now."

"Except for one thing," Finnerty growled. "According to the kid's dad, the kid couldn't have done anything, remember?"

"You believe that shit?"

"We saw Alex Lonsdale the night he wrecked himself, remember? By rights, that kid should have been dead. Jesus, Tom, half his head was caved in. But he's not dead. So who am I to say how they saved him? Maybe they did exactly what Doc Lonsdale says they did."

"All right," Jackson replied. Though he still wasn't accepting the strange tale they'd heard, he was willing to go along with it for the sake of conversation. "So what's your idea?"

"That maybe the kid was programmed to kill after all, and was also programmed to forget what he'd done, after he'd done it."

"Now you're reaching," Jackson replied.

"Except it accounts for the discrepancy in our notes. Remember how you wrote down that Alex said he parked across from Jake's last night, and I wrote down that he said he parked in the lot next door?"

"So? One of us heard wrong."

"What if we didn't? What if we both heard it right, and we both wrote it down right? What if he told us both things?"

Jackson frowned in the darkness. "Then he was lying."

"Maybe not," Finnerty mused. "What if he went down to Jake's, parked across the street, then changed his mind and went up to Mrs. Benson's? He kills her, then goes back to Jake's, and parks in the lot. But he forgets what he did in between the two arrivals, because that's what he's been programmed to do. When he tells us everything he remembers about last night, he remembers parking both places, so that's what he tells us. We didn't make any mistakes, and he didn't lie. He just doesn't remember what he did."

"That's crazy—"

"What's happening in this town is crazy," Finnerty rasped. "But at least that theory fits the facts. Or at least what we think are the facts."

"So he'll come home, because he doesn't remember what he's done?"

"Right. Why shouldn't he come home? As far as he knows, nothing's wrong."

"But what if he does remember?" Jackson asked. "What if he knows exactly what he's doing, and just doesn't care?"

"Then," Finnerty said, his voice grim, "we might have to do exactly what his father suggested. We might have to kill him."

Jackson took two more nervous drags on his cigarette, then stubbed it out in the ashtray. "Roscoe? I don't think I could do it," he said finally. "If it comes down to it, I'm just not sure I could shoot anyone."

"Well, let's hope it won't come down to that," Roscoe Finnerty replied. Then, giving in to his exhaustion, he slid deeper in his seat and closed his eyes. "Wake me up if anything happens."

"Kim!"

Carol Cochran tried to make the word commanding, but her voice cracked with fear. Nonetheless, Kim turned to gaze at her curiously. "Come here, Kim," she pleaded. Still Kim hesitated, and gazed up at Alex, her face screwed into a worried frown.

"Did you hurt yourself, Alex?" she asked, her eyes fixing on the cut over his eye.

Alex nodded.

"How?"

"I . . . I don't know," Alex admitted, then turned to look into the kitchen, where Carol and Lisa seemed frozen in place. "It's all right," Alex said. "I'm not going to hurt you."

As he spoke the words, Carol took a step forward. "Kim, I told you to come here!"

Kim glanced uncertainly from her mother to Alex, then back to her mother. She backed slowly into the dining room, then turned and dashed on into the kitchen.

When her younger daughter was in her arms, Carol's strength seemed to come back to her. "Go away, Alex," she said, the steadiness in her voice surprising even herself. "Just go away and leave us alone."

Alex nodded, but moved slowly through the dining room until he came to the kitchen door, the gun still clutched in his right hand.

From her chair, Lisa watched Alex's eyes, and her fear, instead of easing, only grew. There was an emptiness to his eyes that she'd never seen before. It was far beyond the strange blankness she'd almost grown used to over the last few months. Now his eyes looked as if they might be the eyes of a dead man. "Go away," she whispered. "Please, Alex, just go away."

"I will," Alex replied. "I just . . . I just wanted to tell you I'm sorry for what's happened."

"Sorry?" Lisa echoed. "How can you be—" And then she broke off her own words, as her eyes suddenly fell on the shotgun. Alex followed her gaze with his own eyes, and his expression became almost puzzled.

"I didn't kill anyone," he said softly. "I mean . . . Alex didn't kill anyone. It was the other."

Lisa and Carol glanced nervously at each other, and Carol shook her head almost imperceptibly.

"I'm not Alex," he went on. "That's what I came to tell you. Alex is dead."

"Dead?" Lisa echoed. "Alex, what are you talking about?"

"He's dead," Alex said again. "He died in the wreck. That's all I came to tell you, so you wouldn't think he'd done anything." His eyes fixed on Lisa, and when he spoke again, his voice was strangled, as if the very act of speaking the words was painful for him. "He loved you," he whispered. "Alex loved you very much. I . . . I don't understand what that means, but I know it's true. Don't blame Alex for what I've done. He couldn't stop it."

Suddenly his eyes filled with tears once again. "He would have stopped it," he whispered. "If so much of him hadn't died—if just a little more of him had lived—I know he would have stopped it."

Carol Cochran shakily rose to her feet. "What, Alex?" she whispered. "What would you have stopped?"

"Not me," Alex breathed. "Him. Alex would have stopped what Dr. Torres did. But I didn't know. He wouldn't let me remember, so I didn't know. But Alex found out. What was left of him found out, and he's trying to stop it. He's still trying, but he might not be able to, because he's dead." His eyes suddenly took on a wildness as they focused on Lisa once more. "Don't you understand?" he begged. "Alex is dead, Lisa!" Then he turned, and shambled back through the dining room and out into the night. A moment later, Carol heard a car door slam and an engine start. And then she heard Kim, and felt the little girl tugging at her arms.

"What's wrong with him?" she asked. "What's wrong with Alex?"

Carol swallowed hard, then held Kim close. "He's sick, honey," she whispered. "He's very sick in his head, that's all." Then she released Kim, and started toward the phone. "I'd better call the police," she said.

"No!" Carol turned back to see Lisa standing up, her expression suddenly clear. "Let him go, Mama," she said softly. "He won't hurt anyone else now. Don't you understand? That's what he was trying to tell us. All he wants to do now is die, and we have to let him." She knelt down, and pulled Kim close. "That wasn't Alex that was just here, Kim," she said softly. "That was someone else. Alex is dead. That's what he was telling us. That he's dead, and we should remember him the way he used to be. The way he was the night he took me to the dance." She hesitated, as her eyes flooded with tears. "Do you remember that night, Kim?"

Kim nodded, but said nothing.

"Then let's remember him that way, sweetheart. Let's remember how he looked all dressed up in his dinner jacket, and let's remember how good he was. All right?"

Kim hesitated, then nodded, and Lisa's gaze shifted to her mother. "Let him go, Mama. Please?" she begged. "He won't hurt anyone. I know he won't."

Carol stood silently watching her daughter for several long seconds, then, at last, moved toward her and embraced her.

"All right," she said softly. Then: "I'm sorry."

"I am too," Lisa replied. "And so is Alex."

"You're sure there's nothing I can do?" Jim Cochran asked.

Marsh opened the front door, and gazed out into the night as if expecting Alex to appear, but there was nothing. "No," he sighed. "Go on back to Carol and the girls. And tell them I understand why they didn't come," he added.

Jim Cochran regarded his friend shrewdly. "I don't believe I told you why they didn't come."

"You told me," Marsh replied with a tight smile. "Maybe not in words, but I understood." He glanced back over his shoulder to the living room, where Ellen was still sitting on the couch. "I'd better get back in," he went on. "I don't think she can stand to be by herself very long."

During the hour that Jim Cochran had been there, Ellen had finally begun to speak, but she was still confused, as if she wasn't exactly sure what had happened.

"Where's Carol?" she had asked half an hour ago. Then she'd peered vacantly around the room.

"She's home," Jim had told her. "Home with the girls. Kim's not feeling too well."

"Oh," Ellen had breathed, then fallen silent again before repeating her question five minutes later.

"She'll be all right," Marsh had assured him. "It's a kind of shock, and she'll pull out of it."

But even as he was about to leave, Jim wasn't sure he should be going at all. To him, Marsh didn't look much better than Ellen.

"Maybe I'd better stay—"

"No. If Alex comes home, I don't know what might happen. But I know I'd rather nobody was here. Except them." He gestured past the patio wall and up the road in the direction of the car Jim knew was still parked there, waiting.

"Okay. But if you need me, call me. All right?"

"All right." And then, without saying anything more, Marsh closed the door.

Jim Cochran crossed the patio, and let himself out through the gate. As he got into his car, he waved toward the two policemen, and one of them waved back. Finally he started the engine, put the car in gear, and backed out into the street.

Thirty seconds later, as he neared the bottom of the hill, he passed another car going up, but it was too dark for him to see Alex Lonsdale behind its wheel.

Alex pulled the car off the road just before he rounded the last curve. By now, he was sure, they would be looking for him, and they would be watching the house. He checked the breech of the shotgun.

There was one shell left.

It would be all he needed.

He got out of the car and quietly shut the door, then left the road and worked his way up the hillside, circling around to approach the house from the rear. In the dim light of the moon, the old house looked as it had so many years ago, and deep in his memory, the voices—Alejandro's voices—began whispering to him once more.

He crept down the slope into the shadows of the house itself, and a moment later had scaled the wall and dropped into the patio.

He stood at the front door.

He hesitated, then twisted the handle and pushed

the door open. Twenty feet away, in the living room, he saw his father.

Not his father.

Alex Lonsdale's father.

Alex Lonsdale was dead.

But Ellen Lonsdale was still alive.

"*Venganza . . . venganza . . .*"

Alejandro de Meléndez y Ruiz was dead, as was Raymond Torres.

And yet, they weren't. They were alive, in Alex Lonsdale's body, and the remnants of Alex Lonsdale's brain.

Alex's father was staring at him.

"Alex?"

He heard the name, as he'd heard it at the Cochrans' such a short time ago. But it wasn't his name.

"No. Not Alex," he whispered. "Someone else."

He raised the shotgun, and began walking slowly into the living room, where the last of the four women— Alex's mother—sat on the sofa, staring at him in terror.

Roscoe Finnerty's entire body twitched, and his eyes jerked open. For just a second he felt disoriented, then his mind focused, and he turned to his partner. "What's going on?"

"Nothin'," Jackson replied. "Cochran took off a few minutes ago, and since then, nothing."

"Unh-unh," Finnerty growled. "Something woke me up."

Jackson lifted one eyebrow a fraction of an inch, but he straightened himself in the seat, lit another cigarette, and scanned the scene on Hacienda Drive. Nothing, as far as he could see, had changed.

Still, he'd long since learned that Finnerty sometimes had a sixth sense about things.

And then he remembered.

A few minutes ago, there'd been a glow, as if a car had been coming up the hill, but it had stopped before coming around the last curve.

He'd assumed it had been a neighbor coming home.

"God damn!" he said aloud. He told his partner what had happened, and Finnerty cursed softly, then opened the car door.

"Come on. Let's take a look."

Both the officers got out of the car and started down the street.

Ellen's eyes focused slowly on Alex. It was like a dream, and she was only able to see little bits at a time.

The blood on his forehead, crusting over a deep gash that almost reached his eye.

The eyes themselves, staring at her unblinkingly, empty of all emotion except one.

Deep in his eyes, she thought she could see a smoldering spark of hatred.

The shotgun. Its barrels were enormous—black holes as empty as Alex's eyes—and they seemed to be staring at her with the same hatred as Alex.

Suddenly Ellen Lonsdale knew she was not looking at her son.

She was looking at someone else, someone who was going to kill her.

"Why?" she whispered. "Why?"

Then, as if her senses were turning on one by one, she heard her husband's voice.

"What is it, Alex? What's wrong?"

"*Venganza . . .*" she heard Alex whisper.

"Vengeance?" Marsh asked. "Vengeance for what?"

"*Ladrones . . . asesinos . . .*"

"No, Alex," Marsh said softly. "You've got it wrong." Wildly Marsh searched his mind for something to say, something that would get through to Alex.

Except it wasn't Alex. Whoever it was, it wasn't Alex.

Where the hell were the cops?

And then the front door flew open, and Finnerty and Jackson were in the entry hall.

Alex's head swung around toward the foyer, and Marsh used the moment. Lunging forward, he grasped the shotgun by the barrel, then threw himself sideways, twisting the gun out of Alex's hands. The force of his weight knocked Alex off balance, and he staggered toward the fireplace, then caught himself on the mantel. A moment later, his eyes met Marsh's.

"Do it," he whispered. "If you loved your son, do it."

Marsh hesitated. "Who are you?" he asked, his voice choking on the words. "Are you Alex?"

"No. I'm someone else. I'm whoever I was programmed to be, and I'll do what I was programmed to do. Alex tried to stop me, but he can't. Do it . . . Father. Please do it for me."

Marsh raised the gun, and as Ellen and the two policemen looked on, he squeezed the trigger.

The gun roared once more, and Alex's body, torn and bleeding, collapsed slowly onto the hearth.

Time stood still.

Ellen's eyes fixed on the body that lay in front of the fireplace, but what she saw was not her son.

It was someone else—someone she had never known— who had lived in her home for a while, and whom she had tried to love, tried to reach. But whoever he was, he was too far away from her, and she had not been able to reach him.

And he was not Alex.

She turned and faced Marsh.

"Thank you," she said softly. Then she rose and went to hold her husband.

One arm still cradling the shotgun, the other around his wife, Marsh finally tore his eyes away from the body of his son and faced the two policemen who stood as if frozen just inside the front door. "I . . . I'm sorry," he whispered, his voice breaking. "I had to . . ." He seemed about to say something else, but didn't. Instead, he let the gun fall to the floor, and held Ellen close. "I just had to, that's all."

Jackson and Finnerty glanced at each other for a split second, and then Finnerty spoke.

"We saw it all, Dr. Lonsdale," he said, his voice

carefully level. "We saw the boy attacking you and your wife—"

"No!" Marsh began, "he didn't attack us—"

But Finnerty ignored him. "He attacked you, and you were struggling for the gun when it went off." When Marsh tried to interrupt him again, he held up his hand. "Please, Dr. Lonsdale. Jackson and I both know what happened." He turned to his partner. "Don't we, Tom?"

Tom Jackson hesitated only a second before nodding his head. "It's like Roscoe says," he said at last. "It was an accident, and we're both witnesses to it. Take your wife upstairs, Dr. Lonsdale."

Without looking again at the body on the hearth, Ellen and Marsh turned away and left the room.

EPILOGUE

María Torres drew her shawl close around her shoulders against the chill of the December morning, then locked the front door of her little house and slowly crossed the street to the cemetery behind the old mission.

The cemetery was bright with flowers, for no one in La Paloma had forgotten what had happened three months earlier. All of them were buried here. Valerie Benson only a few yards from Marty Lewis, and Cynthia and Carolyn Evans, side by side, a little further north. All their graves, as they were every day, were covered with fresh flowers.

In the southeast corner, set apart from the other graves, lay Alex Lonsdale. On his grave only a single flower lay—the white rose delivered each day by the florist. María paused at Alex's grave, and wondered how long the roses would come, how long it would be before the Lonsdales, three months gone from La

Paloma, forgot about their son. For them, María was sure, there would be other children, and when those children came, the roses would stop.

Then it would be up to her. Long after his parents had stopped honoring his memory, she would still come and leave a flower for Alejandro.

She moved on into the oldest section of the cemetery, where her parents and grandparents were buried, and where now, finally returned to his family, her son lay as well. She stood at the foot of Ramón's grave for several minutes, and, as she always did, tried to understand what part he had played in what she had come to think of as the days of vengeance. But, as always, it was a mystery to her. Somehow, though, the saints had touched him, and he had fulfilled his destiny, and she honored his memory as she honored the memory of Alejandro de Meléndez y Ruiz. She whispered a prayer for her son, then left the cemetery. For her, there was still work to be done.

She trudged slowly through the village, feeling the burden of her age with every step, pausing once more in the Square, partly to rest, but partly, too, to repeat one more prayer for Don Roberto. Then, when she was rested, she went on.

She turned up Hacienda Drive, and was glad that today, at least, she needn't climb all the way up to the hacienda. It was empty again, and now she only went there once a week to wipe the dust away from its polished oaken floors and wrought-iron sconces. The furniture was gone, but she didn't miss it. In her mind's eye it was still as it had always been. Her ghosts were still there. Soon, she was sure, she would go to join them, and though her body would lie in the cemetery, her spirit would return to the hacienda which had always been her true home.

Today, though, she would not go to the hacienda. Today she would go to one of the other houses—the house where Alejandro had died—to speak to the new people.

They had only come to La Paloma last week, and she had heard that they needed a housekeeper.

She came to the last curve before the house would come into view, and paused to catch her breath. Then she walked on, and a moment later, saw the house.

It was as it should have been. Along the garden wall, neatly spaced between the tile insets, were small vines, well-trimmed and espaliered. From the outside, at least, the house looked as it had looked a century ago.

María stepped through the gate into the little patio, then knocked at the front door and waited. As she was about to knock again, the door opened, and a woman appeared.

A blond woman, with bright blue eyes and a smiling face.

A *gringo* woman.

"Mrs. Torres?" the woman asked, and María nodded. "I'm so glad to meet you," the woman went on. "I'm Donna Ruiz."

María felt her heart skip a beat, and her legs suddenly felt weak. She reached out and steadied herself on the door frame.

"Ruiz . . ." she whispered. "*No es posible . . .*"

The woman's smile widened. "It's all right," she said. "I know I don't look like a Ruiz. And of course I'm not. I was a Riley before I married Paul." She took María's arm and drew her into the house, closing the door behind her. A moment later they were in the living room. "Isn't this wonderful? Paul says it's exactly the kind of house he's always wanted to live in, and that it's really authentic. He says it must be over a hundred years old."

"More," María said softly, her eyes going to the hearth where Alejandro had died so short a time ago. "It was built for one of the overseers."

Donna Ruiz looked puzzled. "Overseers?"

"From the hacienda, before the . . . before the *americanos* came."

"How interesting," Donna replied. "It sounds like you know the house well."

"Sí," María said. "I cleaned for Señora Lonsdale."

Donna's smile faded. "Oh, dear. I didn't know . . . Perhaps you'd rather not work here."

María shook her head. "It is all right. I worked here before. I will work here again. And someday, I will go back to the hacienda."

The last of Donna Ruiz's smile disappeared, and she shook her head sadly. "It must have been awful. Just awful. That poor boy." She hesitated; then: "It almost seems like it would have been better if he'd died in the accident, doesn't it? To go through all he went through, and end up . . ." Her voice trailed off; then she took a deep breath and stood up. "Well. Perhaps we should go through the house, and I can tell you what I want done."

María heaved herself to her feet and silently followed Donna Ruiz through the rooms on the first floor, wondering why the *gringo* women always assumed that she couldn't see what needed to be done in a house. Did they think she never cleaned her own house? Or did they just think she was stupid?

The rooms were all as they had been the last time she had been here, and Señora Ruiz wanted the same things done that Señora Lonsdale had wanted.

The cleaning supplies were where they had always been, as were the vacuum cleaner and the dust rags, the mops and the brooms.

And all of it, of course, was explained to her in detail, as if she hadn't heard it all a hundred times before, hadn't known it all long before these women were even born.

At last they went upstairs, and one by one Donna Ruiz showed her all the rooms María Torres already knew. Finally they came to the room at the end of the hall, the room that had been Alejandro's. They paused, and Donna Ruiz knocked at the door.

"It's okay," a voice called from within. "Come on in, Mom."

Donna Ruiz opened the door, and María gazed into the room. All the furniture was still there—Alejandro's desk and bed, the bookshelves and the rug, all as they had been when the Lonsdales left.

Sitting at the desk, working on a model airplane, was a boy who looked to be about thirteen. He grinned at his mother, then, seeing that she wasn't alone, stood up. "Are you the cleaning lady?" he asked.

María nodded, her old eyes studying him. His eyes were dark, and his hair, nearly black, was thick and curly. "*Cómo se llama?*" she asked.

"Roberto," the boy replied. "But everybody calls me Bobby."

"Roberto," María repeated, her heart once again beating faster. "It is a good name."

"And he's fascinated with history," Donna Ruiz said. She turned to her son. "María seems to know all about the house and the town. I'll bet if you asked her, she could tell you everything that's ever happened here."

Bobby Ruiz turned eager eyes toward María. "Could you?" he asked. "Do you really know all about the town?"

María hesitated only an instant, then nodded. "*Sí*," she said softly. "I know all the old legends, and I will tell them all to you." She smiled gently. "I will tell them to you, and you will understand them. All of them. And someday, you will live in the hacienda. Would you like that?"

The boy's eyes burned brightly. "Yes," he said. "I'd like that very much."

"Then I will take you there," María replied. "I will take you there, and someday it will be yours."

A moment later, María was gone, and Bobby Ruiz was alone in his room. He went to his bed and lay down on his back so that he could gaze at the ceiling, but he saw nothing. Instead, he listened to the sounds in his head, the whisperings in Spanish that he had been hearing since the first time he came into this room. But now, after talking to María Torres, he understood the whisperings.

Soon, he knew, the killings would begin again. . . .

ABOUT THE AUTHOR

JOHN SAUL's first novel, *Suffer the Children*, was published in 1977 to instant bestsellerdom. *Punish the Sinners, Cry for the Strangers, Comes the Blind Fury, When the Wind Blows. The God Project* and *Nathaniel*, each a national bestseller, followed. Now, John Saul's trademark setting, a sleepy, isolated town where suddenly no one is safe, forms the background for this master storyteller's most chilling novel yet. John Saul lives in Bellevue, Washington, where he is at work on his next novel.

RELAX!
SIT DOWN
and Catch Up On Your Reading!

DON'T MISS
THESE CURRENT
Bantam Bestsellers

SPECIAL
MONEY SAVING
OFFER

Now you can have an up-to-date listing of Bantam's hundreds of titles plus take advantage of our unique and exciting bonus book offer. A special offer which gives you the opportunity to purchase a Bantam book for only 50¢. Here's how!

By ordering any five books at the regular price per order, you can also choose any other single book listed (up to a $4.95 value) for just 50¢. Some restrictions do apply, but for further details why not send for Bantam's listing of titles today!

Just send us your name and address plus 50¢ to defray the postage and handling costs.